"Hammer in hand, Richard Chizmar's everything's already been done. An absolutely chilling mash-up of styles, media, biography, and legend. ELASTIC, UNSETTLING, BRILLIANT. And here you thought you knew the names of every genre."
—JOSH MALERMAN

"Brilliant . . . absolutely fascinating, totally compelling, and immensely poignant. I DARE YOU NOT TO FINISH IT IN ONE SITTING. This one will stay with me!"
—C. J. TUDOR

"RIVETING. CHILLING. *Chasing the Boogeyman* is an unflinching look at a real-life monster and the ordinary heroes obsessed with stopping him."
—RILEY SAGER

"Wonderful . . . A KNOTTY MYSTERY WITH AN ELEGANT RESOLUTION AT ITS HEART. . . . It feels so original, dizzy-making in its expert layering of fact and fiction. . . . A hymn to both innocence and growing up."
—CATRIONA WARD

"A meticulously remembered, BEAUTIFULLY CRAFTED hometown nightmare that reminds readers that nostalgia cuts both ways; sure, it can keep our past alive, but it can also be the shadow man standing at the foot of your bed. . . . FOR TRUE CRIME AND HORROR FANS, THIS ONE'S ESSENTIAL."
—*LIBRARY JOURNAL* (starred review)

ADDITIONAL PRAISE FOR
CHASING THE BOOGEYMAN

"Chizmar demonstrates the full power of his impressive storytelling reach. A fascinating conceit paired with deeply human writing creates a thriller that conjures writers as disparate as Stephen King and Michelle McNamara. The result is a marvelous mind game of nuanced, layered storytelling."

—Michael Koryta, *New York Times* bestselling author of *Never Far Away*

"Chizmar presents himself as a print version of Norman Rockwell, if the artist had devoted himself to the creepy things that hide under the bed."

—Linwood Barclay, *New York Times* bestselling author of *Find You First*

"If Ray Bradbury had written *In Cold Blood*, it would probably look a lot like Richard Chizmar's masterful *Chasing the Boogeyman*, a perfectly written and unnervingly suspenseful thriller about a series of murders that tear apart the fabric of a picturesque Maryland town and the writer who puts everything on the line to solve them. This is a mind-bendingly engaging book. Be prepared for the hairs on the back of your neck to be standing at attention as you devour every rich page."

—David Bell, bestselling author of *The Request*

"Perfect for fans of true crime, meticulously orchestrated, and clever beyond measure, *Chasing the Boogeyman* will leave you guessing long after you've read the last page."

—Alma Katsu, acclaimed author of *The Hunger* and *Red Widow*

"Impressive. . . . a smart, entertaining ride."

—*Publishers Weekly*

"We're all chasing the Boogeyman, aren't we? The Boogeyman's the past, the truth, our fragile memories that knit the two together. What Richard Chizmar's done for us in *Chasing the Boogeyman* is give that narrative a taut dramatic line he balances on, never quite tipping one way or the other, just stepping sure-footed all the way to the end—showing us that this is a walk we can all take, if we have the nerve."

—Stephen Graham Jones, *New York Times* bestselling author of *The Only Good Indians*

"Chizmar's *Chasing the Boogeyman* has been written upon missing person flyers and published on telephone poles. HAVE YOU READ THIS STORY? For your own safety, you should. . . . The Boogeyman will soon enter the pantheon of suburban legends that fill our backyards like summer fireflies, his name whispered into ears all over. Pray you keep yours."

—Clay McLeod Chapman, bestselling author of *The Remaking*

"Chizmar takes creepy to a whole new level. . . . A solid true crime facsimile, mixing background detail with action, suspense, and a compelling pace. As metafiction, the book excels: the proximity to reality adds an unshakable level of unease, and it is injected with just the right amount of self-reflection to forge an ironically honest, emotional connection with the reader. The result is strikingly original, a story that will thrill fans of intimately investigated nonfiction like Michelle McNamara's *I'll Be Gone in the Dark* and self-aware, psychological suspense like Oyinkan Braithwaite's *My Sister, the Serial Killer*."

—*Booklist*

CHASING
THE
BOOGEYMAN

A Novel

RICHARD CHIZMAR

GALLERY BOOKS

New York   London   Toronto   Sydney   New Delhi

G

Gallery Books
An Imprint of Simon & Schuster, Inc.
1230 Avenue of the Americas
New York, NY 10020

First Gallery Books trade paperback edition July 2022

GALLERY BOOKS and colophon are registered trademarks of Simon & Schuster, Inc.

For information about special discounts for bulk purchases, please contact Simon & Schuster Special Sales at 1-866-506-1949 or business@simonandschuster.com.

The Simon & Schuster Speakers Bureau can bring authors to your live event. For more information or to book an event, contact the Simon & Schuster Speakers Bureau at 1-866-248-3049 or visit our website at www.simonspeakers.com.

Interior design by Davina Mock-Maniscalco

Manufactured in the United States of America

10 9 8 7 6 5

Library of Congress Cataloging-in-Publication Data is available.

ISBN 978-1-9821-7516-0
ISBN 978-1-9821-7517-7 (pbk)
ISBN 978-1-9821-7518-4 (ebook)

For Kara.
Again.

a note to readers

*C*hasing the Boogeyman is a work of fiction, an homage to my hometown and my passion for true crime. There are slices of life depicted throughout that are very much inspired by my personal history, but other events and real people and places and publications are used fictitiously, and to provide verisimilitude to this crime story. Other names, characters, settings, publications, and events come directly from my imagination, admittedly at times not a very nice place to inhabit.

contents

foreword

James Renner

I write about crime, and sometimes I chase serial killers across the country. I cut my teeth at the *Free Times* in Cleveland, where I worked as an investigative journalist at a time when young women were disappearing on the west side of town. We all knew there was a murderer in our midst, but nobody could find him. I spent a month researching the cases of victims Amanda Berry and Gina DeJesus. One of Amanda's ex-boyfriends looked good for it, but the police had no evidence. Then one day, in 2013, I was watching my son tumble around in his gymnastics class when I got a text from an old source in the Cleveland Police Department—Amanda and Gina just walked out of a house on the West Side. And a third woman is here. By the end of the day, Ariel Castro was in custody. When I went back through my notes, Castro's name was there. His daughter was the last person with Gina DeJesus before she was abducted. My editor had asked me not to interview her because, at the time, she was a minor. I will always wonder what might have happened if I never listened to him.

The summer after they caught Castro, I took my family to Ocean City, Maryland, on vacation. I needed a break from it all and intended to get caught up on some Stephen King and John Irving novels while my kids built sandcastles on the beach. The condo had this old dining room table with an annoying wobble, and on the second day I was motivated to fix it. I surveyed the owner's bookshelves for the right-sized paperback, and in that way happened across a sun-faded copy of Richard Chizmar's true-crime book, *Chasing the Boogeyman*. I started leafing through it and quickly forgot about the table. By dinner, I was obsessed with the details revealed in the book and the horrible unsolved murders that rocked the town of Edgewood in 1988. By midnight, I'd finished it.

I took *Chasing the Boogeyman* with me when we left. I guess that's stealing, but I reasoned this was a better fate for the book than holding up the corner of a dining room table. When I got home, I puttered around the internet for a bit to find out if they'd ever caught the guy, but all I could find were old articles on LexisNexis. No updates for the last ten years. I was surprised, though, to find that Chizmar had become a publisher himself, with some Stephen King titles, no less. I even had an old issue of his magazine, *Cemetery Dance*, from back in college, and it had his contact info listed on the editorial page.

On a whim, I decided to email Chizmar. Any updates on the Boogeyman mystery? I took a picture of my pilfered copy of his book and sent it along as an attachment, and included my phone number. Five minutes later, my phone rang. It was Chiz. I think we talked about the murders for two or three hours that night. Twenty-some years later, he still remembered every detail, every source he'd spoken to. It was still an obsession, I could tell. I had planned to write a feature story about his quest as a young man to find the killer, but other stories, newer stories, got in the way.

Then came that morning in September 2019 when I saw "The Boogeyman" trending on Twitter. I clicked the link, thinking it was a promotion for some new horror movie, a part of me trying not to get my hopes up, and sure enough, it concerned the Edgewood murders. I felt my body go numb when I saw the name of the man police had just arrested. It was the last person I'd expected.

Chizmar didn't answer the phone that day, or for the rest of the week. I got the details from Carly Albright's updates in the *Washington Post*. There was a feeling of palpable relief in the air, and it reminded me of when the Golden State Killer was apprehended. When a monster is finally caught against all odds, it feels like magic. The author J. R. R. Tolkien had a word for that feeling—*eucatastrophe*. The opposite of catastrophe, and all the more important because it's even rarer.

I've been waiting for Richard Chizmar's final words on the matter. I heard he actually interviewed the killer in prison, and I was anxious to hear what he'd discovered. So it's quite an honor to be asked to introduce this long-overdue final edition of his book.

If I've learned anything from Chizmar's journey though, it's that, in the end, patience and hope win out over evil and indifference. Almost all the time. I hope you will agree.

—*James Renner*
March 3, 2020

James Renner is the author of *True Crime Addict*, the controversial book on the Maura Murray disappearance, as well as the novels *The Man from Primrose Lane* and, most recently, *Muse*. He got his start as a crime beat reporter in Cleveland. He currently hosts the *Philosophy of Crime* podcast.

introduction

"What kind of monster does that?"

When I first started clipping newspaper articles and jotting down notes about the tragic events that transpired in my hometown of Edgewood, Maryland, during the summer and autumn of 1988, I had no thoughts of one day turning those scattered observations into a full-length book.

Many of my closest friends and colleagues have a hard time believing this to be true, but I promise that is the case.

Perhaps *something* working deep in the basement of my subconscious had an inkling there might be a story here to tell, but the surface-world Rich Chizmar, a fresh-faced twenty-two-year-old—who on an early June afternoon loaded up his meager belongings (including my beloved Apple Macintosh computer, which I'm still paying for in monthly installments) into the back seat and trunk of his dirt-brown Toyota Corolla and headed north on I-95 to his parents' house at the corner of Hanson and Tupelo Roads—had no clue whatsoever.

All I knew was this: three days earlier, a few blocks from where I'd grown up, a young girl had been taken from her bedroom in the middle of the night. Her savaged body was discovered in nearby woods the next morning. The local police had no suspects.

I learned most of this information from a pair of newspaper articles and the evening news. Initially, reporters were suitably vague about the condition of the girl's body, but an old friend's uncle was a Harford County sheriff, and he spilled all the grisly details. "Jesus Christ, Rich. What kind of monster does that?" my friend had asked, as if my lifelong interest in the macabre made me some kind of an expert on deviant behavior.

I had no answer for him that day, and now, more than a year later, I still don't. Call me naive, but I believe some things just aren't meant to be understood. So much of life—and death—is a mystery.

My father was his typically quiet self when we spoke on the phone the evening before my homecoming—he was mostly concerned with what I wanted for dinner my first night back so he could pick up groceries at the commissary—but my mother was a mess. "We've known the Gallaghers for over twenty years," she said, voice cracking with emotion. "They moved here shortly after we did. Joshua was just a toddler and poor Natasha hadn't even been born. You should reach out to Josh when you get home. I can't imagine what it must feel like to lose a baby sister . . . especially like that. Can you? You'll come with us to the funeral, won't you? You and Josh graduated together, right?" On and on like that.

I assured her that no, I couldn't imagine losing a baby sister (it didn't matter one bit that I was the youngest of the Chizmar children and therefore didn't have a baby sister; that clearly wasn't the point), and yes, of course I'd go with them to the funeral, and yes, Josh and I had in fact graduated together, although we hadn't been particularly close, the two of us running with different crowds.

Even at such a relatively young age, I was already well on my way to becoming a reformed Catholic, but my folks were about as devout as they came, especially my mom. When the world around her suffered—

a deadly earthquake in Asia, floods in South America, a distant second cousin diagnosed with treatable cancer; it didn't matter how near or far—my mother suffered right alongside each and every one of them. She'd always been that way.

Almost breathless by this point in the conversation, Mom went on to say that she and Norma Gentile, our elderly next-door neighbor, had gone to mass every morning for the past week to pray for the Gallagher family. They'd also walked over a platter of homemade fried chicken and coleslaw to show their support. I could hear my father's muffled voice in the background then, chastising my mother for keeping me on the phone for so long, and she scolded him right back with an emphatic "Oh, you hush." When she got back on the line, she apologized for being so upset and chewing my ear off, declaring that nothing like this had ever happened in Edgewood. Before I could muster much of a response, she said goodnight and hung up the phone.

Late the next afternoon, as I steered my overloaded Toyota off the I-95 exit ramp and headed for Hanson Road, the radio newswoman pretty much echoed my mother's claim. There'd always been plenty of crime to go around in a town like Edgewood—assault and battery, breaking and entering, theft, any number of drug-related offenses, as well as the occasional homicide—but no one could remember anything remotely this violent or depraved. It was almost as if an invisible switch had been thrown, the reporter claimed, and we now existed in a different place and time. Our little town had lost what remained of its innocence.

Sitting beside me on the passenger seat that day was my diploma from the University of Maryland School of Journalism, still rolled up in the cardboard mailing tube in which the college had mailed it. I hadn't bothered buying a frame. To my parents' disappointment, I hadn't even bothered walking across the stage at my graduation ceremony earlier in the month.

After four-and-a-half seemingly endless years, I'd had enough of formal education. It was time to get out in the real world and do *something* with myself.

There was only one small problem.

What that *something* was, I wasn't entirely sure.

I'd published a folder full of newspaper articles during the past couple of years, mostly sports stories and a handful of public interest features in my college paper. I'd also gotten lucky and managed to crack my hometown weekly, Hartford County's *Aegis* (twice), and the *Baltimore Sun* (once). As a lifelong Baltimore Orioles fan, I was particularly proud of the Earl Weaver feature I'd written for the *Sun*. Unlike my diploma, it was neatly framed and carefully bubble-wrapped in the back seat of my car.

So, armed with my impressive body of clippings and hot-off-the-press journalism degree, you'd think I'd be anxious to get settled in at home and launch right into an aggressive job search.

And you would be wrong.

You see, somewhere along the way, amid all those stuffy classroom lessons about how to write a proper lede and when to utilize an unnamed source and how to interview a reluctant subject, I fell head over heels in love with a different kind of writing. The kind that came with a whole lot fewer rules and no harried bosses barking in your ear to "hurry the hell up, Chizmar, we need to go to press!"

That's right, I'm talking about the bane of every real journalist's existence—the hippy-dippy, Peter Pan world of Make Believe: fiction.

But wait, it's even worse than that. I'm talking about *genre* fiction. Crime, mystery, suspense, and that black sheep of them all: horror.

I'd already managed to sell a half-dozen short stories to small-press publications located around the country. Magazines with illustrious names like *Scifant*, *Desert Sun*, *StarSong*, and *Witness to the Bizarre*. Magazines with circulations in the mid-to-low three-digit range that often arrived in my PO Box with sloppily stapled bindings and painfully amateurish black-and-white artwork on the front covers; magazines that paid a penny per word if you were lucky, but oftentimes, nothing at all.

As further evidence of youthful ignorance and bravado, I'd actually taken my love affair with genre fiction a step further, by recently announcing the start-up of my very own horror and suspense magazine, an ambitious quarterly going by the questionable-at-best title of *Cemetery Dance* (stolen from the name of the second short story I'd ever written, for which I'd received compliments from roughly a dozen editors regarding the evocative title of that particular tale and exactly zero compliments regarding the quality of the story itself). The debut issue of *Cemetery Dance* was scheduled to be released in a matter of months—December 1988—and as usual, I was in over my head. An awful lot of long days and long nights of on-the-job training awaited me.

But first came the hard part—explaining to my old-fashioned, by-the-book, conservative parents that I didn't even plan to assemble a résumé, much less look for a real job. Instead, I had a different master plan in mind: First, I'd take up residence in my old bedroom on the second floor of my childhood home. Then I'd spend the next seven months sharing their dinner table most every night, preparing for my impending marriage (and subsequent move to Baltimore City so that Kara, my bride-to-be, could finish her undergraduate work at Johns Hopkins University before moving on to physical therapy school, thus insuring that at least one of us would eventually earn a steady income), and lounging around in my sweatpants or pajamas while I worked on my little magazine and wrote stories about bad guys and monsters.

Talk about a Can't-Miss Plan, right?

Fortunately, my mother and father soon revealed themselves to be saints on a whole new level (they still are to this day), and for reasons unknown to intelligent man, they agreed to support my plan and expressed their unwavering faith in me.

So, there you have it . . . that's how I found myself in the early days of summer 1988, sitting behind my writing desk beneath a window overlooking the side yard of the house I grew up in. Every time I took a break from the computer screen and glanced outside, I imagined the ghosts of my childhood friends sprinting shirtless across the lawn, whooping with laughter and disappearing into the wavering shadows beneath the towering weeping willow whose spindly branches had snagged so many of our taped-up Wiffle balls and provided hours of cooling shade in which to play marbles and eat pizza subs and trade baseball cards. I'd even kissed my first girl under that tree when I was eleven years old. Her name was Rhonda, and I've never forgotten her.

But that was the past, and as golden-hued and sweetly nostalgic as those images painted my daydreams, I quickly realized the here and now was a shiny new gift sitting right there in front of me, just waiting to be opened.

As the humidity-drenched days ticked by and the words on the screen added up, the decision to move back home felt truer and truer inside my soul, almost as if a kind of predestination was taking place—and frankly, that surprised me. When Kara—a bubbly, patient, green-eyed beauty (who coincidentally also came from a large Edgewood family)—first suggested I move home for the months leading up to our wedding, I thought she'd lost her mind. I loved my parents with all my heart, but I hadn't lived at home for longer than a weeklong holiday break since I'd been seventeen, five long years earlier. I carried with me legitimate fears that the three of us might drive each other crazy living under the same roof again, and my mother might even resort to poisoning me one evening at dinner.

But as luck would have it, Kara possessed a razor-keen intuition to go along with that million-dollar smile of hers—and as was to become routine in the years that followed, she was right about everything.

The seven months I spent on Hanson Road were just what I needed. In a way, for me, they formed a kind of bridge to adulthood—and both the good and the bad that came along with it.

First, the good: I worked hard in the comfortable silence of my old bedroom and got better at my craft. A handful of stories sold, and the first issue of *Cemetery Dance* arrived on time and on budget, proving a moderate success. I saw people I hadn't seen in years. Rekindled old friendships. I got to help my father mow the lawn and trim the bushes that summer, and rake the leaves and clear the gutters that fall. We tinkered in his garage workshop and watched Orioles games in the basement while sharing paper plates stacked with cheese and crackers and frosty six-packs of Coors. I watched the bathroom scale tip upward as I feasted on my mother's home cooking, and the sound of my parents' laughter as they watched television sitcoms in the dark of their bedroom became my nighttime lullaby.

But then there was the bad; the unimaginably, indescribably bad, hovering above all those wonderful memories like an angry, slate-gray thunderstorm sky. Four innocent girls murdered. Four families ripped apart. And a town held hostage by a faceless madman, a monster far more frightening and evil than anything I could imagine in one of my stories.

For a brief time, not long after the third murder, I tried to tell myself that I didn't know any of the girls that well, not really. But it didn't matter—and I knew it. They were our neighbors. They were friends of friends, siblings of friends, or in some cases, children of friends. And they were from Edgewood. The one place in the world I knew and loved the most.

I've had plenty of time since then to think about it—a little more than a year and a half, to be exact—and I believe the woman disc jockey on the radio that long-ago June afternoon was right when she'd said it was as if we'd experienced a loss of our innocence. After everything that'd happened, it felt like we could never go back to the way it was before.

And maybe we shouldn't.

Maybe that's what grieving is all about: never forgetting what we've lost.

I can't explain how or why it happened the way it did, the timing of me being back there on Hanson Road when the murders occurred. I don't know whether it was fate (as many in my life would like to believe) or simple misfortune. Ultimately, the reasons why don't matter.

I *was* there.

I was witness.

And, somehow, the monster's story became my own.

– Richard Chizmar
June 20, 1990

one

The Town

"It was during those long, slow, breathless walks up that gravel driveway that I first began telling scary stories to my friends . . ."

1

Before I get to the Boogeyman and his reign of terror during the summer and fall of 1988, I want to tell you about the town where I grew up. It's important that you carry with you a clear picture of the place—and the people who live there—as you read the story that follows, so you can understand exactly what it is we all lost. There is a John Milton quote that I think of often while driving the streets of my hometown: *"Innocence, once lost, can never be regained. Darkness, once gazed upon, can never be lost."*

For the citizens of Edgewood, this was our time of darkness.

2

I believe that most small towns wear two faces: a public one comprised of verifiable facts involving historical timelines, demographics, matters of economy and geography; and a hidden, considerably more private face formed by a fragile spiderweb of stories, memories, rumors, and secrets passed down from generation to generation, whispered by those who know the town best.

Edgewood, Maryland, located twenty-five miles northeast of Baltimore in southern Harford County, was no exception. Situated in the top center of an inverted triangular peninsula created by the Chesapeake Bay to the south, the Gunpowder River to the west, and the Bush River to the east, Edgewood was originally home to a number of Native Americans, most notably the Powhatan and Susquehannock tribes. Captain John Smith was among the first to navigate the Bush River, naming it "Willowbyes Flu" after his beloved hometown in England. In 1732, the Presbury Meetinghouse was established on the river's shoreline as one of the first Methodist churches in America.

A railroad system constructed through the area in 1835 provided distribution for local agricultural markets, and the railroad's extension in the mid-1850s provided a foundation for the town of Edgewood's development. The wooden railroad bridge crossing the nearby Gunpowder River was burned in April 1861 during the Baltimore riots, and Confederate soldiers burned it a second time in July 1864.

Although the population of Edgewood was a mere three-dozen full-time residents in 1878, the railroad and neighboring countryside's lush farmland contributed to eventual growth. Before long, there was an abundance of new homes in the area, including a number of extravagant residences, many erected by businessmen commuting daily to Baltimore via train. A schoolhouse, post office, hotel, general store, and blacksmith were soon established within the town's borders.

The Edgewood train station also experienced increased popularity because of its proximity to valuable hunting grounds for numerous species of waterfowl. Soon, gentlemen sportsmen from northeastern cities as far-ranging as New York and Boston traveled to Edgewood to take part in the hunt. General George Cadwalader, a colorful war hero and respected Philadelphia lawyer, gradually acquired large plots of property in the area, consisting of almost eight thousand acres, and invited affluent and influential friends to visit. He leased waterfront land to various hunting clubs and established more than a dozen farms on the property. Hardworking tenant farmers paid Cadwalader a healthy percentage of their seasonal crops.

Another prominent figure in Edgewood's early days was Herman W. "Boss" Hanson. A prosperous gentleman farmer and longtime member of the Maryland House of Delegates, Hanson was also a shrewd businessman. Tomatoes were his company's most profitable crop and at one point, he operated four canneries in the area and purchased all the other local farmers' tomatoes to fill orders. The canned fruit was marketed under the Queen Brand and sold all over the country, eventually even shipping overseas.

The only real drama in the town's history up until that point arrived in the summer of 1903, when a group of armed outlaws attempted to rob a payroll train docked at the Edgewood Station. A fierce gunfight erupted with the local constable and his men, resulting in the death of two lawmen, a civilian employee of the payroll company, and all six of the outlaws. A local newspaper reporter counted over two hundred and fifty bullet holes in the station's walls. Fortunately, such violence was rare in the still-rural town.

A short distance down the tracks was the Magnolia Station, named for the lovely magnolia trees that flourished there. Across from the station was Magnolia Meadows, a popular resort for picnics, outdoor events, and excursion parties from Baltimore. A spacious pavilion centered in the grove was used for dances and weddings, and by the early 1900s, Magnolia boasted a post office, church, schoolhouse, canning house, general store, shoe shop, and barbershop.

The pastoral life of those living in and around Edgewood changed dramatically in October 1917, when the U.S. government took possession of all the land south of the railroad tracks to create Edgewood Arsenal military complex. Thousands of people flocked to the area to construct a number of facilities designed to handle the various aspects of chemical weaponry. The government built massive plants to produce such toxic chemicals as mustard gas, chlorine, chloropicrin, and phosgene. They even produced gas masks for horses, donkeys, and dogs. Peak employment during July 1918 totaled 8,342 civilians and 7,175 military personnel.

While wealthy residents such as General Cadwalader were reimbursed for their lost property, local tenant farmers and sharecroppers received no such payments. A number of Black farmers relocated to establish a small community of modest homes in the Magnolia area known as Dembytown. A general store, a two-room schoolhouse, and a ramshackle jazz club called the Black Hole were erected in a trio of narrow clapboard buildings along the northeastern border of Dembytown. The club burned down in 1920 under suspicious circumstances.

The burgeoning military presence soon transformed Edgewood. Schools, housing, and a multitude of businesses spread across the area. World War II brought yet another wave of military personnel and civilians to town. A modernized train station was hurriedly built to handle the great influx of people. Additional civilian barracks and off-post housing units were constructed in numerous Edgewood locations, including a twenty-six-acre development named Cedar Drive. The overflow of new residents, coupled with the completion of Route 40, a four-lane highway cutting through Edgewood, spurred further economic development. Edgewood Meadows, a sprawling community of single-family homes, was established in the early 1950s. Old Edgewood Road and Hanson Road bisected the sprawling development, and both roadways were soon dotted with commercial establishments. Farther south on Hanson Road, a sprawling community of affordable town houses, the Courts of Harford Square, was constructed, replacing over a hundred acres of fertile farmland. Sitting upon a grassy hill overlooking the new development stood the original "Hanson House" built by Thomas Hanson in the early 1800s. The grand Victorian home featured fifty-one windows and seven gables, and was the first house in Edgewood to enjoy indoor plumbing. In 1963, the Edgewood Public Library opened on Hanson Road across from the bustling Acme supermarket. Later that same year, the Edgewood exit on Interstate 95 opened, spawning even greater numbers of residential neighborhoods. To support the influx of young students in the area, three spacious schools—a high school, middle school, and elementary school—were built on 102 acres along Willoughby Beach Road.

But with every boom there comes the inevitable bust—and in the years following the United States military's involvement in Vietnam, a number of weapons testing programs at Edgewood Arsenal were either downsized or canceled altogether. Troops and civilian personnel were transferred to other bases along the East Coast and, soon after, numerous remote sections of the Arsenal took on the appearance of a ghost town. For several years, there were well-publicized rumors that the U.S. government planned to open a paratrooper school in the abandoned areas, but those plans never materialized.

By the late 1980s, the unincorporated community of Edgewood covered almost seventeen square miles. Population hovered at nearly 18,000 people—68% White, 27% African American, and 3.5% Hispanic. The median household income was a slightly below national average, $40,500. The average household was 2.81 occupants, and the average family size was 3.21.

This was the public face of Edgewood, Maryland.

3

This is the Edgewood I know and love:

I grew up in a modest two-story house with green shutters and a sloping driveway at the corner of Hanson and Tupelo Roads. That house and the sidewalks, streets, and yards that surrounded it were my entire world from the time I was five years old until I left for college at the age of seventeen. My parents still live there today.

I was the youngest of five children—following in the footsteps of three sisters (Rita, Mary, and Nancy) and the eldest of the bunch, my brother (John)—by a margin of nearly eight years. In other words, I was probably a mistake. I've never actually asked my parents if that was the case, but I've heard it enough times from my siblings to mostly believe it to be true. Regardless, it never really mattered.

My father (retired U.S. Air Force, a quiet, hardworking man of decency and integrity) and my mother (a diminutive-in-stature caregiver of the first order, and still very much the Ecuadorian beauty my father married) treated their children with equal measures of love and understanding and patience. Well, almost. I must admit that as the youngest—and some say the cutest—not to mention the last of the Chizmar clan to live under their roof, I very well may be my parents' favorite.

But I digress.

The white-painted front door and large bay window of our house peered out upon Hanson Road, one of the busiest-traveled roadways in all of Edgewood. The speed limit sign posted directly across the street read 25 mph, but few drivers obeyed that particular law. The right side of our house bordered Tupelo Road, a much quieter, tree-lined avenue that stretched all the way from Tupelo Court across the street to Presbury United Methodist Church on Edgewood Road.

A small, enclosed breezeway connected our dining room to a single-car garage. The garage was my father's private place, his sanctuary. Growing up, I was alternately intimidated and fascinated by it. For whatever reason, it always reminded me of the magical and chaotic sorcerer's workshop in the Disney movie *Fantasia*. A narrow homemade workbench lined much of the far wall. Hanging above it, covering every available inch of mounted pegboard, were dozens of tools and gadgets, mysteriously labeled and organized in ways I still don't understand to this day. At opposite ends of the bench, tucked against the wall and stacked atop each other, were four cube-shaped organizers featuring rows of small plastic drawers, each neatly labeled and filled with various-sized nuts, bolts, nails, and washers. Attached to either end at the front of the bench was a pair of large steel vises. Underneath were tidy stacks of pre-cut lumber, a number of plastic buckets, and a couple of old step-stools. The garage's remaining wall space was taken up by sheets of leaning plywood, old furniture awaiting repair, and large, dangerous-looking machinery: a table saw with gleaming metal teeth, a twin-belt sander, a router, and drill press. To my friends and me, the machines all resembled sophisticated instruments of torture. Higher up on the walls hung shelf upon shelf, also homemade, stacked with small card-board boxes, glass jars, and old coffee cans labeled with strips of mask-ing tape bearing my father's all-caps handwriting: *ROPE. TAPE. WIRE. BRACKETS. CLAMPS. BALL BEARINGS.* In other words, the stuff of magic when you're eight years old.

Unfortunately, the rest of the house wasn't nearly as interesting. A small kitchen, dining room, living room, and foyer occupied the first floor. An antique stereo cabinet, housing my father's impressive collec-tion of jazz records, was centered beneath the bay window, and several mahogany bookcases lined the walls. The sofa and accompanying arm-chair were inexplicably green. Upstairs, there were three modest-sized bedrooms and a bathroom. My bedroom was situated in the far corner with windows facing both the side and back yards. On the lowest level was a prone-to-flooding basement with dark paneled walls, sectional sofa, his and her recliners, a black-and-white marble coffee table on which my father played solitaire most every evening, an RCA television, and a spectacular hand-carved cuckoo clock centered on the back wall.

One of my favorite places in the house was the large screened-in back porch accessible through a sliding glass door off the rear of the dining room. I spent countless summer evenings on that porch—reading comics and paperback books, sorting baseball and football cards, or playing board games with friends. My mother would bring out a pitcher of homemade lemonade and chocolate chip cookies still warm and gooey from the oven, and my friends and I would feel like kings of the world. We also had sleepovers out there when the weather was warm enough.

Despite my early love of reading, not to mention obsessively watching scary movies and westerns on TV, I was an outdoors boy. From the day we moved in, I spent countless hours beneath the ageless weeping willow tree that stood watch in our side yard, pretending I was Cy Young Award–winning pitcher Jim Palmer of the Baltimore Orioles. I'd use the heels of my old tennis shoes to carve out a pitcher's rubber in the grass, and then I'd go into my best trademark high-leg-kick wind-up and hurl fastball after fastball at a square patch of bare concrete wall, located dangerously close to the basement window. I still consider it a small miracle that I never once broke that window, but the green shutter bordering the window's left edge paid dearly for my youthful arrogance. Dented and battered beyond recognition from hundreds of errant throws—high and inside to my imaginary right-handed batters—it barely managed to cling to the wall with a pair of bent and rusty nails. That beat-up shutter remains a sore subject to this day between my father and me.

The sidewalk that ran in front of my house, parallel to Hanson Road, had thirty-three cracks of various sizes and shapes. The sidewalk that ran alongside Tupelo had nineteen. I knew those walkways like the back of my hand. I'd walked, skateboarded, or biked them every day for twelve years. When we were young boys, my friends and I built ramps with concrete blocks and wooden boards salvaged from construction sites or "borrowed" from my father's workshop, and jumped them on our bikes. More often than not, we were bare-chested with nary a helmet in sight. Once, we even convinced a little kid who lived a few blocks away to do it blindfolded. That didn't end well, and we never tried it again. Sometimes we upped the ante, soaring over trash cans or plastic bags filled with grass and leaves. Other times, we lay down side by side on the sidewalk and jumped over each other. Believe me when I say that lying on your back on a sun-blasted slab of concrete with your arms at your sides and your eyes closed, letting your idiot friend who truly believes he's Evel Knievel hurtle over you on a bicycle, is the apex of blind adolescent loyalty.

One summer afternoon, my buddy Norman's older sister, Melody—a local force to be reckoned with as she already had her driver's license and smoked unfiltered cigarettes—swung her Trans Am into the driveway next door, got out, and implored us to let her take a turn. After initially refusing, Norm finally relented and handed over his bright-green, chopper-style Huffy bicycle. I remember it like it was yesterday. David Bowie was blaring from the midnight-black Trans Am's speakers as Melody rode all the way up the hill on Tupelo and didn't turn around until she'd reached the fire hydrant at the corner of Cherry Court. Then, she'd started pedaling. Fast. Too fast. My friends and I stood on the curb, slack-jawed with awe, as she hit the base of the ramp at a good twenty-five miles per hour and hurtled through space at least fifteen or twenty feet up in the air, her long, dirty-blond hair streaming out behind her like a superhero cape. When the Huffy's tires met the earth again with a loud *twack*, we all cheered and then quickly went quiet again as the tires immediately began to shimmy and wobble out of control. Before any of us could shout a warning to watch out for the traffic on Hanson Road, the bike—with Melody now hanging on for dear life—crashed into the stop sign at the corner, flinging her onto the sidewalk like a rag doll. En masse, we sprinted to her side, certain that we were about to see our first dead body. Instead, she propped herself up on one skinned elbow, her splayed legs and right forearm a pulpy mess of bloody road rash, and started laughing. We couldn't believe it. Not only was she still alive, she thought the whole damn thing was hilarious. Talk about a freaking legend.

Norm was the only one unimpressed. Furious because the frame of his bike—a recent birthday present from his parents—was twisted into an ugly and clearly unrepairable pretzel shape, he let loose with a barrage of colorful language. Most of which I heard about later because, I have to admit, I was barely paying attention. Instead, I stood there in my side yard, eyes wide, staring down at the deliciously tan flesh of Melody's bare torso, which had been generously exposed when the orange tank top she was wearing had been pushed up and torn away after contacting the sidewalk. Above that flat, smooth, tanned tummy of hers, I could just make out a deep-red sliver of lacey bra cupping a pale mound of bare breast—the first brassiere and boob this nine-year-old had ever laid eyes on in real life. My eyes were glued to all of this like a dirty old man at a crowded beach until she finally made it to her feet, brushed herself off, climbed back into her Trans Am, and drove away. It was one of the greatest days of my young life.

My father was a big believer that people should take good care of the things they owned. It was a matter of pride with him. Our cars were always washed and waxed, and the interior and exterior of the house was uniformly tidy. But I think he reserved his most special attention for the lawn. He'd fertilize in the spring and fall, trim the bushes and trees on a regular basis, pick up fallen limbs after summer thunderstorms, edge the grass along the sidewalks (he was particularly conscientious about this task, oftentimes carving deep trenches on each side of the walkways that inevitably snagged our bike tires, causing more than a handful of spectacular, high-speed accidents; I'm still not convinced this wasn't intentional on his part), and mow the grass once a week like clockwork with an almost religious fervor.

As luck would have it, we had one of the largest yards in the neighborhood and, much to my father's chagrin, it served as a frequent playground for my friends. We played everything from Wiffle ball and kickball to miniature golf and war. Permanent base paths, in the shape of a diamond, were worn into my father's precious lawn. Old dog-chewed Frisbees and trash can lids served as bases. The sagging telephone wire that stretched across Tupelo Road served as automatic home run territory. The ground often shook under our feet as we played, and the muffled *thump* of faraway explosions could be heard as weapon testing operations commenced at Edgewood Arsenal. It wasn't unusual for squadrons of fighter planes or helicopters to fly above our heads on their way to or from Aberdeen Proving Ground—where my father worked the early shift as an aircraft mechanic. When that happened, we inevitably stopped whatever we were doing and pretended to shoot them down with invisible machine guns and bazookas.

I often set up magic shows in the breezeway, charging attendees ten cents a head, and makeshift carnivals in the side yard, using old, discarded toys and comic books as game prizes—all in an attempt to pry loose change from the younger kids' pockets. I also set up a card table on the sidewalk at the corner of Hanson and Tupelo and hawked waxed paper cups of ice-cold lemonade to passing drivers.

A mature plum tree and a tangled cluster of crab apple trees grew in the front corner of the yard, supplying us with plenty of ammunition for our frequent neighborhood battles. The trees also provided perfect cover for bombing cars. If there was one weakness I had as a young man, one bad habit I was unable to break no matter how many times I'd been caught and lectured and punished, it was throwing crab apples or dirt clods or snowballs at passing traffic. I have no explanation for this failing of character other than to say if you've ever lain on your stomach in the cool summer grass waiting for an approaching vehicle, sprung to your feet, hurled a small round object at said vehicle, and then listened to the beautiful *boom* of impact, then you know exactly what I'm talking about. It was even more fun when the drivers pulled over and chased us. For us Hanson Road boys, those were treasured moments of sheer, unbridled joy and adrenaline, and we longed to relive them over and over again. There was a lengthy period of time when I think my flabbergasted father fully believed I was heading for reform school or maybe even prison due to my addiction. After a while, he gave up talking to me about the subject. My sweet mother tried to steer me back with "Why don't you boys chase fireflies or play marbles?" but by that time those were kiddie games and held little interest. No one was more relieved than my folks when I finally gave up the habit for good only a short time before I left for college.

If the house with green shutters and the ancient weeping willow tree represented the center of my world growing up—the hub of my "wheel of life," as I later began to think of it—then each road, big or small, leading away from that house resembled a spoke in that ever-turning wheel, every one of them fanning out in a different direction, eventually running out of space to roam, and serving to collectively define the outer boundaries of my beloved hometown.

Regardless of what any map might show, for me, the town of Edgewood stretched from the Courts of Harford Square (about a mile north of my house along Hanson Road) to the shoreline of Flying Point Park bordering the Bush River (a couple miles south of the high school, which was located exactly one mile from my driveway). Yes, the old cliché holds true: my friends and I walked a mile to and from school every day until we were old enough to drive. We'd barely missed, by a block and a half, the cutoff to ride the bus, but we didn't really mind. The long walk gave us more time to screw around before and after school, and delayed the inevitable drudgery of homework. It also gave us additional opportunities to throw small round objects at passing cars, or even better, at school buses.

I was blessed with an army of companions growing up, but my closest friends, my true partners in crime, were Jimmy and Jeffrey Cavanaugh, who lived two houses farther up the hill from me on Hanson Road. The Cavanaughs were crafty and mischievous and a hell of a lot of fun to be around. Brian and Craig Anderson lived right next door to them. Daredevils both, the Anderson brothers were too alike and hot-tempered to really get along on a consistent basis. Two memorable incidents best defined this dynamic. In one instance, a heated argument led to Craig storming upstairs into the kitchen, where he grabbed a dirty steak knife from the sink and returned downstairs to stab Brian in the upper thigh. To his credit, it was Craig who bandaged his older brother's leg that day and eventually phoned the ambulance. In the second, Craig, in a moment of pure rage one blisteringly hot summer afternoon, actually dropped his shorts to his ankles and squatted in the middle of Hanson Road, defecated into his cupped hand, and proceeded to chase down his fleeing brother, flinging a handful of fresh poo onto Brian's shirtless back like an ill-tempered monkey in the zoo. I know it sounds disgusting and far-fetched in equal measure, but I was there to witness it—and what an astounding sight it was to behold. I'll never forget it.

Jimmy and Brian were a year behind me in school (Jeff and Craig several years behind their older, but not much wiser, siblings), so the three of us were especially close. Based on advanced age and the ingrained bossiness that comes along with having three older sisters, I usually assumed the leadership role of our small neighborhood crew. Jimmy and Brian never seemed to mind, and I can't remember a single plan of theirs that we didn't enthusiastically embrace as well. Depending on whom you asked, we were either the Three Musketeers or the Three Stooges. People knew us and we knew them—every single kid in our section of Edgewood and most of the grown-ups existed on our daily radar. And we knew *stuff*, too. We knew where the pretty girls lived, where the shortcuts were, which cigarette machines in which gas stations always had extra packs of matches left over in the tray (an invaluable currency of which there was perhaps only one equal: firecrackers), which dumpsters held the most returnable soda bottles, and which tree houses held hidden caches of dirty magazines. We knew which parents spanked their kids and which ones drank too much; which neighbors with swimming pools attended church on Sunday mornings—meaning it was safe for us to pool-hop—and when we were older, which stores would sell us alcohol, where the cops hid with radar guns, and which parking lots were safe for making out with a girl.

A typical summer day for us ran the gamut of youthful adventure. We played every outdoor sport known to man, and some others that we invented out of sheer boredom. We popped tar bubbles on the road with our toes. Cheated at Marco Polo in the Cavanaughs' aboveground swimming pool. Fished in the nearby creeks, ponds, and rivers. Explored the endless woods, and built secret underground forts. Sometimes, our good friend Steve Sines would join us and bring along his father's .22 semiautomatic rifle. We'd spend long afternoons hunting for crows and vultures in the woods or shooting at empty cans and bottles. Other times, we'd practice responsible gun safety by pointing at each other's shoes and yelling, "Jump!" before pulling the trigger and blasting the dirt where our friend's feet had stood only seconds earlier. It's a miracle we still have all our toes.

Other days, we might shimmy up a drainage pipe onto the roof of Cedar Drive Elementary and pretend we were standing on a snow-covered mountaintop in a faraway land. Or we'd climb a similar drainage pipe to the top of the Texaco gas station at the junction of Hanson and Edgewood Roads and moon the passing drivers (that particular stunt screeched to a regretful halt one memorable afternoon when my father spotted the glare of our skinny, pale asses on his way home from work. I was grounded for a week).

You have to understand this about living in a small town like Edgewood: boredom made for strange bedfellows, and there was often little rhyme or reason to the things we did. One summer, along with our old friend Carlos Vargas, we created an exclusive group called the Daredevil Club. For some unknown reason, the initiation rites involved throwing miniature Matchbox cars into random neighbors' swimming pools under the cover of darkness. Another time, we became weirdly obsessed with collecting toads in empty peanut butter jars. I also once spent an entire July afternoon walking around shirtless with a dead, six-foot-long black snake hanging around my neck. I even tried to enter several stores, but was turned away. No one—including myself—knows why I did this, but it didn't really matter. It was all fun in the moment.

The Edgewood Shopping Plaza, located several blocks from our houses and directly across the street from the library, also provided many hours of interesting entertainment. There was Plaza Drugs, where we bought most of our candy and all of our comic books and baseball and football cards. I also purchased every one of my Mother's Day gifts at that store from the time I was old enough to walk there by myself until I turned sixteen and got my driver's license. There was a liquor store that also sold the most amazing pizza subs (over a foot long and melted to cheesy perfection) for a couple of bucks, and a laundromat with an old-fashioned candy machine in the back that dispensed packs of Bubble Yum for the unbelievably low price of a dime (a pack ran twenty-five cents in most other places, so I pumped handfuls of dimes into that machine several times a week and then sold the individual pieces for a nickel each at school, thus earning a lovely profit that inevitably went back into more pizza subs). Saving the best for last, there was an honest-to-God pool hall (owned by our friend Brook Hawkins's father) where we played pinball and learned to shoot eight-ball and searched for quarters that the drunks dropped onto the filthy carpet. The lights were dim, the tipplers plentiful, and there were almost always coins to be found.

Outside, at the bottom of the shopping center's parking lot, a group of older boys had built a ten-foot skateboard ramp with eighteen inches of vert, and thanks to the rows of streetlights, we rode that ramp day and night. Sometimes carloads of girls even showed up to watch and cheer us on.

Suffice to say, the Cavanaughs and Andersons didn't spend much time at the library across the street, but you couldn't keep me away. I'd kick back in the overstuffed chairs in the Adult section and devour book after book. General George Armstrong Custer was a favorite early subject, as was almost anything about the Old West, the Civil War, and unexplained phenomena. I found myself attracted to mysteries and crime stories, and wholeheartedly believed in ghosts and werewolves, the Loch Ness Monster and Bigfoot.

One Saturday afternoon, a bona fide Bigfoot hunter from somewhere out west came to town and set up a large exhibit in a back corner of the library. A slow talking, stoop-backed fellow with an unruly salt-and-pepper mustache and one long bushy eyebrow, he gave a fascinating talk, and shared with us photographs and maps and drawings and even a clump of authentic Bigfoot fur attached to a bulletin board with a thumbtack. I'd somehow convinced Jimmy to go along with me that day, and we sat in the center of the front row, paying rapt attention. When the talk was finished, Jimmy and I huddled in between two rows of nearby bookshelves, put our heads together, and came up with a plan. We quickly returned to the exhibit area, where the guest speaker was posing for photographs and chatting with a handful of admirers. Jimmy gave me a nod and proceeded to activate step one of said plan by creating a diversion—to this day, I can't recall exactly what that entailed, but I believe it may have involved dropping to the floor and faking a seizure. Once a concerned crowd had gathered around my flopping friend, I slipped behind the exhibit table and snatched several strands of authentic Bigfoot hair and stuffed them deep into my pocket. Minutes later, we made our escape and no one was the wiser. I tell this story here for the first time with an unapologetic mixture of pride and shame. I still have no idea what became of that clump of authentic Bigfoot hair. If I had to guess, I can envision my mother probably finding it in one of my desk drawers, wrinkling her nose and shaking her head as she threw it away.

For me, after hanging out at either the library or the Edgewood Shopping Plaza, there were two ways to get back home again. The first involved crossing Edgewood Road at the main traffic light and traveling several blocks along Hanson Road. This was the route we'd take if we were riding bikes or skateboards. But if we were walking, we always took the shortcut.

That involved crossing a dangerous section of Edgewood Road right next to the shopping center and walking up the long gravel driveway of the dreaded Meyers House. Once past that monstrosity, we'd cut across a pair of backyards—one small, one not-so-small—and find ourselves standing on the sidewalk alongside Tupelo Road, a mere one block away from my house.

Every small town has a haunted house—a place where horrific things were rumored to have happened, where bad things still lingered, and your heart trip-hammered and arm hairs stood on end every time you walked past it. For us, that was the Meyers House. Built more than two hundred years before any of us were born, and purported to be the original home of a nineteenth-century coven of witches, the Meyers House was a massive Victorian structure with a wide, deeply shadowed wraparound porch, twin gabled peaks, and dozens of windows that watched over the town with a foreboding intensity. During the day, the place was bearably unsettling. You felt the house watching you, measuring you, but you also knew (hoped) that it wouldn't actually make a move. Not in broad daylight—it was smarter and more sinister than that.

At night it was an altogether different story. The house loomed over us in the darkness, hungry and alert and sly, and to dare walk past it was a terrifying odyssey that only the bravest of neighborhood kids would even consider undertaking. "Brave" certainly wasn't a word many people would've used to describe us, but we did it anyway out of a combination of pure laziness (a shortcut was a shortcut, after all) and a masochistic desire to torture ourselves.

It was during those long, slow, breathless walks up that gravel driveway that I first began telling scary stories to my friends. I'd start slowly with a series of mundane incidents, building the narrative gradually, sprinkling interesting tidbits along the way, and timing the pace so that the most awful and terrifying shocks would occur just as we were passing close to the house. Most often, by that point, it was Jimmy who was begging me, "*Please stop, for God's sake, Chiz, just stop it!*" I rarely listened. Sometimes, I'd even glance over my shoulder, eyes bulging at a horrible sight unseen, and let loose with a bloodcurdling scream. Then I'd take off, running for home. By the time we hit the corner of Hanson and Tupelo, our screams had usually turned to paralyzing laughter, and we couldn't wait until the next time to endure it all again.

As it went with most small towns, Edgewood had plenty of odd stories and full-blown legends making the rounds. Some years ago, when I was in elementary school, a young girl, distraught over an unwanted pregnancy, supposedly killed herself by standing on the railroad tracks behind the high school and allowing a speeding train to run her down. Since then, many witnesses claim to have seen or heard the girl's ghost roaming around in the nearby woods. A close and dependable friend of ours, Bob Eiring, swears to this day that he saw a group of white-robed scientists conducting an experiment on an honest-to-God alien when he snuck into an off-limits area on Edgewood Arsenal and peeked into a warehouse window. He claimed the creature had a head the size of a bicycle tire and light-blue powdery skin. We didn't believe him at first, but he spent a couple weeks at the library sifting through old newspaper files and came back with a stack of black-and-white photocopied articles from the 1960s and '70s reporting similar rumors about top-secret extraterrestrial studies being conducted at the Arsenal. So his veracity couldn't be easily challenged. Not with all that evidence.

No one seemed to know when the Rubberband Man first made an appearance in Edgewood—I asked my sisters, and they'd originally heard about him back when they were teenagers—but all the kids I knew were scared to death of him. It was unclear if the Rubberband Man was actually human or some sort of supernatural creature or perhaps even a mutated mistake that had escaped from a laboratory at Edgewood Arsenal. If you listened to the whispers—and it goes without saying that we sure as hell did—the Rubberband Man was almost seven feet tall and painfully thin. His arms were like twigs and hung stiffly at his side. His hair was midnight dark and short and bristly. His eyes were black slits and his mouth was a grim, straight line. No one had ever seen his teeth. No one, that is, who'd ever lived to tell about it. The Rubberband Man was always dressed in dark clothes and liked to prowl secluded playgrounds and open fields at dusk, looking for children to steal away and devour. Once, when I was seven, I'd been playing hide-and-seek with friends at the church playground down the street from my house. There was a pair of brightly painted concrete tunnels, each about twelve feet long, positioned not far from the swings. When we were really little, we used to pretend that they were submarines. That evening, I hid inside one of the tunnels. After a while, when no one came to find me, I peeked outside and will swear on a stack of Bibles that I spotted a freakishly tall, lanky figure emerging from the woods across the way. After fifteen or twenty yards, the figure abruptly changed direction and started trudging toward the playground. Suddenly very afraid, I ducked back inside the tunnel and scooted toward the middle, remaining perfectly still. A few minutes later, I smelled a terrible, sour stench, like a basket of rotted fruit left out in the sun too long. I held my breath, trying not to gag, and remained motionless as a pair of spider-thin legs dressed in tattered black pants shuffled past the mouth of the tunnel. I waited what felt like an hour until I could no longer hear the footsteps, and then counted to fifty inside my head just to be sure before making a frantic break for the road. I found my friends fooling around in front of Bob Eiring's house and told them what'd happened. A short time later, we all returned to the playground with Brian Anderson's father at our side. There was no sign of the strange figure anywhere. But I'm not crazy. I know what I saw. And smelled.

And then, of course, there was the Phantom Fondler. I was away at college when it all started, but I'd been able to keep up with the story, thanks to weekly issues of the *Aegis* that my mom saved for me. In fact, it was a reporter from the *Aegis* who first came up with the "Phantom Fondler" moniker. Since August 1986, someone had entered the homes of at least two-dozen Edgewood women and touched their feet, legs, stomach, and hair while they were sleeping. In each case, when the woman awakened, the man fled from the house and disappeared into the night. Thus far, local police had been unable to capture or identify the assailant.

These stories—and many others I could tell you—offer a mere glimpse into the darker nature of my hometown. Despite my somewhat biased viewpoint, my vision of Edgewood was not entirely colored by the haze of nostalgia or the golden-tinted memories of Norman Rockwellian Americana bliss. As in most small towns, there was crime and violence, treachery and secrets, tragedy and disappointment. There was a wrong side of the tracks to live on, and places where you didn't want to find yourself alone after dark. When I first got to college, I was shocked to find that most of the guys in my dormitory had never been in a fistfight before; I'd been in a dozen or more by the time I graduated high school. Speaking of which, the principal had been arrested for embezzlement during my sophomore year and actually sentenced to real prison time. A couple of years earlier, a middle school teacher had been arrested for a string of armed bank robberies in Maryland, Pennsylvania, and Delaware, crimes committed during his days off.

Unlike the majority of Harford County, and due to our proximity to Edgewood Arsenal, we were a diverse community, thanks to the large number of military families that moved in and out with increasing frequency. A large population of African Americans and Hispanics called Edgewood home and attended schools there, and even in these modern, supposedly enlightened times, their very presence was enough to intimidate certain people. When I was old enough to drive, more than a handful of the out-of-town girls I dated weren't allowed to attend parties or sporting events in Edgewood. "No offense" was the usual excuse their parents told me. I smiled politely and took the girls there anyway. My senior year, when the Edgewood High School lacrosse team won its first state championship in school history, students from the nearby and much-more-affluent Fallston taunted us from the bleachers, chanting, *"It's all riiight, it's okaaay, you'll all work for us one dayyy!"* That kind of elitist attitude only served to strengthen the Edgewood bond—it was us against the world, and we liked it that way. We were more than just a community—we were a family. No, we didn't drive fancy cars and live in huge houses with manicured yards. Our parents didn't belong to country clubs or business organizations; they were members of the American Legion and the PTA. And for me and my friends, that was perfectly okay; a source of blue-collar pride, and the way it was supposed to be.

———

There are two special memories of Edgewood that remain forever imprinted on my soul. The first occurred when I was only five, not long after we moved here. It was a chilly night in December and several inches of freshly fallen snow blanketed the ground. After dinner, my father and I shrugged on our heavy winter coats, ski caps, gloves, and boots, and headed outside. Most of the driveways and sidewalks had been shoveled clean. Christmas lights glowed in the windows and along the rooftops of a handful of houses lining Hanson Road. There was little traffic, and a peaceful hush hung in the air. Hand in hand, neither of us saying much, my father and I walked up Tupelo, past Cherry Court and Juniper Drive, until we reached the corner at the top of the big hill on Bayberry. My father turned to his left and stared down the hill. Watching him, I did the same—and was stunned by what I saw. Every house, as far as I could see, on both sides of the street, was lit up by multicolored Christmas lights, many of them blinking cheerily. Front yards of glistening snow shone with a kaleidoscope of brilliant colors— red and green, blue and yellow, silver and gold. A cluster of carolers sang "Silent Night" in the front yard of one of the houses, and a big plastic

Santa surrounded by flying reindeer swayed in a gentle breeze atop the roof of another nearby house.

I live here, I remember thinking. *This place is my home . . . and it's magic, and I never want to leave.* My father, sensing my breathless wonder, squeezed my hand. I did the same right back, and after standing there for a while longer, we wandered down the street together, taking in the sights.

Coincidentally, the second special memory I've tucked safely away also occurred on a snowy winter evening. I was fifteen, and my friends and I had spent a long, chilly afternoon sledding on the series of hills surrounding Cedar Drive Elementary School just down the street from our houses. A water tower stood at the summit of the largest hill, and its long, spindly legs always filled my head with menacing images of rampaging aliens from one of my all-time favorite movies, *The War of the Worlds.* I'd had frequent nightmares about that tower when I was little, but I was older and braver now, and all alone on the hill, my friends having gone home a short time earlier for dinner. A handful of other neighborhood kids had stayed behind with me, but at some point in the past twenty minutes or so, they too had vanished and I'd been too busy having fun to notice. Hungry, tired, and half-frozen, I took one final trip down the hill and started for home.

As I reached the peak of one of the smaller hills at the base of the tower, it began to snow again, and through the trees I caught sight of my house in the distance, some three blocks away. Blinking red Christmas bulbs glowed along the gutters of the roof. The tall, bushy trees on each side of the driveway were draped with pinpricks of twinkling green. Rectangles of pale light shone in the bay window and pair of smaller basement windows. I stopped walking, catching my breath, transfixed. I imagined my mother preparing dinner in the kitchen, humming to a Christmas song on the radio, my father downstairs on the sofa, watching the news and playing a game of solitaire. I stood there motionless in the falling snow and glanced around—there were no cars moving on Hanson Road, not a single person in sight, the world all around me completely silent except for the rhythmic ticks of icy snowflakes landing on my waterlogged coat. It was a lonely feeling—a somehow melancholy feeling. I looked up at my house again—and for the first time in my young life, it hit me.

Standing there in that frozen moment of space and time, I realized how vast the world around me really was and that one day soon I'd be leaving this place I'd always called home, to venture out on my own. My friends would also be scattered to the four winds, and some I would never see or talk to again. Our parents and brothers and sisters would grow old and eventually we'd have to say goodbye to them, too. Nothing would ever be the same.

My breath caught in my throat, and suddenly my eyes misted and my legs wavered. All at once, I was five years old again, only this time my father wasn't standing next to me, reaching over to take hold of my hand. I remember telling myself in that moment that everything was going to be okay, that I was going to grow up and be happy and one day become a writer, and the words I put down on paper were going to help people make sense of this world.

I've no idea how much longer I stood there in the midst of the snowstorm. All I remember is that at some point, and without realizing what I was doing, I started walking again, my sled tucked underneath my arm, and eventually I made it home in time for dinner.

Although I've often thought about that moment over the years, I've never spoken or written about it until now.

(A great deal of the historical insight included in the first section of this chapter can be found within the pages of two fine books: *Edgewood, Maryland: Then and Now* by Jeffrey Zalbreith; and *Images of America: Edgewood* by Joseph F. Murray, Arthur K. Stuempfle, and Amy L. Stuempfle. I highly recommend both volumes.)

ABOVE: Edgewood Meadows sign at the junction of Bayberry Drive and Edgewood Road *(Photo courtesy of the author)*

LEFT: Weapons testing at Edgewood Arsenal
(Photo courtesy of The Baltimore Sun*)*

RIGHT: The old Edgewood railroad station *(Photo courtesy of* The Aegis*)*

LEFT: The Meyers House
(Photo courtesy of Alex Baliko)

ABOVE: Cedar Drive military housing *(Photo courtesy of the author)*

LEFT: The Edgewood Library *(Photo courtesy of The Aegis)*

ABOVE: The author's home on Hanson Road *(Photo courtesy of the author)*

two

The First Girl

"After all, didn't killers often return to the scene of the crime, observing the damage they'd caused?"

1

The first time I remember seeing Natasha Gallagher was at Sunday morning mass with her family. I was twelve years old at the time, so that would've made Natasha six. It was just my parents and me at church that day—all of my older siblings were out of the house by then—and we'd purposely sat in the back row because my father had tickets to the Baltimore Colts game and was determined to make a quick escape as soon as ten o'clock service ended.

The Gallaghers arrived a few minutes late. I heard the heavy doors creak open behind me and glanced over my shoulder. Young Josh stood in between his parents, looking every bit as thrilled to be there as I'm sure I did, and little Natasha stood off to the side, holding hands with her mother. She was wearing a polka-dot dress and her long blond hair was pulled back in pigtails. The family took a few tentative steps down the center aisle and paused, craning their necks, looking for a place to sit. My father immediately motioned them over, shooing Mom and me toward the middle of the pew. The Gallaghers, one after the other, scooted in next to us. Once everyone had settled in, I casually leaned forward and took a closer look. Josh gazed over with sleepy eyes and gave me a cool-as-ice nod that James Dean and Elvis would've been proud of. Sitting on his left, Natasha broke into a big, gap-toothed grin and wiggled her fingers at me in an exaggerated wave. I immediately sat back and stared straight ahead, my face and ears growing warm. Girls, of all ages, seemed to have that effect on me. I hated it.

The next time I saw her, it was summertime, and she was skipping down the sidewalk in front of my house, swinging her arms high above her head, singing the *Scooby-Doo* theme song in a high-pitched, nasally voice. She passed within fifteen feet of me that day without ever knowing I was there.

An old oak tree—gone several years now—grew in the center of my front yard, conveniently obscuring the porch from passing traffic, its thick network of leafy branches overhanging the sidewalk. I'd taken to climbing that tree and perching myself ten or fifteen feet above the ground, usually with a Stephen King paperback to keep me company. I liked the feeling of being invisible to the world, of watching the steady flow of cars and occasional pedestrians passing below, knowing they had no idea I was there, practically close enough to reach out and touch them. I sat there, hidden and silent, imagining what their lives were like and where they were going and if they were happy or sad, thinking good thoughts or bad ones.

I knew the words to the song she was singing by heart—*Scooby-Doo* was my favorite Saturday morning cartoon growing up—and considered joining in, but I didn't want to scare her, so I kept quiet and let her go on her way. She reached the end of the sidewalk at the corner of Tupelo, stopped walking (and singing), looked both ways, and then crossed the street. Once she was safely on the other side, she started skipping and singing again, continuing down Hanson at an even jauntier pace. I glanced at my book, turned to a new chapter, and when I looked up again, she was gone.

Later that same summer, Natasha and two of her friends stopped by my lemonade stand. All three had wet hair and towels draped around their necks, so I figured they'd just come from swimming. One of her friends announced she didn't have any money, so Natasha pulled out a small change purse and paid for all three of them. Unlike the time I'd seen her in church, she seemed almost shy, barely making eye contact or speaking a word. Until she climbed back on her bike, looked over her shoulder at me, and said, "See you later, Richie Rich." Surprised that she knew my name, I stood there and watched as they pedaled away.

It was 1982 and I was a senior in high school the last time I saw her. It was the week before Christmas break, and Jimmy Cavanaugh and I were sitting on the top row of bleachers inside the gymnasium. Down on the floor, wrestlers from Edgewood and Bel Air were going through their warm-ups. Van Halen blared from the loudspeakers. Fifteen minutes before the match was scheduled to start, the home team's student section was already packed and on their feet. Next to me, Jimmy was busy being Jimmy, stretching a piece of gum out of his mouth and twirling it around the tip of his finger, daring me to dare him to toss it into the bird's nest of curly hair on the sophomore in front of us.

I saw Mr. Gallagher first, shedding his heavy winter jacket as he walked into the gym. His wife and daughter were right behind him, all of them rosy-cheeked and still shivering from the frigid walk across the parking lot. Natasha slipped off her pink ski cap, and long shiny waves of blond hair cascaded down her shoulders. She'd grown taller since I'd seen her last and was well on her way to becoming a little heartbreaker. It was a good thing her brother Josh was around to keep the middle school boys in line.

Mr. Gallagher waved to someone in the crowd, and all three of them started walking single file toward the bleachers on the opposite side of the gym. Halfway there, Natasha abruptly changed direction, veering closer to the padded, red-and-white Edgewood Rams wrestling mat centered on the floor.

I saw Josh then, lying on his back at the far left corner of the mat, legs tucked underneath him, back and arms stretched into what should've been an impossible position. Natasha stopped in front of him and said something. He looked up in surprise. Instead of being irritated by his younger sister's interruption, as I'd expected, Josh quickly got to his feet, a big smile brightening his face, and wrapped his arms around her. When they finished hugging, they high-fived, and Natasha hurried away after her parents.

I remembered thinking at the time: *Maybe sisters aren't so bad after all.* Then AC/DC came over the loudspeakers and, just like that, the thought was gone and I was back to stopping Jimmy from sticking his gum in an unsuspecting girl's hair.

2

During the five years I was away at college, Natasha Gallagher certainly grew up. At five foot four and barely one hundred pounds, she evolved into a natural and gifted gymnast. She adored the sport and was disciplined in her craft, practicing five times a week at Harford Gymnastics in the William Paca Business Center. Floor routine and balance beam were her specialties. She also loved cheerleading and was the only freshman in her class to make the varsity squad at Edgewood High. If you asked Natasha's family and friends to tell you something memorable about her, they would paint a picture of a beautiful and perpetually happy teenager. She was addicted to cinnamon chewing gum and colorful hair barrettes, and was madly in love with life. She loved to laugh and make others do the same. A terrible singer, she never let that stop her from being the loudest in the group. She was goofy and hyper and not the least bit self-conscious, rare for a girl her age. She liked to doodle and daydream. She loved flowers and helping her mother in the garden. And for such a talented athlete, she was endearingly clumsy off the gymnastic mat. Natasha was the kind of girl who picked up trash when she found it on the ground and told strangers to have a wonderful day. She often cried while watching movies and gave the best hugs.

So said her obituary.

3

I was helping my roommates haul furniture out of the unnatural disaster zone that was our three-bedroom apartment, located on the outskirts of the University of Maryland campus, when I first heard the news that Natasha Gallagher had been killed.

I'd lost a coin toss earlier in the morning and was on my way to pick up Chinese food for all of us when a quickie news story came on the car radio. I almost slammed on the brakes in the middle of Greenbelt Road when I heard the reporter mention "young girl from the suburb of Edgewood" and the victim's last name. Praying I was mistaken, I called home as soon as I got back to the apartment and spoke with my father. He didn't know much more than I did, just enough to confirm that it had indeed been our neighbor Natasha. The conversation was brief and somber.

It was all over the evening news and on the front page of several local newspapers the next morning. Later that afternoon, I called a couple of old friends and got the rest of the story.

This is what I learned:

Two nights earlier—Thursday, June 2, 1988—Natasha Gallagher, age fifteen, spent the evening with her mother and father watching television in their basement family room until 9:00 p.m. Once the program ended, she'd said goodnight and gone upstairs to get ready for bed. It was summer vacation and nine o'clock was early for her, but Natasha had been swimming at a friend's house most of the afternoon. She was sunburned and exhausted.

At approximately 9:10, she yelled a second goodnight from the top of the stairwell, and Mr. and Mrs. Gallagher heard her walk down the hall and close her bedroom door. About an hour later, they turned off the television, went upstairs and double-checked the front door was locked, and went to sleep. It was just the three of them in the house. Josh, who'd dropped out of college during his sophomore year after a shoulder injury from wrestling, now lived in a rented town house in nearby Joppatowne, where he worked full-time at Andersen's Hardware.

The next morning, after seeing her husband off to work and loading the dishwasher, Catherine Gallagher glanced at the kitchen clock and was surprised to see that it was almost nine. Natasha was taking care of the neighbors' dogs while they were away on vacation, and it wasn't like her to oversleep. *The kitchen radio's kind of loud this morning. Maybe she's up and in the shower already, and I just didn't hear her*, Mrs. Gallagher thought as she walked down the hallway, going out of her way to give her daughter the benefit of the doubt.

Finding the bathroom empty, an irritated Mrs. Gallagher knocked on Natasha's bedroom door, twice, and when there was no response, she opened it and went inside. Her daughter's bed was empty. The clean shorts and T-shirt she'd laid out the night before were still draped over the chair in front of her desk. Her favorite yellow flip-flops sat on the floor at the base of her bed.

Mrs. Gallagher, no longer irritated but now confused, started to turn away when she noticed something odd about the window. For the past week, an early summer hot spell had settled over Edgewood, with temperatures hovering in the high eighties. Natasha had begged her father to turn on the central air-conditioning, but to no one's surprise, he'd refused. "Not until the first week of July, you know that's the rule," he'd lectured her. "What do you think, we're made of money?" Natasha had pouted, but only for a short time and without any real enthusiasm.

Mrs. Gallagher slowly approached the window. It was slid almost all the way open, the sheer curtains rustling in the muggy morning breeze—but that's not what caught her eye. The screen was missing.

She walked closer and immediately noticed a dark smear, no larger than a dime, on the windowsill. Unable to stop herself, she reached out and touched it, and her fingertip came away stained a dullish red. She lifted her hand closer to her face. *It looked an awful lot like blood*, she told the police later, *but I couldn't be sure.*

The first butterflies of panic stirring inside her, Mrs. Gallagher leaned over the windowsill, careful not to get any of the red stuff on her blouse, and peered outside. A short distance below, on the lawn, lay the screen to the window. It was twisted almost in half.

Mrs. Gallagher, heart hammering in her chest, forcing herself not to run, returned to the kitchen and phoned her husband at the office.

It was 9:07 a.m.

4

The first two police officers arrived at the Gallagher residence on Hawthorne Drive at 9:20 a.m. They found Catherine Gallagher pacing back and forth in the driveway. Her face was streaked with tears and her hands were clasped tightly together in front of her, but she managed to fill them in with clear-voiced efficiency. The Maryland State Police troopers, in their report, later described her as "frightened and agitated, but in complete control. Her chain of events was clear and consistent."

One of the troopers escorted Mrs. Gallagher back inside the house and, after requesting that she wait in the living room, conducted a brief examination of Natasha's bedroom. The second officer went to the side yard and, careful not to disturb anything, inspected the open bedroom window and the damaged screen on the ground.

As the trooper returned to the front of the house, a pair of Harford County Sheriff's cruisers pulled to the curb. Before heading inside to join his partner in questioning Mrs. Gallagher, the trooper quickly brought the arriving officers up to speed and asked them to begin searching the surrounding area. By this point, a small crowd of neighbors had gathered outside on the sidewalk.

By 9:29 a.m., Russell Gallagher arrived at the residence, parking his Cadillac in the driveway and rushing inside. Neighbors reported hearing angry shouting from inside the house, and it was later learned that Mr. Gallagher needed to be restrained in order to prevent him from disturbing the crime scene in his daughter's bedroom.

At 9:41 a.m., Joshua Gallagher, whom his mother had also phoned, arrived at the house. He'd made the normally fifteen-minute drive from Joppatowne in just under ten minutes. Josh spoke briefly with several of the waiting neighbors on the sidewalk, and then he went inside.

5

At 10:07 a.m., less than forty-five minutes after the first officers arrived at Hawthorne Drive, Natasha Gallagher's body was discovered in the woods behind her house by a member of the Harford County Sheriff's Department. Still dressed in the matching light-blue shorts and tank top she'd worn to bed the night before, Natasha was propped up against a tree with her ankles crossed and her hands resting in her lap. She'd suffered severe bruising and swelling around her neck, a fractured cheekbone, a pair of black eyes, and the thumb and ring finger on her right hand had been broken. The coroner determined that the majority of her injuries most likely occurred during a prolonged struggle. What hadn't occurred during the struggle was this: at some point, her left ear had been sliced off by a sharp blade of unknown design. No signs of either a weapon or the severed ear were located at the crime scene. Preliminary reports listed cause of death as strangulation. Approximate time of death had yet to be determined.

6

The rumors started almost immediately.

Neighbors called neighbors and gossiped over backyard fences and cups of coffee or tea. Strangers and friends alike chatted at the bar or in the frozen food aisle at Santoni's grocery store or while waiting in line at the post office. Kids overheard their parents talking about it and repeated what they'd heard on ball fields and playgrounds.

By the time I'd gotten home three days later, I'd already heard a half-dozen different theories regarding what had happened to Natasha Gallagher.

The most prevalent belief was that Edgewood's mysterious Phantom Fondler had finally escalated from voyeuristic creeping and touching to cold-blooded murder and mutilation. There was even widespread speculation that he might do it again, and sooner rather than later. Local police were quick to refute these claims and requested that the public remain vigilant yet calm. Desperate to say *something*, they even provided surprising new details regarding the Fondler investigation for the first time in nearly six months.

"At this time, we do not believe there is any connection," said Major Buck Flemings of the Harford County Sheriff's Department. "For a variety of reasons, which we're currently unable to make public, we believe these crimes have been committed by two very different individuals. In fact, during the course of our lengthy investigation, we recently thought we knew who the Fondler was. We had a suspect who was incarcerated on an unrelated charge, and the incidents ceased. We believed at that time he was probably the man we were looking for.

"This individual was released for a short time and then incarcerated once more," Flemings said. "The incidents started up again while he was free, seeming to confirm our suspicions, but then they continued even though the guy we were looking at was once again back in custody. Now . . . we don't know what to think."

In another surprise admission, Flemings went on to report that the latest fondling incident occurred a mere two weeks earlier but was never publicized at the request of the sheriff's department. "It was the same pattern as before. The woman woke up to find a man standing over her in her bedroom. He was touching her hair and face. She cried out, and the man took off.

"So now we're back to square one. We don't know if it's been the same guy all along, or if it's some kind of copycat running around. We *do* know that nothing much has changed. What he did two weeks ago is the same thing he did in 1986 and 1987. It's the exact same M.O., and bears no evidential resemblance to the case involving Natasha Gallagher. But you can rest assured, every one of my officers is working around the clock to solve this horrific crime."

Another theory floating around town that proved particularly unsettling involved Natasha Gallagher's father. According to several close neighbors, Russell Gallagher exhibited excessively strange behavior in the days that followed the discovery of Natasha's body. Normally stoic and steadfast—some would even say abrasively masculine—Mr. Gallagher was barely able to drag himself out of bed over the course of the next forty-eight hours. "It was like he was in a trance or something," one neighbor claimed. "He cried the entire time I was there and just kept mumbling, 'I'm sorry, I'm sorry.' His eyes were so swollen he could barely keep them open."

Initially, Mrs. Gallagher was all but abandoned to deal with the parade of police officers, detectives, neighbors, and media that swarmed in and out of her house all day long, but Josh quickly stepped up and established boundaries, and her younger sister from Orlando, Florida, flew in later that week to help. According to Rose Elliott, who'd lived next door to the Gallaghers for as long as anyone could remember, Mrs. Gallagher even considered checking her husband into the hospital. That's how desperate she'd become.

For most people, Mr. Gallagher's behavior could be explained away by the obvious fact that the man's only daughter had been violently murdered just days earlier. He was clearly distraught and suffering from unimaginable pain. In addition, it was widely understood that Mr. Gallagher placed the bulk of the blame for Natasha's death on his own shoulders. After all, he was the one who hadn't allowed her to turn on the air-conditioning in the house. He was the reason her window had been left open that fateful night.

"There's not a single rational thought," said Frank Logan, one of Russell Gallagher's coworkers at the insurance agency, "that points to Russ having anything to do with his daughter's murder. To claim otherwise is utterly ridiculous and irresponsible."

But certain other people were quick to point out that even in the days leading up to Natasha's murder, Mr. Gallagher had been acting rather strange. "It was the oddest thing," one local said. "He picked an argument with me just last week. Out of the blue, he accused me of letting my dogs do their business in his yard. I've lived down the street from the Gallaghers for fifteen years and I've never once let one of my dogs take a crap on their lawn. He was really upset about it, too. I have no idea what got into him."

Another Hawthorne Drive resident offered up similar concerns. "He's usually pretty quiet and keeps to himself. I mean, he's friendly enough, waves hello, wishes you a 'good day,' that sort of thing. But lately he's seemed nervous and distracted. And talking a whole lot more than usual, almost like he was covering up for something."

For other townspeople, suspicion immediately focused on Lenny Baxter. Lenny was a decorated Vietnam veteran who spent his days picking up litter along Edgewood Road and doing yard work if he could find someone to hire him. Lenny never begged for money and didn't accept handouts. He'd once lived with his mother on Perry Avenue, not far from the high school, but after her death in the late seventies, he'd been unable to keep up with the mortgage payments and had lost the house. Most of the year—spring, summer, and fall—he lived in a tent in the woods behind the post office. There were rumors he'd booby-trapped the area around his campsite, but I didn't believe them. No one I talked to knew where he went during the winter months.

The thing about Lenny was this: although at first glance he certainly appeared to be strong enough to strangle a young girl, he also walked with a pronounced limp, thanks to an old hip injury, and could barely look people in the eye when he spoke, much less hold a real conversation. He also smelled pretty bad and was in the process of losing most of his teeth. The idea of Lenny Baxter luring Natasha Gallagher out of her house and into the woods seemed a bit far-fetched. The idea of him doing it without leaving behind a slew of evidence seemed downright impossible; a theory based solely on convenience and nothing more. There wasn't a sliver of doubt in my mind that if Lenny Baxter had committed the crime, he'd already be locked up.

Other less popular rumors also surfaced. One story involved a hidden diary discovered in a shoebox in Natasha's bedroom detailing a series of secret rendezvous with an older boy. Yet another described an ongoing argument with a jealous girlfriend suddenly turned violent. None of these local tales possessed a hint of evidence backing them up, but still there remained whispers, as expected.

That first week back in Edgewood, I spoke with pretty much anyone and everyone willing to talk to me about Natasha Gallagher's murder— old friends and acquaintances, the teller at my bank and the counter lady at the post office, longtime neighbors and complete strangers. I also found myself eavesdropping on other people's conversations. I wasn't proud of this fact, but I couldn't wrap my head around the reality that a girl I knew—however peripherally—had been killed just up the street from where I'd grown up. It felt like a movie. It felt like a nightmare.

7

The funeral service was delayed until the following Friday. I assumed this was because the family had to wait for Natasha's body to be released by the coroner's office, which was pretty damn gruesome to consider. My mother was right—I couldn't imagine something like this happening to us.

I'd only been to a handful of funerals in my life—a couple of uncles and a good friend's mother who'd passed away from cancer during our last year of high school—but I'd still managed to create a strict set of expectations for such events. The first was that there was very little talking, and what there was of it was done in hushed tones and a crude form of sign language. My second preconceived notion was that the weather would inevitably match the mood of the attendees—dark and stormy and depressing. A cold rain was practically a given.

The morning of Natasha Gallagher's funeral service dawned sunny and mild. Scattered wisps of thin white clouds scudded across a brilliant blue sky, the kind that begged for picnics at the beach and flying kites and boat rides on the river. It felt wrong, almost obscene.

The service took place at Prince of Peace on Willoughby Beach Road, the same church where I'd first laid eyes on Natasha. Father Francis gave the mass—unbearably solemn and well attended—and did his best to try to make sense of what had happened. I think he also went out of his way to make the ceremony as brief as possible; there was enough pain and suffering in that room to fill a dozen such services.

My parents and I sat toward the front of the church with the Gentiles from next door, my mother and Norma exchanging balled-up tissues throughout the sermon. Mr. and Mrs. Gallagher and Josh sat a few rows ahead of us, along with a bunch of people I didn't recognize, but assumed were relatives. Despite the stories I'd heard around town, Mr. Gallagher appeared rigid and composed. Perhaps he was all cried out by that time. Mrs. Gallagher sobbed throughout, head bowed and slender shoulders trembling. At one point, Josh slid his arm around his mother, and she rested her head on his shoulder. That was when I almost lost it. I wished Kara were there with me, but she was taking summer classes at Hopkins and couldn't afford to miss her first lab.

In a selfish attempt to distract myself from the family's sorrow, I pretended to stretch and casually glanced around the church. Almost every pew was filled. I recognized dozens of familiar faces from the neighborhood (many of them wrinkled and fleshier, others thinner, all of them older), friends of my parents I hadn't seen in years, former teachers and coaches, and a handful of old friends from high school—albeit none of the guys from my youthful inner circle. Most of them were gone now. The Cavanaughs had moved away to South Carolina right after Jeff finished high school. Brian Anderson was taking summer classes at college in West Virginia. I didn't know what Craig was up to; none of us did. Steve Sines had joined the air force and was currently stationed up north in Maine. Carlos Vargas now lived outside Washington, D.C., where he'd just started working as an engineer. Tommy Noel and a handful of others were working full-time at the Arsenal. Most of the rest were scattered around the country like dandelion seeds in the wind. It suddenly made me sad to think about.

I felt a bony elbow poke me in the rib cage and turned around to find my father staring at me with that familiar "pay attention" look etched across his face. I gave him a guilty nod and started listening to Father Francis again.

But just before my father scolded me, I'd noticed two men I'd never seen before, sitting at the rear of the church. They wore dark suits and blank expressions on their faces. Their jutting chins pointed straight ahead toward Father Francis, but their eyes were actively scanning the crowd. *Police*, I immediately thought, a shiver tickling my shoulder blades. It made perfect sense. After all, didn't killers often return to the scene of the crime, observing the damage they'd caused?

8

In the humidity-drenched summer days that followed Natasha Gallagher's funeral, several intriguing developments began to take place.

For reasons unknown, whenever I made a trip to the post office or Frank's Pizza out on Route 40 or the grocery store on Edgewood Road to pick up something for my mom, I found myself driving the long way home. Instead of taking the Route 24 bypass off 40 or cruising a direct path down Hanson Road, I opted to go the back way, driving a series of less-traveled side streets, which inevitably led me straight to Hawthorne Drive—and right past the Gallaghers' house.

The first time I cruised by, Mr. Gallagher had just pulled into the driveway and was getting out of his car with a brown paper bag in his hand. Slumping down in the driver's seat, I accelerated by the house. A large, bright red ribbon had been attached to a tree trunk in the Gallaghers' front yard. Runners of yellow police tape blocked off a portion of the side yard beneath Natasha's bedroom window. The next time I drove past, a couple of days later, both the ribbon and police tape were gone. By the following week, a homemade memorial of flowers and candles and photographs had taken its place at the base of the tree.

I'm not entirely sure why I started driving by Natasha's house. Human nature? Maybe. Morbid curiosity? Probably. Budding obsession? Definitely. I was ashamed to admit such a thing, but what else could it be? I filled my days and nights with stories and novels and movies that peered into the deep, dark wells of human evil. Hell, I wanted to make a career of such excursions. So, didn't it make sense that those fascinations should transfer over to real life? I honestly wasn't sure, and didn't like to think about it.

Around this time, I also started calling Carly Albright. She was a childhood friend of Kara's—I knew her as a smart, cheerful girl who wore bright red eyeglasses and talked too loud—but we'd never been particularly close. The two of them had grown up right down the street from each other in Long Bar Harbor, a mostly waterfront community located just off Route 40, but they'd eventually grown apart when Carly's family moved to a larger house in downtown Edgewood and Carly transferred to John Carroll, a private Bel Air Catholic high school, during her freshman year.

Now, after graduating from Goucher College, Carly was back at home in Edgewood, living with her parents, and working for the *Aegis*. According to her, it was mostly busy work, writing community notices about yard sales and church bazaars and free first-aid clinics at the YMCA. Toss in the occasional obituary or high school sports piece, and you had one seriously bored rookie journalist.

And that's where my initial interest in Carly stemmed from—despite her misgivings, she was an actual working journalist. She was walking the walk and had access to the newsroom and the wire services and seasoned reporters who'd been covering big stories for decades. I was fascinated with the idea that she was only twenty-two years old and drawing a full-time paycheck from a real newspaper. Ironically, she shared similar feelings about me and my fancy degree from the University of Maryland ("You know they have one of the top three journalism programs in the entire country," she once told me at a party), and even more so about my handful of short fiction sales. So, yes, you could say we had a bit of a mutual admiration society going on, and in the weeks to come, Carly would not only prove to be an invaluable source of information, but also grow to be a good and trusted friend.

Not all the developments were of a personal nature. Much to the community's relief, it'd been reported earlier in the week that Natasha Gallagher had not been sexually assaulted—before or after her murder. The time of death had also been narrowed down to shortly after midnight, indicating that she'd probably been taken from the house not long after she'd gone upstairs to bed.

The subject of just *how* Natasha had been stolen away from her bedroom without her parents hearing sounds of a struggle, or any sounds at all for that matter, was now the number two question on everybody's mind. Number one, of course, being: *Who had committed this horrible crime?*

The police offered no answers—although, naturally, the most common theory pointed to Natasha knowing her assailant and leaving her bedroom voluntarily—and as the days passed, neither law enforcement officials nor the media provided any new information related to the murder.

"It's frustrating," said Martha Blackburn, longtime Edgewood resident, when asked by a reporter from the *Baltimore Sun*. "All we get from them is 'it's an active investigation and we're working around the clock pursuing various leads.' Well, of course they are. One of our kids was murdered two weeks ago. What else are they going to do?

"What we really want to know is, do they have any suspects? Was it someone from around here, or a stranger? Do they think he'll do it again? I have three children of my own, you know . . ."

Meanwhile, on the home front, my mother could barely stand to talk about what had happened—the handful of times she did take part in the conversation invariably ended with her tearing up and excusing herself to go lie down—but my father had his own theory. He believed the killer was someone Natasha knew in a cursory manner, meaning not well enough to go along with willingly, but just enough so that she didn't cry out in alarm when the person first climbed through her bedroom window. "Probably someone who lives in a nearby town," he explained, "but not an actual neighbor. Also, most likely someone young, close to your age, Rich." He was convinced that, once inside her bedroom, the person used some type of chemical, like chloroform, to render Natasha unconscious, and then carried her out the window into the woods. He insisted that the police should be looking at people like the lifeguards from the YMCA pool or store clerks, and checking to see if Natasha had gone to any local summer camps and then investigating the counselors.

I guess it was as good a theory as any—truthfully, better than most I'd heard—but there'd been no public mention of any kind of chemicals or drugs being detected during Natasha's autopsy, and without having access to police reports, it was impossible to know for sure. The rest of it made a lot of sense, though. Most fifteen-year-olds live a vastly different life than what their parents see on a daily basis. Words unsaid, thoughts unexpressed, secrets both big and small—they were all just part of being a teenager.

Although initially surprised that my father had given the idea so much careful thought, I later decided that I shouldn't have been. My father was the one who'd passed down his love of hard-boiled detective novels. This was the man who had a complete run of vintage Gold Medal paperbacks lined up on a bookshelf in the basement. He adored the old, black-and-white whodunits on television and often recorded them to watch again later.

Before long, I even found myself wondering if perhaps my father had taken the long way home from work a time or two.

9

There was one rather fascinating item that, at the time, was never made public by either the police or the media. In fact, I wasn't sure if anyone in the press even knew about it until a few weeks later when Carly spilled the beans and confirmed many of the details. I first heard about it from an acquaintance that was related to someone heavily involved with the ongoing investigation. One too many pitchers of Bud Light, and he just blurted it out. I was sworn to secrecy at the time, and kept my word, even after Carly separately confided in me. I just sat and listened to her and played dumb—something I discovered I had a particular talent for doing.

The scoop was this: On the morning Natasha Gallagher's body was discovered, several bystanders and police noticed something odd in front of the Gallaghers' house. Someone had used blue chalk to draw a hopscotch grid on the sidewalk. Instead of the usual sequential numbering of one to ten, the person had drawn the number three inside each of the blocks. Detectives verified with Mr. and Mrs. Gallagher, as well as their daughter's circle of friends, that Natasha hadn't played hopscotch since before her tenth birthday. No chalk of any color was found in the Gallaghers' garage or Natasha's bedroom. It was also quickly confirmed that no young children lived within a four-house radius of the Gallaghers' rancher, and those children who did reside farther away on the street all denied drawing the grid.

The detectives believed with absolute certainty that neither Natasha Gallagher nor any other local child had drawn the hopscotch grid on the sidewalk.

So, then, who did?

And what, if anything, did it mean?

RIGHT: Natasha Gallagher
(Photo courtesy of Catherine Gallagher)

LEFT: Natasha Gallagher
(Photo courtesy of Catherine Gallagher)

RIGHT: The hopscotch grid
found on the sidewalk in front
of the Gallagher residence
*(Photo courtesy of
Logan Reynolds)*

ABOVE: Gallagher residence crime scene *(Photo courtesy of* The Aegis*)*

ABOVE: Damaged screen from Natasha Gallagher's bedroom window
(Photo courtesy of The Aegis*)*

ABOVE: Wooded area behind the Gallagher residence
(Photo courtesy of the author)

ABOVE: Location where Natasha Gallagher's body was discovered
(Photo courtesy of the author)

three

Kacey

"What if there really is a boogeyman?"

1

Kacey Robinson and Riley Holt, both fifteen, had been best friends since their days at Cedar Drive Elementary School. They grew up two blocks away from each other—Kacey in a sprawling rancher on Cherry Road, Riley in a two-story colonial on the corner of Bayberry and Tupelo—and many people meeting them for the first time believed them to be sisters. Both girls had long dark hair, big brown eyes, bright easy smiles, and even sunnier personalities. Kacey and Riley had made a pact when they were in middle school—after graduation, they'd both attend Clemson University (orange was Kacey's favorite color) and travel the world together before starting their careers as veterinarians. After five years, they'd pool their savings and open up their own clinic. The girls' favorite part of the year was summer vacation because they were allowed to stay up late and have sleepovers at each other's houses. They watched movies and played board games and, just lately, talked a lot about boys and pretty clothes. Riley was an only child, and she adored the noisy but loving chaos that inhabited the Robinson home on a typical summer evening. Kacey had three siblings—a brother one year older and two younger sisters.

Even with what had happened just eighteen days earlier, Riley wasn't worried when she rang the Robinsons' doorbell at a few minutes past 9:00 p.m. on Monday, June 20, 1988. In fact, she was in a particularly fine mood because she was planning on spending the night at her friend's house and they were going to make popcorn and watch *Grease* for what had to be their fiftieth time. They both had major crushes on John Travolta.

"Hey, there," a smiling Mr. Robinson said, opening the front door and finding Riley, standing on the porch, a pink L.L.Bean knapsack slung over one shoulder. His smile faltered a little when he glanced behind Riley. "Kacey isn't with you?"

"She *was*," Riley answered. "We were watching TV and playing cards at my house, but then we headed over here."

Mr. Robinson put out his hands, palms up, as if to say: *Well, then, where in the heck is she?*

Riley giggled. "I forgot my glasses and had to run home to get them," she said. "When I got back outside, she wasn't there anymore. I just figured she walked the rest of the way by herself."

Mr. Robinson turned and leaned back into the doorway. "Honey! Is Kacey here?"

Mrs. Robinson's muffled voice came from somewhere inside the house: "Don't think so!" Then, after a brief pause: "Janie says she went to Riley's!"

Mr. Robinson turned back to Riley and shrugged his shoulders. "She's not here."

"That's weird."

"Could she have stopped at someone else's house on the way? Maybe Lily's?"

"I guess so, but we had plans for tonight. Just me and her."

A strange look came over his face. "Where was she when you ran back inside for your glasses?"

"Like two houses down from mine," Riley answered. "Right in front of the Crofts'. I was only gone for like three or four minutes."

"And you didn't see anyone else? No one driving by or walking around?" Mr. Robinson was talking faster now, his voice growing louder.

"No," she said quickly. "I mean . . . I don't think so. I wasn't really paying attention or anything." She covered her mouth with her hand. "Oh my God, you don't think someone—"

"I don't know what I think," Mr. Robinson said, walking off the porch and peering up and down the dark neighborhood. There were no cars moving on the street. Not a person in sight. Somewhere far away, a dog was barking.

"Maybe we should call the police," Riley said.

"Not yet." Mr. Robinson cut across the yard and began jogging in the direction of Riley's house. Over his shoulder: "Go inside and tell my wife I'm going to look for Kacey. Tell her to send David in the car."

Riley nodded her head, beginning to cry, and as she walked into the house, she heard Mr. Robinson shouting Kacey's name.

2

Mr. Robinson's Harley-Davidson T-shirt was drenched with sweat and he was gasping for breath by the time he reached the Holts' driveway. It wasn't that far from his own house, maybe a quarter mile or so, but he was out of shape and had practically sprinted the entire way.

There'd been no sign of his daughter anywhere.

Now he was scared.

"*Kacey!*" he shouted again, cupping his hands around his mouth. The barking dog was his only answer.

He turned and started back toward his house, moving slower now, taking a closer look at his surroundings. *So many damn rows of shrubbery,* he later told the police. *So many fences and trees for someone to hide behind.*

"Shit," he suddenly said aloud to the empty street. "I should've knocked on the Holts' door. Maybe she went back there looking for Riley . . ."

The words died in his throat when he saw it. Up ahead, maybe twenty feet in the distance, framed in a pale circle of light from an overhead streetlamp, was a shoe.

He quickly closed the distance and picked it up, not thinking about the police or tampering with evidence or much of anything at all, just picturing his daughter's sweet face and praying he was wrong.

But he wasn't.

It was Kacey's bright green Chuck Taylor high-top sneaker, the one for her left foot, the reason they'd started calling her their little Irish leprechaun. Clutching his daughter's shoe against his chest, Mr. Robinson took off running for home.

3

The Baliko brothers lived right down the street from Kacey Robinson, and I learned most of what happened that night from Alex, the older of the two. Alex's father was a close friend of Mr. Robinson's—they often went fishing and crabbing together and bowled in the same league every other Friday night—and he'd gotten the details directly from Mr. Robinson. The story was shared with Alex a few days later on their way to the hardware store, and Alex told me he'd never seen his dad look or sound so wrecked. It really frightened him at the time.

I heard the rest of the details of that night from Carly Albright, various media reports, and the actual radio calls between the state police and sheriff's department.

A week earlier, I'd used a 25 percent–off coupon my father had lying around to purchase a police scanner from Radio Shack in the Edgewood Shopping Plaza. I mostly listened at night while I was writing. My sister Mary, a surprise dinner guest earlier that same week, claimed it was ghoulish and that I was subconsciously hoping for something else bad to happen, like those reporters on the Weather Channel during hurricane season. "They don't even bother to hide their excitement," she complained. "It's gross."

My sister wasn't exactly right about my reasoning for buying the scanner, but she wasn't entirely wrong, either. I certainly wasn't hoping for anything bad to happen . . . but I *was* waiting for something. I didn't know what or when, but I undeniably felt *expectant*. I could feel it in the air all around me—a buzzing, almost electrical sensation of foreboding menace. As the long days of summer passed, the same haunting words surfaced in my mind time and again:

There's a storm coming.

4

Officer Aaron Hubbard was very familiar with the area surrounding Cedar Drive Elementary. His family had moved to Edgewood from Ohio when he was ten years old, and he'd attended the school for one year before graduating on to sixth grade at the middle school. As a teenager, he'd spent countless hours roaming the grassy fields around Cedar Drive, playing baseball, basketball and football, hide-and-seek and war and kick-the-can. He'd also had plenty of friends who'd lived in the military housing just up the hill and would often go there to hang out after the school day was finished. He'd even learned to drive a stick shift by practicing in his father's five-speed Subaru on the one-and-a-half-mile road that looped around the elementary school, kindergarten building, and adjacent ball fields.

On the night of Kacey Robinson's disappearance, it was Officer

Hubbard's job to search his old stomping grounds. He circled the loop several times, slowing down and directing the spotlight attached to his cruiser at the usual areas of interest: doorways and windows lost in shadow, the pitch-black tree line that bordered the edge of the road across the way, behind a scattering of dumpsters, and in between several rows of parked buses.

Everything looked in order, so he swung his cruiser into the elementary school parking lot and radioed Shirley Rafferty back at the station to let her know he was going to complete the remainder of his search on foot. He exited his vehicle, flashlight in hand, at 11:27 p.m.

Officer Hubbard's father, recently retired from the Maryland State Police after more than thirty years of service in nearby Cecil County, had made a point of teaching his son the finer points of conducting a night search on foot. Back in the late fifties, during his second year on the job, Mr. Hubbard had interrupted a burglary in progress at a warehouse loading dock and almost been killed. The academy covered this—and every other type of potential conflict scenario—in painstaking detail, but Mr. Hubbard wasn't taking any chances. "The moment you set foot outside your cruiser, you're exposed," he'd lectured his only son. "And when you're exposed, what else are you?"

"You're vulnerable," his son would dutifully answer, trying his best to sound reassuring and confident. He knew his father worried about him, and he knew firsthand how that kind of worry could wear you down. All he had to do was look at his mother to see proof of that.

You're vulnerable. Those two words fluttered through Officer Hubbard's mind as he slowly walked to the rear of the elementary school. He gripped his flashlight in his left hand, the bright beam cutting through the shadows ahead of him, and rested his right hand atop his holstered sidearm. He moved as stealthily as he could.

After circling the building and tugging on several doors to confirm they were locked, Officer Hubbard trudged up the hill toward the baseball diamond and playground. Upgraded just a few years earlier, the ball field featured brand-new dugouts and an electronic scoreboard. Stretching out in foul-ball territory down the left-field line, the playground occupied nearly a full acre of open ground.

Officer Hubbard flashed his light into the first-base dugout to make sure no one was hiding in there, and then cut across the pitcher's mound to check out the opposing team's bench area. When he found it empty, he eased himself out of the gate, trying not to make too much noise, and entered the playground.

He swept the area with his flashlight beam and spotted the girl right away, lying at the bottom of the taller of two sliding boards. Her eyes were open and bulging. Her thin arms were crossed atop her chest, her bare feet dangling several inches above the ground.

His father's eternal warning rushed back at him: *You're vulnerable.*

Unholstering his weapon and scanning the darkness, Officer Hubbard keyed the radio unit hanging across his chest and informed Shirley that he'd found Kacey Robinson.

5

Early the next morning, all four local television networks carried live footage from the playground. Kacey Robinson's body had been removed by then, but there was still plenty to gawk at. More than a dozen uniformed officers and detectives remained at the scene, several crouched in the dirt sifting for clues, others standing around talking in small groups. Despite both access roads leading into Cedar Drive being closed to civilian traffic, a large crowd of lookie-loos gathered behind temporary barricades, many of them sipping morning coffees and smoking cigarettes. A handful snapped photographs with disposable cameras. They'd all walked there, many from the shoulder of Hanson Road, where they'd parked their cars, others from nearby homes.

The handful of on-air news personalities—three women and one man—wore grave expressions on their faces and spoke in respectfully hushed tones. Although a sheriff's department spokesman had provided a brief statement thirty minutes earlier, he'd declined to confirm the victim's identity.

Still, there was little doubt among the horde of onlookers and captivated television viewers watching from home. Word traveled fast in a small town like Edgewood.

By the time dinner tables had been cleared and the evening news hit local airwaves, the tragic details had been confirmed:

The deceased was officially identified as Kacey Lynn Robinson, fifteen years of age, resident of Edgewood, Maryland. Sometime between the hours of 10 p.m. and midnight, she'd been killed by an unknown assailant, and both the nature of her injuries and the positioning of her body—each of the networks was now using the word "posed"—bore striking resemblances to the case involving Natasha Gallagher.

However, it wasn't until the next morning that a lengthy article published in the *Baltimore Sun* revealed the true extent of the hideous crime. According to a police spokesman, Kacey Robinson exhibited numerous facial and head injuries, as well as defensive wounds on her hands and arms. She also suffered a deep bite mark on one of her breasts and her left ear had been severed. Official cause of death was strangulation.

There was no mention of sexual assault. That would come later.

6

The weekly edition of the *Aegis*—released that Wednesday morning— brought news of an even darker nature. A bold headline screamed across the top of the front page:

TWO LOCAL GIRLS DEAD—WAS IT THE BOOGEYMAN?

Centered underneath were large black-and-white photographs of Kacey Robinson and Natasha Gallagher. Both girls were smiling. While the Gallagher family declined to comment for the article, Mrs. Robinson had plenty to say.

"It happened back in May, during the last week of school," she explained. "My two youngest daughters share a bedroom. Janie, my seven-year-old, has a big imagination and often has bad dreams, especially if she's seen something unsettling on television.

"She came into our bedroom in the middle of the night and told me and my husband that the boogeyman was trying to get into her window and could she please sleep the rest of the night with us. We told her there was no such thing as the boogeyman and it was just another nightmare, but we'd make an exception this time and let her stay.

"The next morning at breakfast, she was back to her happy little self and even admitted that she'd been watching a crime show on television right before bedtime. I didn't really think about it again after that— until I heard the news about Natasha Gallagher.

"At that point, my husband called the police and told them the whole story. Detectives came out to the house later that day and searched the yard and checked for fingerprints. They didn't find anything and told us that most likely we'd been right—that our daughter had probably just had a bad dream.

"But what if all of us are wrong and Janie's right? What if someone really did try to break into her bedroom window that night? What if there really is a boogeyman . . . and he came back and got Kacey?"

7

The funeral was held on Saturday morning, and this time a steady rain fell from an ash-gray sky, distant thunder rumbling overhead. I didn't go, but my parents did, sharing a ride with Norma and Bernie Gentile.

I was fighting off a summer cold, so I slept in that morning, hung over on NyQuil and lemon-flavored throat lozenges. Besides, the Robinson children were much younger than me, and I didn't know Mr. Robinson at all and just barely recognized his wife from the one summer I'd worked at a grocery store. Kara, who was tolerating my increasing chatter about the murders with a noticeable lack of enthusiasm, said I was just making up excuses not to go, and she was probably right. Dammit.

I'd received an acceptance letter in the mail the day before, notifying me of my first short fiction sale of the summer. The title of the story was "Roses and Raindrops," about a series of mysterious killings in a small, rural town. The bad guys in this particular tale were supernatural in nature and always left behind a single red rose as a calling card. *New Blood* was the name of the magazine that had bought it. Over the past eighteen months I'd racked up nearly a dozen rejections trying to crack its glossy pages, so I should've been elated with the news. Instead, I hadn't even mentioned it to anyone other than Kara. I was afraid they'd ask me what the story was about, and I'd be too ashamed to tell the truth.

Later that morning, before my parents returned from Kacey Robinson's service, I dragged myself out of bed and drove to the 7-Eleven on Willoughby Beach Road. I told myself I was only going there because I had a craving for a strawberry Slurpee, but I knew that wasn't the truth. If there was one spot in Edgewood that assumed the role of the traditional small-town general store, it was this place. Only instead of the town elders crowding around an old-fashioned woodstove each morning to exchange the latest news and gossip, Edgewood's crew of oldtimers conducted their business at the rear of the store, in front of a long row of automatic coffee machines.

On any given morning, there were usually anywhere from a half-to-a-baker's-dozen men huddled back there, sipping on cups of steaming coffee and puffing on unfiltered cigarettes. Average age was in their sixties. Occupations ranged from electrician and attorney to retired professor and state trooper. There was a core group of regulars, three or four who never missed a day. Fred Anderson, Brian and Craig's father, was one of them. He was always hanging around back there, and this morning was no exception.

I said a quick hello to Mr. Anderson and pretended to have trouble working the Slurpee machine, eavesdropping the entire time. The main topic of conversation was the funeral service, since most of the men's wives were in attendance. I took a good look at the group and wondered what it said about all of us that we were here, wasting our time in a 7-Eleven, while our better halves were honoring the memory of a fallen community member.

Talk soon shifted to the ongoing police investigation and the possible identity of the killer. Most of the men present felt it was an outsider committing the murders, someone with a grudge against pretty young girls. Fred Anderson stridently disagreed. He believed it had to be a local, someone with intimate knowledge of the people and places in Edgewood.

I secured a lid on my Slurpee and eased closer to the group. Feeling brave, I waited for a lull in the conversation, and then bit the bullet. I asked if they had any specific ideas about who the killer might be, a name. The place went silent—the *you could hear a pin drop* kind—and they all just stared at me like I had two heads sitting atop my shoulders. No one uttered a word. Nothing. Nervously swallowing a mouthful of strawberry Slurpee, I nodded awkwardly and went on my way to the cash register, my face burning with embarrassment.

The big news came two days later, on Monday, when Channel 11 aired exclusive footage of a suspect being escorted into the sheriff's station. As far as anyone knew, it was the first time a person of interest had been hauled downtown. The Channel 11 newswoman reported that the man's name was Henry Thornton, age twenty-seven, of Havre de Grace. In addition to cutting grass and doing miscellaneous yard work for several of his neighbors, Thornton worked as a deliveryman for Domino's

Pizza franchises in both Aberdeen and Edgewood. On the night of Natasha Gallagher's murder, Thornton had made late-night deliveries to both Hawthorne Drive and—the next block over—Harewood Drive.

When pressed for a statement, State Trooper Seth Higgins said, "We've spoken with literally dozens of people who we believe may be helpful to our investigation. Mr. Thornton is just one of those individuals, and it's unfortunate that the media has chosen to make such a big deal of it."

Even with news of a possible suspect in custody, people remained on edge. Two young girls had been violently murdered in the heart of downtown Edgewood, their bodies mutilated and grotesquely posed. Local newspapers jockeyed for attention—and increased sales—with garish, tabloid-style headlines:

SERIAL KILLER LOOSE IN EDGEWOOD?

THE BOOGEYMAN STRIKES AGAIN

**POLICE HAVE NO LUCK
TRACKING DOWN VAN GOGH KILLER**

The television news stations were even less dignified in their frenzied pursuit of ratings. Breaking news segments interrupted regular programming throughout the day, and you could barely run out to the grocery store or gas station without a reporter ambushing you and shoving a microphone in your face. Before long, the entire town was caught up in it.

Residents who rarely locked their doors were now double- and triple-checking them numerous times a day. The sales of dead bolts and home security systems went through the roof. Residents paid to have peepholes installed in their front doors and added motion-detector spotlights around their houses. Gun sales spiked at sporting goods stores and pawnshops, as did frantic calls to 911.

One Cherry Court resident—it was never confirmed, but word on the street was that it was Hugo Biermann, a retired naval officer—even booby-trapped the flower garden beneath his daughters' bedroom windows with a pair of steel bear traps. Supposedly, this precaution led to a visit from a member of the sheriff's department, and Biermann was forced to return the traps to his garage.

Early the following week, I took a break from writing and met Carly Albright for lunch at Loughlin's Pub. On my way to the restaurant, I passed a pair of camera crews shooting footage in the neighborhood. Kids on bicycles raced up and down the street, hooting and hollering, trying their best to get on the six o'clock news.

Carly and I had been trading phone calls with increasing frequency, but this was the first time we'd made plans to actually meet in person. As usual, the bar and dining room were packed with military and civilian personnel from Edgewood Arsenal located just a quarter mile up the road. We sat at a small table in the corner and, with lowered voices, caught up on the latest developments.

According to Carly, pizza deliveryman Henry Thornton had been released after more than six hours of questioning. For whatever reason, the police had become convinced of the man's innocence within the first couple of hours and had spent the remaining time determining if he'd witnessed anything of importance on the night Natasha Gallagher had been killed. Unfortunately, he'd been of little help.

Another theory the police were actively exploring, she told me, was the possibility that the killer was using the Edgewood train station to slip in and out of town. They were looking into train schedules and passenger ticketing to determine if there might be some kind of a pattern.

Finally, after swearing me to secrecy and several false starts, Carly eventually revealed that the new number one suspect was Kacey Robinson's ex-boyfriend, Johnathon Dail, a seventeen-year-old who'd been in trouble before for underage drinking and disturbing the peace. An odd pairing, they'd only dated for a few weeks during the school year before

Kacey's parents forced her to break it off. The boy lived with his aunt and uncle on the water at the end of Willoughby Beach Road, but neither had seen him in almost two weeks. They believed he'd gone to Ocean City with friends, but couldn't be certain. Police were actively searching for the boy.

A short time later, Carly and I cut through the bar on our way out and caught the last thirty seconds of the lead story on the afternoon news. A tearful Riley Holt stood in front of her parents at the bottom of their driveway. "I just miss her so much," the teen sobbed before the camera. "I wish every single day that she was still here. I wish I'd never left her alone . . ." With that, Riley broke down with emotion and the program cut back to a frowning anchorman.

The next day, the public was introduced to the detective in charge of the investigation via a televised press conference held on the steps of the Harford County Sheriff's Department. My first impression of the man was this: African American, late-forties/early-fifties, tall, stern (like a high school principal), confident, cheap Men's Wearhouse suit.

"Good morning," he spoke into the microphone. "My name is Detective Sergeant Lyle Harper. I'm going to make a brief statement and that will be it for today. We will not be answering any follow-up questions."

Groans sounded from the members of the media in attendance. The detective immediately lifted his hands. "But I will be making another statement tomorrow or later this weekend, and will be happy to answer your questions then."

The detective cleared his throat before continuing. "Shortly before midnight, last Monday, June 20, the body of fifteen-year-old Kacey Robinson was discovered on the grounds of the Cedar Drive Elementary School. She had been reported missing by her parents earlier in the night at approximately 9:00 p.m. The coroner and investigating officers found striking similarities between the wounds suffered by Ms. Robinson and those of an earlier victim from the Edgewood area, fifte-year-old Natasha Gallagher. In both cases, strangulation was determined as the cause of death, and the bodies appeared to have been purposely displayed in similar positions. However, several significant differences exist with these two cases."

Detective Harper shuffled the papers from which he was reading and cleared his throat once more.

"Evidence found on and around Kacey Robinson's body, including bite marks, scratches, swelling, and bruising, indicate that she'd been sexually assaulted before her death. This is a marked difference from the case of Natasha Gallagher."

One of the reporters standing up front shouted a question, but Detective Harper ignored it.

"We are unable at the present time to determine if there is a single individual responsible for both of these crimes or if it's the work of multiple perpetrators. In that regard, I'd like to caution both the media and the public when it comes to the use of buzz-friendly monikers such as 'serial killer' or 'boogeyman.' Local law enforcement is relying on the public to remain calm and vigilant so that we will be able to properly conduct our investigation. In closing, we encourage all residents of Edgewood to be cautious, to be safe, and to notify us immediately if they see or hear anything out of the ordinary. Thank you, and I promise we'll have more information available soon."

8

That night at the dinner table, the subject of Detective Harper's press conference came up. My father felt the detective had made a strong first impression, doing a fine job projecting a balance of confidence and authority. He thought we were in good hands. To my surprise, my mother seriously disagreed and launched into a five-minute tirade wherein she criticized everything from the way the detective was dressed to the way he swayed back and forth as he spoke to his disclosure of the fact that

Kacey Robinson had been sexually assaulted. "Just imagine how that poor family must've felt hearing those terrible things being broadcast to the entire world. What's the point of doing such a thing?"

I was tempted to explain that the public had a right to such knowledge, especially when people were afraid and vulnerable and looking for answers, but I was smarter than that and kept my mouth shut. It wasn't an argument my father or I—or anyone else, for that matter—was going to win.

As we were clearing our dirty dishes from the table, the kitchen telephone rang. Neither of my parents made a move to answer it, and I noticed a strange look pass between them.

"What?" I said, looking back and forth. "Fine, I'll get it." I slid my plate onto the counter and grabbed the receiver off the hook. "Hello?"

There was no response.

"Hello?"

Again, only silence. I hung up and looked at my parents. "Nobody there."

"Again with that," my father said. "Your mom had a couple of hang-ups earlier. It kind of creeped her out."

She shivered and hugged herself. "I could hear someone breathing on the other end, but they wouldn't say anything."

"Probably kids playing a prank," I said, shrugging.

My father nodded. "That's what I said."

"It was unsettling," my mother replied. "Three times now. No telling who it could be."

"Who do you think it is, Mom?" I asked, trying not to smile. "The boogeyman?"

My mother swatted me on the shoulder with a dishrag. "That's not funny."

"Owww." I put up my hands, still trying not to smile. "I'm sorry, okay? I was just kidding."

"Well, I'm not laughing. It's terrible what's been happening. And *you*"—she pointed at me—"with all those people calling the house to talk to you about it, and those awful books piled up on your desk. *The Encyclopedia of Serial Killers?* Sweet Jesus, you're lucky I didn't toss it in the trash."

I leaned over then and hugged my mom, all four feet ten inches of her. "Now you sound like Mary. She called me a ghoul the other night."

Her eyes widened. "She called you *what?* Wait until I talk to that girl."

I kissed her on the cheek and glanced at my father. He was smiling and shaking his head.

9

Later that night, my father knocked on my bedroom door and poked his head into the room. "You busy?"

I looked up from my computer screen. "Just rereading an old story. What's up?"

He walked in and sat on the edge of the bed. "Do me a favor?"

"Sure. What do you need?"

"For you to be careful."

"Careful with what?" I asked, genuinely confused.

"For starters, with all those questions you've been asking around town."

I started to protest, but he stopped me.

"I know you're interested in . . . this sort of thing, and that's fine. Your mom makes a lot of noise about it, but she's okay with it too. Mainly because she knows you have a good head on your shoulders. She also knows how much you love this stuff" . . . he gestured to the *'Salem's Lot* poster hanging above my bed—"but we just want you to be cautious. This is real life, Rich, and it's obviously a sensitive subject, and some people might not like you asking those kinds of questions."

"You talking about whoever's calling the house and hanging up?"

He looked at me and shrugged his shoulders.

"Okay. I promise I'll be careful. Tell Mom to stop worrying."

He gave me a look. "That's never gonna happen, and you know it." We both laughed.

He stood up from the bed, glancing at the *'Salem's Lot* poster again. "I don't know how you can sleep with that thing in here. That is one nasty-looking zombie."

"Jesus, Dad," I said, feigning outrage. "That's a vampire."

He took another look. "Umm, yeah, that's what I meant. One nasty-looking vampire."

"Good niiight," I said, starting to laugh again.

"'Night, son." And he closed the door behind him.

10

I knew my father was right. I had to be careful. I mean, what was I even doing? Brand-new degree or not, I wasn't a journalist. I didn't work for a newspaper. I didn't have a book deal. As I'd explained earlier to Carly, I was simply . . . curious.

Which is why I soon found myself driving by the playground almost every afternoon. Cedar Drive was along my direct route to the post office—it pretty much marked the halfway point—so it was only natural that I would. Right?

The temporary barricades had been removed and the playground was once again open to the public. But I never saw more than a handful of kids playing there, and always with at least one watchful adult standing close by. I guessed it would take a long time for things to return to normal, if they ever did.

At the bottom of the sliding board where Kacey Robinson had been found was a shrine of fresh flowers and stuffed animals and homemade signs. Candles had been burned there at some point, a scattering of waxy nubs forming a loose ring around the makeshift memorial. Several times I was tempted to park my car and take a closer look, but I never did.

11

The Wednesday before the Fourth of July, Carly stopped by the house and we sat on the front porch with glasses of iced tea. There wasn't a cloud in the sky, and the hot sun shined down without a hint of mercy. Carly made sure the door was closed behind us, and then she once again made me swear to keep what she was about to tell me a secret. I swore and swore again, and she finally told me:

Just as the police had asked the media to withhold from the general public the existence of the hopscotch grid they'd found on the sidewalk in front of the Gallaghers' house, they'd also asked them to hold something back about the Robinson case.

Attached to a telephone pole directly across the street from the Robinsons' house was a square white cardboard sign featuring a small photo of what looked like an adult poodle. HAVE YOU SEEN THIS DOG? was printed above the photo. A phone number was listed below: 671-4444.

Neither the Robinsons nor the Perkinses, who lived across the street, had ever seen such a dog, nor did they have any idea who posted the sign. In fact, no one else living on Cherry Road had, either. Detectives canvassed the surrounding neighborhood and were unable to locate any additional signs. Soon after, someone tried calling the number at the bottom of the sign, but there was no dial tone—just dead air. At that point they checked with the phone company, and, in short order, a representative confirmed that no such number existed.

12

Something else the police hadn't made public—and with good reason—was their increasing frustration due to the complete lack of evidence present at either crime scene. It was extremely unusual for this type of violent crime to be committed with such uncanny precision and self-preservation. "It's like the guy sliced open a hole in the night," one state trooper complained off the record, "and disappeared back into it."

Not a single fingerprint that didn't belong to Natasha Gallagher or an immediate family member was found in her bedroom or on the glass panes or wooden frame of her window. As suspected, the blood trace on the windowsill belonged to Natasha. Because of recent high temperatures, the ground below her window was dry and hard. No footprints or disturbances were found in the grass. No one in the neighborhood saw anything unusual the night Natasha was taken. No strange cars cruising the streets or parked in out-of-the-way spots. No one lurking in the shadows or even walking a dog along the sidewalk near the Gallaghers' residence. As for Natasha Gallagher's body, despite the personal nature and ferocity of the attack, not even a sliver of evidence—no hair or fiber samples, no traces of the killer's blood, saliva, or DNA—was discovered.

The Kacey Robinson case was proving every bit as difficult. A Bayberry Drive resident claimed to have heard a revving car engine around the time of Kacey's disappearance, but by the time she got to the window, the street was empty. None of the other neighbors heard or saw a thing. In addition, nothing of interest was found on the Chuck Taylor sneaker that Mr. Robinson discovered in the roadway, and the missing right shoe had yet to be located. Crime scene technicians lifted more than a dozen usable unique prints from the playground sliding board, but most were those of small children. Nothing else unusual or useful was found on the sliding board itself or the surrounding grounds. Kacey Robinson was sexually assaulted a short time before her death, but the killer almost certainly wore a condom.

No semen or saliva had been present. Even the bite mark had been wiped clean.

And then there was the apparent lack of any significant connections between the two victims. Both girls were fifteen years of age, Caucasian, came from solid, two-parent families, had at least one sibling, and lived in relatively close proximity to each other. Both were attractive and bright and had long hair. But that's pretty much where the common ground ended. Edgewood was a small town, so the two girls knew each other through school and shared a handful of mutual friends, but had rarely socialized or spent time together—either by themselves or within a group. They had never spoken on the telephone or attended each other's birthday parties. Neither had ever dated or admitted to a crush on the same boy. Natasha Gallagher was a cheerleader; Kacey Robinson was the president of the Math Club. Detectives were actively searching for the slightest hint of any additional connective threads, anything that might tie the two girls together in some other way, but thus far had come up empty.

The police and sheriff's department were also starting to feel pressure from the media. Following the death of Kacey Robinson, the small town of Edgewood was no longer just a local story. CNN and the Associated Press now had teams in place and were reporting daily on the situation. Out-of-state news crews taking footage on neighborhood streets had become a common sight around town.

Fortunately, the "Van Gogh Killer" nickname that had first made an appearance in a *Baltimore Sun* headline failed to achieve any level of traction among the public. But "The Boogeyman" was a different story—by the end of June, most members of the media and the vast majority of interested viewers (especially those under the age of thirty) were referring to Edgewood's unknown slayer as exactly that. The police loathed the moniker. They felt it was sensationalistic and in poor taste. And although they were warned by their superiors on a near daily basis not to use it publicly, the police had their own secret nickname for the killer: "The Ghost."

RIGHT: Best friends Kacey Robinson and Riley Holt in Ocean City, Maryland *(Photo courtesy of Rebecca Holt)*

LEFT: Kacey Robinson *(Photo courtesy of Robert Robinson)*

RIGHT: The sidewalk location where Riley Holt last saw Kacey Robinson *(Photo courtesy of the author)*

LEFT: Cedar Drive playground crime scene *(Photo courtesy of The Baltimore Sun)*

ABOVE: Channel 11 reporter at crime scene *(Photo courtesy of Logan Reynolds)*

four

Suspicion Mounts

"Because it makes for a better story . . ."

1

As the month of June came to a sweltering end—and good riddance to it—and the Fourth of July weekend approached, Kara finally got a break from school and we were able to spend some time together. Ever since summer classes had begun, she'd been like a phantom in my life. A tired voice on the other end of a telephone. I missed her.

On Friday, July 1, we got takeout from the Venetian Palace on Route 40—on the way out of the parking lot, I noticed someone had spray-painted THE BOOGEYMAN LIVES on the side of the restaurant's dumpster—and ate dinner at the picnic table in Kara's backyard. There was a nice breeze coming off the river, and for the first time in almost a month, the evening was mild and pleasant. We discussed going to a late movie but decided to save that for another night. We were both tired after a long week. Instead, we drove to the Harford Mall, stood in line at Friendly's for double-dip ice cream cones, and window-shopped while we ate.

Until then, we'd managed to avoid talking about the girls' murders. There'd been plenty of other subjects to catch up on, including ongoing preparations for our January wedding. But as we made our way through the mall, bumping into occasional friends and neighbors, overhearing snippets of strangers' conversations, it became impossible to ignore any longer.

"Everything feels different, doesn't it?" Kara remarked.

I nodded. "Everything *is* different."

"Look around. Hardly anyone's smiling or laughing."

I glanced at a group of teenagers milling about outside the food court—she was right. The kids looked tense and preoccupied. One girl—a thin brunette with long, curly hair—looked like she'd recently been crying. Her boyfriend was holding her close, trying to console her.

"Everyone's talking about it at school," Kara said. "My lab partner asked if I lived in Haddonfield, the town from *Halloween*."

I cracked a smile. I couldn't help it.

"It's not funny, Rich."

"Not funny," I agreed, swallowing my grin as fast as I could. "But kind of clever."

"You heard they canceled the carnival?"

"What about the parade?"

"Last I heard it was still on, although it probably shouldn't be. The Fourth will be the two-week anniversary of Kacey Robinson's murder."

I quickly calculated the dates in my head, confirming her timeline. With the onslaught of recent media attention, it felt like the murder had occurred two months ago instead of mere days.

"It doesn't seem long enough," she continued. "Almost feels disrespectful. And what if something else happens because so many people are out celebrating? Half of them drunk and clueless to begin with."

"The sheriff said there'll be extra patrols the entire holiday weekend."

"You know who I thought of when I saw him say that on TV?"

"Who?"

"The stupid mayor from *Jaws*." In a poor imitation of a man's voice: "'. . . . a large predator that supposedly killed some bathers. But, as you can see, it's a beautiful day, the beaches are open, and people are having a wonderful time.'"

I smiled at that. Once Kara got going, there was no stopping her.

"I'm just glad we'll be out on the bay for a couple days," she said, sighing. "Far away from all this."

"Me too." I reached for her hand. After a long week of writing, I was looking forward to spending time with Kara and her family, fishing and waterskiing and camping out on the beach.

Walking back to the car, we spotted a Channel 13 news crew interviewing an older couple in the parking lot and steered clear. No need to go any further down that rabbit hole. The daily news programs were filled with interviews featuring wide-eyed locals, all of them answering the same handful of questions: *Do you believe there's a serial killer in Edgewood? Do you feel safe in your community? Did you know either of the victims or anyone in the families?*

Although there'd been two more televised press conferences following Kacey Robinson's murder, as well as numerous on-air interviews with police officials, very few additional details had been released. A local bank chain had established a $10,000 reward for any information leading to the killer's arrest, and the Harford County Sheriff's Department had set up an anonymous tip-line for residents to call. Police also addressed recent news of the formation of an Edgewood neighborhood watch program, which I worried could lead to real trouble of a different kind.

"While we certainly appreciate any help the public can provide in this investigation," Detective Harper had said in a prepared statement, "we also need to caution residents to follow several basic rules of conduct. First, absolutely no firearms of any type will be permitted on patrol. No exceptions will be made, and we will prosecute to the fullest extent of the law anyone who disobeys this order. Secondly, and of equal importance, no members of the neighborhood watch should, under any circumstances, act on observed suspicious activity. Their only job at that point is to immediately and safely contact police. Third, if any items of interest are discovered, they should not, under any circumstances, remove or touch the item . . ."

2

After dropping Kara off at her parents' house, I drove by Cedar Drive on my way home. It was just past 9:00 p.m., and the playground was dark and silent. In the glare of my headlights, I noticed that the shrine to Kacey Robinson at the bottom of the sliding board had at least doubled in size since my last visit. More flowers and stuffed animals, and a lot more homemade signs, many of them bearing heartbreaking photographs of Kacey. As I was pulling away, a police car cruised past, heading in the opposite direction. The officer stared at me long and hard. I nodded and flipped him a wave. I'm pretty sure he saw me, but he didn't wave back.

Once I got home, I said a quick hello to my folks, who were watching television in their bedroom, grabbed the John Saul paperback I was reading from the end table next to my bed, and went downstairs to the screened-in back porch. I managed to read two short chapters before my thoughts pulled me away. I closed the book and returned to the kitchen, looking for the cordless phone. A few minutes later, settled comfortably on the porch again, I called Carly Albright, and we picked up our conversation from earlier in the week about the mysterious set of numbers contained in the hopscotch grid and lost dog sign. None of it made any sense.

"What else could they mean?" I asked.

"Nothing I can think of," she answered. "Threes and fours are the dominant numbers. Third and fourth murders? He's done this before? I don't know. That's all I can come up with."

"I feel like it has to be something smarter than that. Something . . . *deeper*."

"Why? Because of Hannibal Lecter?" The Thomas Harris novel *The Silence of the Lambs* had been published to great fanfare earlier that summer. She knew I was a fan, so before I could argue my point, she went on. "He's a made-up character, Rich. You know as well as I do, most of these guys aren't geniuses. Not even close."

"I know, I know." I took a deep breath and tried to find the right words. "It just feels like . . . if he's been careful enough to not leave behind a speck of evidence, and daring enough to taunt the police with these number patterns, then it's reasonable to believe he's pretty damn smart."

"Or that you just *want* him to be smart. We don't even know the person who did this is the same person who left behind the hopscotch grid and the sign. It could all be some kind of bizarre joke."

"Why the hell would I want him to be smart?"

"Because it makes for a better story," she replied without hesitation.

I started to argue again but stopped myself. Maybe she was right. Maybe I just wanted this monster to be brilliant and remarkable and memorable—like a character from a goddamn novel or movie. The more I thought about it, the more I realized that I needed to take a good, long look in the mirror.

Carly's younger sister picked up the extension and asked to use the phone, so we wrapped up our conversation, made plans to catch up later in the weekend, and said our goodnights.

I reopened my book and managed to read another paragraph before closing it again. Staring out at the side yard and Tupelo Road, I imagined large groups of desperate, angry people roaming the dark streets of Edgewood, searching dimly lit alleyways and shadowy intersections. Kara's brother knew someone participating in the neighborhood watch. The guy had purchased military-grade walkie-talkies and night-vision goggles. I'd heard from a friend that another watch group was pulling around a wagon filled with ice and beer on their nightly patrols. And several of the men were carrying stun guns.

It struck me then how dead quiet the streets were. It was officially the start of the Fourth of July weekend, and Hanson Road was utterly silent. Muffled conversations from family cookouts and loud splashes from drunken fathers doing cannonballs in backyard pools should've been echoing across neighborhood fences. Kids should've been outside running around with sparklers and chasing fireflies. Fireworks and bottle rockets should've been exploding overhead, lighting up the sky.

I sat out back for a long time that night, missing those happy sounds and sights, thinking about the Gallagher and Robinson families just down the road from me, and the words that Carly had spoken earlier on the telephone, feeling slightly ashamed.

Because it makes for a better story.

3

Early the next morning, my father asked if I would pick up some gas for the lawn mower and Weed eater. After breakfast, I loaded up the pair of five-gallon cans he always kept stored in the corner of the garage and drove to the Texaco station.

When I pulled up to the pumps, Josh Gallagher was parked right in front of me, filling up his old Mustang. I hadn't seen him since his sister's funeral and immediately wished I'd chosen a different gas station. I had a bad habit of putting my foot in my mouth when I got nervous, and the last thing I wanted to do was say something wrong and upset him.

As it turned out, I didn't need to worry about it. No sooner had I turned off the engine and gotten out of the car than Coach Parks, my high school basketball and lacrosse coach, pulled up to the pump next to us. He practically bounded out of his pickup truck.

"Chiz!" he said, a big grin spreading across his chubby face. "Long time, no see!"

"Hey, Coach. How've you been?"

He walked over and gave me a high five that made my fingers ache. "You know me, Chiz. Not too high, not too low. Doing okay."

Coach Parks glanced at the car in front of us then, and I saw his eyes widen. "Oh, hey Josh, I didn't see you there."

Josh finished placing the nozzle back onto the pump and looked over at us. "Mr. Parks," he said with a nod. "What's up, Rich?"

I tried to keep my face blank. "Not much, Josh. How you doing?"

He shrugged, and I silently cursed myself. *Duh, nice going. How the hell did I think he was doing?* He surprised me with what he said next. "I saw you and your mom and dad at the funeral. Appreciate you all coming."

I opened my mouth to respond, but the words wouldn't come. I tried again. "I'm . . . really sorry about what happened."

"Me too," Coach said, his voice sounding very different than it had just sixty seconds earlier. "And I'm sorry I wasn't able to make the service. We were camping with my brother's family and didn't hear the news until we got back."

"No worries," Josh said, his face unreadable. He pulled a set of keys out of his jeans pocket. "I better get going. My mom's waiting for me to take her grocery shopping."

"Give your folks my best," Coach said.

Another nod. "Will do."

I lifted my hand in an awkward wave. "Take it easy."

Josh yanked the car door closed and fired up the engine. It made my Toyota Corolla sound like my mother's sewing machine. We watched him speed away and merge into traffic on Edgewood Road. Once the Mustang had disappeared from sight, I blew out a deep breath.

"You're not kidding," Coach said. "What a terrible thing."

I opened the trunk and hauled out the gas cans. After placing them on the ground in front of me, I was reaching for the pump handle when Coach asked, "Police talk to you yet?"

My hand froze. "About what?"

"About what happened to Josh's sister."

I was about to ask if he was pulling my leg, but I could tell by the expression on his face that he was dead serious. "*Me?* Why would they want to talk to me? I wasn't even here when it happened. I was back in College Park."

"I don't know. They talked to me. I just figured they were doing the same to everyone from that part of town. I heard they interviewed Alex Baliko and his brother. Charlie Emge. Danny and Tommy Noel. Tim Deptol."

I looked at him in surprise. "What'd they ask you?"

He ran his fingers through his thinning hair, a nervous gesture I recognized from years of playing ball for him. "They mainly wanted to know what I thought of Natasha. Was she as well-liked and -behaved as everyone claimed she was? Did I know of anyone at the school who was jealous of her or didn't like her?" He made a face. "They also asked when was the last time I'd seen her and where I was the night she was killed."

"Jesus."

"Yeah, can you believe that? I can't tell you how relieved I was to say that I was on vacation with my family. Like, I was glad I had a real alibi, you know?"

"Did they ask you anything else?"

"Not really. Fortunately, it was pretty quick." He laughed. "Don't get me wrong, I still almost crapped my pants."

"I bet."

He gave me a hearty slap on the back, and as usual I pretended like it didn't hurt. "Don't worry, Chizzy. I'm sure the cops'll get around to you eventually."

4

As luck would have it, "eventually" came the very next day.

My parents had gone to 10:00 a.m. mass at Prince of Peace, so I was alone in the kitchen when someone knocked at the front door. I looked out the peephole and immediately recognized the tall man standing on the porch as someone whose face I'd seen a lot of lately on television. I opened the door and invited Detective Harper inside. Surprisingly, at first, I didn't feel anxious at all. Not even with the head honcho of the entire investigation sitting right there on my living room sofa waiting to interview me. In fact, I barely even glanced at his badge and ID when he pulled them from his jacket pocket.

Detective Harper was much more soft-spoken in person than he came across on TV, and extremely polite. He promised it wouldn't take more than fifteen or twenty minutes of my time, and it didn't. When we were finished, he flipped closed the small spiral notebook in which he'd been taking notes and thanked me. Then he handed me a business card and left.

When my parents returned home from church a short time later, I didn't mention a word about my visitor. I'd already decided that would have to wait until later.

To the best of my recollection, this is how the interview went:

DETECTIVE HARPER: Let's start with your personal details. Name. Age. Address. Occupation.

ME: My name is Richard Chizmar. I'm twenty-two years old. 920 Hanson Road is my residence until January, when I'm getting married and moving to Roland Park in Baltimore. I live here with my parents. I just graduated in May from the University of Maryland. I'm a writer and an editor. Well, trying to be.

DETECTIVE HARPER: Congratulations on your upcoming wedding.

ME: Thank you.

DETECTIVE HARPER: And you grew up here in Edgewood?

ME: We moved here from Texas when I was five. After my father retired from the air force.

DETECTIVE HARPER: Is it just you and your parents? Or do you have siblings?

ME: I have three sisters and a brother, all much older. They've been out of the house since I was nine or ten.

DETECTIVE HARPER: Did you know either of the girls who were killed recently—Natasha Gallagher or Kacey Robinson?

ME: I knew Natasha a little bit from seeing her around the neighborhood. But I hadn't seen her since before I left for college, freshman year. I went to high school with her brother, but we didn't hang out or anything. I didn't know Kacey Robinson at all.

DETECTIVE HARPER: Never driven by Kacey in the neighborhood? Run into her at the grocery store?

ME: If I did, I wouldn't know it. I didn't even know what she looked like until I saw her picture on the news and in the paper.

DETECTIVE HARPER: You say you went to school with Joshua Gallagher. What can you tell me about him?

ME: Umm, good guy, I guess? We had a couple classes together junior year. I'd see him out at parties from time to time. He wrestled and hung out with a bunch of guys from the team. I've probably only run into him maybe four or five times since we graduated.

DETECTIVE HARPER: Do you know if he's ever been in any kind of trouble? Anyone he's had problems with?

ME: No, nothing like that.

DETECTIVE HARPER: How about the rest of the Gallagher and Robinson families? Any contact?

ME: I sort of know Mr. and Mrs. Gallagher from around the neighborhood and church, when I used to go. Good enough to say hello to if we run into each other in a store, or wave at if one of us drives by. I know Mrs. Robinson from when I used to bag groceries at the commissary on Post. That was the summer before my junior year of high school. She used to come into the store like twice a week. I don't think I've ever met Mr. Robinson.

DETECTIVE HARPER: Can you tell me where you were on the night of June 2, 1988, the night Natasha Gallagher was attacked and killed?

ME: I was still back at school, in my apartment.

DETECTIVE HARPER: In College Park?

ME: Yes, well, actually Greenbelt, right outside College Park. My roommates and I lived in an apartment complex called Brittany Place.

DETECTIVE HARPER: And you were at your apartment with your roommates on the night of June 2?

ME: Yes, sir. We'd just started cleaning it out earlier that week because our lease was ending.

DETECTIVE HARPER: How many roommates?

ME: Three.

DETECTIVE HARPER: And all three were at the apartment that night?

ME: Actually, just one of them. The other two had gone home to visit their families.

DETECTIVE HARPER: Would you be able to provide me with your roommates' names and contact information?

ME: They're Bill Caughron. David Whitty. Fred Answell. I can grab my address book when we're finished and get you their phone numbers and addresses.

DETECTIVE HARPER: Which roommate was with you on the night of June 2?

ME: Bill Caughron. He's also from Edgewood. His mom still lives on Perry Avenue.

DETECTIVE HARPER: And he'll be able to verify that you were with him on the evening of June 2?

ME: Absolutely.

DETECTIVE HARPER: This is all just standard procedure, Mr. Chizmar. We're asking the same questions to literally dozens of residents. I don't mean to make you uncomfortable.

ME: I'm okay. It's all just a little . . . unsettling.

DETECTIVE HARPER: Would it make you feel better if I told you I even asked your mailman the same handful of questions?

ME: Old Mr. Rory?

DETECTIVE HARPER: The Gallaghers and Robinsons are both on his delivery route, so yeah, I had to talk to him.

ME: I guess that makes me feel a little better.

DETECTIVE HARPER: I understand. I do. We're almost finished here. Your roommate Bill, he was with you the entire night?

ME: Pretty much. He left to go to his girlfriend's at some point, but that was pretty late.

DETECTIVE HARPER: About what time was that?

ME: I think it was around eleven, maybe a little later.

DETECTIVE HARPER: And did he stay the night at his girlfriend's or come back to the apartment?

ME: He stayed overnight.

DETECTIVE HARPER: Can you tell me his girlfriend's name?

ME: Sure. It's Daniella Appelt.

DETECTIVE HARPER: Now, as I understand it, you'd made an earlier trip here to Edgewood not long before June 2?

ME: I did. It would've been sometime during the last week of May. I'd borrowed a friend's truck and brought home my desk and a bookshelf and a few other pieces of furniture.

DETECTIVE HARPER: How long of a drive is it from Greenbelt to Edgewood?

ME: Depends on the time of day. Usually about an hour. Longer if there's D.C. traffic.

DETECTIVE HARPER: How about the evening of June 20, the night Kacey Robinson was killed?

ME: I was here at home—in my bedroom working and listening to my police scanner. I heard the initial calls go out after

Mr. Robinson called the station. I stayed up listening the rest of the night. My parents can verify that.

DETECTIVE HARPER: And you never left the house that night?

ME: No, I didn't.

DETECTIVE HARPER: Okay, a couple more questions and we can wrap it up. Since you've been back from College Park . . . sorry, Greenbelt . . . have you seen or experienced anything strange here in Edgewood? Anything at all?

ME: Nothing I can think of. I've mainly been cooped up in my bedroom working.

DETECTIVE HARPER: Fair enough. By the way, you said you were a writer . . . what kind of writing do you do?

ME: Umm . . . fiction, mostly. Mystery. Suspense. Crime. Horror.

DETECTIVE HARPER: Horror, huh? Like serial killers?

ME: Sometimes.

DETECTIVE HARPER: Thanks. I really appreciate your time, Mr. Chizmar.

5

After Detective Harper left, I walked outside and picked up the newspaper from the bottom of the driveway. Sitting on the front stoop, I was looking for the sports section to catch up on yesterday's box scores, when a headline just below the front-page fold caught my eye.

CROPPING EARS: A LONG AND SORDID HISTORY

I couldn't believe the old-school *Baltimore Sun* had printed such a sensational headline—and on the front page, no less. The article's byline read Mark Knauss, a name I didn't recognize. I immediately started reading and by the time I reached the jump at the bottom of the page, I couldn't turn fast enough to page fourteen to finish the article. It was fascinating.

According to the author, cropping—the act of removing a person's ears as a form of punishment—was documented as far back as ancient Assyrian law and the Babylonian Code of Hammurabi. In England, during the early sixteenth century, Henry VIII amended existing vagrancy laws so that first offenses would now be punished with three days in the stocks, second offenses with cropping, and third offenses with hanging. Cropping also took place in the United States in the late eighteenth century—punishing such crimes as perjury, libel, arson, and counterfeiting—most notably in Pennsylvania and Tennessee.

The practice of cutting off the ears of conquered adversaries dated all the way back to the time of the Crusades, but didn't become more prevalent until Native Americans began performing the ritual mutilation of fallen enemies on the battlefield.

During the United States' involvement in the Vietnam War, many controversial stories began to surface in the media detailing incidents of American troops mutilating deceased North Vietnamese soldiers and civilians, including the severing of ears. This practice originally began in the early years of the war when U.S. advisers working with indigenous troops such as the Montagnards offered a small cash bounty for Vietcong troops killed. In order to collect, they had to present proof of the kill, and it was decided that an ear would suffice. Combat photographs and film footage of American troops committing these atrocities and wearing necklaces comprised of dozens of severed ears sparked cries of outrage back home in the States.

More recently, in 1986, nine murder victims in Miami, Florida, were found with their ears severed. While local law enforcement originally believed the grisly acts to be the work of a serial killer, an arrest in connection with an unrelated homicide led police to suspect the killings were tied to a religious sect called the Nation of Yahweh.

The original founder, Hulon Mitchell Jr., Yahweh, "wanted White devils to be killed in retribution or revenge for any Black person that was murdered out in the community," said Daniel Borrego, a former Miami-Dade homicide detective.

Cult members revealed that in order to become "Death Angels"—highly respected enforcers responsible for keeping other followers in line—they were required by Yahweh to "bring me the ears of the White devil."

Finally, there was Robert Berdella, a Missouri serial killer known as "The Kansas City Butcher" and "The Collector." Between 1984 and 1987, Berdella kidnapped, raped, tortured, and killed at least six men. He often imprisoned his victims for periods of up to six weeks. In addition to severing their ears, he committed numerous other atrocities, including pouring drain cleaner in eyes, inserting needles under fingernails, and binding wrists with piano wire.

Jesus.

As I finished reading the article, several crystal-clear thoughts settled in my mind: (1) While interesting, none of this information offered even a hint as to why someone had sliced off Natasha Gallagher's and Kacey Robinson's ears; (2) The words I'd just read had left a nasty taste in my mouth, and I really needed to brush my teeth and take a shower; and finally (3) There was no way in hell I was going to let my mom read this article.

Before I went back inside, I walked to the driveway and tossed the newspaper into the garbage can.

6

Later that afternoon, Carly Albright called, and she had news.

Kacey Robinson's ex-boyfriend had been located in Ocean City, Maryland, where he'd spent the last several weeks working at a beach stand on Fourth Street, renting umbrellas, chairs, and bodyboards. He had a rock-solid alibi for the night of June 20 and was no longer considered a person of interest. He'd reportedly told the detectives, "All those assholes back in Edgewood should mind their own business. I wasn't anywhere near that fucking dump and don't plan on going back any time soon, either." He sounded like a real charmer.

Before we hung up, she passed on two more items of interest: one of her most-trusted sources had revealed that a small baggie of marijuana had been found hidden in Natasha Gallagher's bedroom. Police didn't think it had anything to do with her murder but were talking with local dealers, just in case. The same source reported that someone had called the tip-line recently, claiming that Kacey Robinson wasn't quite as sunshine perfect as everyone believed she was. Evidently, Kacey had a very bad habit that only her closest friends were aware of: she was a kleptomaniac.

7

After dinner, I spent some time in the garage organizing my fishing gear in preparation for the next morning's boat trip with Kara's family. I'd just finished spooling new monofilament on my favorite reel when my father swung open the breezeway door and told me I had a call. He handed me the cordless phone.

"Thanks," I whispered. "Who is it?"

"They didn't say."

I lifted the phone to my ear. "Hello?"

No response.

"Hello?" I said, louder this time. Sometimes the cordless got poor reception out in the garage.

Again, only the soft hiss of an open line.

"Hello?" Irritated now.

And then I heard a soft *click*—and the drone of a dial tone.

I pressed the off button on the phone and looked at my father. "Think we had a bad connection."

He looked at me with doubt in his eyes. "You sure about that?"

"Not exactly. You didn't recognize the voice?"

He shook his head. "It was a man. Normal-sounding. Specifically asked for Richard."

"Huh."

"Maybe he'll call back."

"Maybe."

"You being careful like I asked?"

"Yeah. I mean, I've been with Kara for the last couple days. Getting a lot of work done before that."

He glanced at my tackle box and fishing rod. "You finished in here?"

"I am." I turned off the overhead light and followed him into the house.

Just before we reached the living room, he turned and lowered his voice. "Let's not mention this to your mother, okay?"

"Absolutely not."

8

That night, although exhausted, I still had trouble falling asleep. I tossed and turned for a while, thinking about the mystery man who'd phoned the house. The previous prank calls could've been chalked up to simple acts of mischief. My friends and I had done it dozens of times growing up. Call a random number, remain silent or say something stupid, and hang up. But this time was different. I had been asked for by name. Then, he'd waited until I'd gotten on the line, listened to my voice, and only then ended the call. *Who the hell was it? Was the call some kind of message? A warning? If so, a warning for what purpose?*

I knew my father was worried, and I didn't blame him. The whole situation was odd . . . and disturbing.

I thought about Detective Harper's business card tucked away in the top drawer of my desk. *Should I call and tell him? Tell him what? That someone was making stupid prank calls and messing with my head? He'd probably crack up laughing and hang up on me as well.*

But then an incident from earlier in the week dawned on me. I'd been out running errands, my first stop being the post office to mail a stack of new short story submissions. Afterward, backing my car out of a tight parking space, I almost bumped into a silver sedan with dark windows parked on the opposite side of the lot. I didn't think anything of it at the time. But then I stopped at Plaza Drugs for a ream of paper and a birthday card my mom had asked me to pick up for Norma Gentile. On the way out, I had to wait for two vehicles to pass before walking across the parking lot to my car. One of them was a silver sedan with tinted windows. My final stop was the First National Bank so I could withdraw forty dollars in cash. While standing in line at the ATM, I noticed an older man with his back to me holding the door open at the Chinese restaurant next door. When a thin woman with short black hair walked out behind him, I realized it was Mr. and Mrs. Robinson, Kacey's parents. I immediately dropped my gaze to the sidewalk in front of me, holding my breath and hoping Mrs. Robinson wouldn't recognize me. All I could think in that moment was: *I didn't even go to their daughter's funeral.* To my relief, they walked directly to their car in the parking lot without so much as a backward glance.

Driving home, I caught the traffic light on Edgewood Road. Still distracted with thoughts of the Robinsons, I waited for the light to turn green and then hung a right, following a UPS truck onto Hanson. Halfway home, I glanced at the rearview mirror and noticed a silver sedan two cars behind me. I slowed down for a better look, but with the sun's glare on the windshield, I couldn't tell who was behind the wheel. By the time I turned into my driveway a couple minutes later, the car had disappeared from sight. A half hour later, absorbed in the writing of a new short story, it was all but forgotten.

Until now.

It was a long time before sleep finally came.

ABOVE: Police questioning residents of Bayberry Drive
(Photo courtesy of Logan Reynolds)

ABOVE: Detective Lyle Harper *(Photo courtesy of The Aegis)*

five

July

"There's a storm coming..."

1

Fortunately, this time, the shark-hating mayor of Amity Island was right.

Edgewood residents turned out in overwhelming numbers for the town's annual Fourth of July celebration, and according to police, not a single arrest was made for a violent crime.

Monday morning dawned with holiday-perfect skies overhead, and it almost felt as if the townspeople arose from their beds in especially boisterous spirits, grateful to have an extra day off from work, and eager and determined to put the recent bad news behind them. The Cub Scouts–sponsored pancake breakfast at the fire hall and the Little League doubleheader afterward were well attended and loudly cheered. Backyard cookouts filled the air with the delicious aroma of hamburgers and hot dogs and barbecued chicken, and the sweet sound of children's laughter. At the end of Willoughby Beach Road, Flying Point Park was a circus. An armada of boats lined the sandy beach, radios blaring, as grown-ups guzzled cold beer out of plastic cups and worked on their sunburns, and children did butt-busters and played tag and Marco Polo in the shallow waters. A short distance downriver, fishermen and crabbers lined an L-shaped pier, casting their baits into the heart of the deep channel in search of big catfish and perch. Dozens of families and packs of teenagers spread out across the park's grassy fields, eating and drinking too much, tossing Frisbees and horseshoes and flying red-white-and-blue kites. The playground swarmed with hordes of wide-eyed, sugar-spiked kids who, despite the scorching sun overhead, showed no signs of slowing down. The summer air was redolent with the fragrant perfume of charcoal grills, suntan lotion, steamed crabs, and freshly cut grass.

Once evening came, people headed downtown and large crowds gathered along both shoulders of Edgewood Road. The high school marching band led off the parade with a rousing rendition of "The Star-Spangled Banner," everyone rising from their lawn chairs and blankets and standing at attention as a line of proud flag bearers passed by. The Little League and softball teams came next, the players dressed in their uniforms, waving their caps at parents and friends and posing for photos. Then, the fire trucks and ambulances and police cars, lights flashing, sirens bleating; a staggered line of tractors advertising local businesses and parade sponsors; squadrons of soldiers from Edgewood Arsenal marching in perfect cadence, the gold buttons on their uniforms sparkling in the setting sun, spinning spit-shined rifles like batons and tossing them high into the air; Miss Maryland and Miss Harford County riding in the back of red-and-white convertible Corvettes, waving and blowing kisses to the crowd, hurling handfuls of candy to the children; and finally, last in line as was tradition, a caravan of open-air Jeeps—American flags attached to the antennas—carrying surviving members of the Edgewood Veterans of Foreign Wars, their dress uniforms and medals and ribbons taken out of storage for all to admire.

As soon as the parade was over, people packed up their belongings and scattered around town to enjoy the rest of the night. Many headed just down the street to the shopping center parking lot, which afforded an unobstructed view of the upcoming fireworks show. Ice cream and snowball vendors waded throughout the crowd, ringing their bells, as packs of giggling children chased after them. Others folded up their blankets and went home to watch the show from front porches and backyard patios. A handful of mostly older folks, exhausted from the day's activities, went straight to their beds and a good night's sleep.

As promised, there were indeed many extra patrols cruising the streets of Edgewood—including members of both the Maryland State Police and Harford County Sheriff's Department. Plainclothes officers infiltrated the crowds throughout the day and night. Others posed as joggers or romantic couples out for a stroll, keeping a close watch over the suburban streets. A handful of arrests were made for driving under the influence, drunken and disorderly conduct, illegal fireworks, and petty vandalism. The day's most serious bust came when two out-of-towners were arrested during the fireworks display for marijuana possession, and an illegal handgun was subsequently discovered in their vehicle's glove compartment.

The night's biggest scare came long after most of the crowds had dispersed and gone home. Rodney Talbot, age forty-three, notorious malcontent and raging alcoholic, skipped out on his bar tab and locked his keys in his car outside of Winters Run Inn. Ironically, the mishap most likely saved Talbot from getting pulled over and spending the night in jail, as a state trooper was parked just down the road on Route 7 in prime position to nail him.

But that's where Rodney Talbot's luck ran out.

Unable to hitch a ride with anyone else at the bar, Talbot staggered his way home through a nearby stretch of swampy woodland, tripping and falling face-first into a creek and stopping twice to vomit.

Once he finally reached his double-wide trailer on Singer Road, he found the front door locked. After banging on the door and calling his wife every horrible name he could think of, and several others he made up on the spot, Talbot went to the rear of the trailer, climbed atop an old picnic table, and attempted to crawl through a narrow bedroom window.

Inside the cramped trailer, Talbot's equally piss-drunk wife, Amanda, awakened from a deep stupor. Not recognizing her husband's mud-streaked face at the window, she immediately believed that here was the Boogeyman, trying to break in and kill her. She'd be damned if she let *that* happen. Amanda grabbed an unloaded twelve-gauge shotgun from inside the closet, and when she couldn't locate a box of shells, she spun the weapon around and repeatedly slammed the heavy wooden stock against the back of the intruder's head. Once she was certain the Boogeyman was unconscious and no longer a threat, she called 911.

Within minutes, sirens blaring, three police cars, an ambulance, and a fire truck pulled up in front of the trailer. One of the officers, who was all too well acquainted with Rodney Talbot's shenanigans, immediately recognized the would-be killer and calmly informed Amanda that she'd nearly murdered her own husband.

Later on, back at the station, the officer couldn't help but shake his head as he shared the story: "I couldn't believe it. I expected her to get upset and start bawling or cussing. Instead, she took a good look at Rodney all sprawled out on the ground and started belly laughing. Five minutes later, she was *still* laughing. Gave me a damn headache. And the thing is, we couldn't even arrest her for being shit-faced and stupid. She was minding her business in her own home, and the gun was legally registered."

2

The Thursday after July Fourth, Carly Albright made an unexpected appearance at my house. My mother answered the door and announced in her sweetest voice, "Richard, there's a *girl* here to see you." When I walked into the foyer, Mom raised her cute little eyebrows at me and smirked. I pretended not to notice. Closing the door behind me, I joined Carly on the porch. Once again, we settled on the top stoop.

"Richie . . . are you not allowed to invite girls inside your house?" Carly asked, smiling.

"Trust me, you don't want to go in. My mom'll force you to eat a three-course lunch and talk your ear off while she does it. How was your Fourth?"

"Spectacular," she said in a deadpan tone of voice. "I started my day by covering the turtle races at the pancake breakfast. Then I interviewed drunks all afternoon and recorded the results of the horseshoe contest. All for five crappy inches of copy in yesterday's paper."

I grimaced. "That *is* rough."

"Fortunately, I had the new Nora Roberts to keep me company the rest of the evening."

"You didn't go to the fireworks? No big date?"

She looked at me. "Rich, I'm ten pounds overweight, a workaholic, and a terrible listener. I haven't had a date in over a year."

I averted my gaze, pretending to watch a dump truck drive by. "Sorry I asked."

"How 'bout you? How was your Fourth?"

I shrugged. "It was good. Finally got to spend some quality time with Kara. Caught some fish. Drank some beer. Got a sunburn."

She glanced at my forehead. "I can see that."

"So . . . what's up?"

She was quiet for a beat, and then said, "I have a favor to ask."

"No problem, what do you need?"

"I pitched a story idea to my editor this morning, and she was actually excited, for a change."

"Okay," I said, waiting for her to finish.

"Well . . . the idea is *you*."

"Huh?"

"You. I'd like to interview you about your writing and the magazine. Just think, if you make it big one day, I'll have been the first."

I blew out a deep breath. I really didn't know if I was ready for my entire hometown to know what I was up to. Looking for an easy out, I asked, "Don't you think the timing might be a little bad for something like this?"

"My editor and I already discussed that. She said as long as we stay away from anything too dark or graphic and don't mention the words 'serial killer,' it should be fine. She thinks the town needs a little good news, and you're it. Local boy makes good, that sort of thing."

"Me, good news. That's a first."

"So what do you say?" she asked, leaning over so I couldn't look away from her.

I thought about it a moment longer. "You're sneaky, you know that? You didn't call and ask because you knew it would be easier for me to say no over the phone."

She flashed me an innocent look. "Why, Mr. Chizmar, I honestly have no idea what you're talking about."

"And when would you like to conduct this little interview of yours?"

She reached into her satchel and pulled out a bulky tape recorder. "How about right now?"

3

I'd just finished hosing off the lawn mower and was pushing it into the sun so it could dry when a grizzled voice called out, "Hey there, Richard. Come on over here for a minute."

I looked up and Mr. Gentile was standing on his front porch looking over at me. He hooked a bony, arthritic finger in my direction and gestured for me to hurry up.

Bernard Gentile—when we were kids, he insisted we call him Mr. Bernie—was in his late eighties and looked every day of it. His face was tanned year-round and deeply creviced. Slight in stature, he stood no more than five foot six, and walked with a badly hunched back that made him appear even shorter. Some of the neighborhood kids called him the Hunchback of Notre Dame when he wasn't around, but I never liked that and told them so. To my adolescent mind, Mr. Gentile was the spitting image of the irascible Mister Magoo, but I never shared that thought with anyone other than my parents. It felt disrespectful. A distinguished navy veteran of two wars (and boy, did he have the medals to prove it), Mr. Gentile was a gentle soul and a first-rate storyteller. When we were young, he regaled us regularly with tales ranging from the Great Depression and the Second World War to old-time jazz clubs and the night he met Elvis Presley. He once summoned Jimmy Cavanaugh and me to his porch and spent the better part of an hour explaining in painstaking detail the reasons why we both would've made excellent Pony Express riders in the Old West. "Tall and skinny," he told us over and over again. "You boys sure fit the mold." The rest of that summer, every time he saw us out in the yard or ran into me at church, he'd repeat those same words with a big smile on his wrinkled face: "There they are! Tall and skinny!"

As I made my way to the porch, I patted the life-sized ceramic donkey that guarded the Gentiles' front lawn on the head for good luck. That donkey had been sitting there in that same spot for pretty much forever. Somewhere in the house, my folks had a black-and-white photograph of me as a toddler, straddling the donkey's back, my dangling legs too short to reach the ground.

"How are you, Mr. Gentile?"

"Right as rain," he croaked, sitting down now. "Right as rain." He waved a liver-spotted hand at a pair of leafy plants hanging from hooks on the porch ceiling. "Do me a favor and haul those down for me, will ya?"

I walked over and got up on my tiptoes and took the plants down one at a time, almost dropping the last one. Those suckers were heavier than they looked.

"Just leave 'em right there," he said, pointing at the far corner of the porch. "I'll haul 'em around back later in the wagon. Norma says they aren't getting enough sun out here."

"I can take them around back for you, no problem."

He put a hand up, stopping me in my tracks. "I'm not crippled, son. Just couldn't reach 'em, and Norma won't let me anywhere near a ladder these days. Not since I gave myself stitches in my head trying to trim that stupid tree." He pointed an elbow at the empty chair next to him. "Have a seat for a few. Want to tell you something."

I took a seat. He stared off into the distance like he was trying to remember something important.

"With everything that's going on, I thought you might find it interesting." Then he looked at me. "It happened back in the sixties, before you and your folks moved next door. I imagine your father was still stationed in Texas back then or maybe even overseas."

I nodded, even though I had no idea.

"You have to understand, Edgewood looked a lot different back then. Route 40 didn't exist and neither did most of 24. Not many of the stores or restaurants around those parts, either.

"It was Nina's sweet sixteen summer; I remember that because Norma threw her one heckuva party." Nina was the Gentiles' only daughter. They also had two sons. All three children much older than me and long ago moved away.

"A young boy who lived in military housing over by Cedar Drive went missing one summer day. He'd been off playing at a nearby creek with his friends. After a while, they'd gone home for lunch and he'd stayed by himself, looking for minnows, his friends said later. Only I guess he hadn't been by himself after all, because when the other kids returned to the creek a half hour or so later, all they found was one of their friend's shoes on the creek bank." He looked at me then. "Sound familiar?"

"Just like Kacey Robinson," I said.

"The boy's parents and friends looked everywhere for him. When they couldn't find him, they called the MPs and the MPs called in the sheriff's department. They searched day and night for over a week before they called it off.

"Anyway, the summer wore on, and except for the boy's family and friends, the incident was pushed pretty much into the background. Life works like that. Something else—good, bad, indifferent—always comes along and helps us on our way.

"But then, sometime in late August, just before the kids put away their bathing suits and baseball mitts and dusted off their schoolbooks, it happened again. Another child went missing. This time, a little Black girl. She'd been playing in her front yard under the supervision of her mother. The phone rang inside the house, and the mom went in for no longer than a minute, she later told police, and when she came out again, the girl was gone. No shoe left behind this time. Not even one of the pretty pink hair ribbons she'd been wearing that day.

"After that, it was pretty much an exact repeat of the first time around. The police were called. Search parties were organized and conducted and eventually called off. And the little girl was never seen or heard from again.

"The town was on edge after that. Lots of suspicion. Folks improperly accused. Tensions rose. Tempers flared. And then, just like before, time passed and things began to go back to normal. The holidays came and went. Students returned to school. No more children disappeared. And then, before everyone knew it, it was summer again." He squinted at me. "You get what I'm telling you?"

I nodded my head, lying. "I think so."

"I figured you would. You're a smart young man. Always have been." Evidently, my intelligence had been greatly overestimated.

A few minutes later, my father called out from the driveway, looking for my help. I jumped at the chance to excuse myself, and as I said goodbye to Mr. Gentile, the overwhelming thought in my head was: *I can't wait to call Carly and tell her the story I just heard.*

4

My conversation with Mr. Gentile occurred on the morning of Saturday, July 9. By noon, I'd already phoned Carly and relayed the chilling story of the two missing Edgewood children. Sharing my excitement, she'd immediately promised to scour the *Aegis*'s back-issue microfiche files to see if she could pull up any additional details.

By early Monday afternoon, Carly and I sat across from each other inside the Edgewood Public Library, an open file folder stuffed with photocopies on the table between us.

I put down the single-page article—dated July 11, 1967—I'd just finished reading and picked up a two-pager stapled in the upper left corner. A child's photograph was centered beneath the headline: **STILL NO SIGN OF MISSING BOY**. This was Peter Sheehan, age seven. I quickly read the article, and when I was finished, Carly asked, "So what do you think?"

"I don't know what to think." I used the tip of my finger to slide the next article on the stack across the table. "Other than the shoe that was left behind, there's not much in common with what's happening now."

"That's what I thought, too. The first victim's male, the second's female. One's White, the other's African American. And no bodies were ever found. We don't even know if they were killed, much less strangled."

"And they were a lot younger than Natasha Gallagher and Kacey Robinson."

"And not a word about anything number-related left behind at the crime scenes." She looked at me. "You disappointed?"

"A little," I said, suddenly feeling foolish. "I really thought the murders might all be connected somehow . . . but there isn't any connection at all, is there?"

She shrugged. "Another hometown human tragedy under mysterious and unsettling circumstances."

"I guess so." After scanning the article, I looked up at her. "You're going to make a fine journalist once they actually let you write something."

Her face lit up. "Wait until you read what I wrote about you!"

"Please, don't remind me."

"You sure I can't convince you to read it ahead of time? It would make me feel better."

"Nope," I said, shaking my head. "Once'll be enough, and I might as well wait to read it when everyone else does."

"If you say so." She picked up the folder, shuffled to the bottom of the pile, and handed me what she found there. "I did find something else kind of interesting," she said. It was an article dated March 1972. The headline read: **TEENAGER KILLED IN EDGEWOOD.** I'd been six years old at the time it was published.

I lowered my voice and read aloud:

"'Late Thursday evening, local police discovered the body of missing fifteen-year-old Amber Harrison of Hanson Road, along the muddy shoreline of Winters Run Creek'—that's a block away from where we're sitting right now."

Carly nodded her head.

"'Ms. Harrison, a freshman from nearby Edgewood High School, had been missing for approximately forty-eight hours, after disappearing during a short walk home from a friend's house located on Cavalry Drive.

"'According to preliminary reports, Ms. Harrison was beaten and strangled—'"

I stopped reading and looked at Carly. "Whoa. Any other victims? Did they catch the person who did it?"

"That's the really interesting part," she said. "I looked everywhere and I couldn't find anything else. Not even a single follow-up article."

"That doesn't make any sense."

"I know. The system's kind of old and lame, so I guess I could've missed something. But then I checked the *Baltimore Sun* and there wasn't even a single mention of it."

"That *is* interesting," I said, thinking.

"Are your Spidey senses tingling?"

I looked at her, surprised. "You're a fan?"

She rolled her eyes and began straightening the stack of photocopies. "What, you think only boys read comics?"

5

The next morning, I woke before dawn with my bladder on the verge of exploding, a direct result of washing down a chili dog with a Double Big Gulp of Coke the night before. As I made my way to the bathroom, just a step above sleepwalking, I heard the crinkle of newspaper and the metallic clink of a spoon stirring coffee. I paused at the top of the stairway and peeked downstairs. I could just make out the dark silhouette of my father hunched over the narrow table in the corner of the kitchen. He looked small, somehow, and lonely sitting there by himself. The house was silent and still, and I flashed back in time to hundreds of other early mornings just like this one. Standing there in my pajamas, I thought: *This is what you do when you have a family. You get up when it's still dark outside and you go to work so the people you love can have a better life. Even when you're sick or tired and don't want to.* I watched him for a while longer, my heart aching in a way I'd never felt before. "Love you, Dad," I whispered in the darkness, and then I crept to the bathroom and back to bed.

6

Two weeks later, on Wednesday, July 27, Carly's article about me was published in the *Aegis*. Despite the fact that my parents had a subscription and home delivery, I bought my own copy at the Wawa and read it alone in my car. I only read it once, and quickly, right there in the parking lot, cringing every time I stumbled upon a direct quote. Kara said later that I looked handsome in the photo and came across as enthusiastic and smart. I, however, was almost positive I looked and sounded like a complete and total idiot. I hated every word, but of course I didn't tell Carly that. Instead I thanked her and told her how proud the article had made my parents, which was undeniably true. Those two were over the moon that their baby boy had made the local paper, and the front page of the People & Places section, at that. Later that evening, Norma and Bernie Gentile stopped by the house and actually asked me to autograph their copy. I thought they were kidding, but they weren't. My mother couldn't stop smiling. The next day, my father went right to the library and made a dozen photocopies of Carly's story, mailing them to relatives all around the world.

There were, however, two pleasant surprises that arose from the article's publication. The first was a late-night phone call from my old pal Jimmy Cavanaugh. His parents had an out-of-state subscription to the *Aegis* and had told him all about it. He phoned to congratulate me and let me know that he'd be in town over the weekend for his cousin's wedding. We ended up chatting for more than an hour and made plans to get together.

The second surprise was a congratulatory call the next morning from Detective Harper. He'd stumbled upon the article—or so he said, going out of his way to sound casual—and really enjoyed it. He just wanted me to know that. Before we hung up, I took a chance and ran an idea by him: "What do you think about me riding along with one of your officers some time? Just to observe and get a feeling of what it's like to be a police officer in a small town like Edgewood." I explained to him that I'd already gone on several ride-alongs the previous year with a friend who was a Baltimore City cop. I knew all about the release forms I'd be asked to sign and what was expected of me. He promised to think about it and get back to me. I wasn't holding my breath.

7

That same Wednesday night, after dinner, my parents walked down the street to visit with Carlos Sr. and Priscilla Vargas. I was all but certain the subject of my newspaper article would come up within the first thirty seconds of conversation.

Meanwhile, Kara and I spent the evening watching a movie in the basement, and then she said an early goodnight and headed home to work on an assignment. Damn. Even two full months after graduation, I still hated school.

Just as I was about to step into the shower, the phone rang. I quickly wrapped a towel around my waist and picked up the receiver in the upstairs hallway.

"Hello?"

"Quick bit of news." Carly Albright's voice sounded muffled and faraway.

"Talk to me."

"A local landscaper, Manny Sawyer, age thirty-one, was taken to the station house this morning at approximately 11:15 a.m. Evidently, he'd worked on a crew that cut down some trees in the Gallaghers' backyard, *and* moved some bushes and did some mulching two houses down from the Robinsons."

"Whoa."

"I know, right? Last I heard, he was still there being interviewed."

"Keep me posted, okay?"

"Will do. See ya."

She hung up. Replacing the receiver, I headed back into the bathroom. I started the shower running, but before I could remove my towel, the phone rang again. *Jesus, Carly*.

I hustled into the hallway and grabbed it off the hook. "Hey, that was fast—"

"What was fast?" A man's voice I didn't recognize.

"Sorry about that, I thought you were someone else."

The man chuckled. Low and gravelly—not a pleasant sound.

"Who is this?" I asked, hoping I sounded calmer than I felt.

No answer, but I could hear him breathing.

"Why do you keep calling here?"

Click.

And then the dial tone.

I lowered my hand and stared at the telephone for a moment. For the first time, I allowed myself to ask the question: *Was that really the Boogeyman?* Then I turned off the shower and ran downstairs to make sure the doors were locked.

8

I t felt just like the good old days.

Car windows down. Radio up. Six-pack of Bud Light on the floorboard of the back seat. And Jimmy Cavanaugh riding shotgun.

"That's wild," he said. "Like one of those scary stories you used to tell us when we were kids. 'A Monster Walks Among Us.'"

I'd just finished bringing him up to speed on Natasha's and Kacey's murders and what Carly Albright had found in that old article in the *Aegis*. We'd spent the past half hour catching up on each other's lives and driving around town, revisiting all of our old haunts. It'd been more than three years since Jimmy's last visit, but not much had changed.

"You know what I miss?" he asked, staring out the window.

"What?"

"The old water tower. Remember when we used to go sledding there?"

"Absolutely."

"Remember the time it sprung a leak and the entire hill iced over? That old guy flew down it on ice skates and almost killed himself!"

I laughed, remembering. "You know that 'old guy' was probably about the same age we are right now?"

"No way," he said, stunned. "You really think so?"

"I do. We're getting old, man."

"And you're getting married," he said, grinning.

"Yes, I am. And you'll be standing right next to me as a groomsman."

"Wouldn't miss it." He looked around for cops and took a swig of his beer. Belched. Gesturing out the window as we drove past the Edgewood Diner, he said, "Now that's one place I *don't* miss. Not even a little bit."

"You and me both," I said. "Haven't stepped foot in there since high school."

"Mel still own it?"

"What do you think?" I said, giving him a look. Mel Fullerton was a grizzly bear of a man—six four, at least two-hundred-and-fifty pounds, ratty beard and mustache, Confederate flag on his baseball cap, pack of Red Man in his jeans pocket. He was also a first-class asshole.

"Remember when we were kids and he always tried to shortchange us?" Jimmy asked.

"Until Mr. Anderson threatened to kick his ass if he ever did it again."

"I would've paid good money to see that."

"Me too," I said, swinging into the narrow parking lot adjacent to First National Bank. I pulled into a spot and turned off my headlights. Staring straight ahead across Edgewood Road and up the long gravel driveway, Jimmy didn't say anything at first, but then I watched as his eyes widened. "Jesus. The Meyers House."

"You didn't think it would be gone, did you?"

"Not exactly," he said, his voice fading. "To tell the truth, I'd almost forgotten about it."

I looked at him to see if he was bullshitting me, and I could tell that he wasn't. My heart ached at the idea of him—or any of us, for that matter—forgetting about such an important piece of our childhood. The idea that such a thing could actually happen had never really occurred to me, and I wasn't sure how to respond. For a split second, I felt an itch growing at the corners of my eyes.

"I used to have nightmares about that house," he said, breaking the silence.

I wanted to tell him that I *still* had occasional nightmares about that house, but decided to keep it to myself. All of a sudden, it didn't feel right sharing that with him. "My father said the owners sold it a couple years ago and someone new lives there now."

"No kidding." He stared out the windshield. "Can you imagine living there?"

"Nope. Not even for a single night."

"God, Brian and Craig dared us to spend the night in the backyard. *'Bet you twenty bucks you can't make it until morning.'* What did we last, an hour?"

"Not even," I said. "Like half an hour. You were so scared you ran home without your sleeping bag."

"That's because I saw a ghost," Jimmy answered with a haughty tone of voice. "I almost peed my pants that night."

We cracked up then, and the sound of our laughter steered me back to a happy place. It felt good to remember simpler times.

Almost as if reading my mind, Jimmy asked, "Does it feel weird living back here again?"

"Yes and no." I shrugged. "It feels weird sleeping in my old room, that's for sure. And the town feels . . . different somehow . . . but that's no surprise these days."

He looked at me. "I guess you've been following the cases pretty closely."

"Why do you say that?" I asked, hoping I didn't sound defensive.

"I don't know." He shifted in his seat. "You always liked . . . mysteries and . . . figuring things out."

"Even the police can't figure this one out, though. We keep hearing they're about to make an arrest, but nothing ever happens. The whole town's on edge."

"Are *you*?"

"A little bit," I admitted. I thought about telling him about the strange phone calls, but didn't. I'm not exactly sure why. "I went jogging the other night—to the end of Hanson and back. I ended up freaking myself out. I kept hearing footsteps behind me and seeing things moving in the shadows."

"Creepy," he said in a mock scary voice.

"It really was. I booked it home."

He laughed and took another drink of his beer.

"Hey, look at that," I said, pointing across the street.

He followed the direction of my finger but didn't say anything.

"Right there. By the side of the house." An indistinct shadow was moving in the darkness, a flickering light guiding the way.

"Is that someone carrying a lantern?"

"Looks like it," I said, whispering now, feeling like I was ten years old again. "Or maybe a flashlight with weak batteries."

"What do you think he's doing?"

"No idea."

"Maybe he's moving a body? Or burying one!"

I watched the light disappear around the back of the house. "You want to walk up there and take a look?"

I heard him swallow. "Do you?"

Grinning, I looked over at my old friend. "You know we're still a couple of idiots, don't you?"

"Speak for yourself, Chiz."

"You hungry?"

"Starving."

I started the car and pulled out of the parking lot. Five minutes later, we were sitting at the bar in Loughlin's, getting change for the jukebox and ordering cheesesteaks and a pitcher of beer.

9

Jimmy farted again and started giggling.

"Jesus," I groaned. "If they don't hear us coming, they'll definitely smell us."

"Sorry," he whispered. "What did I tell you? Don't let me order the onion rings."

"You shouldn't have ordered three pitchers of beer."

"That too." Stifling another giggle.

It was nearly midnight, and against my better judgment, we were back at the Meyers House. On foot this time. Jimmy was hammered and in rare form. I was mostly sober and drowning in regret. It was late and chilly and just beginning to rain.

Back when we were kids, Jimmy had a way of convincing me to do stupid things. Really stupid things. When I was young, despite the fact that I'd once paid nine dollars and fifty cents for a magic feather, I didn't consider myself naive or an easy target. In fact, I was usually the one doing the talking-into when it came to our frequent misadventures. But I guess you could say Jimmy Cavanaugh was my kryptonite. He just had this way about him—it's like he could erase my memory of past nightmares and convince me that whatever he was talking about was the coolest, most reasonable idea in the world. *Hey, Rich, do me a favor—* that was a specialty of his—*and hold that pine cone up and let me shoot it with this BB gun. Don't worry, your fingers are safe. Hey, Chiz, I dare you to climb that tree and swing down from that vine like Tarzan. Do me a favor, Rich, take this stick and poke that hornet's nest. I'm pretty sure it's empty.* I swear it was like he was some kind of demented magician casting spells over me purely for his entertainment.

And now, after all these years, he was back at it.

Up ahead, the Meyers House loomed over us, its pointed rooftop vanishing into a starless sky. Every window along the front of the house was dark. Not even the porch light was turned on. A whole crew of bloodthirsty killers could be sitting up there on the porch, sharpening their knives and just waiting for us, and we'd never know it. Listening to the not-so-stealthy sound of gravel crunching beneath our shoes, I knew that anyone would have long ago heard our approach.

"Hold on," Jimmy said quietly. "I gotta pee."

"Again?"

He didn't answer. It was too dark to see more than two or three feet in front of my nose, but I heard him walk a little farther away, and then the sound of a zipper being lowered, followed by a loud sigh, and finally, a steady stream splattering the gravel.

"At least pee in the grass, for chrissakes," I said.

From the darkness next to me, "Too late," and then the sound of a zipper going up, and the gurgly squelch of another wet fart. "Excuse me. Sorry." More giggling.

I'm in hell, I thought, not really meaning it.

"Hey," he called out in a low voice from somewhere in front of me. "Do me a favor."

"Nope. Don't even ask. Whatever it is, the answer's no."

"All I was gonna say was keep talking so I can find you. It's spooky as shit out here in the dark by myself."

"Oh."

"What'd you think I was gonna say?"

"Something remarkably stupid, most likely."

"Keep talking, I think I'm almost there."

"You know what? I should just take off. Leave you all alone out here in—*owww!*"

One of Jimmy's hands had swum out of the darkness in front of my face and poked me in the eye. A split second later, I heard a *whoosh*, and his other hand slapped me in the ear.

"There you are," he whispered, oblivious to my pain. Even with my one good eye, I couldn't quite make out his face, but he was standing close enough for me to smell his oniony breath and the sour stench of urine. I was pretty sure he'd peed all over his shoes.

"If you did that on purpose," I said, "you're walking home."

"Did what on purpose?"

"Never mind. This is ridiculous. We're getting soaked. Let's just go back to the car."

"What's that?"

"What's what?"

"Right there."

"If you're pointing somewhere, I can't see. It's too damn dark."

"Up there on the left, behind the Balikos' house."

Squinting into the darkness, I could just make out a halo of dim light coming from the rear of the house and the rough outline of a shed in the corner of the yard. "I don't see anything."

"Keep looking."

I kept watching and just when I was convinced that Jimmy was up to his old tricks, there it was—something small and pale and round moving parallel to the driveway maybe thirty-five yards ahead of us.

"You see it?" he asked, his voice suddenly steady.

"What the hell is that?"

Whatever it was, it was coming closer. Floating above the ground. Backlit by the patio lights of the houses behind it. A moment later, we heard approaching footsteps rustling in the tall grass bordering the driveway.

"It's a face," he whispered.

We ran, just like countless times before, as if all the demons in hell were chasing after us. Which, in that moment, just might have been the truth.

10

Later, in the car, the heater blasting.

"That was one of the creepiest fucking things I've ever seen," Jimmy said, rubbing his hands together. "You think we should call the police?"

"And tell them what?"

"That we saw some creepy-ass albino dude sneaking around in the dark. Maybe it was the killer."

"I don't know," I said. "We've both been drinking. I'm not sure we'd make very reliable witnesses."

"Didn't you say they had an anonymous hotline?"

I was impressed that he remembered. "Okay, but you do the talking. You're not from around here anymore. They won't recognize your voice."

Pulling up to the curb in front of Plaza Drugs, I reached into the center console and handed him a quarter for the pay phone and my pair of winter gloves.

"What are these for?" he asked.

"No fingerprints."

He snapped his fingers. "Smart."

As he was getting out of the car, I said, "You know the guy we saw might not have been an albino."

Jimmy just looked at me.

"He might've been wearing a mask."

11

I watched the news and scanned the newspaper for days afterward. I'd told Carly what had happened, and she put her ear to the ground to see if there were any whispers. I drove by the Meyers House at least three or four times a day.

Nothing.

12

On the final evening of July, I found myself standing at the bottom of my driveway, staring up the hill at a regiment of dark clouds marching over the horizon. It'd been a quiet month thus far in the town of Edgewood, but I sensed that peace and quiet would soon be coming to an end.

There's a storm coming.

Those four words had been echoing through my head for weeks now.

Growing up, one of my most treasured memories was working alongside my father in the garage. Many of my friends whom I met later in life would find this strange—and with good reason.

When I told people that I wasn't very mechanically inclined, it was somewhat of a lofty understatement. And, if they didn't already know this about me, they learned it soon enough. No matter how hard I tried, I couldn't figure out how to set up a VCR, much less assemble a piece of furniture. IKEA was my sworn enemy. Car engines—hell, engines of any kind—might as well have been the human brain as far as I was concerned. They were both an eternal mystery to me.

During my childhood—and still to this day—my father standing out in the driveway with his head buried underneath the hood of one of our family cars was a common sight for passing motorists and pedestrians. Me standing by his side helping out? Not so much. We tried. We really did. But it inevitably went something like this:

Minute one: Rich standing off to the side, arms crossed in front of him, rocking on his heels with excitement. Paying close attention. Maybe even asking a question or two.

Minute three: Rich leaning now, using his fingers to tap out the rhythm to the latest Old Spice commercial on the rocker panel of the car, mere inches from where his father's head is positioned.

Minute five: Rich fidgeting like he's going to pee his pants at any moment. Paying more attention to a pair of fat squirrels playing chase on the telephone wire stretching across Hanson Road than to what his father is trying to oh so patiently teach him.

Minute eight: Rich spinning in tight circles back-and-forth across the driveway like an F5 human tornado, all the while making chimpanzee sounds like Cornelius from Planet of the Apes *(a film I've always loved), unable to hear a word his father is saying as he asks Rich to hand him a three-eighths-inch wrench.*

Minute ten: Rich, now completely still and silent, arms hanging dejectedly at his side, eyes lowered. His father standing in front of him, a complex mixture of love and frustration etched upon his reddening face. Finally, his father takes a deep breath and mutters those three magic words: "You can go." And before his father can change his mind, Rich is tearing up the hill toward Jimmy's and Brian's houses, hollering over his shoulder as he goes, "Thanks, Dad! Love you!"

And that's pretty much how it went. Every single time. Until finally, one day we just accepted it and stopped trying.

Fortunately, working *inside* the garage, on one of my father's frequent "projects," was an altogether different experience. I mentioned earlier that the garage had always reminded me of the mysterious and chaotic sorcerer's workshop from Walt Disney's *Fantasia*. That was never more the case than on those long summer evenings after dinner when my dad would busy himself with building or repairing various objects at his workbench. He was the graying wizard, wise and patient and not entirely of this world—and I was his eager apprentice.

He'd ask me to grab a two-by-four from the stack along the back wall or a box of wire from the shelf, and I would hop to it. He'd lower his head and set to work, and I'd be right there next to him, peering around his back, studying, careful not to nudge an elbow while he was performing delicate surgery on a brand-new footstool for my mom or the messy guts of a neighbor's broken-down television.

For some reason, my most memorable nights out in the garage were almost always accompanied by thunderstorms. While we tinkered away inside, the sky overhead would slowly writhe and boil, shifting and swirling until it resembled the dark purplish shade of one of the many ugly bruises that littered my lanky, ten-year-old body. Long, grumbling peals of distant thunder crept ever closer, like armies of giants on the move. My father loved the sound of thunder and would often turn off the Orioles game playing on the radio just so we could hear it better.

Before long, he'd look up at me and announce, "What do you say we take a break and watch the storm roll in?" and then without another word, he'd drop what he was doing onto the workbench and stroll outside onto the driveway. He'd usually lean back against one of the cars and fix his gaze directly up Hanson Road. Following right behind him, I'd imitate his every move.

Our house was located at the bottom of a natural trough formed by the intersection of Hanson and Tupelo Roads. Sometimes, during big storms, the roadway there would flood, accumulating as much as two or three feet of standing water. When that happened, the pump in our basement was forced to work overtime, and my father had to stay awake throughout the night to make sure it didn't clog.

In the opposite direction, going up the hill, stood the Gentile and Cavanaugh and Anderson houses, Brian and Craig's next-door neighbor's split-level marking the summit of a steep incline.

My father and I, the wizard and his apprentice, would stand outside in the driveway—sometimes talking about the Orioles or one of my friends or a book one of us was reading; many times not talking at all— and watch the storm come over that hill into the heart of Edgewood. On special nights, it felt like we were doing more than just watching; it felt like we were welcoming it with open arms.

First, the wind picked up, whispering among the treetops and tousling our hair. Then, the rumbling of thunder grew louder and sharper and flashes of lightning stabbed at the skyline. The light dimmed another notch, as the skies overhead grew angrier. And then the burnt smell of ozone assaulted us, and the aroma of damp earth filled the air. That's when we knew: it was pouring somewhere close by, and getting closer. Finally, that tingling, electrical *buzz* began to dance in the air around us, a dangerous sensation of crackling intensity that made the tiny, tan hairs on our forearms stand at attention.

The first fat drops of rain began to fall soon after. Scattered at first; swollen and heavy and hungry for earth; splatting on our faces, seeping into our hair; staining the roofs and hoods of the cars and the concrete driveway at our feet; all the while, beating a deep staccato rhythm, erasing the everyday sounds of the world from around us.

My father and I stood side by side, embracing every sweet moment, heads tilted, eyes closed, drinking in the cacophony of the storm; just the two of us now—the Lords of Edgewood.

Then, without warning, we found ourselves standing beneath a majestic waterfall. The entire world had transformed, and we were at its mercy—and my mother was standing at the mouth of the open garage, yelling at us to stop being fools and get inside before we caught pneumonia, and my father and I couldn't stop laughing, too lost in the waterfall to listen, too consumed with greeting the storm . . .

Thunder growled overhead. Lightning speared the horizon. Gazing around the dying light enveloping Hanson Road, I blinked, and the whispers of memory faded away. I was no longer a child. It was the final day of July 1988. And I felt it singing deep in my bones: *there's a storm coming*.

ABOVE: Fourth of July parade *(Photo courtesy of Deborah Lynn)*

ABOVE: Winning (9-to-10-year-old division) squad of
the Fourth of July tournament *(Photo courtesy of* The Aegis*)*

ABOVE: The long gravel driveway leading to the Meyers House
(Photo courtesy of Alex Balikó)

ABOVE: The Edgewood Marching Band
(Photo courtesy of Bernard L. Wehage)

six

The House of Mannequins

"Their heads had been shaved, and their hair replaced by cheap wigs."

1

Within minutes of sitting inside Detective Lyle Harper's unmarked brown sedan, I realized who he reminded me of: Danny Glover. Same deep, gravelly voice; same boisterous laugh; same sad puppy-dog eyes. I wasn't sure why I hadn't made the connection earlier when I first met with him in my living room—nerves, probably—but the similarities made me instantly like him. Glover had always been one of my favorite actors.

To say that I'd been surprised a day earlier when the detective called to not only approve my request for a ride-along, but to offer to take me himself, would be an immense understatement. Initially puzzled as to why he'd extend such a privilege, I decided to keep my big mouth shut and enjoy the ride, maybe learn something in the process.

Thus far—thirty minutes into what was estimated to be a four-hour shift—I was definitely doing both of those things. Detective Harper was not only a wealth of information and a true professional, but also funny as hell. He'd already covered his three children—two older girls and a boy my age—and his frequent misadventures in single parenting when they'd been younger. Clearly, dating the teenage daughter of a homicide detective was not for the faint of heart. I was suddenly very grateful that Kara's father sold insurance. Despite the rigors of his career, Harper had recently remarried and seemed to have a good life. And his children still adored him, which he claimed was a small miracle.

I think I reminded Harper of his son, Benjamin, who was a professional musician. During the day, he taught private lessons on the piano, guitar, and saxophone. At night, he played with a pair of well-respected bands—jazz and contemporary—in various clubs and restaurants throughout the D.C. area. So far, it'd been a struggle financially, but the detective claimed he'd never seen his son happier or more dedicated, so as a father, he was hanging on to that and being as supportive as he could.

Once the small talk was out of the way, Harper got down to business, explaining that he'd spent the majority of the afternoon going over written statements from family and friends and neighbors of the victims, searching for anything of interest that might've been missed earlier. I asked him how many times he'd already read each statement, and he gave me a look that said, *You don't even want to know*. Once he finished reading, he'd made follow-up phone calls to a handful of interviewees to ask additional questions.

Now the plan for the rest of the evening was to patrol the streets of Edgewood—starting on the outskirts along Route 40 and slowly circling our way into the heart of downtown, and then turning around and working our way back out again—investigating anyone and anything Detective Harper deemed of interest.

2

It was strange seeing the streets of my hometown from inside a police car. It didn't feel quite real, almost like the windshield was a television screen and I was sitting in the basement with my father watching one of his cop shows. Speaking of my father, he was back at home sulking because he hadn't been invited to come along. Like I had any say in the matter. I stared out the passenger window and once again, that sense of expectation swelled within me, as if some important event was lurking just beyond the horizon. *There's a storm coming.*

Without being asked, Detective Harper spent the first part of our drive teaching me what the various call-signals meant each time a new one was transmitted over the police scanner. I told him I'd purchased my own scanner to listen to while writing at night, and he didn't seem even a little bit surprised. Later, I realized why: I'd already told him about buying a scanner when he'd come to the house for our initial interview. Which probably explained why he was going to so much trouble to fill me in on all the call-signals. It was a nice thing for him to do.

Harper had another surprise in store for me, too. He'd actually dug up and read my article about Earl Weaver in the *Baltimore Sun*. I didn't know whether to be nervous about that or flattered. When I asked him why he'd done it, he smiled and said, "I'm a detective. I do my homework."

As we crossed over the Route 24 bridge, we spotted a man and young boy with fishing rods, standing on the bank of Winters Run. A small campfire burned in a clearing behind them.

"What do you think they're going for down there?" he asked, tapping the brake pedal.

"Sunnies. Yellow perch. Cat. Maybe largemouth or crappie if they're using live minnows."

He looked over at me, impressed. "You're a fisherman."

"Almost every day growing up."

"And now?"

"Not really. We used to sneak onto the University of Maryland golf course once in a while and fish the ponds. Caught a couple of keepers in the bay over Fourth of July. But that's about it."

"I'm strictly a freshwater guy," he said. "Like to get out two or three times a week when I can." He looked at me. "Haven't been out much lately."

He switched on the turn signal and swung a left onto Edgewood Road. I watched the houses blur by as we made our way up the long, winding hill into town. Summoning my courage, I asked, "So . . . on a night like this, you're driving around and looking for what exactly?"

"To be honest, I'm doing as much thinking as I am looking. If that makes any sense."

I nodded. "I think it does."

"I don't usually do a wide canvass like this. That's left up to the uniforms." He pulled into the bank parking lot and stopped no more than fifteen feet away from where Jimmy and I had parked a week earlier. I suddenly had a sinking feeling in my stomach. "But sometimes it helps to get out from behind the desk, away from the phone and all that paperwork."

"So, while you're driving . . . you're thinking about all the details of the case? Trying to make things fit?"

"That's right," he said. "Also thinking about what we might've missed. What's sitting right there in front of our noses that we haven't yet noticed for one reason or another."

"Does that happen a lot? You guys missing something and then coming back and finding it later?"

"Huh, all the time," he said, shaking his head. "People think detective work is exciting and glamorous, full of gun battles and car chases. The truth is it's rarely any of those things." He reached over and turned down the volume on the scanner. "It's drudgery—sifting through hundreds, sometimes thousands of pages of reports and photographs, watching hours of security footage, knocking on doors and making phone calls and talking to people who are either too eager to talk, but have nothing to say, or have crucial information, but refuse to talk at all."

"That doesn't sound very exciting."

"Trust me, it's not."

"How long have you been doing it?"

He answered right away. "This October will be nineteen years."

I whistled. "Almost as long as I've been alive."

"Let me ask you something," he said, pointing across the street at the gravel driveway leading up to the Meyers House. *Shit, here it comes*, I thought. "I saw a bunch of kids walking up there the other day. Where do you think they were going?"

Instant relief flooded over me. "Um . . . it depends," I said, suddenly thinking about the man we'd seen creeping around in the dark. "It's either a shortcut to Cherry or Tupelo. If you walk about three-quarters of the way up and cut through one of the backyards on the left, you get to Cherry. If you walk all the way up and cut across the big house's backyard and keep going through the Pattersons' backyard, you get to Tupelo. Five or six houses up the street from my parents'."

"And everyone who lives around here knows about it?"

I shrugged. "All the kids do. That's part of living here."

The detective seemed to think about that for a moment, and then he backed out of the parking space and merged onto Edgewood Road. Reaching the intersection by the Texaco station, he made a right turn onto Hanson. When he slowed the car a half mile later, I knew where he was taking us.

"What can you tell me about this area?" he asked, hanging a left onto the loop that circled Cedar Drive.

I glanced at Kacey Robinson's memorial at the bottom of the sliding board. It'd finally stopped multiplying in size. Almost dusk now, there were only two people—a mom and daughter, it appeared—playing on the swings. A large dog was leashed to the base of the jungle gym maybe ten yards away from them. The rest of the playground was deserted and lost in shadow.

"Let's see," I said, looking around and pointing out the landmarks. "We used to sled over there when we were kids. The big baseball field and playground hadn't been built yet. Played football right over there by the military apartments. If you cut through that field," I said, gesturing to the opposite side of the road, "then through the Goodes' backyard, you'll end up in Tupelo Court, right across the street from my house."

"How about the Boys and Girls Club—was that open back then?"

"Nope. It was just a big empty parking lot. We used to hang out there when we were older and drink beer or take girls up there."

As we approached the elementary school on our left, I pointed at the tree line directly across the street from where the buses were parked. A narrow path had been carved into the woods. It opened into deep pools of darkness. "There's another shortcut right through there. Comes out behind the new office building across from 7-Eleven."

"The one at the corner of Edgewood and Willoughby Beach?"

"That's right. Seven-Eleven was the first place around here with a Space Invaders machine. When I was nine, I used to take off at a sprint after dinner with a single quarter in my pocket. Down Hanson, cut across Cedar Drive, through those woods, and up the hill. I'd play my one game and book it home as fast as I could in the dark so my parents wouldn't know I was gone."

"That's a long-ass haul for a game of Space Invaders."

I laughed. "Tell me about it. Especially when you get killed all three times in the first minute or two. What can I say—I was a little obsessed."

As we reached the stop sign at the far end of Cedar Drive, Detective Harper braked to a stop and sat motionless behind the wheel. There was no traffic on the road ahead, but still we didn't budge. I studied the cluster of bushes across the street in case the detective was tracking movement I wasn't aware of—but there was nothing. Finally, he hit the gas, turning right, and headed in the direction of the high school. When he spoke again, his voice was quiet and cautious.

"So I know, in order to come along tonight, you had to agree not to ask me anything specific about the case," he said. "But I'd like to ask *you* a question or two if you'd be willing to answer."

"Okay," I said, a nervous cramp blooming in the pit of my stomach.

He looked over at me and smiled, but it never quite reached his eyes. "Relax, Rich. It's not a big deal. I'm just looking for a . . . different perspective."

"Okay," I said again.

"Are you aware of any racial tensions here in Edgewood?"

"Not really." I shrugged. "I mean, nothing out of the ordinary. We're a pretty diverse community and always have been."

"Yet both victims have been young White girls."

"Well, yeah." I looked at him. "Do you think that's strange?"

"Do you?"

"I guess not. I just figured that means the killer himself is White. Most serial killers don't cross racial lines when selecting their victims."

He raised his eyebrows. "I see I'm not the only one who's done his homework. Where did you learn that?"

"I don't remember exactly. Probably one of the books I've read."

He hung a left onto Willoughby Beach Road. "Okay, next question . . . if you were a bad guy from out of town and were looking to steal a young girl off the streets of Edgewood, where would you do it? First place that comes to mind."

I lowered my head and closed my eyes. Putting on my writer's cap, I thought about what he was asking me. "Somewhere without a lot of people. A park, early in the morning or at dusk. One of the back roads or down by the water. Closing time at one of the bars or restaurants." I opened my eyes. "Sorry, that was more than one."

"No, that's good," he said. "Real good. I just didn't want you to over-think it." He pulled into the parking lot in front of the middle school and turned off the sedan's headlights. It was full dark now, fireflies speckling the night sky. Warm yellow light spilled from the windows of the houses across the street, and you could just make out the dim, flickering glow of television screens in living rooms and dens. "Now, tell me this . . . if you're an out-of-towner, an outsider, where's the very *last* place you'd go to abduct a young girl in Edgewood?"

"A neighborhood," I replied without hesitation.

He nodded his head but didn't say anything, just kept staring out into the darkness. For a moment I thought I'd said something wrong, but then it occurred to me what he was doing. "You really believe the killer's a local, don't you?"

"I think he's probably lived here his entire life." Harper looked at me. "You're not convinced?"

"I don't know what to believe," I said, looking away. *Or maybe I just didn't want to believe it.*

3

"Have you ever been scared while doing your job? Not the some-one-might-shoot-me or I'm-in-danger kind of scared. I'm talking about chills-running-down-your-spine-because-this-is-spooky-as-hell scared."

We were on our way back to the station when it occurred to me that this ride-along had probably been more for Detective Harper's benefit than my own. Not that I really minded. We'd covered the town, front to back, three times. I'd seen parts of Edgewood I hadn't visited since I was a kid. We'd even gotten out and walked the river-bank for a while. I'd definitely learned a lot and enjoyed the detective's company, but somehow he'd managed to pump me for more informa-tion than I'd been able to get out of him. With the night almost over, I figured I might as well try to squeeze in a last-minute question or two of my own.

"Sure," he said. "I've had some moments like that."

"What was the worst one?"

He was quiet for a moment, thinking, then: "The House of Manne-quins."

"Oooo, that *does* sound creepy. What happened?"

The traffic light turned green and we accelerated through the intersection.

"It was late one night, back when I was working in the city. My partner and I answered a call from a lady concerned about her neighbor. She lived right down the street from old Memorial Stadium, and for the last day or so, she'd been hearing these weird voices and banging noises coming from inside the row house next door. She'd tried ringing the bell and knocking a bunch of times, but no one answered. Her neighbor's name was Thomas McGuire. She said he was in his sixties and nice enough, but also kind of strange. He talked to himself a lot, and believed in UFOs and crystals and stuff like that.

"Anyway, we checked it out. I took the front, and my partner went around back. Sure enough, no one came to the door. I tried to peek inside the window, but there were heavy curtains blocking the view. Right about then my radio squawked, and it was my partner, telling me to get my ass around back.

"I found him standing at a half-open window, peering through a gap he'd made in the curtains. Even in the dark, I could see that his face had gone pale and he had his service revolver in his hand. He stepped aside and I took a look.

"Candles were burning inside the house. Hundreds of them, everywhere, including all over the floor. Spread out among the candles were dozens of naked bodies, all of them propped up in various poses. Sitting at the dining room table. Leaning against the kitchen counter. Standing with their backs against the wall. Their mouths had been smeared with red lipstick and their glassy eyes sparkled in the candlelight.

"'What the hell is this shit?' I said, backing away from the window.

"'You smell it?' my partner whispered. 'You smell the blood?'

"I unholstered my sidearm. 'You call it in?'

"'Yeah,' he said.

"A sound came from inside the house then. Someone crying. My partner didn't wait. He kicked in the door. 'Police!' he shouted, pointing his weapon. 'Mr. McGuire! Are you here?!'

"We took one step into the kitchen and froze. The stench of fresh blood was overwhelming. Flickering shadows surrounded us. Up close, it only took a second for us to realize that the bodies weren't human—they were mannequins. But mannequins didn't bleed. *So then where was the smell coming from?* There were dozens of those things scattered throughout the house. Four sitting on the living room sofa, two with their legs crossed. Three more huddled as if in conversation next to the TV. I poked my head into the downstairs bathroom and goddamn there was a mannequin sitting on the toilet, another primping in front of the mirror. We moved into the living room and they were all around us, watching our approach with those dead, shiny eyes, and then even more lining the stairway leading upstairs. The bedrooms were filled with them. A couple spooning on the bed in one room, a half dozen engaged in an orgy in another, a child-sized mannequin standing alone in the shower with the water running, two more sitting cross-legged on the floor at the end of the hallway. And, everywhere we looked, candles burning on every available surface.

"By the time we returned downstairs, our backup had arrived, and they were every bit as freaked out as we were. They followed us single-file into the basement, where the stench of blood and decay was the strongest. And right there, among all the burning candles, the washer and dryer, these rows of cardboard boxes stacked up against the wall, this tangled mess of at least twenty old bicycles, and two dozen or so mannequins, we found the bodies of three women, all in their forties. Two were prostitutes and the third was a day-care worker who'd been reported missing three days earlier. They were naked, disemboweled, hanging from the ceiling. Their heads had been shaved, and their hair replaced by cheap wigs. In the opposite corner of the basement, behind this big pile of junk, we found Thomas McGuire. He was naked too, curled into a fetal position. Sobbing. Every inch of his body smeared with the blood of his victims. A fourth body, the guy's ex-wife, was dis-covered later in the trunk of his car. That one had been there for a few days as well."

"Jesus," I said, feeling sick to my stomach. "When did this happen?"

He answered immediately: "October 9, 1976."

We didn't talk the rest of the way back to the station.

4

That's not funny," I said.

Carly Albright sat across the table, smiling, clearly enjoying herself. It was early the next afternoon, and we were sitting at what was fast becoming our regular corner table at Loughlin's Pub.

"All I'm saying is that it's a pretty common tactic that police use. You see it in the movies all the time. They pretend to get close to a sus-pect in order to draw them in and create trust."

"That's not what he was doing. He was a legit nice guy."

She ignored me. "And then the suspect gets a little too comfortable, makes a mistake, and *boom* they're busted."

"That's not how it went. And busted for what? I haven't done any-thing wrong."

"Does he know that?" she asked, raising her eyebrows.

"He actually asked for my opinion on stuff relating to the case."

"Classic misdirection."

"Oh, never mind." I picked at the plate of chicken nachos sitting between us. "You're impossible."

"All I'm saying is that Detective Harper might not be the buddy cop that you're making him out to be."

"I never said he was! I simply said he was nice."

"Well . . . I'm not so sure you should trust him. He has a job to do and he's under a lot of pressure."

"Now you sound like my mother."

Carly stacked several loaded nachos on top of each other, crammed them into her mouth, and started chewing. "Suit yourself," she mumbled, crumbs flying everywhere.

5

Later that night, just before heading upstairs to get some writing done, I went into the garage, pressed the button on the automatic door opener, and walked outside to haul the garbage cans to the curb.

I was halfway down the driveway before I realized how dark it was. Glancing at the front porch, I noticed that the exterior light was off—either my father had forgotten to turn it on after dinner (which almost never happened) or the bulb had burned out. The moon and stars overhead, shrouded behind heavy cloud cover, offered little help. Hanson Road was silent and still, unnaturally so, and the sound of my footsteps was eerily loud. By the time I'd positioned both cans at the curb for early-morning pickup, the back of my neck was bathed in cold sweat and I could hear the thumping of my heart inside my chest. My eyes darted nervously back and forth into the shadows.

And then I knew—I didn't know *how* I knew with such absolute certainty, but I did—the Boogeyman was hiding nearby, watching me.

Instead of turning and fleeing for the open mouth of the garage—*What if he'd slipped inside while my back was turned and was waiting for me in the darkness?*—I stood there frozen in fear at the bottom of the driveway, my right hand still gripping the handle of one of the trash cans.

My mind suddenly flashed back to a story I'd once heard—a story about a good man not much younger than I was now, but considerably braver.

———

I'd spent the summer before my senior year of high school working as a laborer on Edgewood Arsenal. The hours sucked, but the daily commute was short and the pay was good. I did a little bit of everything—mowing and trimming grass, repairing broken playground equipment, laying asphalt. But my most memorable task that summer was shredding government documents.

Each morning a truck pulled up and delivered several pallets of cardboard boxes containing thousands of sheets of paper that needed to be destroyed. My supervisor—a soft-spoken African American gentleman named Lonny—and I unloaded the boxes, stacking them at the head of an industrial shredder that very much resembled a wood chipper with a long, narrow conveyor belt leading to its hungry metal teeth.

We then took turns feeding the machine, one of us carefully staggering stacks of documents atop the belt so the gnashing teeth wouldn't jam, and the other emptying tangles of shredded confetti from the collection basket into a number of nearby dumpsters. The work itself was long and boring. From time to time, we stumbled upon something interesting—black-and-white photographs of blown-up vehicles after multiple rounds of long-range weapons testing was my personal favorite—but for the most part, it was a dull and monotonous routine.

Despite the drudgery, Lonny and I didn't have a whole lot to say to each other in the beginning. We were both quiet by nature, and on the surface, we couldn't have been more different. I was a skinny seventeen-year-old White dude from the suburbs getting ready to graduate in the spring and head off to college. He was a husband and father in his early thirties, muscular and with dreadlocks, from a small backwoods town in western Texas.

But that all changed one afternoon when Lonny noticed the book I was reading at lunch. I no longer remember the exact title, but the subject matter was the Vietnam War.

"You reading that for school?" he asked in that thick drawl of his.

"Just for myself. I read a lot of history books."

"Learning anything interesting?"

"A ton," I said. "Mostly what a clusterfuck it was over there. I still can't

believe they sent kids like me to fight in those jungles. I can't even imagine what it must have felt like."

He looked at me then, really *looked at me*—and later, when I thought back on that conversation, it was clear he was deciding in that moment whether or not to trust me with his story. "I was there," he finally said, eyes lowered.

And that's all it took.

For the next several weeks, he shared his story with me, and I peppered him with a barrage of questions. I learned about weapons (why the U.S. grunts preferred the enemy's AK-47 rifles to their own M16s), firefights (anywhere from thirty seconds to five minutes of hell on earth), wartime racism (how the African American soldiers almost always got stuck walking point when out on patrol, and how they always ended up lugging around the heavy M60 machine gun known as "The Pig"), but mostly I learned about the friends he'd made and lost during his tour of duty (his "brothers," he called them). It was a powerful and emotional experience—for both of us—and one I soon learned he hadn't shared with many people. I felt honored.

Of all the stories Lonny told me that summer, one in particular always stood out. He'd been in-country for less than a week when he was ordered to walk point for the first time. He was green as hell and didn't have a clue what he was doing, but that didn't matter. It was his turn. It was a night patrol, and another company had made contact with the enemy in that same area just days earlier. A couple hours in, while climbing a steep trail, Lonny held up a fist, signaling for the men following behind him to stop. He didn't see anything waiting in the dark jungle ahead, but he felt *it*—with every fiber of his being, he felt the enemy hiding nearby, watching them at that very moment. The word he used to describe that feeling was "hinky"—he went on to say that he would experience it over and over again during his time in Vietnam, a kind of instinctual survival trait—and he had no idea from where it came. He told me that, squatting there on that dark trail, he felt the tiny hairs on his forearms rise to attention, the sweat drenching his *uniform instantly turn ice-cold, and a bad taste come into his mouth. The taste of fear. Thirty seconds later, he was in the middle of his first firefight . . .*

———————

Standing at the bottom of my driveway, still holding on to that trash can lid as if it were some kind of lifeline, I tasted that same primal fear flood my mouth, threatening to drown me. Eyes scanning the shadows, I couldn't spot anything out of the ordinary—but I knew better. Everything around me felt *hinky.*

He was out there in the darkness.

Somewhere.

Close.

I have no idea how much time passed before a line of cars crested the hill on Hanson Road, illuminating my frantic retreat into the garage and the safety of my house beyond. It could have been forty-five seconds, or more like five or ten minutes. My brain had thrown a cog and temporarily stopped working.

All I knew was this: neither before that night nor since have I ever felt such stark fear completely paralyze my mind and body. And I've never again known with such certainty that I was in the presence of pure evil.

ABOVE: Major Buck Flemings (left) and Detective Lyle Harper
(Photo courtesy of Logan Reynolds)

ABOVE: Cedar Drive military housing *(Photo courtesy of the author)*

ABOVE: Cedar Drive Elementary School *(Photo courtesy of the author)*

seven

Maddy

*"By the middle of August, most residents of Edgewood
were in a state of full-fledged hysteria."*

1

On the morning of August 10, I was sitting in a rotating barber chair getting my hair cut, listening to a bunch of grumpy old men—not one of them under the age of seventy, including Big Ray, who was busy trimming my sideburns—argue about the forthcoming presidential election, when the news came on the radio: another Edgewood girl had gone missing.

Her name was Madeline Wilcox, and she was eighteen years old. Maddy, as she was known to family and friends, lived with her parents at the end of Hanson Road, four blocks east of the library. Beautiful and spirited, she was set to graduate from Edgewood High School the following spring, but only if she managed to pass the two make-up classes she was taking this summer. So far, so good—at the time of her disappearance, she had earned Bs in both classes. Maddy's older sister, Chrissy, was spending her first summer off from college working as a lifeguard in nearby Dewey Beach. Maddy had plans to visit her the following weekend.

Earlier in the morning, as was her routine, Mrs. Wilcox carried up a load of laundry from the basement, and, on the way down the hallway, cracked open her daughter's bedroom door to wake her. To her surprise and immediate concern, Maddy wasn't there and her bed didn't appear to have been slept in.

The night before, Maddy had driven some friends to a party in Joppatowne, but Mrs. Wilcox was an early sleeper and had been in bed by nine thirty, so she hadn't heard if her daughter made it home in time for her midnight curfew. Her husband was away on a three-day business trip, so he wasn't any help either. Mrs. Wilcox looked around the empty bedroom and suddenly thought: *What if Maddy never made it home last night?*

She placed the laundry basket on the bed and went to the front window. Peering outside, she spotted her daughter's candy apple red Camaro sitting at the bottom of the driveway. She immediately breathed a sigh of relief. *Thank you, Lord, she made it safe and sound.*

Walking downstairs, she glanced at the small crystal bowl on the foyer table, checking for her daughter's car keys. They weren't there. She later told police that's when a bad feeling washed over her.

Hurrying outside in her bare feet, Mrs. Wilcox was halfway across the lawn when she noticed the Camaro's driver's-side door was slightly ajar and the interior light was on. Her fear deepened.

Fighting back tears, she was reaching for the door handle when her right foot landed on something sharp in the grass. She yelped and looked down: it was her daughter's key chain.

That's when the tears flowed freely, and she ran back inside to phone the police.

2

As I stared at Madeline Wilcox's face on the afternoon news, it came to me why her name had sounded so damn familiar when I'd first heard it broadcast over the radio.

An old friend and teammate from my lacrosse days, Johnny Pullin, had once dated Madeline's older sister for a couple of months. At first I couldn't remember the sister's name or even what she looked like, but boy oh boy, I definitely remembered Madeline. Despite the fact that I'd only met her on two occasions, she'd made quite the lasting impression.

Both times had been at the Rocks, a twisty stretch of Deer Creek located in northern Harford County, where generations of local teenagers had escaped to drink beer, do cannonballs off the old railroad bridge, and ride the rapids on inflatable tubes.

Johnny Pullin and I had been eighteen that summer, which would've made Madeline no older than fourteen. But that hadn't slowed her down one bit. The pretty young girl I remembered had cussed like a sailor, flirted like a homecoming queen, and worn all of us out with her brash, know-it-all attitude. I'd even caught her sneaking beers out of my cooler.

Carly had done some quick asking around the morning of the disappearance, and, at first glance, it appeared not much had changed in the past four years. Madeline Wilcox was a below-average student and had been in frequent trouble for smoking on school property and cutting classes. In fact, she'd had to repeat the ninth grade due to an excessive number of unexcused absences.

There were, however, numerous indications that she'd recently been making changes in her lifestyle and was finally headed in the right direction. She was going to summer school and had gotten a job working three days a week as an aide at a Bel Air nursing home. Her bosses had only good things to say about her performance. Many of the neighbors also spoke highly of her, praising her friendly attitude and thoughtfulness. Mrs. Peters, an elderly woman next door who'd recently lost her husband to cancer, said that Madeline had shoveled the snow from her driveway all last winter without ever being asked, and when the woman had tried to pay her for the work, the teenager had refused to accept a single penny. According to her friends, she'd recently quit smoking and was saving the money she used to spend on cigarettes to buy a golden retriever puppy at the end of the summer. She planned to name it Sawyer.

3

After arriving at the scene, crime-lab technicians immediately began working over Madeline Wilcox's Camaro, dusting for prints and scouring the dash, seats, and floor mats for trace evidence. Uniformed police and detectives canvassed door-to-door along both sides of Hanson Road and spread out onto surrounding streets. Additional officers—along with two teams of dogs—began searching the woods that bordered many of the backyards along this stretch of Hanson. Winters Run snaked through much of that heavily forested area, eventually passing under historic Ricker's Bridge as it wound its way north toward Route 24 and beyond.

Detectives spoke at length with both of Madeline Wilcox's friends who were supposed to have accompanied her to the party the night before. Frannie Keele and Kendall Grant explained that the three of them had changed their minds because they were tired, and had decided to skip the party. Instead, they'd spent the evening at Kendall's house a few blocks away, eating pizza that'd been delivered by Gus's and playing video games. Madeline had left at five minutes before midnight to make the short drive home. According to the girls, she'd been in a good mood throughout the night.

Mr. Wilcox caught a flight back from New York within an hour of his distraught wife's phone call. A sheriff's deputy was waiting for him at BWI Airport to bring him home. At twenty minutes past one, breaking news reports interrupted episodes of *All My Children*, *The Young and the Restless*, and *Days of Our Lives* for tens of thousands of local viewers. Mr. and Mrs. Wilcox stood side by side on the front porch of their house. Detective Lyle Harper stood behind them, looking suitably grim. A sobbing Mrs. Wilcox stared directly into the camera and pleaded with whoever took their daughter to please return her unharmed. "Maddy is such a sweet girl," the mother said, tears staining her quivering cheeks. "She means everything to our family. Please let Maddy come home." A stone-faced Mr. Wilcox put a steadying hand on his wife's shoulder, but didn't say a word.

When they were finished, three of the four networks returned to regular programming, but the Channel 13 news team remained on-air, first interviewing Frannie Keele and Kendall Grant, and then wrapping up with a neighbor from down the street.

It wasn't long before someone made up a HAVE YOU SEEN THIS GIRL? poster featuring Madeline's photograph, a brief description (5'5", 120 pounds, blond hair, green eyes, small scar above left eye, butterfly tattoo on right ankle), as well as contact information for the Harford County Sheriff's Department. By dinner, practically every business in Edgewood had at least one poster plastered on its front door or storefront window.

That evening, Kara and I joined a group of about thirty or forty civilian volunteers in searching a wooded area that ran parallel to much of Perry Avenue, the next street over. Plans were also solidified to check out the ball fields and woods behind the three schools on Willoughby Beach Road the following morning. I'd talked my father out of coming— the last thing he needed to do was take a day off work and come out here and catch poison ivy with the rest of us—but I saw plenty of other familiar faces from the neighborhood. Mr. Vargas was there with several other dads from Bayberry Court; Coach Parks and his wife; Carly

Albright and her mom, both wearing bright orange vests like it was the middle of deer season; Mrs. Tannenbaum from the front desk at the Edgewood Library; Jim Solomon from the Texaco station; and a trio of old high school wrestling teammates: Len Stiller, Frank Hapney, and Josh Gallagher.

Several times during the search, I stole sideways glances at Josh. I couldn't imagine the courage it must have taken for him to be out here with the rest of us. Kara made a point of going over and saying hello and asking about his parents, but not me. I just left him alone and kept beating the bushes.

Dusk soon fell, and after almost three hours in the woods, it grew too dark to see much of anything, so we gave up. To the best of my knowledge, none of the searchers found anything remotely connected to Madeline Wilcox's disappearance. The only real excitement came when Jim Solomon discovered a brand-new box of .22 cartridges some kid had probably dropped a week earlier, and Frank Hapney accidentally kicked over a hornet's nest and got stung a half-dozen times on his arms and legs.

It was during the next morning's search that several rumors began to spread. The first and least palatable was that Madeline Wilcox was having an affair with a married man, and the illicit relationship had led to her disappearance. Whether people believed it was the unidentified husband she was allegedly seeing who stole her away or the angry wife, I never heard.

The most popular theory to make the rounds that day was the growing suspicion that Madeline Wilcox may have simply run away from home. Evidently, she'd done so several times before—once traveling as far south as North Carolina—and many townspeople were now convinced she'd done it yet again.

"Think about it, Chiz," Kurt Reynolds said, as a group of us trudged across an open field in a long human chain, five or six feet separating one person from the next. "The Boogeyman kills his victims and sets 'em up so someone finds 'em right away. This ain't that. It's already been something like thirty-six hours."

Kurt had graduated a year ahead of me and never was the sharpest stick in the bunch. Jimmy Cavanaugh had once sold him a baggie of pencil shavings for ten dollars, and Kurt had actually rolled it and smoked it. He was a volunteer fireman now, and his entire crew was participating in the search. Kara hadn't been able to make it because of school, so I was stuck with this guy all morning. I loved Kara more than life itself, but right now the blame for my raging headache lay squarely in her lap.

Lowering my voice, I asked, "What if we just haven't found the body yet?"

"Well now, that's the thing, ain't it? The Boogeyman *wants* us to find the bodies. Why would he start hiding 'em now?" He gave his odd-shaped head a vigorous shake. "No sirree. If she was dead, we'd a found her by now. She's probably sitting on a beach somewhere with a cold beer in one hand and a fatty in the other."

Of course, I disagreed with my old friend's expert criminal analysis, but I kept my opinion to myself. I knew better than to argue with this knucklehead. A short time later, when the opportunity presented itself, I pretended to lag behind the group and then stealthily shifted over a handful of spots in line. Instead of five or six feet separating Kurt and me, it was now more like thirty, and I couldn't hear a single word the guy was saying. Miraculously, within a half hour, my headache was gone.

Madeline Wilcox's boyfriend must've been listening to the same scandalous rumors circulating about her disappearance. He was clean-cut and well-spoken, and when Channel 11 interviewed him that evening on the six o'clock news, he was plenty pissed off.

"It's ridiculous that we have people even considering such a thing, much less speaking openly about it. Not only ridiculous, but slanderous. All of our energy and resources, the police and community alike, should be focused on finding Maddy."

He narrowed his blue eyes at the camera. "I promise you she did not vanish on her own accord. She did not leave by choice. She was excited to go back to school and graduate, even more excited to apply for college. We'd just made plans the other day to go visit her sister at the beach . . ."

Before the news cut away to commercial, a short video clip appeared onscreen showing a staggered group of searchers emerging from the woods behind the high school. The Channel 11 anchor confirmed what I'd surmised earlier—despite the strong turnout, none of the day's searches had managed to unearth anything of interest. Staring at the television, I recognized Kurt Reynolds's lopsided gait at the front of the crowd. He looked like one of George Romero's shambling zombies from *Night of the Living Dead*. On his immediate left was Danny Earnshaw, one of my sister Nancy's old classmates. He ran a successful law office on Route 40 now. Then I spotted my old baseball cap and gray *Twilight Zone* T-shirt in the crowd, and not far behind me—a surprise. I did a double-take and moved closer to the television screen to confirm what I was seeing. Walking at a brisk pace, almost catching up to me now, was Mr. Gallagher. He carried a long walking stick, and a bright orange floppy hat—one of those freebie giveaways from an Orioles game—was perched atop his head. I stared at him, wondering how we hadn't managed to cross paths during the search, until a crying baby in a Pampers commercial took his place on the television.

4

A pair of local fishermen discovered Madeline Wilcox's body beneath Ricker's Bridge at approximately 8:23 a.m. on Friday, August 12— precisely forty-eight hours after she'd first been listed as a missing person.

As they approached their regular fishing spot, both men initially believed they'd stumbled upon a homeless woman sleeping, or perhaps a drunken college girl passed out. They often found signs of partying under the bridge—empty beer cans and bottles, cigarette butts, the occasional used condom—and they figured the woman was most likely sleeping it off after a particularly wild night. Her back was propped up against the old stone foundation, long legs splayed out in front of her, and her hands rested peacefully atop her stomach. Then, as they drew closer, the men realized it wasn't a woman at all—it was a teenage girl. Her open eyes were bulging, her neck was swollen and bruised, and she was naked below the waist. She didn't appear to be breathing. That's when they ran for help.

Although the media wasn't able to report many of the official details until the following day's news cycle—by now, most members of the police department were in no mood to cooperate with journalists, local or otherwise—it didn't really matter. Word spread like wildfire around the streets of Edgewood.

Madeline Wilcox had been beaten, sexually assaulted, and strangled to death. Investigators had found three deep bite marks scattered across her chest and torso. Like Natasha Gallagher and Kacey Robinson before her, Madeline's left ear had been severed and her body posed after death. Once again, there was no sign of the missing ear at the crime scene. Red marks circled her wrists and ankles, evidence of ligatures that had been removed. The killer had hidden Madeline Wilcox away, abused and tortured her at his leisure, and then disposed of her body once he was sated.

To make matters worse—if that were possible—the police now knew for certain that the killer was playing games with them. The area surrounding Ricker's Bridge, including the shadowy confines located beneath its stone arch, had been thoroughly covered by the authorities on two separate occasions. The first time had occurred the morning of Madeline's disappearance, within hours of her mother's frantic phone call to 911. The second time had occurred the following afternoon, when nearly two dozen police cadets had been trucked in from the academy in downtown Baltimore to aid in the search.

Both times the area had been deemed clear, which could only mean one thing. At some point, the killer had doubled back and purposely dumped the body beneath the bridge to send police a very clear message: *I'm watching your every move and I'm smarter than all of you.*

5

Law enforcement officials grew increasingly tight-lipped after the death of Madeline Wilcox. No longer able to deny the obvious, they privately acknowledged what three murders in the span of sixty days signified: Edgewood had a serial killer. And instead of closing in on the madman, they were falling further behind with each passing day. And now, the Boogeyman was laughing at them.

Thus far, Carly had had no luck finding out if the perpetrator had left behind anything involving numbers. Her usual sources claimed they'd been stonewalled by *their* usual sources. I'd run into Detective Harper in the McDonald's parking lot a couple days earlier, but he'd practically growled at me when I'd said hello. It wasn't like I could just come out and ask him anyway. He had no idea I knew about the hopscotch grid and missing dog sign, and would most likely be angry as hell if he ever found out.

Finally, eight long days after Madeline Wilcox's body was found, a crack appeared in the police's wall of secrecy, and Carly got the scoop we'd been waiting for.

Each block of the mysterious hopscotch grid discovered after the first murder was filled in with the number three. The number that appeared most often on the missing dog poster found after the second murder was four. This time, in the course of conducting her autopsy, the coroner had discovered something peculiar lodged deep in Madeline Wilcox's throat: *five pennies.*

6

Later that week, I stopped at 7-Eleven to grab a quick snack on my way home from the library. Chili dogs were on special—two for $1.99, including a small fountain drink. *Lunch on a budget*, as my father liked to say.

On the sidewalk out front, I ran into Parker Sanders, an old friend who was two years behind me in school. He was on his way out the door with a Big Gulp in one hand and a bag of M&Ms in the other.

"Eating healthy, I see."

"You know it," he said. "Hey, I heard you guys are playing basketball again down at the high school."

"You should come on out."

"Tell Pruitt to call me next time you play. He still has my number." Flipping me a wave, he climbed into his car.

Fat chance of that happening, I thought, watching him drive away. Jeff Pruitt couldn't stand the guy.

My stomach growling, I turned to go inside and bumped into a man holding the door open for an exiting customer.

"Sorry," I said, backing up to give him space. "I wasn't paying attention."

"No problem at all," he said, continuing on his way to the parking lot.

My mouth went instantly dry. I stood there, frozen, afraid to turn around and look. I'd only heard the mysterious caller's voice one time, and only three words at that—"*What was fast?*"—but I was almost certain I'd just heard it a second time.

Finally breaking my paralysis, I walked into the store and waited until I heard the heavy glass door close behind me, and then I risked a glance over my shoulder. The man appeared to be in his mid-thirties, tall and stocky, with short dark hair hidden beneath a faded Atlanta Braves baseball cap. He was sitting behind the wheel of a yellow Volkswagen

Bug and was now wearing sunglasses. I couldn't tell if he was looking at me or not. A moment later, he backed up and drove away.

I should follow him. See where he lives.

But my legs wouldn't budge.

My appetite for chili dogs gone, I paid for a Snickers and a carton of chocolate milk, and went home.

7

By the middle of August, most residents of Edgewood were in a state of full-fledged hysteria. Gun sales soared once again, and following a July lull, there was now a lengthy waiting list for the installation of home security systems. The Hair Cuttery in the mall and local beauty parlors were booked solid with appointment slots filled until late September—the media had been quick to point out that all three of the Boogeyman's victims had beautiful manes of long, flowing hair, so now women of all ages were rushing out to get short haircuts. Almost overnight, at least within the cozy confines of Harford County, the Joan of Arc and Dorothy Hamill hairstyles of the '70s were once again all the rage.

And then there were those folks—their numbers seeming to increase with each passing day—who claimed that guns and security systems were of no help when it came to stopping the Boogeyman. Citing the horrific nature of the murders, along with the puzzling lack of evidence left behind, a small but vocal group of residents were now convinced that this serial killer was not a human being at all, but rather some kind of supernatural creature. "How else do you explain it?" one wide-eyed gentleman told a Channel 2 reporter live on the air. "These girls are being stolen away right out from under their parents' noses, from the safety of their own homes and neighborhoods, brutally maimed and killed, and then returned for public viewing. Nothing human is capable of that kind of sleight of hand. Something else—something not of this world—is clearly at work here."

The very next afternoon, a woman wearing a pink terry-cloth bathrobe and curlers in her hair—"absolutely scandalous," my mother commented at my side—told a news crew from Channel 13 that something had activated the motion detector spotlight in her backyard the night before. When she rushed to her upstairs bedroom window, she spotted a dark figure loping across the lawn. The woman claimed it was at least seven feet tall and had a single, pointed horn protruding from the center of its sloping forehead, and when it reached the privacy fence that encircled the backyard, it simply took flight and disappeared into the night sky. Of course, her husband had been sleeping at the time, and hadn't seen a thing.

Watching these lurid stories—and so many others like them—unfold daily on television, I couldn't help but think: *They're just like scenes out of a horror movie . . . only this time, they're absolutely real.*

The next morning, Carly called and asked me to stop by the newspaper office. An un-aired video from a Channel 11 newscast had been making the rounds there, and she wanted me to take a look. Once I arrived, she escorted me into the break room where a television and VCR sat atop an old wooden desk that had seen better days. The room smelled of coffee and cologne and stale cigarette smoke. Carly pressed play, and a familiar face flashed onto the screen: Blanche Waters, the elderly African American woman who lived just around the corner from my parents. I'd cut her grass and shoveled snow off her driveway from the time I was twelve until I'd left for college. Leaning on her cane, she looked like a child standing next to the reporter. "My grand-daddy used to tell the story of Henry Lee Jones, a runaway slave who struck a deal with the devil. In exchange for helping Henry and his family escape north, the devil demanded that Henry kill the plantation owner's ten-year-old daughter, a sweet-natured girl who'd never once hurt a soul." Mrs. Waters sneezed and proceeded to give her nose a good, long *honking* with a balled-up handkerchief. Once she was finished, she gave the hankie a careful inspection, and then unceremoniously stuffed it back into the pocket of her blouse. The reporter holding the microphone glanced at the camera and raised his bushy eyebrows in amusement. The old woman continued: "Henry Lee did the deed that very night, strangling the girl to death in her bed, but it turned out the devil had tricked him. Oh, he kept the first part of the bargain, all right; he helped Henry and his family make safe passage. But then he pulled a fast one, cursing Henry Lee with eternal life and an unquenchable bloodthirst for innocent young White girls. Not long after, Henry's wife took their two children and fled in the middle of the night, and they were never heard from again. Legend has it that Henry Lee Jones is still out there to this day, possessed by the devil's hateful rage, roaming the countryside and strangling young girls to death. My granddaddy's long gone to the grave by now, bless his gentle soul, but I believe he was speaking the truth." She turned then and stared directly into the camera. "Henry Lee Jones has come to Edgewood, and he's hungry. How else, with so many Blacks and Hispanics residing here, do you explain three dead *White* girls?" The videotape ended then.

"Jesus," I said, looking up at Carly.

"Can you imagine if they'd put that on the evening news?"

I shook my head. "I'm actually a little surprised they didn't."

"Me too."

"I'm glad my parents will never see it. They adore Mrs. Waters. Hell, I do too. I've known her since I was a kid." I sighed. "At least, I *thought* I knew her."

Carly picked up the remote and turned off the television. "I think we're going to find out very quickly just how much we *don't* know in this town."

8

In the days following the death of Madeline Wilcox, the national press invaded Edgewood in full force, with news teams coming from as far away as Florida, Chicago, Boston, and Canada. It wasn't unusual to take an afternoon drive and see residents on one side of the street talking to a camera crew, and residents on the opposite side of the street being interviewed by police detectives. Law enforcement and media helicopters circling overhead soon became an everyday occurrence.

Parents from neighboring towns in Harford County had no compunctions—moral or otherwise—about forbidding their children from setting foot in Edgewood, especially after dark, propping up the murders as incontrovertible proof that "the town is a dangerous cesspool of sin and degradation, populated by noneducated, low-income drug abusers." Those stinging words came from the bright red lips of a big-haired woman named Kemper Billington, who just happened to be the vice president of Fallston High School's PTA, during a live interview with a Channel 11 news team. Adding fuel to the fire, the *Aegis* ran a particularly offensive editorial regarding the burgeoning budget costs of the police investigation, drawing more than a dozen irate letters to the editor—including one from *Aegis* employee Carly Albright—and scores of subscription cancellations.

The cycle of gossip continued unabated. Just as they had after the first two murders, rumors once again began to run rampant throughout the town, the most colorful involving a theory that there was a satanic cult operating just below the surface of Harford County society. Stories of cows and dogs being mysteriously and brutally slaughtered dominated late-night conversations, as did one particularly gruesome tale about an alleged grave-robbing incident that'd taken place at Edgewood Memorial Gardens earlier in the summer. The murders of the three young Edgewood girls were now being attributed to a new wave of initiation rites for the cult's Satanic High Council. Alleged members of the council included the chief of police, the vice principal at Edgewood Middle School, and the captain of the varsity cheerleading squad's well-endowed stepmother. A late-night anonymous phone call made to the tip-line informed police where they could find a makeshift altar deep in the woods behind the shopping center. A team of detectives checked it out and came away thoroughly unimpressed.

Another piece of gossip that quickly gained traction was a report that police were now searching for two men working in tandem. A serial killer team working hand in hand seemed the most plausible explanation for how the girls had been taken from such familiar surroundings without a single clue being left behind. One man entered Natasha Gallagher's bedroom, rendered her unconscious, and handed her out the window to a second person. One man distracted Kacey Robinson and Madeline Wilcox while an accomplice moved in and knocked them unconscious.

According to Carly Albright, neither story carried much credence. As far as she knew, investigators were still searching for a lone killer, believing strongly that the three murders' M.O.s were too identical and disciplined in nature to be the work of multiple perpetrators.

There was, Carly explained, one interesting trend beginning to emerge in Edgewood, and, just as the satanic panic and multiple serial killer theories could be attributed to a recent increase in gossip—somewhere along the line, suspicion had begun to replace caution—so too could this new pattern of behavior. In the days following Madeline Wilcox's death, there'd been a sudden sharp increase in the number of verbal arguments and physical altercations occurring between local residents. Loose lips and drunken slurs led to fistfights in parking lots and front yards. Joking around turned serious and then violent. Old feuds were rekindled, and new ones started. A rash of false accusations broke out, and it took an official warning from police to tamp it down. The tip-line took in calls at a record pace, but most of them were trivial nonsense, and law enforcement was considering shutting the whole thing down.

I had personally witnessed this new dynamic during one of my infrequent morning jogs. Making my way up Perry Avenue, I came across a group of kids on bikes and skateboards. In the middle of a roughly formed circle, two boys were fighting. They couldn't have been more than eleven years old. I rushed in and broke it up.

"I know who your parents are!" I lied. "Now shake hands and make up, and I won't tell them what I just saw."

"I ain't shaking that fucker's hand," the smallest of the two boys snarled.

"Why not?" I asked.

"He's telling everyone my father's the Boogeyman."

And then there was the curfew. Beginning on Monday, August 15, by order of the Harford County Sheriff's Department, all residents of Edgewood were required to be off the streets by no later than 10:00 p.m. Exceptions were being made for night-shift and health-care workers, and security company employees. Gas stations, restaurants, and bars all closed early with, surprisingly, only a handful of complaints from their owners.

Once Madeline's body had been released by the coroner's office, the Wilcox family opted for a private funeral at a small church on the Eastern Shore, for which I was both grateful and relieved. After speaking to a handful of friends and neighbors, I realized it was pretty obvious that most people shared my reaction—there'd already been enough funerals in Edgewood this summer.

Despite the turmoil swirling throughout the rest of town, 920 Hanson Road remained a safe haven. While my mother reacted to Maddy's death with predictable bouts of grief and reflection, she also stayed surprisingly calm about the situation. She told me one night after dinner that she was doing all she could to remain faithful and optimistic, sending casseroles and trays of cookies and brownies to the police station to help feed the officers working overtime, and praying as hard and as often as she could. She resolutely believed it was all in God's hands now, and although she didn't come right out and say it, I think for whatever reason she also believed that the murders were finally over.

My father wasn't quite so sure. He woke me early one Saturday morning and quietly asked for my help installing new locks on the outside basement door, as well as the door at the rear of the garage.

Still, most nights, the three of us talked and laughed and shared a dinner table, and I went to bed counting my blessings that two such kind people had found each other in this world and made me a part of their lives.

As the month wore on, I thought the long days and pressure at work was finally starting to get to Carly. She'd been moody all week and short with me on the phone. I eventually asked if she needed a break from our calls and the whole Boogeyman business in general. To my surprise, she started crying, letting it all pour out while giving me the whole story.

Earlier in the week, while working on an article in her bedroom, she'd heard something at the window. When she got up and looked outside, she was almost positive she saw a dark figure scurrying away into the darkness. The next day, while making her way around town for work, she started to feel strange, convinced that someone was following her. That evening, the nightmares started. Bad ones. She'd barely slept all week, and the stress and exhaustion were taking their toll. She apologized, but I told her there was no need and that I understood. What I didn't tell her was that I was experiencing similar feelings of paranoia and having nightmares of my own.

9

On Friday afternoon, August 19, Detective Lyle Harper and Major Buck Flemings from the Harford County Sheriff's Department held a joint press conference on the steps of the courthouse. More than thirty-five news organizations from all over the country attended. Major Flemings spoke first, announcing the formation of a brand-new task force consisting of members from the sheriff's department, state police, and Federal Bureau of Investigation. Detective Harper would be heading up the task force, and as he stepped up to the podium next, I immediately noticed how tired and thin he looked. I couldn't help but think of his wife at home and three adult children scattered around the state, and I hoped they were rallying around him to offer their support. He looked like he needed it.

Harper spoke for a short time, concluding with a grim-faced promise that the task force was "working around the clock to put an end to the senseless killings in Edgewood."

When he was finished, I glanced at my mother on the sofa, bracing myself for another round of criticism directed at the detective. Despite my frequent reassurances, she was still wary of the man.

Instead, I found her with her head bowed and eyes closed, lips moving inaudibly, clasping her rosary in her hands.

ABOVE: Madeline Wilcox *(Photo courtesy of Frannie Keele)*

ABOVE: Madeline Wilcox driveway crime scene *(Photo courtesy of Logan Reynolds)*

LEFT: HAVE YOU SEEN THIS GIRL? poster
(Photo courtesy of the author)

ABOVE: Madeline Wilcox
(Photo courtesy of Frannie Keele)

ABOVE: Police and residents searching a field near Hanson Road
(Photo courtesy of The Aegis*)*

ABOVE: Police and residents searching tree line *(Photo courtesy of* The Aegis*)*

ABOVE: Detectives examining crime scene at Ricker's Bridge
(Photo courtesy of The Baltimore Sun*)*

eight

The Boogeyman

"And if it wasn't the Boogeyman at your window,
then who was it?"

1

Curious as always, and unable to locate much information in my home set of *Encyclopedia Britannica*, I visited the library later that week and researched the origins of the Boogeyman.

While many books and magazine articles on folklore and the supernatural provided valuable details, the majority of my notes came from a single volume: *Monsters and Myths* by Robert Carruthers Jr.; Lemming Publications; New York, New York; 1974.

The following is a brief summary:

Spelled a variety of different ways, including *bogeyman*, *bogyman*, and *bogieman*, the Boogeyman is a mythical creature most commonly used by adults to frighten children into good behavior. The first known reference to a "Bogeyman" is considered to be the hobgoblins described in England in the 1500s. The word "bogey" is derived from the Middle English "bogge/bugge" meaning "something frightening" or "scarecrow." It may've also been influenced by the Old English term "bugbear"—"bug" meaning "goblin" or "scarecrow," and "bear" representing an evil demon in the form of a bear that feasts on small children. While the description of the

Boogeyman usually differs on a cultural level, there are often shared characteristics to the creatures, including claws, talons, red eyes, and sharp teeth. Some are even described to have horns and hooves. Boogeyman-like creatures are almost universal, common to the folklore of most all countries. Sack Man, El Coco, Babau, Buba, Bagu, and Babaroga are just a handful of the names they go by.

2

On Friday, September 9, the police got the break they'd been waiting for.

Seventeen-year-old Annie Riggs was one of Edgewood High School's most accomplished students. President of the senior class, she earned straight As across the board and was captain of the varsity field hockey and lacrosse teams. She had a broad, contagious smile and an even bigger heart. Humble in nature and possessing a self-deprecating sense of humor, Annie was well-liked by students and faculty alike.

That Friday evening marked the end of the first week of high school—only four days long, thanks to the Labor Day holiday on Monday—as well as the first full week of field hockey practice. Annie stayed late after Friday's practice to talk with her coaches about a new offensive set and the team's first scrimmage the following Monday afternoon. At approximately 7:15 p.m., she left the school and began walking home. A short time later, along a quiet stretch of Sequoia Drive, a masked assailant attacked her from behind. A struggle ensued, and she was able to break free and run to a nearby house for help.

Despite the presence of dozens of reporters in town, news of the attempted abduction did not hit airwaves until early the following morning. For once, the handful of residents involved kept their mouths shut.

On Monday, September 12, Carly Albright secured a copy of Annie

Riggs's handwritten police statement. It's reprinted here, in its entirety, for the first time:

I was the last girl in the locker room after practice because I'd stayed late. Usually I get a ride home with a friend or one of my parents, but my teammates were long gone and my mom and dad were at a work dinner. I put on a sweatshirt and my watch and necklace and grabbed my backpack from my locker. That's when I noticed how really late it was. I left the school through the side gym doors. I saw Mr. Harris on my way out and told him I'd see him on Monday. I knew it was going to rain and I could hear thunder, but even after looking at my watch, I was still surprised at how dark it was. It was like a ghost town outside. The parking lot was nearly empty, and I didn't see anyone else when I crossed Willoughby Beach Road. Further down the street, there was an old couple getting into their car at the church, but that was it. By the time I got to Sequoia, it was really thundering and lightning. A white Jeep turned the corner up ahead and slowed down, and for a minute I thought it was my friend Lori Anderson stopping to give me a ride. But it wasn't her, and whoever it was just kept on going. I looked over my shoulder and watched the Jeep drive away and that's when I got a weird feeling like someone was following me. I kept looking over my shoulder but didn't see anyone. Then I started hearing things. Footsteps behind me on the sidewalk. A tree branch snapping like someone had stepped on it. But every time I looked around, no one was there. By that time, I figured I was just being paranoid and felt pretty stupid, but that didn't stop me from walking faster. (A little while ago, the really tall detective—I can't remember his name—asked if I had experienced anything strange or unusual in the past couple months, and I told him no. But now I remember that that's not really true. Another day, right before classes started, I hit the

*hockey ball around with a couple of friends at the school, and
I got the same weird feeling when I was walking home. Like
someone was following me. But it was the middle of a sunny day,
so I never really felt scared or in any kind of danger. I'd actually
kinda forgotten about it until right this minute.) Anyway, by that
time, I'd gotten to the part of Sequoia where there are no houses
or streetlights, just what's left of that old garage and all those
overgrown trees and bushes. The wind was really starting to pick
up and the temperature was dropping fast. I thought I heard
footsteps again, so I checked over my shoulder one more time.
Same thing. No one there. I was starting to feel like an idiot. I was
only a block and a half away from home, and I told myself that I
wasn't going to look again. No matter what. It wasn't like I was
ten years old or something. But then I was sure I heard it again.
Footsteps. Right behind me. Louder this time. I forced myself not
to look. Walked even faster. And they went away. I actually kinda
giggled, thinking I'd won, and then, out of habit I guess, I glanced
over my shoulder—and he was right there. A man. Very tall. Very
big. Dark pants and dark long-sleeve shirt. And he was wearing
a mask. It looked like the mask from that movie* The Town That
Dreaded Sundown. *My friends and I rented it a bunch of times.
Kind of like a cloth sack with eyeholes. Before I could run or
scream or do anything, he grabbed me around my neck from
behind and lifted me off the ground. I dropped my backpack, and
then right away we were moving backward toward the trees. He
was very strong. I started screaming and trying to punch and
kick him, but he was hard to reach because he was behind me. He
shoved a hand over my mouth to stop me from screaming. He was
wearing some kind of gloves, but I didn't get a look at what kind.
At one point, I bit his hand really hard, and I remember the glove
tasted like rubber, but he didn't even seem to notice. I mean, it
had to hurt, but he didn't make a sound. The arm around my neck*

started to tighten and I could tell I was going to pass out soon. That's when I remembered the little canister of pepper spray my mom had given me. It's not much bigger than a tube of ChapStick, and I'd put it inside my sweatshirt pocket when I was in the locker room. I grabbed it and reached behind me and started spraying—for what felt like a really long time. At first, I thought it wasn't working or I was missing his face. He didn't slow down, or let go, or scream. He didn't do anything except keep dragging me farther away from home. I remember actually thinking, I'M GOING TO DIE. But then all of a sudden, the arm around my neck was gone and I was on the ground looking up at him, and the man was shaking his head, kind of like a dog that's just gone swimming, and then he ripped the mask off and started clawing at his eyes. Then all of a sudden, he just ran away. I only saw his face for a second, and from the side, but I noticed that he had short dark hair and a really pronounced chin. I got up and ran to the closest house. When I was banging on the door, I realized that the man had never once said a word, even after I'd sprayed him. I could hear him breathing and gasping for air, but that's it. He never made any intelligible sound. I mean, how is that even possible? I'm pretty sure that's all I remember right now.

3

When the news hit the following morning, it struck with the force of a tsunami.

Although a police spokesman was quick to caution that the attack on Annie Riggs had yet to be officially tied to the murders of the other three Edgewood girls, the public wasn't buying it at all. Annie Riggs was young, attractive, and wore her shiny brown hair long and wavy. That's all it took in most people's eyes.

By lunchtime, a police sketch of the assailant—along with a photograph of the mask he'd worn—had been broadcast across local networks, as well as CNN. Within hours, 911 and the tip-line were flooded. An elderly man recognized the person in the sketch—it was his son-in-law. A music teacher from the elementary school was certain it was her gynecologist. Another woman stated in no uncertain terms that it had to be her ex-husband. On and on it went.

The mask left behind was constructed of rough burlap. Ragged eye and mouth slits had been cut out with sharp scissors or some kind of razor, and short lengths of twine had been laced up the back to secure it in place. The Harford County Crime Lab was currently running a barrage of tests on it.

I couldn't be absolutely positive, but I felt there was at least a decent possibility it was what Jimmy Cavanaugh and I had seen floating toward us in the darkness that night outside of the Meyers House. Later that afternoon, at home in South Carolina, Jimmy got a good look at the mask on CNN and called to tell me he felt the same way.

Annie Riggs was interviewed for hours, as well as examined from head to toe—fingernails scraped; mouth swabbed; face and hair and clothing picked at, combed over, and vacuumed. For the first time, police had an eyewitness, and they were all over her. After reviewing her written statement, a team of detectives encouraged her to search her mind for anything she might have missed, emphasizing that no observation was too minor to bring to their attention. That's when she remembered her attacker's strange odor. She claimed it was unlike anything else she'd ever smelled before, but struggled to be more specific after that. "It didn't stink like B.O. or sweat," she explained. "It was something else, something . . . indescribable." When pressed further, Annie went on to say that it was an organic, almost earthy smell coming from the man himself; she didn't believe it came from his clothes or mask or gloves. And that was the best explanation she was able to muster.

In the meantime, every inch of the one-acre lot of overgrown brush and uncut weeds on Sequoia Drive was relentlessly searched, as were all the surrounding yards and roadways. At the rear of the lot, behind the remnants of the old garage, a narrow path created by parallel rows of head-high shrubbery led to Holly Avenue, where the police believed the man had most likely parked his vehicle. Willoughby Beach Road, a quick escape route, waited a mere two blocks away.

Detective Harper and a majority of the task force members felt re-energized and optimistic, thanks to Annie Riggs's brave actions. After months of coming up empty, they not only now had a witness, but finally a piece of concrete evidence. Other police officials, however, those whose job security was left up to the whims of the voters, were less enthusiastic. Thousands of dollars and hundreds of man-hours had been expended to catch this monster, and the closest they'd been able to come was thanks to a five-foot-six, one-hundred-and-ten-pound field hockey player who'd just had her braces removed four months earlier.

Speaking of Annie Riggs, she became a national celebrity overnight. The media hadn't yet decided whether to crown her as "The Girl Who Beat the Boogeyman" or "The Lone Survivor," so for now, they were calling her both. One out-of-state newspaper printed Annie's junior class yearbook photo next to a photograph of the mask beneath a 36-point headline that read: **BEAUTY AND THE BEAST.** Closer to home, many of Annie's friends and schoolmates had nicknamed her "Ripley" after Sigourney Weaver's badass character in the *Alien* films. Many of those same friends and schoolmates spent the afternoon and evening relating personal stories about Annie on live television. So far, Annie's parents had been flooded with requests from over one hundred media outlets, most notably CNN, the Associated Press, the *New York Times*, *Newsweek*, *People*, *Entertainment Tonight*, and the *Tonight Show*. They'd turned each and every one of them down, claiming their daughter needed to rest and recuperate from the ordeal.

As dusk approached, the already steady volume of 911 calls saw a marked increase. A man behaving suspiciously was reported on Bayberry

Drive. Several residents called in about a green pickup truck driving too slowly along Perry Avenue. Citizens spotted the masked man behind every tree and telephone pole, lurking in every dark corner of every back-yard. Gunshots echoed throughout the town as jittery homeowners fired at shadows. It was a miracle no one was killed.

I sat out on the front porch with my father for almost an hour and watched police cruisers speed up and down Hanson Road, many of them with their spotlights dancing across yards and behind parked cars. I stopped counting after thirty of them. That disconnected sensation of watching a movie rushed back at me, and I shared how I was feeling with my dad, explaining that I'd felt something similar on the night of my ride-along with Detective Harper. My father respectfully disagreed. He said it felt like we were actually *in* a movie. I had to admit he had a point.

Earlier at dinner, even my dear mother had jumped into the fray. She'd been adamant that the police sketch was the spitting image of the thirty-year-old son belonging to the woman who cut her hair. His name was Vince, and he'd been in trouble before with the law. For what, she didn't know, but she'd met him at the beauty salon on several occasions and was almost certain it was the same person. What she didn't remember, though, was that I too had once met Vince, and based on my recollection, the guy looked nothing like the man in the sketch. Fortunately, to my father's and my own great relief, we'd been able to talk her out of calling the tip-line and passing on her suspicions.

Shortly after dinner, the phone rang. At first I didn't think any-thing of it. There hadn't been any more prank calls since the night my parents had gone to visit Carlos and Prissy Vargas—the night the Boogeyman had finally spoken to me. But then I saw the look come over my mother's face after she lifted the receiver to her ear and said, "Hello," and I knew something was wrong. She immediately slammed the phone back onto its cradle. My father and I stood there, staring at her, neither of us saying a word. She looked at us with fury in her eyes.

"Your little prankster must be in a particularly good mood tonight," she said. "All he did was laugh and laugh. I wonder why." Before we could respond, she stomped upstairs, leaving us to do the dinner dishes.

4

The next day's lunchtime newscasts were filled with one jaw-dropping misadventure after the other—all from the night before. Evidently, Detective Harper's task force had had an interesting time of it.

In story number one, a longtime resident of Sunshine Avenue, down along the river, tossed a string of ladyfinger firecrackers into his backyard in an attempt to scare away a bunch of noisy geese. His neighbor, believing he'd just heard automatic gunfire, grabbed his .45 from an end-table drawer and ran outside to investigate. On his way, he tripped over a poolside lawn chair in the dark and accidentally shot himself in the leg. The neighbor with the pesky geese, hearing the gunshot and screams coming from next door, hopped the fence and used his shirt to tie a tourniquet around the man's leg before calling for an ambulance. Pretty damn heroic, if you ask me.

Story number two involved three local teenagers who'd gotten drunk off a stolen bottle of Jack Daniels and come up with the brilliant idea of fashioning their own versions of the killer's mask and spreading out among their neighborhood to peer into people's windows. Their little stunt resulted in a half-dozen phone calls to 911, including one from a frightened homeowner who feared he was having a heart attack, and a dangerous close call when another not-so-frightened homeowner, armed with a machete, charged into his backyard and nearly chopped one of the teenagers to pieces. The three boys—I found out later that the ringleader was none other than the younger brother of my not-so-dear old friend and volunteer fireman Kurt

Reynolds—spent a long night in separate holding cells before their parents showed up at the station to bail them out.

The third and most compelling story involved a state trooper on foot patrol not far from the Meyers House. Walking along Cherry Road, he'd quite literally stumbled upon a man wearing dark clothes emerging from a resident's backyard. "I tripped over an uneven section of sidewalk," he later told his supervisor, "and saw that my shoelace was loose. I bent down to retie it, and when I stood up again, there he was—a man coming out of the bushes no more than twenty feet in front of me. He saw me about the same time that I spotted him, and we both just stood there for a moment, staring at each other. I finally identified myself and ordered him to remain right where he was, but he took off down the street."

Radioing in for backup, the trooper engaged in a foot chase. The suspect cut through another backyard and the trooper followed. Over fences, around swimming pools, crashing through bushes and sprinting across empty streets. Twice, the trooper almost caught up with the mystery man, only to once again lose sight of him. Finally, in an unlit backyard, the trooper was forced to disengage after being unexpectedly attacked—not by the fleeing man, but by a chained-up German shepherd that almost made a meal out of both his legs. An exhausted-looking police spokeswoman seemed to go out of her way to point out that the suspect was most likely not the man they were searching for in connection with the attack on Annie Riggs. Little more than twenty-four hours had passed since the Riggs attack, and law enforcement was convinced that the would-be killer wouldn't be so brazen as to try again so soon.

"So then who the heck are *they* looking for?" my dad asked later that afternoon as we were putting away yard tools in the garage. "And in broad daylight?" I glanced across the street at the Hoffmans' house just in time to see a pair of uniformed officers climb over the split-rail fence and disappear into our neighbors' backyard.

5

My mother never learned how to drive. Growing up in a wealthy family in Quito, Ecuador—wealthy by local standards of the time, that is; quite a huge difference from our own country's standards—she was escorted to school and wherever else she needed to go by the family's driver. Later, in her twenties, after she met and married my father, in her words, she "just never got around to taking the test and getting a driver's license." Her inability to legally drive was something my siblings and I had a great deal of fun with in younger days, but she never seemed to mind. She took our frequent teasing in stride and got back at us by refusing to ride with anyone other than my father—except when faced with desperate circumstances, which was why she allowed me the honor of driving her to Santoni's later that Sunday afternoon. My father was busy helping a neighbor, she needed additional ingredients for tonight's dinner, and she clearly didn't trust me to pick them up by myself.

We walked side by side, up and down the grocery store aisles, filling the small basket I carried with whatever she pointed at on the shelves. In between stops, we said hello to what felt like the entire town of Edgewood. Between church, neighborhood activities, and monthly bingo nights at the community center, my mom was friendly with just about everyone. By the time we left the store thirty-five minutes later, we knew who in town was sick, who was pregnant, who was headed to what college in the fall, who'd just gotten a promotion at work, and who'd just gotten fired for the second time in as many months. I was exhausted.

As we were walking across the parking lot, I noticed someone standing on the sidewalk in front of the bank, peering at us from behind a light pole. A tall man, he was wearing a baseball cap and sunglasses. When the man realized I was staring at him, he quickly turned away and disappeared around the corner. I wasn't 100 percent certain, but pretty damn close: the man spying on us was Detective Harper.

On our way out of the parking lot, I drove past the bank and took a closer look. The detective—if it had indeed been him—was nowhere in sight. *Why in the hell would he have been watching me? Or had he been staking out the shopping center and it was just a coincidence that I came along?*

That night, while lying in bed, I watched as the eleven o'clock news came on television. The news anchor introduced her opening story, and of course, it was related to local hero Annie Riggs and the ongoing hunt for the Boogeyman. As Detective Harper's forlorn face flashed onscreen and his deep baritone voice filled my bedroom, I picked up the remote control, turned off the TV, and went to sleep.

6

By the time September rolled around, I had fallen into a new routine. After a goodnight phone call with Kara, I'd work on the magazine—mostly reading the slush pile, proofreading, and laying out ads—until I could no longer keep my eyes open. It was usually after midnight when I turned off my desk lamp and crawled into bed. Most mornings, I awoke around eight thirty. Some days, depending on the weather and my mood, I'd go for a run or shoot some hoops, and then come home and shower and get to writing. Other days, I'd start off slow and easy, reading a couple chapters in bed before heading downstairs, still dressed in my pajamas, for a bowl of cereal and the morning paper.

On Wednesday, September 14, my mother knocked on my bedroom door at 7:25 a.m., waking me from a deep slumber. Even if I hadn't glanced at the alarm clock and seen how early it was, I would've known by the expression on her face that it was important.

"Carly's on the phone," she said, reaching out with the cordless. "She asked me to wake you. She sounds upset."

I took the phone. "Hello?"

"You need to come here right now," Carly said, voice shaking.

"Where's here?" I asked, yawning.

"My house. Please hurry."

And then she hung up.

7

Carly lived with her parents on the other side of Edgewood Meadows, about halfway between the library and the high school. It took me less than ten minutes to get dressed, find my car keys, and speed to her house.

When I pulled up, she was sitting on the front porch, chin resting on her folded hands. Her eyes were puffy and red.

"What's wrong?" I asked as soon as I got out of the car.

She struggled to her feet, looking so exhausted and childlike I suddenly wanted to hug her. "Last night, right after I turned off the lights to go to sleep, I heard something at my window again." She looked around like maybe her neighbors were standing outside on their lawns eavesdropping. Seemingly content that no one was listening, she went on. "I was too scared to even get up and check it out this time. The room was dark, the window was dark, and for a second I was sure someone was hiding under my bed and they were going to reach up and grab me." She started coughing, covering her mouth with a hand that was shaking.

"Take your time," I said.

"A couple minutes later, I heard the same noise—a scraping sound, like someone was trying to pry off the screen—and I knew I wasn't imagining it. I pulled the blanket up to my eyes and just laid there. I couldn't move; couldn't open my mouth to call out to my parents; couldn't do anything. I was completely frozen. After a while the scraping noise went away . . . but it was at least three or four hours before I finally closed my eyes and fell asleep."

I glanced at the side of the house. "Why don't you wait here and I'll go check out your window?"

Shaking her head, she said, "I already did that. I didn't find anything."

"Okay, then how about we go grab something to eat, and afterwards I'll drop you off back here and you can try to catch up on some sleep?"

"Listen to me . . . I didn't find anything on the window, but a little later, when I came outside to go to work, *this* was waiting for me."

She stepped aside then, giving me a clear look behind her. In the center of the front porch, inches away from the Albrights' MARYLAND IS FOR CRABS doormat, someone had drawn a sad face in blue chalk. Right underneath it were three numbers: 666.

"What are we going to do?" she said, starting to cry.

Never taking my eyes off the chalk drawing: "I think it's time we called Detective Harper."

8

As expected, he wasn't pleased.

First, Harper read us the riot act for sticking our noses where they didn't belong and potentially mucking up an active investigation. Next, he explained in meticulous detail why the hopscotch grid, pet poster, and pennies were critical pieces of evidence that the public could not, under any circumstances, be made aware of. Finally, he made us promise that we wouldn't breathe a word of it to anyone, going on and on in that scary cop voice of his about how we were jeopardizing all the hard work his troopers had done.

"And to think I trusted you," he said, glaring in my direction. "I won't make that mistake again." Standing there on the front lawn, I wished I could disappear.

And that, as it turned out, was the easy part.

The hard part came when it was time for Carly to call her father at work—before one of the neighbors beat her to the punch—and explain why there was a Crime Lab van parked in their driveway and a team of detectives swarming all over their front porch and side yard. Her dad, surprisingly calm considering the news, immediately phoned her mom, and they were both parked at the curb within thirty minutes. Mrs. Albright wasn't nearly as chill. If looks could kill, I'd be a dead man. After giving Carly a hug and making sure she was okay, she went inside with her daughter to talk to Detective Harper. Before the door closed, I overheard Mr. Albright telling the detective that it had been dark when they'd left for work that morning, and neither of them had noticed the chalk drawing on the porch.

It got even more difficult later that morning when it was my turn to pick up the phone and tell my parents what had happened. Suffice to say, there were unpleasant words exchanged (many of them muttered in unintelligible Spanish) and more than a few frightened tears.

To make matters worse—if that were possible—Carly's mom emerged from the house a short time later and made it painfully clear that she wasn't happy with me, either. As far as she was concerned, my selfish curiosity had contributed to making her daughter the target of a sadistic serial killer who'd already tortured and murdered three young girls. And now he knew where the Albrights lived.

For the second time that morning, I was dragged behind the woodshed by my ears and given a verbal lashing. "I had a feeling you'd be trouble," Mrs. Albright snapped, waggling a finger in my face. "Carly's working hard to build a respectable career and she doesn't need some horror junkie dragging her into this mess. And you have a fiancée . . . you shouldn't even be hanging around with my daughter."

Despite her shaky condition earlier that morning, Carly stepped up to the plate and took one for the team. Big-time. I was so damn proud of her. First, she went after Detective Harper: "I was the one who worked my inside sources for information about the investigation. Richard had nothing to do with that." When Detective Harper pressed Carly to reveal those anonymous sources, she refused, citing standards of confidentiality. She also held firm and claimed we were well within our rights to pursue our own journalistic investigation as long as it didn't interfere with any of the work the police were doing. Then it was her mom's turn: "And how dare you speak to my friend like that. I'm a grown woman perfectly capable of deciding whom I work and spend time with. As for his fiancée, her name is Kara, and I adore her. Not once has Richard acted like anything less than a gentleman."

Did I mention how proud I was of her?

Once the dust had settled, surprising news awaited us. Although Carly hadn't found anything of interest in the side yard earlier that morning, the detectives sure as hell did. A narrow flowerbed bordered by small round stones ran along the entire length of the left side of the Albrights' rancher. The ground there had been mulched, but summer storms had washed much of it away. In a bare patch of topsoil, directly beneath Carly's bedroom window, detectives discovered a near perfect boot imprint. A lab technician immediately set to work, taking photographs of the imprint from every available angle. After confirming with Carly and her parents that no one in the family owned a pair of boots with that particular tread pattern, a second technician—using a small bucket of water, a bag of powdery dental stone, and some type of spray fixative—made a casting impression of the boot imprint. I'd witnessed the procedure a number of times before on television—usually performed by professional Bigfoot hunters in the wilds of the Pacific Northwest—but I'd never observed it in person. The whole process was fascinating, and despite the gloomy mood of the day, I found myself wishing that my father had been there with me.

Driving home later that afternoon, I found myself circling the block, stalling. I knew I was too old to be sent to my room or grounded—for chrissakes, I was getting married in a few months—but I have to admit the idea did occur to me. I was also afraid my mom might cut me off from her cooking the rest of my time at home, but that didn't happen either. Even down the road, when things went from bad to worse to downright horrible, she kept right on feeding me.

As for Carly, her life changed in rather dramatic fashion. Detective Harper assigned a rotating shift of troopers to watch over the Albrights' house for a period of three weeks, as well as around-the-clock surveillance on Carly herself. While my name—and any mention of the front porch chalk drawing—had been kept out of all media reports, Carly, of course, wasn't quite so lucky. She was front and center for all of it, the latest star in the Boogeyman's Grand Guignol production, and the press hungered for a piece of her. "It felt gross," she told me later, "to be on the other end of all those microphones and flashing cameras. I hated that they were waiting for me like vultures outside my house and the office." It didn't take long before she stopped talking to the media altogether.

If there was a single bright spot to come out of all this mess, it was that soon after, Carly Albright was given a promotion at the newspaper. The *Aegis*, in all of their opportunistic wisdom and greed, realized that they had a staff writer under contract who was now intimately tied to the paper's number one story: the Boogeyman. Goodbye community events and obituaries; hello front-page features and pay raise.

In the days that followed, I was often tempted to ask Detective Harper if he'd been watching me that evening at the shopping center, or if any of his men drove a silver sedan with dark windows—but I never summoned the courage. It was embarrassing enough that he'd started referring to Carly and me as Nancy Drew and Joe Hardy (from the Hardy Boys mysteries I'd loved so much as a child). I did, however, finally break down and tell him about the prank calls we'd been receiving. He asked if the person had threatened me, or any member of my family, and when I told him no, not really, he appeared to move on without giving the matter a second thought.

9

Kara wasn't nearly as dismissive about the phone calls, especially in light of what had just gone down at Carly's house. It was dusk, and we were sitting in the still warm grass beneath the weeping willow tree, watching fireflies dance across the side yard, when she brought it up again.

"I don't understand why they don't just tap your phone," she complained. "It's been going on ever since you came home. That's not a coincidence. The guy even said your name, for goodness' sake."

"But that's all he did. He didn't threaten me. Didn't threaten my mom or dad."

"You don't think him taunting you is the same thing as a threat?"

I offered a half-hearted shrug. I was tired and had a headache and was anxious to change the subject.

"How about the message he left on Carly's doorstep? You think that's a threat?"

"I get what you're saying. I do. I'm just not sure what you want me to do about it."

"For starters, you can tell Detective Harper to get off his ass and do his job."

"I tried that." I glanced at her in the darkness. "You really think it's the Boogeyman calling the house and not just someone messing around?"

"I do," she said with no hesitation. "I think he's playing games with you."

"Why would he do that? And why me of all people?"

She crossed her legs and turned to me, taking my hand in hers. "*Why?* Because he's a sicko who gets off on scaring and hurting people. *Why you?* I don't know . . . maybe because he knows you're a horror writer. Or maybe he knows you personally."

"Don't even say that."

"He picked you for a reason, Rich," she said, giving my hand a squeeze. "And now Carly. I'm starting to get really freaked out."

"Don't be," I said. "Everything will be okay."

I didn't entirely believe it, but I didn't know what else to say.

10

A few days later, I answered the door and found a smiling Carly Albright standing on my porch. Actually, standing wasn't quite accurate—she was dancing in place, feet shuffling back and forth, like a little girl on the verge of peeing her pants.

"It wasn't him!" she said.

"Who wasn't him?"

"The man at my house . . . the man who drew on my porch . . . it wasn't the Boogeyman!"

I stepped outside. "What are you talking about?"

"Detective Harper just left my house. He said one of the neighbors behind us had security footage of a man cutting through their yard the night it happened. The homeowner recognized the man's face; he was part of a landscaping crew she'd recently hired.

"The detectives went over and talked to the guy, and he admitted it right away. Detective Harper said he almost seemed relieved to have been caught."

"So how do they know he wasn't involved with the murders?"

"Rock-solid alibis for two of the three nights. Plus, he looks nothing like the police sketch. He's really short and scrawny and his ears are pierced. He said the whole thing was just a stupid joke. The guy's a hard-core metalhead, into satanic rock: Ozzy, Danzig, Black Sabbath, Darkthrone, the whole thing. He got all pissed off when the *Aegis* ran that article about satanic cults—he thought we were making fun of them. When he found out that someone in the neighborhood worked for the paper, he thought it'd be funny to get stoned and sneak over and draw a six-six-six on my porch. He was planning to draw a pentagram on the driveway, too, but chickened out. He told the police he just wanted to scare me."

"Jesus," I said. "So the blue chalk and the numbers . . . that was all just a freaking coincidence?"

"Yes!"

"That's pretty hard to believe."

"I know, but apparently it's true. How crazy is that? The guy said he wanted to use spray paint, but couldn't find any, so he borrowed the chalk from one of his roommates. He even took the detectives into the roommate's bedroom and showed them the box of blue chalk that was in a desk drawer."

"They check out his roommate?"

"Yeah, he was clean, too."

"This is insane," I said. "So no more cop parked out in front of your house? No more hunky bodyguards?"

Her smiled faded. "Well, that's where it gets kinda interesting."

"How so?"

"Satan's little helper has a size twelve-and-a-half foot."

I looked at her. "What the hell does that mean?"

She sighed like I was an idiot. "The guy they just talked to wears a size twelve and a half. The boot print under my window was a ten."

"Ohhh," I said, understanding now. "So, it was two different people that night."

"They think so," she said. "The metalhead swears he didn't go any-where near my window, and the detectives didn't find any boots in his closet that matched the tread pattern . . . so they're gonna keep watching the house—and me—for another week or so. Just in case."

"Meaning they're not entirely convinced that it *wasn't* the killer sneaking around outside your window."

"Maybe . . . but probably not. What are the chances two weirdos were creeping around my house on the exact same night?"

"What are the chances some random dude decides to play a prank involving blue chalk and the number six?"

"Touché," she said, tilting her head to the side, thinking.

"And if it wasn't the Boogeyman at your window, then who was it?"

"Kids fooling around. The Phantom Fondler. Hell, maybe I'm just sleep-deprived. Imagined the whole thing."

"You didn't imagine the boot print, Carly."

She nodded. "It was probably just kids messing around."

"I hope you're right."

"Yeah," she said, her eyes focusing on something in the distance. "Me too."

11

The rest of September passed quietly.

ABOVE: Edgewood High School
(Photo courtesy of the author)

ABOVE: Annie Riggs
*(Photo courtesy of Molly
Riggs)*

RIGHT: The abandoned lot
where Annie Riggs
was attacked
*(Photo courtesy
of Carly Albright)*

LEFT: The killer's
mask found on
Sequoia Drive
*(Photo courtesy of
Logan Reynolds)*

ABOVE: Task force members revealing the killer's mask to media members
(Photo courtesy of The Baltimore Sun*)*

LEFT: Police sketch of the killer
(Photo courtesy of Alex McVey)

RIGHT: The mysterious chalk drawing on the Albrights' front porch
(Photo courtesy of Logan Reynolds)

nine

October Country

"... an act of madness."

1

*F*irst of all, *it was October, a rare month for boys ..."*
   Of all the breathtaking passages of lyrical wonder that Ray Bradbury has gifted readers with during his lifetime, those eleven words from the opening of his seminal novel, *Something Wicked This Way Comes*, may very well be my favorite.

   Bradbury goes on to describe a mythical landscape, an October Country, where Autumn is King and Mischief is Queen and anything is possible. The good, bad, miraculous, and unimaginable—it's all right there, waiting for you in the month of October, hovering just beyond the reach of your fingertips.

   Ever since I was a child, it was my favorite time of year—a season of absolute magic. The air smelled of ripe apples and dying leaves and wood smoke. The wind made you ache in some place deeper than your bones. The sky overhead was layered with rich shades of orange and yellow and purple and red and a host of swirling colors too beautiful to be named. The harvest moon—swollen and magnificent, and so close on the horizon you could almost reach out and touch it—paid its annual visit and left you yearning for more. Clouds drifted by, peeking over their shoulders, reluctant to make way for winter's footfalls. Naked tree branches reached out as you walked past, skeletal fingers hungering for your touch, and packs of fallen leaves crunched beneath your wandering feet, their boundless brethren skittering past you in the chill autumn breeze like miniature ghosts haunting the landscape. Dusks and twilights lingered. Midnights stayed forever. Fat jack-o'-lanterns flashed jagged grins from porch railings and windows, flickering orange eyes tracking your every move.

And then it happened.

The most magical day of all arrived.

Not only for the young, but also the young of heart.

Night crept over the town like a silent thief, and it was finally here.

Halloween.

2

In the town of Edgewood, Monday, October 31, dawned clear and cold with a sense of hopeful optimism blanketing the streets.

It had been nearly two months since Annie Riggs's narrow escape on Sequoia Drive, and in that time, there had been no further attacks. The local media, eager to keep the story (and newsstand sales) alive, made scant mention of this fact, focusing instead on the latest possible sightings and the occasional interview with a low-ranking member of the task force—any excuse to keep those magic words "The Boogeyman" in their headlines. The fake-tan and chiseled faces of the national press, meanwhile, slowly abandoned ship, hotel room and expense account costs ballooning too high to stick around town without additional violence and bloodshed to cover. The police went about their business, mostly quietly. Every week or so, a spokesperson surfaced to make a brief official statement—all of them sounding pretty much the same at this point; the task force was working around the clock and citizens were to maintain vigilance. It'd been nearly a month since Detective Harper last held a press conference. On that occasion, he'd spoken for only a handful of minutes before revealing an updated police sketch of Annie Riggs's assailant. Other than thickening the man's eyebrows and thinning his upper lip, it looked pretty much exactly the same as the original.

As for the townspeople of Edgewood, most believed (or at least told themselves so) that the killer had finally moved on. It'd been fifty-two days since anything bad had happened. After losing his anonymity the night of the Annie Riggs attack, and nearly being captured some time later during a neighborhood foot chase with police, the Boogeyman would have to be a careless fool to stick around and try anything else. And he'd already shown he wasn't that at all.

Regardless of the surge of optimism felt by many residents, the curfew remained in place—albeit, as of three weeks earlier, a slightly relaxed one of 11:00 p.m.—and a handful of special ordinances had been established for Halloween night. The board of directors for the Edgewood Shopping Plaza announced a trick-or-treating alternative for younger children. From 5:00–7:00 p.m., each of the stores would hand out treats, and participating families were encouraged to give out candy of their own in the parking lot. In addition, children under the age of twelve were not permitted on neighborhood streets without adult supervision, and all trick-or-treaters, regardless of age, had to be off the streets by 9:00 p.m. For the second week in a row, *Halloween 4: The Return of Michael Myers* was the main attraction at the Edgewood Movie Theater, but all late showings had been canceled. If you wanted to celebrate Halloween night with a tub of buttered popcorn and Michael Myers's latest slow-walk murder spree, you had to get in line for either the 5:00 or 7:15 p.m. screenings, or you were shit out of luck.

Fortunately, the month of October had been a quiet one for Carly Albright as well. Just what the doctor ordered. The press finally gave up on getting her to talk, and despite the occasional nightmare, there appeared to be no more Boogeyman-related excitement or intrigue at the Albrights' house. No more chalk drawings. No more creepers outside her window. No more police cars parked in front of the house. The concluding theory was that the boot print the police had found in the flower garden outside her bedroom most likely belonged to a random neighborhood kid. Thinking back on my toad-hunting days, when my friends and I'd hit pretty much every single window-well in Edgewood Meadows, I figured there was a decent enough chance they were right. Although she'd yet to be nominated for a Pulitzer—which, even though she denied it, was her secret life ambition—Carly was enjoying covering real news, for a change, and seeing her byline in the weekly *Aegis*. Her editor had even assigned her an electronic pager so she could be on call 24/7, which sounded like a horrible fate to me, but Carly sure didn't think so. She was happier about that damn beeper than she was for her pay raise.

October had been kind to me, too. Feeling especially inspired as of late, I'd been fortunate enough to place three more short stories, a new personal best for a single month. None of those tales were about to be nominated for a Pulitzer, either—or any other award, for that matter—but they'd sold to decent enough markets I could be proud of. I was gaining confidence as a writer, and without the constant distraction of chasing the Boogeyman's shadow, I was able to spend longer and more productive stints in front of the keyboard. I'd even stopped listening to the police scanner most nights.

From time to time though, I still felt as if I were being watched when I was out in public, and I could've sworn I'd spotted that same silver sedan behind me one evening on Route 40, but thus far there'd been no repeat of that awful night when I'd taken out the trash and somehow *known* that the Boogeyman was lurking nearby. The prank phone calls that had plagued the Chizmar household had slowed dramatically over the past couple of months, all of them silent hang-ups. I was starting to believe once again that it was just a random caller, a bored teenager getting his rocks off by trying to scare me. He'd probably seen the article in the *Aegis* and figured me to be an easy target.

Even my mother was in much better spirits, practically back to her old and relaxed sweet self. As was tradition, she'd spent most of the afternoon in the kitchen, baking fresh bread and making meatballs alongside her secret-recipe tomato sauce. For as long as I could remember, we'd always invited friends and neighbors over on Halloween night. Everyone feasted on heaping plates of spaghetti and meatballs and salad, and once the kids headed out trick-or-treating, the grownups piled into the living room and basement to sit around and talk or watch college football on TV. Whoever happened to be sitting closest to the front door, usually one of my parents or my crazy uncle Ted, was responsible for handing out candy each time the doorbell rang. I remember always being amazed upon my return to the house several hours later—my pillowcase stuffed with treats almost too heavy to carry—only to see that most of the grown-ups were still sitting around and talking. Whatever could they possibly have to jaw about for so long?

3

By five thirty that particular Halloween evening, our house was packed. The living room and basement were standing room only, and the kitchen wasn't much better. Norma and Bernie Gentile sat at the dining room table, along with my sister Mary, her husband, Glenn, and my uncle Ted and aunt Pat. All of them stuffing their faces and trying not to talk with their mouths full.

Kara and I sat on folding chairs in the foyer, a big bowl of candy balanced on a TV table between us. It was almost full dark outside, and scores of trick-or-treaters were already on the prowl. We'd been busy for at least the past twenty minutes—football players and fairies, astronauts and aliens, princesses and Smurfs—but had barely made a dent in the mound of candy.

I hadn't dressed up for the occasion (unless you counted gray sweatpants and a sweatshirt as a costume), but as usual Kara had pulled out all the stops. That was just one of the many things I loved about her. She embraced and celebrated life to the fullest extent. Whether it was dressing up as the cutest court jester you've ever seen (as she'd done this year) or taking weeks to find someone the perfect Christmas gift or pulling her car over to the side of the road to watch a winter sunset, Kara was able to find beauty and grace and meaning in so many everyday moments. If I was shadows and moonbeams and tales of death and horror, she was sunshine and laughter and the yellow brick road from *The Wizard of Oz*. We balanced each other.

Shortly after seven, Kara announced she was braving a return trip to the kitchen to grab refills on our drinks, and left me alone at the door. Within minutes, led by Darth Vader and Elvis Presley, the largest pack of the night streamed up the driveway, giggling, skipping, burping, and squeezed onto the porch. Elvis rang the doorbell. Taking the bowl with me, I stepped outside and began tossing handfuls of candy into pillowcases, grocery bags, and plastic pumpkins. As the horde of trick-or-treaters moved on amid a chorus of shouted thank-yous, I happened to glance across the street. A lone dark figure stood scarecrow-still on the sidewalk in front of the Hoffmans' house. Too tall to be a child and making no attempt to conceal his presence, the man appeared to be watching me. *Probably a bored dad waiting for his kid*, I thought. *Maybe even an undercover cop; they're out in full force tonight. Or better yet, Detective Harper spying on me again.*

I was about to turn away when a pickup truck swung around the corner of Tupelo, the beams of its headlights washing over the Hoffmans' front yard. I saw him clearly then. It wasn't Detective Harper.

The man was dressed in dark clothing, and he was wearing a mask—one that very much resembled the crudely made mask I'd recently seen on television and in the newspaper. My mouth went instantly dry, and I felt cold sweat break out along the back of my neck.

The stranger just stood there, motionless, arms at his side, staring.

A camera suddenly flashed at the bottom of the driveway, stealing away my attention. "Just one more," a frazzled mother begged. The Incredible Hulk and Superman stuck out their tongues and struck a pose—and the camera flashed again. When I returned my gaze across the street, the masked man was gone.

"Everything okay?" Kara asked, arriving at the door with our drinks.

"All good," I said, stepping inside. I took a long swig of lemonade and didn't say a word about what I'd just seen. *Probably just a prank*, I told myself. *Like the scene in* Halloween II *when one of the guys dresses up like Michael Myers.*

As the night wore on, Kara and I assumed the role of gatekeepers at 920 Hanson Road, greeting late arrivals at the door and hugging departing guests goodbye. The Gentiles were the first to leave, hurrying next door to hand out full-size Baby Ruth candy bars, something they'd done ever since I was a little kid. Before they walked away, Mr. Bernie pulled a shiny silver dollar from his coat pocket and flipped it to me without a word. My uncle Ted—my father's younger brother and still the biggest kid I've ever known—tried to give me a wedgie on his way out the door, but settled for a noogie, instead. Aunt Pat scolded him all the way back to their car. Shortly after seven thirty, Carly Albright, Mickey Mouse ears perched jauntily atop her head, stopped by and helped us hand out candy to the never-ending parade of trick-or-treaters. Listening to her and Kara catch up, a plate of spaghetti balanced in Carly's lap, was my favorite part of the evening. It was easy to see why the two of them had once been so close.

Later, in bed, I realized that the Boogeyman hadn't come up in conversation a single time that evening. I couldn't remember the last time that'd happened with more than a few people gathered in the same room. Despite the unnerving incident that'd occurred earlier in the night—by then I'd mostly convinced myself it was just another stupid prank—this realization made me smile, and soon after, as I drifted off to sleep, those familiar haunting words—*A storm is coming*—resurfaced in my head . . . only this time, I found myself wondering if perhaps the storm hadn't finally passed us by.

4

The next morning, I woke up feeling refreshed and energetic, ready to knock out a long session at the keyboard. I was working on a new story about a father and son. For a change, it wasn't scary and wasn't supposed to be. More than anything, it was a slice-of-life tale, capturing a moment in time that really meant something to me. I suspected that the story was about my own father, but it wasn't exactly clear yet. I was anxious to find out.

I headed downstairs to grab a bowl of Wheaties to take back up to my desk, and knew that something horrible had happened the moment I saw my mother's face.

"What's wrong?" I asked.

She looked away from me, staring out the kitchen window into the backyard. "A girl never made it home last night."

5

Sixteen-year-old Cassidy Burch lived with her mother and younger sister in an end-of-row town house in the Courts of Harford Square. Her father, a truck driver, had been killed three years earlier in an accident on I-95. While diminutive in stature—five four and one-hundred-and-ten pounds—Cassidy had a bright smile and outgoing personality that filled up any room she chose to enter. A sophomore at Edgewood High School, Cassidy played junior varsity field hockey and was treasurer of the Latin Club. She worked hard in the classroom for her B average and held down a part-time job at Burger King on Route 40. Cassidy Burch had sparkling blue eyes and beautiful, long blond hair.

At around 5:30 p.m. on Halloween night, while her mother remained at home to hand out candy, Cassidy took her eleven-year-old sister, Maggie, trick-or-treating. Maggie was dressed as Buttercup from her favorite movie, *The Princess Bride*, which she'd seen three times last year at the theater. She looked every bit of a lovely princess, with her long, blond, braided hair and flowing homemade gown, and received many compliments. The sisters roamed the neighborhood for almost ninety minutes, filling two plastic pumpkins with treats before finally returning home.

While Buttercup began sorting her mountain of candy on the dining room table, Cassidy went upstairs to change clothes.

At 7:20 p.m., a car horn sounded in front of the Burches' town house. Cassidy bounded down the stairs, her red velvet hooded cloak fanning out behind her like Wonder Woman's cape. A mid-length gray skirt, white leggings, and black saddle shoes completing the picture, Little Red Riding Hood hugged her mother and sister goodbye and headed off to a party with her best friend, seventeen-year-old Cindy Gibbons.

It wasn't really a party. Jessica Lepp had convinced her parents to allow her to have a small group of friends over—eight, maybe ten kids—with two conditions: no sleepovers because it was a school night, and everyone had to be out of the house by 10:45. Jessica's mother insisted that she would not be to blame for any of the girls missing curfew. The Lepps lived on Larch Drive, a five-minute car ride from the Courts of Harford Square. Steep and winding, Larch Drive—at its highest point—bisected Hanson Road, a mere fifty yards up the street from my parents' house.

Most of the girls wore costumes that night—a sexy vampire, a nerd with taped eyeglasses, Catwoman, and a pair of cheerleaders. They gathered in the Lepps' basement and danced to '70s disco and snacked on bags of pretzels and chips. After a while, Jessica put *A Nightmare on Elm Street* on the VCR, and they all crammed themselves onto the sofa and love seat, many of the girls—including Cassidy—covering their eyes during the scary parts. It was good old-fashioned, innocent fun. No boys, no drinking or smoking, no mean-spirited gossiping. Just a lot of giggling and the occasional belch from too much soda.

At 10:45, as promised, the girls began to leave. Cassidy and Cindy stayed after for a short time, helping their friend clean up pizza boxes, paper plates, and empty soda cans from the basement. Mrs. Lepp made a point of thanking them both and shooed them out the door at 10:55. From the front porch, she watched them get into Cindy's car and drive away.

At that exact same moment, Cassidy's mother was sitting up in bed, a historical romance novel resting in her lap, staring at the alarm clock. As she watched the minutes tick by, Mrs. Burch listened for the sound of a car pulling up in front of the town house. She'd performed this same routine on many other nights, and it was never easy on her nerves. *One day that girl will understand what it feels like to be a mom*, she often thought, as she lay there worrying herself sick.

Watching the clock click over to 11:00, and still no Cassidy, she started chewing on her fingernails, a horrible habit she was determined to quit. Starting tomorrow.

At 11:02, Mrs. Burch heard a car door open, a few seconds of muffled rock music, and then the door slam closed. She exhaled a deep sigh of relief and returned her attention to the book she was reading. The heroine in the story was about to confront a gang of armed hooligans who were planning to ransack her family's cabin, and Mrs. Burch was anxious to learn how it turned out.

She read to the bottom of the next page before realizing she hadn't heard the sound of Cassidy's key sliding into the lock, or the sound of the front door opening and closing, or the sound of the dead bolt being engaged.

Hopping out of bed like her feet were on fire, she hurried downstairs, calling out her daughter's name. The foyer was empty, the interior light still on, and the front door was locked up tight. She swung it open and stepped out onto the porch, calling out Cassidy's name again. No answer. She studied the length of well-lit parking lot on her right and scanned the dark expanse of empty field on her left. The night was silent. Nothing moved.

Hurrying back inside, Mrs. Burch found the cordless phone on the sofa where she'd left it earlier and called the Lepps. Jessica's mother answered on the first ring and assured Mrs. Burch that she'd watched from her front porch no more than ten minutes ago as Cassidy and Cindy drove away. *Maybe they stopped at the Stop and Shop for gas or something*, she offered. Mrs. Burch thanked her and hung up.

Frantic now, she called the Gibbonses next. Cindy picked up right away, sounding out of breath. She told Mrs. Burch that she'd just gotten home after dropping off Cassidy and had hurried inside to answer the phone before it woke up her parents.

"You dropped her right in front of the house?" Mrs. Burch asked.

"What do you mean?" Cindy replied, confused. "I always do."

"I know that, but . . . five minutes ago . . . that was you and Cassidy out front?"

"I mean, it might've been a little longer than five minutes, but yeah, I dropped her off and came straight home."

"Did you see Cassidy after she got out of the car? Did you see anything at all?"

Cindy hesitated before answering. "I usually wait until she gets inside . . . but I think I just drove away this time. I didn't want to be late 'cause of curfew."

"And you didn't see—"

"Wait a minute," Cindy said, her voice rising. "Are you saying Cassidy didn't get in the house? She's not there with you?"

"That's exactly what I'm saying."

"Oh my God!" Sounding upset now. "Oh my God. I think I better wake up my parents."

"You do that, honey. I'm going to call the police."

6

All this happened just down the road from where I was sleeping.

7

After a brief search, police discovered the body of Cassidy Burch at 2:27 a.m. at the Edgewood Memorial Gardens cemetery on Trimble Road. The rookie state trooper who found her not far from the main entrance initially believed he'd stumbled upon the scene of a Halloween prank, as the body was laid out in front of a headstone and surrounded by a number of still-lit jack-o'-lanterns. Partially dressed in her Little Red Riding Hood costume, Cassidy Burch had been beaten, sexually assaulted, and strangled. Her left ear had been severed and was missing from the scene. Nearly a dozen bite marks covered her body, as if the killer had attacked in a frenzied bloodlust. One veteran trooper described it as "an act of madness."

ABOVE: Cassidy Burch *(Photo courtesy of Candice Burch)*

ABOVE: Cassidy Burch *(Photo courtesy of Candice Burch)*

ABOVE: Edgewood Memorial Gardens *(Photo courtesy of the author)*

ABOVE: Police and detectives searching for evidence near the Burches' Courts of Harford Square town house *(Photo courtesy of Logan Reynolds)*

ten

Aftermath

*"He likes how it feels to kill,
and he'll do it again if we don't stop him."*

1

The town of Edgewood woke up the Tuesday morning after Halloween to a nightmare.

Breaking news broadcasts interrupted early morning talk shows on all four local television networks, and the grisly details of Cassidy Burch's murder dominated drive-time airwaves on every local radio station. Anxious to share the news, neighbors rushed to pick up their telephones and gathered in small groups on porches and driveways. Many residents got in their cars and drove out to the cemetery but were turned away by police barricades blocking the lone entrance road. By midmorning, most everyone in town had heard: the Boogeyman was back.

After consoling my mother in the kitchen, I rushed upstairs and phoned Carly Albright. She was away from her desk, so I left a voice message, and she called right back. She was as stunned as I was with the news. I told her about the man in the mask I'd seen across the street from my house the night before, and she scolded me for not telling her earlier. Fortunately, she was in a hurry or I really would have gotten an earful. Speaking fast, she said she was about to head over to the high school to interview the principal and several faculty members. Classes for the day had been canceled for students, but teachers were still required to come in. We made plans to talk later that evening, and off she went.

The local noon news broadcast led with live footage of Detective Harper giving a brief statement just outside the cemetery's front gate: "At this time, I can confirm that the body of sixteen-year-old Cassidy Burch was discovered earlier this morning on the grounds of the Edgewood Memorial Gardens."

As the detective continued talking, the camera zoomed over his shoulder, focusing on a small group of officers walking among the headstones at the opposite end of the cemetery. Each of them carried a small bundle of red flags affixed to fifteen-inch wire stakes. Before the camera panned away, it captured one of the officers kneeling down and examining something on the ground at his feet, and then sticking a flag in the grass to mark the spot before moving on.

"We'd like to request that you extend to the Burch family sufficient time and privacy to grieve this tragic loss," Detective Harper continued. "Task force members are currently pursuing a number of vital leads. We'll have more information available later this evening. Thank you."

I felt lost and restless the remainder of the afternoon. I couldn't stop thinking about the man in the mask. It'd been around 7:00 p.m. when I first noticed him watching me from across the street. The police believed that Cassidy Burch was killed shortly after she was dropped off at around 11:00 p.m. Four hours. *Had the Boogeyman paid me a visit last night, and then simply moved on down the road to stalk and kill his latest victim?* The thought was almost too much to bear.

Unable to sit still for longer than a few minutes at a time, I knew trying to write was a lost cause and I didn't trust myself enough to properly edit the handful of articles I had on hand for the magazine. After a while, I simply left and went for a drive. Avoiding the cemetery and Courts of Harford Square, I aimlessly circled the other half of Edgewood, cruising past the shopping center, 7-Eleven, and high school, where I spotted Carly's car parked right out front in the visitors' lot. After sitting in my car and staring into space for a half hour or so at the water's edge by Flying Point Park, I topped off my gas tank at the Texaco station and did one final loop before heading back. Without even realizing I was doing it, I drove past the houses of the first three murder victims on my way home.

The evening news—which I watched in the basement with my parents—offered few additional details about Cassidy Burch's murder. Police were busy with their investigation and reluctant to speak on camera, especially since they had nothing new to add. Video footage showing nearly a dozen uniformed officers searching the grassy field next to the Burches' town house soon gave way to a montage of Cassidy's tearful friends and neighbors sharing personal anecdotes about the slain teenager. A dark-haired girl named Mallory held up a watercolor painting of a sunset, explaining that Cassidy had finished it in art class the year before and just recently surprised her with it as a birthday present. Another classmate, Lindsey, talked about how generous Cassidy was, always helping her out with her calculus homework, and how Cassidy doted on her little sister, Maggie. A middle-aged man, who lived in the same town house court as the Burches, echoed those kind thoughts, before adding that he believed Satanists were responsible for Cassidy's death. He claimed to have witnessed gangs of drugged-up teenagers dressed all in black with upside-down crucifix earrings and pentagram tattoos on their arms roaming around at night. "They left that poor girl's body in the boneyard. What more proof do the cops need?" I found it interesting that Cindy Gibbons, the girl who had dropped off Cassidy the night of her murder, never made an appearance on any of the networks. She also hadn't returned any of Carly's phone calls. *Probably still too upset,* I thought, changing the channel.

After a commercial break, the silver-haired anchor on Channel 11 gave the sheaf of papers he was holding a dramatic shuffle and began to run down a long list of what he called "breaking developments." Effective immediately, a town-wide curfew of 9:00 p.m. would be strictly enforced. A number of bars and restaurants announced they were closing early, as well as several local retailers including Walmart, Baskin-Robbins, Radio Shack, and Santoni's. In addition, all classes at Edgewood High School were canceled for the remainder of the week. The middle and elementary schools would remain open, but attendance would not be mandatory and would be left up to the discretion of each student's parents or guardians. The high school announced tentative plans to reopen the following Wednesday, November 9—Tuesday was Election Day—and promised to bring in a staff of grief counselors to help students cope with the tragedy.

Later that night, I climbed the stairs to my bedroom feeling numb and exhausted. I didn't know Cassidy Burch, her mom, or her little sister. As far as I knew, I'd never run into any of them in a store or on the street, or anywhere else, for that matter. Unlike Cassidy's friends on television, I'd never heard the girl sing or paint or laugh. I didn't even know what her voice sounded like.

So then why was my heart aching so deeply? Why did I feel so angry? Cassidy Burch was the Boogeyman's fourth victim. Why did it feel so different this time? Was I feeling guilty because I'd seen the man in the mask shortly before the murder and hadn't said anything? Or, Jesus, after all these years . . . was I finally turning into my mother?

I crawled into bed and phoned Kara for what had to be the fifth time that evening. Despite having an exam the next morning and a pile of homework, she did her best to cheer me up before saying goodnight. Carly Albright called a short time later, just as she'd promised, but I'd already turned off my bedside light and the ringer, and gone to sleep.

2

When I caught up with Carly early the next morning, she was in a lousy, sleep-deprived mood. None of her usual sources had been able to find out what the killer had left behind this time at the Cassidy Burch crime scene. Obviously Detective Harper had given his men hell about leaking any information to the media, and now no one was talking.

Carly believed that the Boogeyman had stuck to his routine and left behind *something* pertaining to the number six, and I agreed. After a short discussion, we decided the most likely conclusion was the pumpkins. The police had been very open with their description of the jack-o'-lanterns that'd been found surrounding the body, but had never once mentioned how many there were. It only made sense, but it felt infuriating and somehow wrong not knowing for certain.

With news of the Boogeyman's return, scores of national media swarmed their way back into town to cover what they were now calling "The Halloween Horror." There was even a rumor that *America's Most Wanted* was headed to Edgewood to stage a re-creation of the latest murder. While most local business owners kept their enthusiasm under wraps, a handful—including that jackass Mel Fullerton at the diner— were openly giddy at the prospect of once again bearing the fruit of all those media expense accounts. I recognized many of the news personalities from seeing their faces on television, and although I wasn't overly impressed with any of them, I almost managed to become a local legend by coming within an inch of backing into *A Current Affair's* own Maury Povich's rental car in the shopping center parking lot. With the dark mood I'd been mired in as of late, I probably would've gotten out of my car and punched him in his smug little face. And if I happened to run into Geraldo Rivera anywhere in town, it was going down.

There was also a story circulating that the FBI was planning to conduct a house-to-house search of the entire town. Civil rights activists had already gathered, picketing the sheriff's station and courthouse.

Many homeowners interviewed on the news claimed they planned to defend their personal property by any means possible, including arming themselves.

Edgewood was turning into a powder keg, ready to blow at any moment.

3

When Edgewood High School reopened the following Wednesday—with George H. W. Bush as president-elect of the United States of America—the guidance counselor's office had been taken over by a pair of grief counselors brought in from Baltimore City. By the end of that first week, a third counselor was added to the staff to help deal with the throng of upset teenagers that continued to stream into the office each day.

Returning high school students were also greeted by the sight of three detectives sitting behind folding tables in the lobby of the old gym. Going grade by grade and class by class, the detectives managed to interview each and every registered student—all 857 of them. It took them almost two weeks.

Afterward, I spoke with a handful of students myself, curious as to what kind of questions they'd been asked. Their responses were unsurprising: *How well did you know the girls who were murdered? Do you know of any problems involving the girls—grudges, rumors, bad breakups, anything? Were the girls especially close to any specific faculty members or other school employees? Have you seen anything strange or unusual around town these past few months?*

Soon after, an interesting story began making its way around town. Supposedly, the police were now focused on a thirty-one-year-old man named Aaron Unger. A well-liked English teacher and assistant soccer coach at Edgewood High School, he'd only moved to the area two years earlier from his hometown in Flint, Michigan. According to several people, including Bernie Gentile, Unger had already been questioned by detectives four times and had yet to provide a legitimate alibi.

Carly Albright chased the story for days and was able to confirm that many of the reported details were, in fact, accurate. But it all fell apart a short time later when she received news that Unger had finally revealed the reason for his initial reluctance in providing police with an alibi. Evidently, he'd spent Halloween night in the company of two paid escorts, and he'd been afraid that if the news became public, he'd (a) lose his teaching job; and (b) be charged with solicitation.

As it turned out, the police decided not to press charges and remained quiet about the whole situation. But in the end it didn't matter. Aaron Unger quit at the conclusion of the school year and moved back home to Michigan.

4

On Friday, November 18, Carly met with acclaimed FBI profiler Robert Neville, and interviewed him for a feature article in the *Aegis*.

The practice of profiling—analyzing criminal cases in order to build psychological and behavioral profiles of potential suspects—had only become prevalent in the law enforcement community a decade earlier, when FBI agent John E. Douglas's work on the Atlanta child murders of 1979–1981 thrust him into the public spotlight.

If John Douglas was widely considered the godfather of criminal profiling—and, indeed, he was—then Robert Neville was quickly earning the title of favorite son.

Young, handsome, and brilliant, Neville wrote an in-depth and controversial profile of the man known as "The Boston Butcher" that led to the 1985 arrest and conviction of a well-loved Massachusetts priest for the murder and rape of seven local prostitutes. A year later, his analysis work on the infamous Chicago suburb "Brady Bunch Murders" earned him his second promotion in as many years and landed him on the cover of *People* magazine.

Despite all the accolades, Carly wasn't a fan. She claimed Neville was sexist and arrogant and had terrible breath. The interview only lasted thirty minutes, but she couldn't wait until it was over. When I asked if she'd shared any of those observations with either Neville or her boss, she failed to recognize the sarcasm and instead gave me a snotty look and snapped, "What do *you* think?" I knew better than to say anything else after that.

The following excerpt from Carly Albright's Q&A with FBI profiler Robert Neville is reprinted here with permission from both the author and the *Aegis*:

CARLY ALBRIGHT: What makes a good criminal profiler?

ROBERT NEVILLE: The ability to step into a criminal's shoes and mind—to see the world with different eyes. Critical thinking, logic, reason, and such. Strong intuition and analytical skills. Emotional detachment. A strong stomach.

CARLY ALBRIGHT: Are you ever haunted by the work you do? Bad dreams? Depression?

ROBERT NEVILLE: No. Some things linger, certainly. But I tend to just reset and move on. I have to.

CARLY ALBRIGHT: Why was it important for you to come to Edgewood in person? Couldn't you have developed a profile of the killer by looking over reports and talking with task force members on the telephone?

ROBERT NEVILLE: I could've done that, yes, but because of the nature of these crimes, it was clear to me that I should be here.

CARLY ALBRIGHT: What do you mean by "the nature of these crimes"?

ROBERT NEVILLE: Make no mistake—the attacks in Edgewood are escalating in violence and depravity. Four murders in 151 days. He likes how it feels to kill, and he'll do it again if we don't stop him.

CARLY ALBRIGHT: And you're certain it's a "him"?

ROBERT NEVILLE: Of course. Even without an eyewitness, I was quite positive it was a man.

CARLY ALBRIGHT: What else can you tell us about the Boogeyman's profile?

ROBERT NEVILLE: Well, he likes being called that. He likes the attention and the notoriety. He knows about those who have come before him. Son of Sam. BTK. The Night Stalker. We've allowed him to feel part of something now.

CARLY ALBRIGHT: What else?

ROBERT NEVILLE: White male. Mid-to-late twenties or thirties. Likely single or divorced. Average or slightly higher than average intelligence. Good physical condition. He's either unemployed or has a job that allows him to move around freely late at night. He either lives nearby in a private setting or he drives a truck or van. He rapes and kills his victims somewhere private and then he dumps them elsewhere.

CARLY ALBRIGHT: So you believe he lives here in Edgewood?

ROBERT NEVILLE: The killer's a local, definitely. He's familiar with these streets and the dumping sites.

CARLY ALBRIGHT: Does he know his victims personally?

ROBERT NEVILLE: Not necessarily. In fact, most likely, no. But once they've caught his eye, once he makes up his mind, he watches them for some time before making his move.

CARLY ALBRIGHT: So you're saying he's driving around town picking random girls?

ROBERT NEVILLE: No. Not at all. He clearly has a type. Young, attractive, popular, long hair. He's angry with these girls. He wants to dominate and destroy them. Why? Occam's razor: the most likely answer is the simplest one. Someone that fits that physical description hurt him in the past. He feels burned or abused or cheated. Perhaps he feels lied to and that he was made to look foolish and weak.

CARLY ALBRIGHT: Why does he bite his victims?

ROBERT NEVILLE: Biting—that's personal, intimate, and demonstrates his power over his victims. The same reason I believe he strangles them instead of using a weapon. He wants these girls—and the public—to know that they're powerless to stop him from doing whatever he wants.

CARLY ALBRIGHT: And the severed ears?

ROBERT NEVILLE: Much of the same. He takes them as souvenirs, mementos. He controls everything. Most likely, over time, he pulls these souvenirs out of their hiding place and relives the experience.

CARLY ALBRIGHT: Why does he pose the bodies?

ROBERT NEVILLE: There could be a number of reasons. It's part of what we call his "signature." Once again, he may be exhibiting his power over his victims. "I not only controlled you in life, but also in death." Or, when the act is completed, he may feel a sense of remorse, however fleeting.

CARLY ALBRIGHT: Several police officers I've spoken with have referred to the killer as "The Ghost." So how do you capture a ghost, Mr. Neville?

ROBERT NEVILLE: Amusing but inaccurate. The man we're looking for has proven elusive, but I assure you he is 100 percent flesh and blood. And he will eventually make a mistake, and we will catch him.

CARLY ALBRIGHT: Do you think he's taunting the police?

ROBERT NEVILLE: I think he's playing a game and he's enjoying it. He likes killing, and he's getting better at it.

5

And there it was in stark black-and-white: *The killer's a local, definitely. He's familiar with these streets and the dumping sites.*

I tossed the newspaper into the trash can and pushed my chair away from the desk. Who was I to argue with the great Robert Neville?

As I walked out of the bedroom and headed downstairs to drive to the post office to check my PO box, it dawned on me why I'd been feeling so unsettled and angry the past couple of weeks. No matter how much I'd wanted it not to be true, deep in my heart, I'd known all along that Detective Harper and Robert Neville were right: *The killer was one of us.*

6

That Sunday morning, while my parents were down the street at Prince of Peace Church, I met some friends behind the high school to play basketball. My former roommate Bill Caughron was there with his older brother, Lee, along with Jeff Pruitt, John Schaech, the Crawford brothers, and a couple of younger guys I didn't know that well who were home from college on Thanksgiving break. We played a quick game of twenty-one to get warmed up, and then ran full-court for the next hour and a half.

It felt good to be outside, sweating my ass off, and catching up with old friends. Just what I needed to get out of the funk I'd been in. Of course, Cassidy Burch's murder was the main topic of conversation. Jeff Pruitt and Kenny and Bobby Crawford had grown up on Boxelder Drive, a two-minute walk from Jessica Lepp's house, where Cassidy and her girlfriends had partied the night she was killed. Bobby knew both Jessica and Cassidy and was still pissed off that Cindy Gibbons hadn't made sure that Cassidy got safely into her house on Halloween night. "I'm not the only one who thinks it's her fault, either. I heard she's even getting death threats."

One of the younger guys said his mom worked with Mrs. Burch, and that she was hanging in there, trying to be strong for Cassidy's little sister. A bunch of the mothers had gotten together and arranged a meal drop-off schedule for the Burches so they wouldn't have to worry about cooking. They were also taking turns running errands for the family.

Thirsty and sore afterward, I stopped at the 7-Eleven on my way home. As usual, it was a packed house in the rear aisle next to the coffee machines. I nodded hello to Mr. Anderson and Larry Noel, said excuse me to the others so I could squeeze by, and made my way to the Slurpee machine at the end of the counter. A little kid with red hair and freckles and a large booger hanging out of his left nostril had beaten me to it and was pouring himself a jumbo Blueberry Smash.

While I waited my turn—trying my damnedest not to stare at the crusty green nose goblin dangling perilously close to the boy's upper lip; every time he breathed in, it disappeared back into his nostril and every time he breathed out, it reappeared—I couldn't help but overhear snippets of nearby conversation.

"Wearing that ugly-ass hat of his . . ."

". . . and he was there again last night. I saw 'em . . ."

"That son of a bitch's too lazy to kill someone."

". . . over by the firehouse . . ."

"My money's still on Stan. He's got a . . ."

". . . ain't that difficult to find out he's got a record longer than my arm."

". . . and if the cops won't do it, we should."

"Four dead White girls and a Black cop . . . what's wrong with that picture?"

One of the men suddenly cleared his throat. Loudly. "You gonna pour yourself a drink or just stand there eavesdropping all morning?"

I blinked and realized the man was talking to me. The redhead with the booger in his nose was nowhere in sight. I looked over and tried to force a smile on my face. All of the men were staring at me. "I wasn't listening. Just daydreaming. Sorry about that."

Ignoring their grumbling, I grabbed a cup and started filling it. When I was finished, I slid a straw out of the box on the counter and took a deep breath. There was only one way to the cash register. Turning sideways to make myself as small as possible, I excused myself again and again and started working my way down the aisle. Until a hard shoulder slammed into my arm, halting my progress.

"You oughta watch where you're going," said a stocky bald man I didn't recognize.

"Leave him alone," someone said from behind me. I turned around and Mr. Anderson was standing there. He smelled like cigarettes and coffee. "How you doing, Rich?"

I swallowed with relief. "I'm okay. How are you?"

"Doing fine," he said. "Wish your parents a happy Thanksgiving for me."

"I will. Please tell Mrs. Joyce I said happy Thanksgiving, too."

He nodded his head, and I started walking again, anxious to get out of there. Just before I cleared the aisle, I heard a quiet voice behind me say, *"That's how you get yourself in trouble, boy."*

I kept walking and didn't look back.

7

The second half of November was a particularly hectic time for the Boogeyman task force. With the holidays waiting just around the corner, people were excited to begin their preparations—grocery shopping for the long Thanksgiving weekend, as well as early gift buying and decorating for Christmas—but they were also nervous wrecks. Calls to both 911 and the tip-line continued to pour in at a record pace.

A man who lived across the street from the elementary school reported hearing footsteps on the roof of his house in the middle of the night.

A resident of Sequoia Drive heard a *thump* outside while doing the dinner dishes. She looked out the kitchen window and saw a dark figure leaping over her backyard fence.

One of the women who worked the counter at the post office left a message on the tip-line describing a mysterious pile of cigarette butts she'd discovered behind her shed. Her embarrassed husband called back an hour later to apologize. The cigarettes were his. For the past month he'd been slipping out of the house several times a day to sneak a smoke, even though he'd sworn to his wife he was quitting.

An accounting instructor from Harford Community College broke down in tears while telling a veteran 911 operator that she'd just heard a woman's scream coming from the field behind her house.

A man claimed his back gate was left open during the night; an angry woman complained that her porch light had been vandalized; a nine-year-old girl called to say her corgi named Elvis was missing from her family's fenced-in backyard.

And Detective Harper and his task force members investigated each and every phone call.

8

Two days before Thanksgiving, Channel 13 broke into a 7:30 p.m. rerun of M*A*S*H with news that, just minutes earlier, a man had walked into the Harford County Sheriff's Department and confessed to the recent murders of four young Edgewood girls.

The news team didn't have a photo of the man or his name, but according to their reporter at the sheriff's office, he appeared to be in his midthirties, tall and solidly built, with short dark hair and a mustache.

That night, the entire town—including my parents and me—went to sleep, hoping and praying that the nightmare was finally over.

Unfortunately, our optimism was short-lived.

The next morning, it was widely reported that the man's confession had been a hoax—he'd actually been in a Pennsylvania prison serving time for a breaking-and-entering conviction when the first two girls had been killed. The unidentified man was currently in police custody, now undergoing a psychiatric examination.

9

I was sitting at the dining room table the morning after Thanksgiving, still dressed in my robe and pajamas, feeling fat and sleepy and reading the newspaper when Carly barged in.

"What are you doing here?" I asked. "How did you get in my house?"

She settled into a chair across from me. "Your mom let me in."

"I didn't hear the doorbell."

"That's because I didn't ring it. Your mom was outside sweeping the sidewalk."

"I think I liked it better when you and my mom didn't know each other."

She smiled. "That woman's a saint."

I couldn't argue with that. "So why are you here?"

"I have something to show you," she said, leaning over and pulling a manila folder out of the side pocket of the oversized Lois Lane purse she'd recently started carrying. She opened the folder and slid four glossy photographs across the table.

"What's this?" I asked, yawning.

"What does it look like?"

I took a closer look. "It looks like you took pictures of the memorials people left behind for the girls. That's kind of creepy."

"Not me. One of our staff photographers."

"Okay," I said. "So what?"

"Look again." She gestured at the photos. "They're in order. Notice anything interesting?"

I studied the first photo for a long time. I was about to tell her I had no flipping idea what she was talking about, when I spotted it—in the lower right corner of the photograph.

I immediately moved on to the second photo. It took a little longer this time, but eventually I found it—in the upper left-hand corner this time.

"Holy shit," I said, looking up at her.

"Pretty cool, huh?"

LEFT: The 7-Eleven on Edgewood Road
(Photo courtesy of the author)

ABOVE: Local news crew interviewing Cassidy Burch's friend Lindsey Pollard
(Photo courtesy of The Baltimore Sun)

eleven

Memorials

*"The image was crudely drawn,
but crystal clear in its depiction . . ."*

1

I gathered the photographs into a neat pile. "You figured all this out by yourself?"

"Is that so hard to believe?" Carly asked, giving me that fussy look of hers. "Wow. You think I need a brilliant *man* at my side like you or Robert Neville, don't you?"

"Umm, no. I was just wondering if anyone else at the newspaper spotted it. Like maybe the photographer."

"Oh," she said, relaxing. "No one knows. Just you."

"And it was all right there this whole time." I sighed. "You realize we have to tell Detective Harper, don't you?"

She frowned. "I was afraid you'd say that."

"You want to do the honors or me?"

"And let you get all the credit?" she said. "Heh, no thanks. I'll make the call."

2

While Carly phoned Detective Harper from the extension in the kitchen, I spread the four photographs out on the dining room table and re-examined them.

They were full-color eight-by-tens—crisp and in focus—and slick to the touch. The first photo had been taken in the Gallaghers' front yard not long after Natasha's funeral. Once the red ribbon someone had tied around the Gallagher's oak tree disappeared, it didn't take long before it was replaced with something a little more elaborate. Someone—most likely a girlfriend—had written FOREVER IN OUR HEARTS, NATASHA in the middle of a large poster board and drawn a big red heart around it. Several small photographs of Natasha had been glued or taped along each side of the heart. The remaining white space on the poster was covered with dozens of handwritten messages—*RIP! I MISS YOU! I'LL LOVE YOU FOREVER! YOU'LL NEVER BE FORGOTTEN*—along with a handful of drawings (hearts, praying hands, birds, rainbows, and sad faces with tears dripping from the eyes). The poster had been nailed or stapled to the base of the tree. Directly above it a large wooden cross, covered with flowers, hung from a nail. Beneath the display, spread out on the lawn, was a small army of colorful stuffed bears and giraffes, elephants and dinosaurs, as well as a staggered row of small glass vases holding withered bouquets of cut flowers and the remnants of nearly a dozen candles.

My eyes moved to the lower right-hand corner of the poster, focusing on a small image sandwiched between a heart broken in two by a jagged crack running down the center and a sad face with an exaggerated frown. The image was crudely drawn, but crystal clear in its depiction: a miniature hopscotch grid. Inside each of the squares was the number three.

I swallowed and moved on to the second photograph: the Kacey Robinson shrine that'd been erected near the base of the sliding board at the Cedar Drive playground. Instead of one large poster, Kacey's memorial was comprised of three smaller homemade signs. I stared at the rectangular sign in the middle. Upper left-hand corner. Right below a photo of Kacey Robinson riding a bicycle with no hands and a big smile on her face, someone had drawn a small replica, maybe four inches high, of the sign found hanging on the telephone pole outside of the Robinson house. HAVE YOU SEEN THIS DOG? was crammed into the space at the top of the sign and CALL 4444 was scrawled along the bottom. In between was a cartoony image of a dog with a big, toothy grin on its face.

My heart still beating a mile a minute, I picked up the third photograph: another front-yard memorial, this one for Madeline Wilcox. Mounds of flowers, several small crosses, and two unopened packs of Marlboro cigarettes lay in the grass in front of a poster-sized photograph of Madeline. She was wearing a yellow sundress and flip-flops, sitting on the hood of a classic car, looking happy and carefree. The poster was at least three-by-five feet, and was attached to a long wooden stake that had been pounded into the ground. A cluster of heart-shaped balloons floated in the breeze above Madeline's head. I stared at the car's front bumper, inches from Madeline's right foot, where the killer had used a strip of clear tape to affix five shiny pennies to the surface of the poster.

Before I could change my mind, I moved on to the last photograph. At the time the picture had been taken, Cassidy Burch's memorial was in its infant stages. Just a handful of homemade signs and sympathy cards attached to the wrought-iron fence posts surrounding the cemetery, as well as some balloons and a single, lonely candle. I'd recently seen video footage on the news, and the shrine had more than quadrupled in size. At the bottom of the largest sympathy card, below the signature of the person who'd left it, the killer had drawn a fat pumpkin with a crooked grin—and six triangular eyes. It looked obscene.

"He's picking us up in fifteen minutes," Carly said over my shoulder—and I nearly screamed.

3

Y ou two are unbelievable, you know that?"

Detective Harper shook his head and looked up from the photographs with a mixture of disbelief and admiration. At least, that's what I hoped the expression on his face meant. It was hard to tell—he might've just been pissed off again.

We were parked outside of the Boys and Girls Club at Cedar Drive, just a few minutes away from my parents' house. Being a gentleman— not to mention a big fat chicken these days when it came to Detective Harper—I'd volunteered to take the back seat and offered the front to Carly, a decision she may've been regretting right about now.

"Aren't you even a little bit impressed?" Carly asked quietly.

He looked at her. Slowly nodded his head. "Yeah. I am."

"But . . . ?"

"But . . . we've already known about the drawings and the pennies for a couple of weeks now."

"You have not!" I blurted out, and immediately regretted it.

The detective swiveled in his seat. "Excuse me?"

"Sorry," I said, lowering my eyes. "I didn't mean to yell. I'm just . . . surprised."

"Well, you shouldn't be. And you—" He was talking to Carly again. "You know you can't write about this. And neither one of you can say a word about it to anyone."

"I know that," she said, pouting.

"And the Hardy Boy in the back seat . . . he knows it too?"

I nodded, not trusting myself to speak.

"You mind if I take these with me?" Harper held up the photographs.

"Help yourself," Carly said. "But can I ask you a question?"

"Go ahead."

"Have you been staking out the memorials? In case he comes back?"

Harper thought about it for a moment before answering. "Every night for the past two weeks."

"All four of them?"

He paused again before answering. "Yes."

"And?"

"And nothing I can share with you."

"C'mon," she said, her tone surprising me. "Me and Joe Hardy back there—"

"Hey!" I said, sitting up again.

"We haven't given you a single reason to doubt us. Not before and not now. We called you today, didn't we? We didn't have to do that. We could've—"

"Okay, okay . . ." He put up his hands in surrender, and then seemed to make up his mind. He exhaled for several seconds before saying: "Look—this all remains confidential, okay?"

"Of course," she said.

He glanced at the back seat.

"Yes, of course," I repeated.

"We only started full-time surveillance on the memorials a couple weeks ago because that's when we first discovered what he was doing. That's our fault. We should've picked up on it earlier. If the public knew, they'd run us out of town, and I wouldn't blame them."

He shifted heavily in his seat. "But even before we figured it out, we had officers keeping an eye on them. Pretty much from day one we made sure to do regular drive-bys."

"Did you see anything?" Carly asked. I looked at her from the back seat, and for the first time it occurred to me that she just might really win that Pulitzer one day.

"We saw enough to ask family and friends and certain members of the media for any photographs or video they might've taken during the vigils that were held at the memorials. Lots of different faces in those crowds. We're still analyzing everything that came in."

"That's smart," she said.

"I'm glad you approve."

She actually giggled then. "So I'm guessing some kind of pattern started to emerge? Repeat visitors? Familiar faces that kept showing up?"

"You'd be surprised," he said, nodding. "Some folks visited or drove by pretty much every single day. We kept a record of those people."

Uh-oh. My face started to get warm.

"Usually they were relatives or friends, people we'd already talked to who had rock-solid alibis."

My hands were sweating.

"But every once in a while, someone interesting came along."

My stomach did a somersault.

"Someone whose behavior we found unusual or even downright odd."

"Odd how?" Carly asked.

"You name it, we saw it. Hysterical bouts of crying. Angry out-bursts. Excessive praying. A handful of folks even took souvenirs along with them when they left. Stuffed animals. Photographs."

I tried to swallow, but my mouth was too dry.

"When that happened, we usually ran a background check and sometimes even assigned a surveillance unit to keep eyes on them, just to see if any other . . . odd behavior came up."

Shit. Ten more seconds of this and I was going to throw up.

"I'm sorry," Carly said suddenly. "I just got paged. I need to call the paper."

Thank God, thank God, thank God. God bless her precious pager!

Detective Harper started the engine and pulled out of the parking lot. A few minutes later, as we swung into my parents' driveway, I glanced at the rearview mirror and saw that he was staring at me. Before I could look away, he gave me a wink.

ABOVE: Carly Albright chasing a story for *The Aegis*
(Photo courtesy of Brooklyn Ewing)

twelve

Shotgun Summer

"It was him."

1

Ever since meeting with Detective Harper a week earlier, something had been bothering me. It'd taken a couple days to get over that sly wink in the rearview mirror and the notion that the police knew all about my frequent drive-bys of the memorials, not to mention, most likely, the victims' houses, too. I obviously wasn't nearly as clever as I thought I was.

And then there was the photograph tucked away inside an envelope in the back of my desk drawer.

I'd found it several months ago in a patch of trampled grass at the base of the tree where Natasha Gallagher's friends and family had erected her memorial. A four-by-four-inch color image of Natasha eating steamed crabs at a poolside picnic table; the photo was faded and wrinkled from exposure to the weather. There was a partial footprint on the back of it and a tiny ragged tear along the top left corner from where it had been stapled or thumbtacked to the poster board. I figured the wind must've blown it free. The September evening I'd stumbled upon it, I'd looked around to make sure no one was watching, and then I'd bent down, pretending to tie my shoe, palmed it, and slipped it into the back pocket of my shorts as I walked away. As Detective Harper noted, odd behavior, to be sure. I didn't understand why I'd stolen the photograph back then, and I didn't understand it any better now. All I knew was that Harper or one of his officers had witnessed the whole damn thing.

But still, that wasn't what was bothering me. Embarrassment's temporary. I've learned that the hard way over the years. It was something else—something important—skating just below the surface of my consciousness, trying its damnedest to break free and make itself known, but thus far unable to.

It was driving me crazy.

I'd even tried an old trick taught to me by an upper-level journalism professor I'd greatly disliked but had begrudgingly come to respect by the end of his class. He'd suggested that, in order to recall important facts or story lines that had somehow slipped away, a writer should make a list of anything and everything—no matter how trivial—that had filled his most recent days.

My list looked something like this:

Thanksgiving
Kara
Mom
Dad
Carly
Detective Harper
Memorials
Boogeyman
Sliding board
Photographs
Cedar Drive
Basketball
Library

Post office
Shopping
Printer
Magazine
Story
Rejection
Bank
Pizza Hut
Stephen King
Movie theater
Carol's Used Bookstore
Oil change
Snow flurries
Cemetery
Boys and Girls Club

I'd thought about adding *skydiving*, *drag racing*, and *white water rafting* just to make my life appear a little more interesting, but decided against it. Not that it mattered. Regardless of how many times I pored over it, the list didn't work, and I was back to square one.

2

I woke up late on the morning of Tuesday, December 6, shrugged on my ratty old brown robe and slippers, and went right to work on a story I'd started the night before. It wasn't a particularly good one, but I liked the main characters quite a bit, and thought it had potential if I nailed the follow-up drafts. The title was "Shotgun Summer," and it followed the exploits of a pair of teenage runaway sweethearts who found themselves mixed up with a gang of violent bank robbers. The boy wanted to get as far away as possible from the bad guys and never look back, but his sixteen-year-old girlfriend had other ideas. She'd gotten a taste of easy money and bloodshed, and discovered that she liked it. I was probably at about the halfway point of the story when I wrote this scene:

Just outside of Toledo, they pulled over at a Phillips 66 to gas up the van. While Jeremy and Trudy walked around back to use the restrooms, Hank went in alone and paid the cashier for thirty bucks of unleaded, plus sodas, cigarettes, and that morning's edition of the Plain Dealer. *The lady behind the register never looked up from the magazine she was reading.*

When Hank returned to the van, he slapped the newspaper down on the dash in front of Leroy and said, "This ain't good." On the front page was a photograph of the bank they'd robbed two days earlier. In the background, on the sidewalk, lay two crumpled bodies.

And just like that, I remembered.

Searching my desk for his business card, I picked up the phone and called Detective Harper.

3

Surprisingly, he wasn't angry with me. In fact, he didn't call me Joe Hardy even once.

I started by describing the incident that'd occurred in front of my house on Halloween night. The man dressed in black, staring at me from across the street. A pickup truck turning the corner and its headlights giving me a good look at the mask the man was wearing.

I told him that while I'd initially been unnerved by the sighting, especially since Cassidy Burch had been murdered later that same night, I also figured it was just another teenager playing a prank—like the kids who'd gotten into trouble a month or so earlier for scaring people in their houses. That's why I hadn't reported it.

But something about that night had stuck in my mind, even now, five weeks later. I just couldn't remember what it was—until this morning.

The woman who had taken the photographs at the bottom of my driveway had been facing in the direction of the man wearing the mask. Depending on how wide she'd framed her photos, there was a decent chance the man would be visible in the background.

All Detective Harper had to do now was find out who the Incredible Hulk and Superman were.

4

I t only took a day.

Sending his men door-to-door along Hanson Road and the surrounding area, Detective Harper was able to track down the woman's identity and address. Her name was Marion Caples, and she lived with her husband and six-year-old son, Bradley, aka the Incredible Hulk, at the bottom of Harewood Drive. Superman was seven-year-old Todd Richardson, her next-door neighbor's son.

Marion Caples hadn't yet sent in the film from Halloween night to be developed, so Detective Harper had the police lab take care of that task on her behalf. The first photograph came out blurry and off-center, which was most likely why I'd heard Mrs. Caples beg the kids for "just one more." The second photo, however, was a 100 percent bull's-eye. You couldn't have asked for better timing. While the Hulk and Superman showed off their muscles and cherry lollipop–stained tongues in the foreground, the man in the mask, awash in the truck's headlights, stood in clear profile behind them.

Initially, Detective Harper claimed he wasn't going to be able to show us the photograph because of the ongoing nature of the investigation. But once Carly reminded him that we'd promised our confidentiality in exchange for more information, he'd relented. That girl was turning into one hell of a reporter.

The photo he slid across his desk the next afternoon was an eight-by-ten enlargement, full-color, and crystal clear. I didn't say much while we were at the station house, but when Carly and I got back in the car, the first words out of my mouth were: "It was *him*. Don't ask me how I know, but I do."

thirteen

Questions

"He turned and saw the outline of the killer's white mask
floating closer in the darkness . . ."

1

On Wednesday, December 14, the town of Edgewood opened its eyes in surprise to six inches of fresh snow on the ground. Schools canceled classes for the day, and many residents called out of work or went in late. The overnight forecast had merely called for a 50 percent chance of flurries, so none of the roads had been treated with salt, and even the plows had gotten a late start. By 10:00 a.m., most streets were still covered. It was a wet snow, perfect for making snowballs, and by late morning, an epic battle was raging on Tupelo Drive. On one side of the road, three boys stood tall behind a chest-high wall of packed snow; on the other side of the road, nearest to my house, five smaller kids mounted valiant charge after charge, only to be mercilessly pummeled and turned back each time. They'd sound a collective retreat, regroup behind a snow-covered car in my neighbor's driveway, reload with a new batch of ammunition, and bravely launch another attack upon the fortress. I watched the whole thing unfold from the safety of my bedroom window for a while, and wistfully thought I'd give just about anything in the world to go outside and join them.

It had been six uneventful weeks since Halloween night and the murder of Cassidy Burch. According to Detective Harper's most recent press conference on the first of the month, the task force was pursuing a number of leads and working closely with agents from the Federal Bureau of Investigation to maintain the highest level of safety within the community. Whatever that meant. All I knew was that I'd definitely noticed fewer patrol cars driving around town since Thanksgiving. My father had mentioned the same thing to me just the day before.

Since the holiday, two additional suspects had been brought in for questioning. The first was a thirty-nine-year-old bus driver from the high school, whose daily pickup and drop-off route included two of the murdered girls' homes. The second was a twenty-six-year-old former Harford Mall security guard who lived with his mother on Hornbeam Road. Several recent harassment complaints had been filed against the man by shoppers—all teenage girls with long hair—and the mall had fired him just after Black Friday.

Carly Albright covered both stories for the *Aegis* and told me that nothing ever came of them. The bus driver had alibis for each of the four murders and the ex-security guard had long, stringy blond hair that didn't match the police sketch, as well as a disability involving his right hand from a long-ago automobile accident. Law enforcement determined there was absolutely no chance this man could've strangled anyone.

Detective Harper hadn't brought up the photograph from Halloween night again, and I hadn't asked about it. I kept expecting to see the image pop up in the newspaper or on one of the nightly newscasts, but so far it hadn't made an appearance or even a mention.

While running errands one afternoon with my mother, I'd noticed the beauty parlor next door to Radio Shack seemed particularly busy. I immediately thought, *Here we go again*, but my mom assured me it was only because of the holiday season and she had it on good authority that the "short hair craze" in Edgewood was over. Around that same time, Carly spoke with Joe French at the pawnshop and he told her that no one was buying guns anymore either. I thought that was good news.

Something else had changed in the six weeks since Halloween night: in all that time, we'd only received one prank call. Whereas before, the calls had begun to slowly dwindle, now they'd practically stopped altogether. I couldn't even remember the last time it'd happened. The week before Thanksgiving, perhaps.

Time seemed to move faster in December, the lure of the holidays and a brand-new year dragging us along with its inexorable pull.

On Friday, December 16, came a momentous occasion in my life. A UPS truck pulled up to the curb in front of 920 Hanson Road, and I helped the driver unload twenty heavy boxes into the garage. At long last, the debut issue of *Cemetery Dance* was a reality. One thousand copies. Forty-eight pages. Several goddamn typos, despite a half-dozen rounds of proofreading.

My father and Kara and I spent the weekend stuffing four hundred subscriber copies into manila envelopes and packing an additional three hundred and fifty copies into various-sized boxes for comic book stores. It would prove to be the first of hundreds of times the three of us worked side by side in pursuit of my big dreams, but I would never forget the feeling of this particular moment.

The following week, it snowed again, and on December 21, I celebrated my twenty-third birthday with Kara and my parents and my sister Mary and her family. Mom baked my favorite chocolate cake with chocolate icing for dessert, and I made a secret wish before blowing out the candles.

Later that evening, Kara and I met Carly Albright and the man who was soon to become her boyfriend—a first-year state trooper from Baltimore County—to grab a drink and exchange Christmas gifts. I'm not much of a bar-hopper, but seeing Carly smiling and laughing with someone who really seemed to care about her was the cherry on top of a wonderful night. Before we said our goodbyes, Carly gave me an engraved fountain pen "to sign contracts and autographs once you're famous," and I gave her a fancy Sony mini-recorder to help her with her interviews. Miraculously, none of us had brought up the Boogeyman that entire evening.

Early the next morning, Kara and I drove down Route 40 to White Marsh Mall to try and finish our Christmas shopping. Evidently, we weren't the only ones who'd woken up with that bright idea. The place was a zoo.

While navigating the throngs of shoppers swarming both the first- and second-level concourses, I began to experience that same eerie sensation of feeling watched, the first time it'd happened in a long time. The next hour passed in a blur of continuous glances over my shoulder and having to say, "I'm sorry, can you repeat that?" to my obviously frustrated fiancée. But no matter how irritated she became with me, I didn't tell her the truth, because I didn't want her to worry.

A short time later, we stopped in the food court for slices of pizza and sodas, and saw Mr. and Mrs. Gallagher in line at the soft pretzel stand. I was pleasantly surprised by how different Mr. Gallagher looked. He was at least ten or fifteen pounds heavier than the last time I'd seen him, and a healthy color had returned to his face. He'd also started wearing glasses and was holding his wife's hand. I decided not to bother them and didn't say hello.

Later still, our shopping finally completed, we ran into Mike Meredith in the parking lot. We'd graduated high school and played lacrosse together. The best goalie I'd ever teamed with, he was also one of the weirdest guys I knew. For that reason, I didn't even bother asking him why his hair was dyed green. Mike was also quite the talker, which is what led to him sharing the news.

"You haven't heard?" he asked.

"Heard what?"

"Whoa, okay. You *really* haven't heard?" he asked again, eyes flashing wide.

"Mike, I don't know what the hell you're talking about."

"Last night . . . the neighborhood watch."

"What about it?"

"Oh, man. It was a shitshow, Chiz."

"How so?"

He shook his head. "It was bad, my friend. No more neighborhood watch, that's for sure."

And then he told us what happened.

2

At approximately 11:15 p.m. on Wednesday night, Mel Fullerton, Ronnie Finley, and Mark Stratton—all members of the Edgewood Neighborhood Watch—were driving in Mel's oversized pickup along Perry Avenue, directly across the street from the high school. It was pretty cold out, and both Mel and Ronnie had spiked their coffee with bourbon. They'd also brought along a twelve-pack of Budweiser, the empties of which they'd dumped about an hour earlier along a dark stretch of Willoughby Beach Road. Their "shift" was set to end in fifteen minutes, and they were tired and grumpy, especially Mel, who'd been in a particularly foul mood the whole time.

They'd just made a left-hand turn onto Hornbeam Road and were heading up the long, sloping hill toward the library and shopping center when someone dressed in dark clothing darted across the road directly in front of the pickup and disappeared into a culvert on the opposite side of the street.

Mel immediately slammed on the brakes and flung open the driver's door, stumbling out onto the road. The other two men followed, Ronnie sprinting down the grassy hill into the culvert, his boots splashing in the shallow, running water.

"Mark, you watch that side," Mel had ordered, pointing to his left, "in case he crawls into the drainage pipe and tries to double back!"

Without a word, Mark had headed off into the darkness, the beam of his flashlight bouncing over the frozen ground.

Mel sidestepped his way down the hill, taking his time so he wouldn't fall. He'd known he was drunk, but hadn't realized how badly until he'd gotten out of the truck. He was breathing heavily, and vapor clouded the air in front of his fleshy face. "Ronnie!" he called into the night.

A barking dog in the distance answered him.

Mel reached the bottom of the rise, and just as his ears registered the sound of running water gurgling over rocks, his foot slipped on one of those rocks, and down he went, sprawling onto his backside in the frigid stream.

"*Son of a bitch!*" he screamed, pushing himself back to his feet and almost falling again. "Ronnie, where the hell are you?!"

No answer—not even the dog this time.

"You okay, boss?" Mark had called out from the other end of the drainage pipe that ran underneath the road.

Great, Mel thought, *probably saw the whole damn thing, and he'll sure as shit be running his mouth tomorrow morning at the diner.* "I'm fine," he said. "Where the hell did Ronnie get to?"

"Beats me."

Mel heard footsteps behind him then, coming down the hill on the opposite side of the stream, slow and stealthy, and if it was Ronnie, why hadn't he said something by now?

Already scared, he turned and saw the outline of the killer's white mask floating closer in the darkness, footsteps coming faster now.

He reached into his jacket pocket and fumbled out the .38 he'd stashed there before he'd left his house. Lifting it chest-high, he commanded, "*Stop right there!*" and then jerked the trigger three times, *boom boom boom*.

"What the hell was that?!" Mark yelled.

"I got him!" Mel answered. "I got the Boogeyman!"

Still holding the gun in front of him, Mel splashed his way across the culvert.

At the same time, an out-of-breath Mark appeared above him, leaning over the guardrail. Spotting the crumpled body on the hillside, he whispered, "Holy shit."

Mel bent over, slowly reaching out with his free hand to unmask the killer, already thinking about what he was going to do with all that reward money, when a scattering of clouds swam free of the moon— and Mel Fullerton realized that there was no mask and he'd just shot and killed Ronnie Finley, his best friend in the world, and he was going away for a very long time.

3

I t felt like I blinked, and Christmas and New Year's were ghosts in the rearview mirror. That's how quickly those next two weeks passed.

Knowing what was ahead of us, Kara and I stayed in on New Year's Eve and watched Dick Clark's midnight countdown on television. My parents had gone to bed earlier, and cuddling under a blanket on the basement sofa, it felt just like old times back when we were dating in high school. I dropped Kara off around 12:30 a.m. and was home snoring in bed before one.

The next evening wasn't nearly as serene. A bunch of the guys—led by Jimmy Cavanaugh and Brian Anderson, both of whom had flown into town earlier that afternoon—showed up at the house and dragged me away for my bachelor party. There soon followed spirited rounds of bowling and poker and too many pitchers of Loughlin's Pub beer to count. After we closed the place down, we got it into our heads that it would be a good idea to throw snowballs at cars out on Route 24. None of us were in any condition to drive, so we walked the mile and a half. It was almost 2:30 a.m. by the time we got in position along the tree line and traffic was sparse. Finally, headlights approached, traveling east and moving at high speed. Calling on years of experience, we waited until just the right moment and, carefully timing our throws, we all fired our snowballs. *Splat splat splat*—three of them hit home! Before we could even begin to celebrate our success, the car screeched to a sudden halt in the middle of the highway and switched on its flashing lights and siren. As luck would have it, we'd just nailed a Harford County Sheriff's cruiser. The driver banged a tight U-turn and started speeding down the wrong side of the highway in our direction. We immediately dropped our remaining snowballs and fled into the woods, barely managing to escape.

The next morning, I woke up in my parents' basement, surrounded by eight of my closest friends. Brian Anderson was shirtless, his chest and shoulders a patchwork of scrapes and scratches he'd suffered during our hasty retreat. One of Jimmy Cavanaugh's sideburns had been mysteriously shaved off and he was missing both of his shoes. Steve Sines, who had made the trip from Maine, had a beauty of a black eye, but no one could remember where in the hell it came from.

As for the guest of honor, I woke up wearing a cardboard box on my head that just hours earlier had housed a twelve-pack of Bud Light. One of my friends—to this day, none of the bastards will own up to it—had drawn a penis on my forehead with permanent magic marker. My poor mom almost fainted when she saw it. And as if the hazy memories of that night weren't enough, I had several Polaroids to commemorate the special occasion. I kept them hidden inside a desk drawer.

4

On Wednesday, January 4, the big day finally arrived: in front of 125 cherished family members and friends, with my nervous father standing at my side as best man, Kara and I exchanged our wedding vows. The ceremony and reception were every bit as wonderful as we'd hoped for, and seeing everyone together in one grand room—laughing, dancing, celebrating—was a precious gift Kara and I knew we'd always carry with us. It was the happiest day of my life—but unfortunately short-lived.

Thanks to the early start of Kara's winter semester, there was no time for a real honeymoon. Instead, we spent an amazing weekend in a cabin retreat tucked away in the snowy mountains of West Virginia before returning home to pack up my stuff and move into our new apartment in Roland Park, a forty-five-minute drive from Edgewood and only a handful of blocks away from Johns Hopkins.

By mid-January we'd settled into our new routines: Kara spent most of her mornings and afternoons on campus, except for Fridays when she only had one early class, and I kept myself busy back at the apartment, writing new stories and working on the second issue of the magazine.

The long days were filled with quiet solitude, giving my mind plenty of time to wander. So, it was only natural that, after all that'd happened, some of those thoughts would take me back to Edgewood.

It had been ten weeks now since the Halloween night murder of Cassidy Burch, and, with the exception of the Mel Fullerton shooting, the town had remained peaceful. Mel was currently free on bail and staying out of the public eye, according to Carly, but the whole thing was a breathtaking mess, complicated by the surprise revelation that Ronnie Finley had been having an affair with Mel's wife. As a result, many folks around town did not believe the shooting was accidental.

I found myself bundling up against the cold and taking long walks after lunch to break up my day and help clear my head. During those walks, I often chewed over the current situation with the Boogeyman. Based on Carly's regular updates, nothing much was happening with the investigation. There was still the occasional report of a night prowler or Peeping Tom, and her next-door neighbor had called the cops just a week earlier to complain about a suspicious BGE meter reader wandering the neighborhood, but that was about it. On a whim, I'd visited the Enoch Pratt Free Library in downtown Baltimore one afternoon and ended up going down a rabbit hole, spending five hours searching their microfiche files for newspaper articles about recent murders in Pennsylvania, Delaware, and Virginia. Just because the killings had stopped in Edgewood didn't mean the Boogeyman hadn't moved on and started again elsewhere. Eyes blurry, I headed back to Roland Park later that afternoon empty-handed.

And still the questions remained: *Why had the killings suddenly stopped? Was the Boogeyman waiting, biding his time before striking again? Or had he finally given up and left town, or maybe even gotten locked up for some unrelated offense?*

I knew Detective Harper was asking himself the same questions day and night, and was in a much better position to formulate answers, but that didn't stop me from wondering. The Boogeyman was a part of my life now—a part of all our lives. It was during those long, midday walks—Bruce Springsteen and the Rolling Stones blaring on my headphones—that I first began contemplating writing a book about the murders. If my former next-door neighbor Bernie Gentile was right, time would continue to march forward, the residents of Edgewood would eventually move on with their lives, and memories of the four dead girls would fade away until they were nothing more than a footnote in the town's history. That didn't feel right to me.

Toward the end of the month, my parents came by for a visit. My father strolled into the apartment cradling two paper bags overflowing with groceries—"Picked up a few extra items at the commissary"—and my mom came in with a month's worth of *Aegis* back issues, as well as a recent copy of *Reader's Digest* with "all the interesting articles marked" for me to read. The four of us shared a late lunch of soup and sandwiches in the cramped kitchenette and caught up on all the latest news. David Goode, who grew up across the street in Tupelo Court, was now engaged to a girl he'd met at college. Tal Taylor, an old high school friend, had recently started a new job with UPS. Norma Gentile was back in the hospital with more hernia trouble, but was expected to fully recover. There'd been no more prank phone calls, my mother was happy to report, and she immediately made the sign of the cross to make sure it stayed that way. Neither of them brought up the Boogeyman—whether by design or accident, I wasn't sure. I almost mentioned that I was thinking of writing about the murders, but in the end I kept my mouth shut. I didn't want to ruin the mood.

Before they left that evening, my mother kissed me on the cheek and slipped an envelope with fifty dollars inside my shirt pocket, so "you and Kara can go out to dinner one night." I tried to give it back, but she wouldn't hear of it. My father gave me an awkward half hug at the curb before climbing into the driver's seat. Five minutes after they drove away, I could still smell his aftershave on my shirt. I already missed them like crazy.

5

Later that same afternoon, Carly called to tell me that the Edgewood High School bus driver was back on the hot seat. His name was Lloyd Bennett, and evidently, his alibis for the nights of the Boogeyman murders weren't quite so ironclad after all. The woman he'd claimed to have been with on all four occasions had lost her nerve and admitted to the police that he was lying. She didn't know where he'd been, but it certainly wasn't with her.

Last Carly had heard, Bennett and his attorney were at the station house being interrogated, and detectives were filing paperwork to get a search warrant for his car and residence.

6

Carly phoned again a few days later to tell me she'd just been assigned a front-page gig focusing on the families of the Boogeyman's victims. She knew that from day one I'd been clipping articles and making notes of my own about the murders—a kind of loosely organized scrapbook or journal—and wanted to know if I'd be interested in co-writing the article with her. She'd already gotten permission from her editor.

I told her I'd sleep on it and let her know. That night, I discussed the idea with Kara, and then I went for a run by myself and thought about it some more. On the one hand, it would make for an interesting challenge and be good experience. On the other hand, book or no book, I had little desire to speak with still-grieving family members and friends, and risk tearing open fresh wounds. I went to bed that night decidedly undecided, but when I woke the next morning, all my indecision had vanished. I suddenly knew: telling the survivors' stories was the right thing to do, and I wanted to be a part of it. I phoned Carly shortly after breakfast and agreed.

We spent much of the next week sitting in hushed living rooms and dens, interviewing family members of the slain girls—with the exception of Mr. and Mrs. Wilcox, who'd sold their home in early January and moved to the Eastern Shore, and Mr. Gallagher, who'd politely declined our invitation. It was a somber, oftentimes tearful experience, but also surprisingly uplifting. Inspired by the overwhelming love and courage I felt in those rooms—within those special people—I found myself looking at the world through a different lens than I had before. It was hard to explain any better than that or even fully understand, but I couldn't wait to see how this experience affected my writing. Talking to Carly, I discovered that she felt very much the same way. "This whole thing has changed me," she told me one evening on our way back to the newspaper office. "I'll never be the same after this."

Once we got started, it only took us three days to write the article. I'd never collaborated before and expected countless headaches and arguments, neither of which ever materialized. On Friday, February 17, two days early, we turned in five thousand words, our maximum word limit.

On February 22, the article was published in the *Aegis* under a banner headline: **THE FAMILIES MOURN AND REMEMBER.** My mother called in tears to tell me how great of a job we'd done, and all three of the families we'd interviewed sent personal notes thanking us for writing such a humane and thoughtful tribute. My father had the first page of the article framed for both Carly and me. Mine still hangs above my desk as a daily reminder of the surviving family members' bravery.

The *Aegis* maintained all publication rights to the article, so I was unable to reprint it here, but our editor, Karen Lockwood, graciously granted permission to reprint selected excerpts from our interview notes.

MRS. CATHERINE GALLAGHER

Albright: How are you and your family coping?

Mrs. Gallagher: The only way we know how: minute by minute, hour by hour, day by day. It's been eight months, and it still feels like every day brings a brand-new challenge.

Chizmar: Has it gotten any easier at all?

Mrs. Gallagher: Yes and no. My husband and I have been going to therapy for almost six months. Grief counseling. It helps. We now have more of the necessary tools to cope with what happened to Natasha. And we've learned how to lean on each other in healthy ways. That's important. God, it was so hard in the beginning. We were both so lost and angry.

Chizmar: Is the anger still there?

Mrs. Gallagher: Oh yes, some days. I'll go four or five days in a row feeling pretty strong, holding on tight to happy memories, and then *bam*, out of the blue, I explode. Just a couple weeks ago, I was loading the dinner dishes into the washer, and I started thinking about the time Nat put in too much detergent and flooded the kitchen with suds. I started laughing at first, and then I was crying. And before I knew what I was doing, I'd thrown a couple of plates against the wall. My husband came running in, scared out of his wits, which I felt horrible about.

Albright: How has your son handled the loss of his sister?

Mrs. Gallagher: Josh doesn't talk about it much. He refused to go to counseling with us, but I know he's hurting just like we are. He gave us the most beautiful Christmas gift—a photo album filled with pictures of Natasha from the time she was a baby up until when she died . . . when she was killed.

MR. ROBERT AND MRS. EVELYN ROBINSON

Albright: What's been the most difficult part of losing your daughter?

Mr. Robinson: All of it. Not hearing her voice. Her laugh. Knowing she was taken a couple hundred yards from our front door and not being able to do anything to stop it.

Mrs. Robinson: For me, the hardest part has been helping Kacey's younger sisters understand what happened. Even now, they have real trouble grasping how and why something like this could happen. To anyone. Bedtime is especially difficult.

Chizmar: How have family and friends helped you cope?

Mrs. Robinson: Everyone's been amazing. I don't know how we would've gotten through the funeral and that first month without everyone holding us up. I don't even remember most of it. The girls' and David's friends have been wonderful.

Albright: Do you think the police will ever catch the man who did this?

Mr. Robinson: I sure as hell hope so, but I'm not holding my breath. Not anymore. When it comes to Kacey's murder, I believe the police are no further along now than they were on the night she was killed.

MRS. CANDICE BURCH

Chizmar: By all accounts—based on the words of everyone I've spoken with and judging from my own time with you—you're an extraordinary woman. You lost your husband several years ago, and now your daughter, yet you remain one of the strongest, most positive women I've ever met.

Mrs. Burch: Well, I thank you for saying that. I have my good days and I have my bad days. Most of those bad days, I keep to myself so nobody has to put up with me. But I also have another daughter, a beautiful little girl with a whole life ahead of her, and I don't plan on letting her suffer any more than she's already had to. We're a team, me and Maggie, and we're going to honor Cassidy's memory every single day by sticking together and trying to make this world a better place.

Albright: Have you been in touch with the police lately? Any recent news at all?

Mrs. Burch: One of the detectives calls me from time to time, usually to ask if Cassidy knew this person or that person. Or if she'd ever been to this place or that place. I ask them every time if they're making any progress, and every time it's the same answer: they're pursuing leads and tracking down people to talk to.

Chizmar: The Wilcox family recently moved away from Edgewood. There's a FOR SALE sign in your front yard. Where are you headed?

Mrs. Burch: Not far at all. Just down [Route] 40 to Havre de Grace. I want us to wake up every day with a fresh view, a fresh start, but Maggie will still be attending Edgewood Middle School in the fall. We were able to work it out with the education board, which is a true blessing.

MISS VALERIE WATSON, English teacher, Edgewood High School

Albright: You taught both Natasha Gallagher and Kacey Robinson, is that right?

Miss Watson: I did. I had Natasha freshman year and Kacey sophomore year.

Albright: What kind of students were they?

Miss Watson: Oh, they were both such special girls, but in different ways. Natasha had so much energy she could barely sit still some days. I used to tease her about it, but she just laughed and said I sounded like her mother. She was a very good student and always looking out for her classmates, just making sure everyone around her was happy is the only way I can describe it. Kacey was the top student in my English class. Whatever the subject was, no matter how difficult, she just got it, and boy could she write. Her papers were college level As. I know she had her heart set on becoming a veterinarian, but she would've made a really great teacher or even a full-time writer. She was brilliant, but she never acted like she was, which is why the other kids adored her so much.

MR. CARL RATCLIFFE, Gallaghers' neighbor

Chizmar: What do you remember most clearly about Natasha?

Mr. Ratcliffe: Her and her friends were always out in the yard doing cartwheels and flips and crazy stuff like that. Always laughing and carrying on and being loud and silly, but never in a disrespectful or annoying way, like so many kids today. She always said hello and goodbye, always asked if we needed help carrying in the groceries. Her parents did a fine job with that young lady. It's such a crying shame what happened.

MRS. JENNIFER STARSIA, Robinsons' neighbor

Albright: What do you remember most clearly about Kacey?

Mrs. Starsia: We have two greyhounds that we rescued from a track down in Florida. She loved those dogs so much and would come over all the time and visit with them. She'd talk to them too, just go on and on, having an actual conversation as if they could understand what she was saying. She was always such a happy girl.

Chizmar: How do you feel about venturing outside after dark these days in your own neighborhood?

Mrs. Starsia: For the longest time after what happened, I just wouldn't go outside by myself at all—day or night. I'm a little better now. Daytime hours are fine, but I usually wait for my husband if I need to go somewhere after dark. We put up a fence in the backyard so we don't really have to walk the dogs anymore. They can run around all they want. And my husband's in charge of taking out the trash now.

MISS ANNIE RIGGS

Albright: This is the first time you've spoken with the media about what happened on the night of September 9. Why did you change your mind and decide to talk?

Miss Riggs: It was always my parents' decision. Right after it happened, we were being bombarded with interview requests, and they were afraid I'd be overwhelmed. They also didn't want me to say anything that might antagonize the person who attacked me. They're still worried about that.

Albright: Do you ever worry that he might come after you again?

Miss Riggs: Sometimes, but I have faith in the police. They've been great. I know they're watching out for me and my family.

Albright: What sticks out in your mind the most about the man who attacked you that night?

Miss Riggs: He just felt . . . wrong. Except for his breathing, he never made a sound the entire time, and when I saw his eyes through the holes in his mask, they were dead, emotionless. I still see them in my dreams sometimes.

MISS RILEY HOLT, Kacey Robinson's best friend

Chizmar: If you had to name one thing you miss most about Kacey, what would it be?

Miss Holt: One thing is too hard, so I'll name two. The first is her smile. It was never fake or phony. You knew she meant it. That was always something I could count on. The second is how generous she was. She would always give you the last piece of gum in the pack, every time.

7

It was my father who called me with the news two days later. I spoke with Carly that same afternoon—after going for a walk to try to make sense of what I'd just heard—and she filled me in on the details.

Late the night before, Natasha Gallagher's father slipped out of bed, careful not to disturb his sleeping wife, and put on his boots and winter jacket. He left the house by a sliding glass door and walked into the woods using a flashlight. Once he reached the spot where his daughter's body had been found, he dropped the flashlight and pulled a .38 revolver from his jacket pocket. He slid the barrel into his mouth and pulled the trigger.

8

On the first Friday of March, I made the drive to Edgewood and spent the afternoon at my parents' house. They had a stack of mail for me that for some reason the post office had failed to forward, and my father needed help repairing a long section of gutter that'd blown free of the roof during a recent storm. When we came back inside from finishing the job, my mom had mugs of hot chocolate waiting for us on the dining room table. It had been more than a month since we'd last seen each other, and it was nice to just sit and talk for a while; I'd missed that. And I'd missed their faces, too. We spoke on the phone several times a week—usually after dinner when I knew they would be sitting together watching television in the basement—but it wasn't the same. I could tell they had similar feelings. The house seemed quieter than usual—the whole neighborhood did, for that matter—and before I left, I snuck upstairs and peeked into my old bedroom. Even though I hadn't been gone that long, my folks had already converted it into a second guest room, but without my desk and bookshelves and posters on the wall, it looked kind of empty and sad.

Shortly after 5:00 p.m., my mom announced that it was time for her to start making dinner, and after assuring her for the third time that no I really couldn't stay, I gave both her and my father hugs goodbye and went on my way.

After all, there was a third reason I'd chosen to visit Edgewood that day, and it was waiting for me just down the road on Route 40.

When I pulled into the Giovanni's parking lot a few minutes before five thirty, snow flurries were dancing in the beams of my headlights. I hurried inside, hoping I was the first to arrive, but guessing I wasn't.

I was right.

Detective Lyle Harper had already been seated. Dressed in a brown suit, he looked an awful lot like the first time I'd seen him on television—maybe a smidge heavier back then, and he'd also been wearing a tie the night of his press conference. He was talking with a waitress when I got to the table. She took my drink order and disappeared into the back.

I'd been pleasantly surprised a few days earlier when Harper accepted my dinner invitation. I wasn't at all sure he would, and wasn't even exactly certain why I'd asked him in the first place. It was just an idea that was floating around inside my head as of late and I decided to finally act on it.

We spent the first thirty minutes or so munching on bruschetta and clams casino, and catching up on our families, newlywed life, and the article that had been published in the *Aegis* a week earlier. The detective was the most relaxed I'd ever seen him. Right before our entrées arrived, he even managed to crack a joke about my frequent drive-bys of the dead girls' houses. Before I could respond, he gave me a wink like that day in the car and burst out laughing.

It was during the main course that we finally got down to business and began talking about the Boogeyman. We kept our voices low for obvious reasons.

"So, Carly told me there's nothing solid on Lloyd Bennett," I said.

"Not yet, but we're working on it."

"He still doesn't have an alibi?"

Harper shoveled in another bite of lasagna. "We're checking out a few things he told us. Interesting guy. We *definitely* have our eye on him."

"I saw a picture of him on the news. Not a bad match for the police sketch."

"Ehh, not a good one, either."

I couldn't argue with that. "I'm sorry about that nasty editorial in the *Sun*," I told him. "Talk about a hatchet job."

He shrugged. "Comes with the territory. I'm used to it."

"The guy who wrote it wouldn't know a crime scene from his asshole. It was pretty obvious he was just fishing for votes."

"That's okay. You can demand a retraction after we catch the guy."

I looked at him closely. *Was there something he wasn't telling me?* "You still think you'll catch him?"

"Yes, I do."

"Even if he doesn't . . . do it again?"

"Yes."

I wasn't sure what to say, so I said nothing at all. Even with this Bennett guy back in the picture, I had my doubts, serious doubts, that the Boogeyman would ever be captured. In fact, if I were forced to place a bet on the final outcome, I'd put my money squarely on the killer's identity forever remaining a secret—just like Jack the Ripper, Zodiac, and the Green River Killer, and any number of other infamous cases.

So then why did he seem so confident?

"Okay, spill. What aren't you telling me?" I finally asked.

He bit off a huge chunk of Italian bread and pointed at his mouth, pretending he couldn't talk. I laughed and tried again. "I'll wait right here until you finish chewing."

"We've almost had him twice now," he said, leaning in closer after draining what was left of his beer. "If there's a next time, we'll get him."

"Twice?" I asked, confused. "The night the officer got bitten by the dog—"

"That was the first time."

"What was the second?"

"Early December. Two of my men had him cornered in a backyard, but he managed to get away. Again. He's like fucking Houdini."

"And you're sure it was him?"

"Yes."

"How can you be so sure?"

He motioned to the waitress for another beer, then said: "Cards on the table. This is all off the record, correct?"

"Of course."

"And you won't share this information with your reporter friend?"

After a slight hesitation, I answered. "You have my word."

"The fucker was wearing a mask. I swear on my badge, it was him."

9

The restaurant parking lot was dusted with snow, and a quick glance at the streetlights confirmed what the hostess had warned us about just minutes earlier: it was coming down harder now. The wind had also picked up, and it tugged at the collar of my lightweight jacket, sending icy fingers down the length of my spine. As we reached Detective Harper's unmarked sedan, I glanced behind us, noticing the twin paths our footsteps had left in the snow. For whatever reason, seeing that gave me the surge of courage I was searching for.

"I enjoyed that, Rich," Harper said, fishing his keys out of his pocket. "Great meal. We'll have to do it again some—"

"What else aren't you telling me?" I asked, cutting him off.

He looked at me in surprise.

"I'm sorry, Detective—but there *is* something else, isn't there?"

He stared at me for a long time, his close-cut hair turning white with flakes of melting snow. Then: "We off the record?"

"Yes, absolutely."

He sighed. "Fine, fuck it. It'll be all over the *Baltimore Sun* soon enough anyway. Someone leaked it to one of their reporters, but we convinced the powers that be to sit on it until April."

"I won't say a word to anyone, I promise."

"We have his DNA."

I gaped at him. "*What?* How did *that* happen?"

"We found a blood trace on a headstone at the cemetery, and another one on Cassidy Burch's Halloween costume. They both came from the same person, and it wasn't Cassidy."

"That's . . . great news!" I said, barely able to contain my excitement.

He nodded, his eyes dark slits. "The son of a bitch finally made a mistake."

10

By the time I pulled out of the Giovanni's parking lot, it was 9:20 p.m. and the snow was coming down sideways. According to the weather lady on 98 Rock, the roads were getting worse by the minute—I'd already seen several plows go by—which made my next decision all the more questionable.

Instead of turning left and heading west on Route 40 toward Kara and the apartment, I found myself making a pair of quick rights and navigating the slippery hill up Edgewood Road. Five minutes later, I stopped at the mouth of Tupelo Court, directly across the street from my parents' house, and turned off my headlights.

Staring at the rectangles of golden light spilling from the basement windows, I pictured them inside, cozy and warm, dressed in pajamas and robes: my father kicked back in his easy chair, a paperback spy novel open on his lap, a crime show playing in the background; my mother nestled under a blanket in her own chair, eyes scanning the latest issue of *Reader's Digest* or sewing a hole in one of my father's work shirts. Perhaps there was a plate of crackers and cheese or sliced apples resting on a TV table between them. Or a pair of empty ice cream bowls—they both had quite a sweet tooth. At 10:00 p.m., when the show was finished, they'd turn off the television, check the doors, and head upstairs to get ready for bed. The door to my old bedroom would be open. The room dark and silent.

A snowplow rumbled past me, its headlights glowering in the swirling darkness like some kind of prehistoric monster. I watched its taillights disappear around the bend in a spray of snow as it headed north toward Cedar Drive—and my thoughts returned to that long-ago winter evening when I was fifteen and stayed out late to catch one more run down the hill on my brand-new sled. I hadn't thought about that night in forever, which was rather strange, considering the crest of the hill I'd stopped on as soon as I caught sight of my house in the distance wasn't very far from the piece of ground upon which Kacey Robinson's body had been discovered at the base of the sliding board.

I was right, you know, I thought, my gaze returning to 920 Hanson Road. *Nothing was ever the same again after that night. The world had changed—had grown—and there was nothing I could do to stop it. We all grew up. Moved away. Lost touch. Even me.*

Right then, sitting alone in my car, heart aching, sudden tears stinging the corners of my eyes, I would've given anything in the world to go back in time and be that crazy teenager again. Walking up Hanson Road with my plastic sled tucked underneath my arm; clothes soaked; heart full; head spinning; a mug of hot chocolate waiting for me on the kitchen table, along with dry clothes and a hug from my smiling mother; the smell of my father's aftershave and the sandpapery feel of the callouses on his hands as he walked by and gave my neck a squeeze, the gentle wisdom of his voice.

For a brief moment, I considered driving across the street, pulling into the driveway, and banging on the front door.

But then a gust of wind buffeted the car, shaking me from my reverie, and a squall of snow corkscrewed across the windshield, obscuring my view—and I knew it was too late.

Another time, I thought, turning on my headlights. *Soon.*

I eased onto the road, back tires fishtailing for traction. Once they began to catch, I leaned on the gas, anticipating the slide, but knowing I would need the extra speed to crest the hill in front of the Andersons' old house. Outside the passenger window, 920 Hanson Road blurred by, and I had just enough time to think: *Who's going to shovel the driveway tomorrow morning?* before I was pumping my brakes on the downward slope of the hill.

Five minutes later, I was following a snowplow west on Route 40, finally headed home, the lights of Edgewood fading away in my rearview mirror.

Richard Chizmar

LEFT: *Cemetery Dance #1 cover*
(Photo courtesy of the author)

ABOVE: The culvert on Hornbeam Road where Mel Fullerton shot and killed Ronnie Finley *(Photo courtesy of the author)*

fourteen

April 2, 1989

". . . remained unsolved."

On Sunday, April 2, 1989, exactly ten months from the night fifteen-year-old Natasha Gallagher disappeared from her bedroom and her battered body was discovered in the woods behind her house, Detective Lyle Harper stood on the front steps of the Harford County Court-house and addressed members of the media. The detective spoke for five-and-a-half minutes and took no questions when he was finished.

The news he shared that afternoon was as disheartening as it was brief: DNA analysis was still in its infancy—the first case to utilize DNA evidence to secure a conviction had just recently occurred in July 1987—and as a result, only a handful of labs were set up for proper test-ing. The current average waiting period for test results was three to five months. In addition, there was no national DNA database in existence.

After a four-and-a-half-month wait, the results had come back earlier in March. No DNA profile matches had been found for the traces of blood that members of the state police had discovered at the Cassidy Burch crime scene. The task force—comprised of members of the Harford County Sheriff's Department, Maryland State Police, and

Federal Bureau of Investigation—promised to continue pursuing active leads and testing additional persons of interest. The tip-line remained open.

The murders of Natasha Gallagher, Kacey Robinson, Madeline Wilcox, and Cassidy Burch—all residents of Edgewood—remained unsolved.

September 2019

1

It's a postcard-perfect early fall afternoon, and I'm cutting the lawn on my riding mower, trying to get as close to the edge of the pond as possible without going in—which has happened before; only once, but trust me, that was enough—when I feel my cell phone vibrate in my pocket. I slide it out and glance at the screen: CARLY ALBRIGHT.

It's been a while since we've last spoken—at least a month, maybe longer—so I stop the mower and cut the engine. A couple of geese honk their approval from across the pond.

"Hello?"

Carly says something in that sassy tone of voice of hers, but I can't understand. My ears are buzzing from the sudden silence, and she's talking too fast. I try again.

"Hello? Carly?"

". . . him!"

"One more time, sorry. I'm outside and—"

"They caught him!"

"Who?"

"*They caught him!*" she repeats, yelling now. "*They caught the Boogeyman!*"

2

I t's been so long since I've heard that name spoken out loud it takes a moment for it to register. A low-budget horror film with that same title went straight to VOD not long ago, and I ran across some ads and a trailer for it online, but other than that, it's been ages.

It's hard to believe that more than thirty years have passed since the Boogeyman's reign of terror in my hometown of Edgewood—but the calendar doesn't lie, no matter how much we may want it to.

A lot has changed over three decades, but some things have remained the same.

Kara and I are still together and going stronger than ever, mostly due to the magnificence of her heart and a bottomless well of patience and understanding. Along the way, we've been blessed with two sons, grown now—Billy, age twenty-one, named after my father; and Noah, age seventeen, named after a dear friend and one of Kara's favorite physical therapy patients, a great and gentle man who once stormed the beach at Normandy and, through acts of unimaginable bravery, saved the lives of many other great men on that historic day.

In the fall and spring, Billy attends Colby College in Maine—about an hour away from our friend Stephen King's house—where he studies English and writing and plays lacrosse. Noah's a high school junior and a math whiz and is already committed to playing lacrosse at Marquette University after graduation. During the summer, we're all together in a two-hundred-year-old refurbished farmhouse we recently purchased in Bel Air, Maryland. The property has a pond and a creek and open fields and woods, and although it's only been a couple of years, it feels like we've been here forever.

I only wish my mother and father could've lived long enough to see it. They would've loved every inch of the place. My mom would've spent hours sitting on the back porch, watching the turtles chase each other in the pond and the hawks circling overhead. She would've adored the many gardens. My dad would've been fascinated with the centuries-old architecture, especially the two-hundred-year-old logs somehow holding up the ceiling in our stone basement, and we would've had to drag him out of the four-car garage every night to come inside for dinner.

It was always the plan to have them come and live with us once they reached their golden years, but you know the old saying about God and making plans. My mother has been gone since February 2001. My father left to be with her six years later on July 7, 2007. I think about and miss them every single day.

Kara's father is also greatly missed, gone just a handful of years now, but her ninety-one-year-old mother is still with us, living in an in-law suite on the first floor of our new home. Much like her youngest daughter, she's feisty and stubborn and full of life, and I think she likes it here with Kara and me and her grandsons. At least I hope she does. We count our blessings every day for this time with her.

Of course, we haven't always been so fortunate and, over the years, we've had to say farewell to a number of cherished loved ones: my eldest sister Rita passed away not long after this book was originally published; my uncle Ted, still one of the finest and funniest men I've ever known; Craig Anderson, my buddy Brian's younger brother; Bernie and Norma Gentile; Michael Meredith; and my old friend Detective Lyle Harper. All of them gone now, but not forgotten.

I came pretty close myself at one time. At the age of twenty-nine, I was diagnosed with testicular cancer. The doctors acted immediately and took care of business over two successful surgeries. When all was said and done, they told me I fell squarely into the 99th percentile for no recurrence of the cancer. With those odds, and a month or so of recovery time under my belt, I felt as good as new. But thank goodness I'm not a betting man, because boy did they get that wrong. Six months later, after experiencing severe pain in my stomach and lower back, and undergoing a lengthy series of scans and X-rays, those same doctors discovered the cancer had returned with a vengeance, spreading to both of my lungs, liver, stomach, and lymph nodes. They immediately scheduled twelve weeks of intensive chemotherapy and gave me a 50 percent chance of survival, barely bothering to disguise the fact that they'd exaggerated those odds in an attempt to keep me encouraged and in the fight.

But they needn't have worried. With my family and friends at my side every step of the way, and God watching over me—yes, I *do* believe He had a hand in my recovery, and yes, I do know my mom is smiling down on me as I type these words—I somehow managed to once again beat the odds. This past July marked twenty-five years of living cancer-free.

Even now, many friends tell me they believe I was saved so that one day I could become a successful writer and share my stories with the world. I always thank them for the kindness and counter with the same response: I believe I was saved so that one day I could become a father to my two boys.

After more than a decade of living in cramped apartments and eating ramen noodles or peanut butter sandwiches for dinner and scrounging loose change from the sofa cushions or floor mats in the car, almost all of the big dreams that originated inside my heart during those early days in Edgewood finally came true. My little magazine, *Cemetery Dance*, is now in its thirty-second year of publication. In 1991 we bit the bullet and expanded the press to include a hardcover book imprint. To date, we've released more than four hundred books. I've written and sold nearly one hundred short stories of my own, as well as a number of books, including *Gwendy's Button Box*, a cautionary dark fairy tale, co-written with Stephen King. Shortly after the book's publication, a reporter asked if I'd ever dreamed I would one day write a book with Stephen King. I smiled and looked him in the eye and told the simple truth: "I've always been a dreamer, but I never ever dreamed that big."

I know exactly how blessed I've been—and continue to be—and not a single day passes that I don't feel an overwhelming sense of gratitude and wonder. If I'm being completely honest, I'm still not sure how it all happened. A lot of luck, a lot of hard work, and the unwavering support and love of a lot of amazing people—that's my best guess.

3

The house is silent by the time I get inside. Kara left an hour ago to run errands, and the boys are away at school. Down the hall, my mother-in-law is napping in her bedroom. Her door is closed. I've forgotten to take my boots off, and as I walk into the family room, I leave a trail of cut grass on the hardwood floor behind me. Sitting down on the sofa, I pick up the remote control from the coffee table. My hands are shaking. Remembering what Carly Albright told me right before we ended our call—and ignoring the near constant vibration of my cell phone inside my pocket—I click on the television and turn to CNN.

The reporter is young and fit with chiseled cheekbones and a hint of dark roots showing in her blow-dried blond hair. The chyron at the bottom of the screen reads: LAURIE WYATT, CNN—HANOVER, PENNSYLVANIA. A banner headline in red lettering runs across the upper right corner of the screen: "THE BOOGEYMAN" IN CUSTODY. Beneath it is the image of a person I do not recognize.

". . . to recap this afternoon's breaking news, members of both the Pennsylvania and Maryland State Police executed a search warrant on a residential home in the 1600 block of Evergreen Way in Hanover,

Pennsylvania, and took fifty-four-year-old Joshua Gallagher into custody, charging him with the 1988 murders of four Edgewood, Maryland, teenagers, including his younger sister, Natasha.

"According to a police spokesperson, Gallagher, a longtime employee of Reuter's Machinery, had been under surveillance for an undisclosed amount of time, while police awaited the results of a DNA test . . ."

4

The 1990 publication of *Chasing the Boogeyman: A True Story of Small-Town Evil* remains, to this day, an oddity in my career. The only nonfiction book I've ever written, it sold a total of 2,650 copies before going out of print in 1995—far from a bestseller, but not abysmal numbers, either, for a small regional publisher that regularly released books about duck decoys and lighthouses.

Over the years, I've seen a handful of copies surface on eBay, usually with broken bindings and tattered dust jackets, selling for not much more than the original cover price. I did, however, once witness a mint signed edition go for a tad over $150 dollars from a well-known online bookseller.

The book still has a small but dedicated group of fans—my oldest son, Billy, adores the damn thing; the page margins in his personal copy are filled with scribbled notes—but I'm not one of them. The story brings back too many painful memories.

The late, great *Locus* and *Rocky Mountain News* book reviewer, Ed Bryant, once wrote: "As the sweltering days of summer passed, Chizmar not only found himself increasingly haunted by the story of his hometown Boogeyman, he found himself actually becoming an integral character in the story, a willing and unafraid participant. As such, when the inevitable time came to sit down and put pen to paper, Chizmar valiantly chose the more difficult, yet infinitely more intimate point of view from which to tell the tale: his own. And through those piercing, at times naive eyes, readers get an earnest and honest snapshot of time and place and conscience that is hard to turn away from."

I suspect that Ed's overly generous review was responsible for selling a large percentage of those 2,650 copies. I also suspect he was in a very kind and charitable mood the day he sat down at his keyboard to write that review. Looking back, I didn't so much choose *any* authorial point of view when it came down to the writing of *Chasing the Boogeyman*; I simply told the story the only way I knew how.

Earlier this week, when my literary agent called with the surprising news that multiple publishers had inquired about an updated version of *Chasing the Boogeyman*, I was tempted to immediately sit at my desk and tackle a complete rewrite. Instead, I gave it some thought and decided that Ed Bryant was right about at least one thing: the story I chose to tell back in 1988 was a snapshot of time and place, as honest and well-crafted as that young writer was capable of performing. And even now, that's good enough for me. As a result, while I've revised large sections of the original manuscript to make for an easier reading experience, I've left the heart and soul of the story alone. Warts and all, as they say.

One final note regarding the original 1990 edition, a curious aside that never fails to bring a smile to my face: the book's initial publication made unlikely heroes of two of my favorite people—my mother and Carly Albright. To this day, I continue to be approached by readers at bookstore signings and appearances and asked if I might have any photographs of my adorable mother to share. As for Carly, she was so flooded with date requests for almost a year after the book's publication that she eventually had to change her phone number. Of course, she bitched and moaned and blamed me for the inconvenience, but I'm pretty sure she enjoyed every damn minute of it.

5

Speaking of Carly Albright, even with her big promotion and pay raise—not to mention her pager—she didn't last very long at the *Aegis*. By her twenty-seventh birthday, she was one of the *Baltimore Sun's* most widely read columnists. From there, she moved on to the *Philadelphia Inquirer* and, after a brief but unhappy stint at *Vanity Fair*, she settled in at the *Washington Post*, where she still works as a senior writer. Carly's personal life was equally prosperous. While in her early thirties, she joined a book club and, at the inaugural gathering, met a very nice man named Walter Scroggins. The two were instantly smitten with each other. Walter, bald and bespectacled, was a former professional football player who now ran a successful physical therapy practice in Rockville, Maryland. A gentle giant, he was kind and funny and never read the newspaper, a habit he'd developed during his playing days. Following a whirlwind, six-month romance, Carly and Walter got married and went on to raise three lovely daughters, each one more stubborn and sassy than the last.

After telling me to go inside and turn on CNN, Carly promises to call back as soon as she has more details, and hangs up on me. It takes her three long hours to eventually make good on that promise, but I never doubt her for a second. After all these years, she's yet to let me down. For the next forty-five minutes, she reads from her extensive notes. This is what she tells me:

Lieutenant Clara McClernan is the detective in charge of cold case files at the Maryland State Police Department. She's closed a number of high-profile murder cases during her years on the street and is known as a thorough and relentless investigator. At some point, she becomes interested in the Boogeyman. She knows of Detective Lyle Harper from reviewing many of his past case reports and listening to the usual talk around the barracks. She respects his body of work and very much enjoys his company the handful of times they meet before his death in

March 2019. Up until his retirement fifteen years earlier—and even after that, if he was being honest—Detective Harper had never stopped thinking about the murders of the four Edgewood girls and the serial killer who evaded justice almost supernaturally for all these years. The last items to be removed from his bulletin board on the day he left his office for the final time were photographs of Natasha Gallagher, Kacey Robinson, Madeline Wilcox, and Cassidy Burch. When asked by Lieutenant McClernan, he was only too happy to hand over his stack of personal notepads involving the open case.

And buried deep inside one of those small spiral pads, McClernan uncovers the first loose thread—and yanks on it.

Following the death of Natasha Gallagher on June 2, 1988, none of the immediate family members were swabbed for DNA. The initial reason for this oversight was the overwhelming nature of the crime. Edgewood was a small town not really prone to such violence—a home abduction that turned into a murder involving mutilation and a posed body was unheard of, and police were scrambling to cover the appropriate bases. The second reason the family was never swabbed at the time of the murder is because of how utterly distraught they were, especially the girl's father. Detective Harper even scribbled a note in that regard: "Need follow-up DNA on dad/mom/brother, but family needs time."

For whatever reasons—perhaps because detectives failed to turn up even a hint of evidence at the Gallagher crime scenes or simply a matter of police oversight—the subject wasn't broached again until the day after the June 20, 1988, murder of Kacey Robinson. At that time, after directing the swabbing of the Robinson family, Detective Harper ordered members of the Harford County Sheriff's Department to follow through with taking samples from the three members of the Gallagher family. On Friday, June 24, a sheriff's deputy swabbed Mr. and Mrs. Gallagher at their home on Hawthorne Drive. The same deputy noted, in his report, that he was unsuccessful in his attempt to attain a sample from Joshua Gallagher because the young man was working off-site, making lumber deliveries all day. Phone messages were left at both his residence and place of employment, directing Mr. Gallagher to return the call in order to set up a brief appointment to be swabbed.

And that is the last mention of it that Lieutenant McClernan is able to find anywhere. As a result, it goes on "her list."

That list grows daily, comprised of black holes and dusty forgotten corners of the investigation that she knows for certain have already been checked and rechecked any number of times, but that's what the cold case grind comes down to. Doing the work again with brand-new eyes and ears. Searching for not only what might've been missed the first time around, but also what might've been viewed in a different light. *Change the light in the room*, she's fond of saying, *and you never know what you might see.*

The number one item on Lieutenant McClernan's list is re-examining a theory that none of the media were privy to back in 1988—the suspicion that the Boogeyman might've been a member of law enforcement. This notion would go a long way toward explaining the lack of a struggle in Natasha Gallagher's bedroom, as well as no cries for help in the other three cases. A Maryland state trooper, Michael Moore (no relation to the award-winning documentary director), had been singled out as a potential suspect. At the time of the murders, he was twice divorced and living off the beaten track in the backwoods of Harford County. Over a period of seven years, several of Moore's ex-girlfriends had called police to report physical and sexual abuse, but then subsequently refused to press charges. Moore was also a decent physical match for the police sketch of the Boogeyman, and there was some underlying confusion about the validity of his DNA profile. Knowing better than to get excited this early in the game, the lieutenant makes a series of phone calls and does some digging. What she comes up with is disappointing, yet not surprising. In April 2001, Moore was arrested for false imprisonment and rape, and is currently serving prison time in Cumberland, Maryland. His DNA profile was updated at the time of his trial and does not match the blood trace left behind at the Cassidy Burch crime scene.

After scratching Moore's name off her list, the lieutenant moves on to item number two: a sheriff's deputy named Harold Foster, who was forced to turn in his badge in 1998 because of drug and theft charges in Baltimore City. Foster's ex-wife, a longtime resident of Fallston, had told her divorce attorney at the time that she wouldn't have been surprised if Foster was responsible for the murders of the three girls in Edgewood (this was prior to the death of Cassidy Burch). According to the ex, Foster had violent sexual fantasies involving choking and biting and didn't have an alibi for any of the three nights in question. Her lawyer relayed the information to a cop friend, and it was deemed good enough to be sent up the chain and entered into a file and investigated. However, a month later, when the DNA sample was discovered at the cemetery, there was no subsequent mention of a follow-up analysis involving Foster's DNA. It had, most likely, just slipped through the cracks. Unfortunately, a series of quick phone calls clears up the issue for Lieutenant McClernan, providing evidence that testing had, in fact, been administered with no match found, effectively eliminating Foster.

Items numbered three through seven on the list are relatively minor in comparison and take only forty-eight hours for the lieutenant to go through. Still, she isn't discouraged. The list is long and still growing. She has time.

So now she comes to item number eight: Joshua Gallagher and the question of his missing DNA sample. She starts by taking a closer look at his alibi. On the night of his sister's murder, Joshua is with Frank Hapney, a co-worker and former classmate. They spend the evening drinking at Loughlin's Pub until approximately 10:00 p.m. and then return to Hapney's Edgewood Road apartment. Once there, they watch television and continue drinking until almost midnight. Joshua leaves at that time and goes home, arriving at his town house around 12:15 a.m.

Considering Natasha Gallagher's estimated time of death, the timeline provided by Joshua Gallagher's alibi is tight—not to mention difficult to verify—but the lieutenant isn't overly concerned. Joshua Gallagher has no priors, no complaints, and is by all accounts a loving son and brother. He's never once appeared on any list of suspects.

As if to prove her point, she opens another folder and stares at Gallagher's twenty-two-year-old face. Compares it to a photocopy of the Boogeyman police sketch. They look nothing alike. Plus, there's this: on the night of her close call, Annie Riggs claimed the killer was a large man—at least six feet tall, muscular and strong. Joshua Gallagher stands five foot, nine inches tall and weighs one-hundred-and-sixty pounds.

Having already run a background check on Gallagher weeks earlier when she first added his name to the list, Lieutenant McClernan knows he's now married with two teenage sons, and lives and works in Hanover, Pennsylvania. He coaches his boys' travel baseball teams during the summer, throws darts in a league on Saturday nights, and is an avid hunter. He seems to have made a decent life for himself. Next, she runs a check on Frank Hapney, just in case she decides she wants to talk with him. No police record. Still lives in Edgewood in a rented house on Willoughby Beach Road. Works full-time at Lowe's Hardware in Bel Air.

Then she looks up the parents, Russell and Catherine Gallagher. She's dismayed to find that Mr. Gallagher committed suicide in early 1989, but once again she's not terribly surprised. Divorce and suicide are all too common among parental survivors of adolescent murder victims. Once feelings of guilt and blame enter the picture, it's difficult to find the way back. And sometimes the other person's simple presence is too painful a reminder of what has been lost. According to the computer file, Mrs. Gallagher is seventy-three years old and still living on Hawthorne Drive in Edgewood. She has never remarried.

Shuffling through Detective Harper's notepads and a stack of old reports, the lieutenant comes across a scattering of handwritten notes regarding Joshua Gallagher. In the first one, Detective Harper mentions that Gallagher only attended three semesters of college in Pennsylvania before returning home to Edgewood. A reason for his early departure is not listed. *Something else to check out*, the lieutenant thinks, and adds it to the list within the list. The second note concerns Gallagher's place of employment at the time of his sister's murder—Andersen's Hardware on Route 40 between Edgewood and Joppatowne. It's no longer open for business, but she knows the store well because her father was once an active woodworker and often purchased lumber and tools from there. Remembering Joshua Gallagher's claim that he was busy delivering lumber on the day his parents were swabbed, the lieutenant jots down a note of her own to check out what kind of vehicles the employees used for such deliveries. It's been over thirty years, but someone has to remember.

The lieutenant places her pen down on the yellow legal pad she's nearly filled and sits back in her chair, face etched in concentration. There was a bad accident ninety minutes earlier on Route 24—a convertible Mustang crossed the center line and collided with a dump truck carrying a full load of gravel—and the barracks is bustling with activity. The lieutenant notices none of it. A moment later, she leans forward, picks up the pen again, and scribbles a single hurried sentence at the bottom of the page: *Natasha Gallagher—first victim and only girl not to be sexually assaulted.* She makes a point to underline *only*. It's an observation that Detective Harper had highlighted numerous times in his notes, but she suddenly feels the itch to dig deeper.

Finally ready to get started in earnest, Lieutenant McClernan picks up the telephone on her desk and dials Joshua Gallagher's house. An answering machine picks up after the third ring and she hangs up. Next, she tries his cell phone—one ring and straight to voice mail. This time, she leaves her name and number and asks Gallagher to get back to her.

To her surprise, he calls back five minutes later. She explains to Gallagher that she's taking another look at his sister's case, as well as the other three murders from 1988. She never once mentions the missing

DNA sample. Soft-spoken and rather awkward, Gallagher sounds stunned that the case is still open. He sounds even more stunned a few minutes later when the lieutenant asks if she can meet with him at his earliest convenience, making it clear that she's willing to make the drive north to Hanover. Without missing a beat, Gallagher tells the detective that he's more than happy to come down to Maryland and meet with her, but it'll have to be the following week; it's smallmouth season and he has a four-day fishing trip planned on the Susquehanna. After making plans to meet at the barracks the following Wednesday at 11:00 a.m., Detective McClernan thanks him for his time and they hang up.

Her next call is to Catherine Gallagher, Joshua's mother. She answers on the first ring, and by 2:00 p.m. that same afternoon, the lieutenant is sitting in the elderly woman's living room, a cup of hot tea in front of her, surrounded by dozens of Hummel figurines and three long-haired cats. Lieutenant McClernan opens the conversation by asking about Natasha, and then as is often the case, she just sits there and listens. Mrs. Gallagher is only too pleased to talk about her daughter's smile and messy bedroom and how she was training to one day try out for the U.S. gymnastics team and the Olympics. She tells the lieutenant all about Natasha's plans to take acting classes in college and move to New York City after graduation. Then she takes out a thick photo album from a drawer underneath the coffee table—her once-happy life frozen in time under laminated pages—and invites Lieutenant McClernan to join her on the sofa to look through it.

Spotting a photo of a young Joshua Gallagher straddling a motorcycle in the driveway, the lieutenant seizes the opportunity to steer the conversation in his direction. Upon hearing her son's name, Mrs. Gallagher immediately points to a photograph on the mantel. Her grandsons, she explains. Andrew and Phillip. They live in Pennsylvania but visit regularly with Joshua and his lovely wife, Samantha. The lieutenant takes a sip of tea and eases into a question about Joshua's time at Penn State. A few minutes later, she has her answers.

Joshua attended college on a wrestling scholarship, but shortly after injuring his shoulder, he decided that the rigors of being a Division One student-athlete were too time-consuming and stressful for his type A personality. After many sleepless nights, he quit the wrestling team and focused on his studies. Soon after, he picked up a part-time warehouse job to help with tuition payments. He also met a girl. Her name was Anna and she came from a wealthy family in the New York suburbs. For a time, they were inseparable. Then, before they knew it, it was the end of the spring semester and time to return to their respective home-towns for the summer. Joshua wanted to remain in Happy Valley to work and rent an apartment for the two of them to share. Anna didn't— she missed her family and wanted to spend the summer at the shore with them. Joshua wasn't happy, but they visited each other over the break and managed to make it work. Until the fall, when they both re-turned to campus, and a restless Joshua figured he'd had enough and it was time to see other people. Anna was utterly crushed. Unable to sleep or focus on her classwork, she eventually dropped out and returned to New York shortly before the Christmas break. Not long after, a de-pressed Joshua called home and explained to his parents that college wasn't really in the cards for him. He was ready to just find a real job and get started on his life. His parents were disappointed, of course, but ultimately supported his decision.

Now, at last, the lieutenant transitions to her final subject of the af-ternoon: Mr. Gallagher. Taking special care to be as sensitive as possible, she asks Mrs. Gallagher about her late husband's state of mind follow-ing the loss of their daughter. As Mrs. Gallagher responds at length, Lieutenant McClernan takes copious notes: "At first, he was completely bereft, unable to function. We considered admitting him into the hospi-tal, but by the morning of Natasha's funeral, he seemed to rebound. We went to therapy together for a long time afterward and it seemed to be working. He was getting better, I'm sure of it. He even started playing golf again on the weekends. Then it all went downhill again. He began to have trouble sleeping, and then he started drinking every night to help him sleep, but that didn't work either. It just made him angrier. I don't know what set it off again, but it had to be something. He . . . changed. I tried to talk to him about it, but he wouldn't let me in. And then he stopped going to counseling. Finally, as a last resort, I made plans to be away from the house one evening after dinner, and I sent Josh over to talk with him. But it didn't help. He was furious that I went behind his back, and if anything, it got even worse after that. A few days later . . . he was gone. And in all these years, I've never figured out what was behind that whole downward slide of his."

On her way back to the barracks—red-eyed and sneezing, thanks to Mrs. Gallagher's demon cats—the lieutenant calls information and gets the number for Penn State University's administration office. Expecting to reach an answering service this late in the afternoon, she's pleasantly surprised when a cheerful-sounding woman answers the phone. The lieutenant explains what she's after and is promptly transferred to the registrar's office. An equally cheerful woman takes down Joshua Gallagher's name and social security number, as well as the lieutenant's cell number, and promises to get back to her as soon as she locates the requested information.

About to toss her cell phone onto the passenger seat and call it a day, Lieutenant McClernan changes her mind and punches in Frank Hapney's home number, the only one she has on file for him. It's 4:55 p.m., so she figures she has a fifty-fifty chance of catching him. This time she comes up a winner—Hapney picks up, and it sounds like he's been drinking.

Five minutes later, she has everything she needs.

Frank Hapney hasn't seen or spoken with Joshua Gallagher in over a decade. He vaguely remembers the night of Natasha Gallagher's murder and recalls speaking to the police later that week to verify Josh's alibi, but he tells the lieutenant the same thing now that he told the detectives back then: He had too much to drink that night and passed out.

He *thinks* he remembers Josh leaving around midnight, but it could've been a lot earlier or even a lot later. There's just no way for him to be certain, especially after all these years. Finally, Lieutenant McClernan asks Hapney about Andersen's Hardware and the eighteen months he and Joshua worked there together. "That's right," Hapney says, slurring his words. "I was pretty new, but Josh had already been there for a while when I first started, and he handled a lot of the deliveries. Some nights, he drove home one of those flatbed trucks with the metal side railings you can adjust, and other nights he took home a panel van. It all depended on what kind of load he was carrying that day."

Lieutenant McClernan falls asleep that night feeling good about number eight on her list. After all, there's not a single thing about Joshua Gallagher that fits the Boogeyman's profile—he's too young at the time of the murders, lives in a town house with neighbors on either side of him, has no known ties to three of the four victims, and looks nothing like the police sketch of the killer. Plus, sororicide—the act of killing one's own sister—is extremely rare when it comes to modern-age serial killers. If the lieutenant's investigation continues in this current direction, then Joshua Gallagher will most likely prove an easy scratch-off, and she'll move on to number nine on her list.

And yet . . . a number of troubling issues have arisen with number eight that just won't leave her alone.

There's the lack of a DNA sample, a questionable alibi, girl troubles, and easy access to a panel van. Not nearly enough to set off her internal alarm system, but definitely enough to sound a couple of loud, sporadic beeps. At the very least, an interesting pattern is beginning to emerge, and Lieutenant McClernan believes the next week or so will provide all the answers she's looking for.

But, as fate would have it, it happens even quicker than that.

Two days later, Jennifer Schall, an administrator from Penn State University, returns McClernan's phone call—and the lieutenant learns the truth about Joshua Gallagher's early exit from college. After a stalking and harassment complaint was filed against Joshua in October 1985 by his ex-girlfriend Anna Garfield—who had broken up with Joshua, and not the other way around—he was placed on probation by the university and warned not to contact her again. When Ms. Garfield filed a second complaint in early December 1985, accusing him of breaking into her dorm room and vandalizing her personal belongings—an incident captured on video by the dorm's hallway security cameras—Joshua Gallagher was summarily expelled from school and permanently barred from the university grounds. Campus security personnel asked Ms. Garfield if she'd like them to contact local police, but she declined and signed a release form stating as such. Because he was eighteen and considered a legal adult, the administration office didn't bother to call Gallagher's parents. A curt one-page letter of dismissal was mailed to the house.

Interesting, Lieutenant McClernan thinks. *After all these years, is Catherine Gallagher lying to protect her son? Or does she still not know the actual truth?*

The lieutenant thanks Jennifer Schall for the information and asks if Penn State keeps past student photos on file—perhaps from old yearbooks or student ID cards. She'd like to take a good look at Anna Garfield's photograph. Jennifer says she'll have to check and promises to get back to her.

After giving Jennifer her email address and ending the call, the lieutenant immediately dials Reuter's Machinery in Hanover and asks to speak with Joshua Gallagher's supervisor. She realizes it's a delicate situation, and the last thing she wants to do is spook Gallagher, but her internal alarm is starting to beep a little louder now, and she needs to know the answer to one important question. After an almost five-minute hold, a gruff-sounding man picks up the extension. The lieutenant explains who she is and claims that she has an important question for Joshua Gallagher regarding his sister's case. She understands he's not at work today, but she's wondering if they might know where she can reach him. The lieutenant isn't at all shocked by the supervisor's answer—and the volume of the alarm bells inside her head immediately cranks up another notch. It seems that Joshua Gallagher isn't fishing for small-mouth on the Susquehanna, after all. In fact, he didn't even bother to call in and take off work until earlier this very morning, when he complained that he was suffering from a severe bout of diarrhea and a temperature of 101.

The lieutenant hangs up the phone and pulls out a manila folder containing Mr. and Mrs. Gallagher's DNA profiles. Staring at the thirty-year-old printouts, she thinks back to the conversation in Catherine Gallagher's living room and something that the older woman had said while paging through the photo album. The comment had struck the lieutenant as rather odd, but she didn't say anything at the time because she didn't want to interrupt the flow of the discussion. She knew from years of hard-won experience that once you stopped someone in the midst of talking about a particularly difficult subject, it was often impossible to get them started again.

The lieutenant picks up the phone, locates the number she's looking for in her notepad, and punches it in. Catherine Gallagher answers after the second ring and sounds genuinely pleased to hear from her. After exchanging pleasantries, Lieutenant McClernan gets right to it.

"I was going through my notes earlier this morning," she says, "and I came across a couple of things I wanted to clarify."

"Of course. Anything I can do to help."

She starts with a throwaway. "You mentioned that your daughter planned to take acting classes in college and move away after she graduated. I know you mentioned where, but I didn't write it down. Was it New York or Los Angeles?"

"Oh, it was New York," Mrs. Gallagher says, a wistful tone seeping into her voice. "She always wanted to star in a Broadway play."

"That's right. I remember now. Thank you."

"You're very welcome."

"I just have one more question for you, Mrs. Gallagher. When you were showing me photographs of your son and daughter, you commented a couple of times about their close resemblance to each other. I believe the word you used was 'uncanny.'"

There's a lengthy pause before the older woman answers, and when she finally does, her voice sounds different. "Oh . . . did I say that?"

"Yes, ma'am, you did. I even wrote it down in my notebook because it struck me as odd. The first time you mentioned it was after you showed me a photo of the two of them at the beach. They were very young, and I believe they were building a sandcastle. The second time was when we were looking at a photograph your husband took during a family visit to Penn State."

"I'm afraid I don't remember. I'm sorry."

"That's okay, Mrs. Gallagher." The lieutenant shuffles some papers to make it sound like she's busy. "So, before I go, the question I have for you is this, and I need you to be honest with me. It's very important right now that you tell me the truth."

"Okay." Voice barely a whisper.

"Your son, Joshua . . . he was adopted, wasn't he?"

The lieutenant hears a sharp intake of air on the other end of the line, and knows that her hunch is right.

"Are you okay, Mrs. Gallagher?"

"It was my husband's decision not to tell Josh."

Lieutenant McClernan sits up in her chair and waits for Mrs. Gallagher to continue.

"He didn't want Josh to feel like an outsider once he grew up. He wanted him to feel like part of the family. And then, a few years later, when Natasha came along—a miracle baby, the doctors called her—and the two of them looked so much alike, it became even easier to keep the secret."

"No one else knows?"

"My sister and an aunt and uncle back in South Carolina, but that's it."

"Joshua still doesn't know?"

"No." Starting to cry now. "We just wanted him to be happy . . ."

After getting off the phone, Lieutenant McClernan scribbles *Adopted—there would be no familial match* along the bottom of Mrs. Gallagher's DNA printout and returns it to the manila folder. She tosses it onto her desk and spends the rest of the morning going over Detective Harper's notebooks. She's already done this a half-dozen times, but thinks one more time can't hurt. A few minutes past noon, she receives an email from Jennifer Schall at Penn State. A faded color photograph is attached. The lieutenant stares at the photo, heart and alarm bells thumping, and thinks, *No wonder Josh was so hung up on her.* Anna Garfield is a beautiful young woman with big brown eyes, full lips, a delicate aristocratic nose, and long, shimmering chestnut hair that falls well past her shoulders.

Bingo.

The lieutenant gets up from her desk and knocks on Captain Bradford's office door. Quickly filling him in on all the details, she leaves her captain to contact the sheriff in Harford County and returns to her desk to call the York County detective squad. York, as well as nearby Lancaster and Adams Counties, comes up a zero. No known teenage girls with long hair have been strangled to death over the past ten years. No severed ears or bite marks or posed crime scenes.

But once the detectives expand the search to include an additional half-dozen counties, they immediately get a hit.

Two years ago, to the northwest in Juniata County, the body of a seventeen-year-old girl with long blond hair was found strangled to death. The victim, Sheila Rafferty, had what resembled a single bite mark on her left shoulder, but the coroner couldn't be certain because the girl had been in the river for so long. Fishermen had stumbled upon her body in shallow water along the rocky banks of the Susquehanna.

Things are clicking into place now. And fast.

When Joshua Gallagher arrives at the Maryland State Police

barracks two days later, he's already the subject of around-the-clock surveillance. He doesn't make a move without detectives knowing exactly what he's doing. Lieutenant McClernan greets Gallagher in the lobby and invites him to sit in the lone chair in front of her desk. They speak for approximately thirty minutes. The lieutenant's demeanor is relaxed and friendly. She asks no difficult questions. Gallagher slumps in his seat, almost appearing to be bored at times. His voice is steady, his responses brief and to the point. At one point, he actually yawns.

A few minutes before they wrap it up, the lieutenant begins to fidget with a small hoop earring dangling from her left ear. Across the room, Detective Janet Ellis sees this signal and immediately gets up from her desk, carrying a manila file folder. Her long brown hair cascades halfway down her back, a clear violation of department regulations. She approaches Lieutenant McClernan's desk and, flashing Joshua Gallagher a friendly smile, says, "Sorry to interrupt, Lieutenant, but here's the file you asked for."

"Thanks so much, Anna," the lieutenant responds, taking the folder.

Joshua Gallagher immediately scoots upright in his chair and struggles to avert his eyes from Detective Ellis as she makes her way back to her desk. Lieutenant McClernan opens the folder and pretends to read what's inside. Peering over the top of the file, she watches the struggle on Gallagher's face. After another thirty seconds or so, she closes the folder and finishes up the conversation.

As Joshua Gallagher walks across the barracks parking lot, Lieutenant McClernan sits behind her desk, staring at the armrests of the chair Gallagher just vacated—and the glistening sheen of perspiration he left behind. Slipping on gloves, the lieutenant gets up, sliding a swab out of the sterile tube in which it's stored, and takes careful samples from each of the armrests.

6

There will be no trial. No flashing cameras outside the courthouse. No dramatic televised proceedings. No daily glimpses of the monster. The Boogeyman. Joshua Gallagher.

He admits all of it, and then some. The four Edgewood girls in 1988, including his own sister, and three others—one in 2001 in western Maryland, and two more in 2006 and 2018 in Pennsylvania.

And the police believe there are even more.

7

On Monday, December 2, 2019, I'm sitting behind my desk in my home office, printing the day's pages, when my cell phone begins to ring. I glance at the caller ID: MD STATE POL. Curious, I answer. "Hello?"

"Is this Richard Chizmar?" A woman's voice.

"Yes, it is. Who's calling?"

"This is Lieutenant McClernan, Maryland State Police."

"I know who you are," I say. "I've seen a lot of you lately."

She laughs. Not a cheerful sound. "I'm pretty sick of myself, too."

"I didn't mean that at all."

"Listen," she says, getting right to it. "I have an unusual proposition to run by you."

"What's that?"

"It's my understanding that you're writing a new book about the Joshua Gallagher case."

"Is that a question?" I ask, unsure of where this is going.

"No."

I wait for more, but she doesn't say anything. "I've been offered a contract to revise the original manuscript and write a new afterword."

"Good for you," she says, sounding like she means it. "I hope you haven't signed the contract yet."

"Why's that?"

"Because I think there's a much bigger payday in your future."

"And why's that?"

"Because Joshua Gallagher wants to talk to you—and only you."

8

The ground rules are simple. I'm not to take anything into the room with me. No paper or writing instrument, no recording devices of any kind. The interview will be video- and audiotaped by the police, and I will have full access to the unedited footage. In addition to my list of questions, the police will supply me with a handful of their own. I retain all print rights to the interview. The video footage, however, remains the sole property of the Maryland State Police. For the duration of the interview, Joshua Gallagher will remain in leg and arm restraints. An armed guard will remain in the room with us at all times. I have sixty minutes to conduct the interview.

9

Interview Date: Thursday, December 5, 2019

Time: 1:30 p.m.

Location: Maryland Penitentiary, Baltimore, MD

[Joshua Gallagher looks nothing like the quietly confident, athletic teenager with whom I attended high school. The years have not been kind to him. He's overweight and unshaven. His mild expression remains unchanged as the guards seat him on the other side of the table. Smelling of perspiration and industrial-strength laundry detergent, he appears neither pleased nor displeased to see me. His right eye suffers from a slight tic. He nervously taps his foot on the floor, jiggling the length of chain that binds his ankles. He doesn't look at all like a man who has admitted to killing seven young women.]

RICHARD CHIZMAR: Why me, Josh? Why am I here?

JOSHUA GALLAGHER: A number of reasons. [clears throat] I've followed your career with great interest. You've done well. I even rented *Road House 2* on Redbox. I've also never forgotten that you came to my sister's funeral.

CHIZMAR: Half the town went to Natasha's funeral.

GALLAGHER: You were there for all of it. You became part of it.

CHIZMAR: When exactly did I become part of it?

GALLAGHER: When you and your reporter friend began questioning half the town. When you started keeping a scrapbook about the murders.

CHIZMAR: I see you read the book.

GALLAGHER: Of course I did.

CHIZMAR: I assume you're the one who started calling my apartment and hanging up on me the week the book was published?

GALLAGHER: I wanted to hear your voice.

CHIZMAR: And it was you calling my parents' house all those times?

GALLAGHER: [nods] Yes.

CHIZMAR: Why?

GALLAGHER: I don't really know. They became part of it all, I guess.

CHIZMAR: It scared the hell out of my mother.

GALLAGHER: I'm sorry. She didn't deserve that. But I guess maybe that was the point: it was to scare you.

CHIZMAR: You wanted me to stop?

GALLAGHER: I don't think so. I don't know what I really wanted.

CHIZMAR: Did you follow me?

GALLAGHER: When?

CHIZMAR: Back in '88. Around Edgewood.

GALLAGHER: [nods] Sometimes. A little later, too.

CHIZMAR: After the book came out?

GALLAGHER: [nods]

CHIZMAR: Where?

GALLAGHER: That's not really important.

CHIZMAR: It is to me.

GALLAGHER: Don't you have other questions for me?

CHIZMAR: [pause] Anna Garfield. Did all of this start with her?

GALLAGHER: [deep breath] Yes and no.

CHIZMAR: Can you explain what that means?

GALLAGHER: I can try. [long pause; the tapping on the floor grows more rapid] Something inside of me is broken. It always has been, as long as I can remember. Something in my head's messed up. It's . . . it's wrong.

CHIZMAR: Go on.

GALLAGHER: I don't know how to explain it better than that. I've read the books. I know how clichéd it sounds, but—

CHIZMAR: Books?

GALLAGHER: Books about killers. Mass murderers.

CHIZMAR: Have those books taught you anything about yourself?

GALLAGHER: [pause] That I'm not alone.

CHIZMAR: Was Natasha the first? Or were there others before her?

GALLAGHER: [shakes head] I'd thought about it. A lot. I came close a couple of times.

CHIZMAR: What stopped you?

GALLAGHER: Fear. I was afraid to cross that line. Scared I'd get caught. Scared I'd like it. So, I settled for other things.

CHIZMAR: Animals?

GALLAGHER: [nods]

CHIZMAR: When did you first begin hurting animals?

GALLAGHER: I was probably eight or nine.

CHIZMAR: What kind of animals?

GALLAGHER: Oh, all kinds. Fish. Frogs. Rabbits. Eventually, cats and dogs. A horse in a field, once. I did that one at night. That was really something.

CHIZMAR: And you knew it was wrong?

GALLAGHER: Yes.

CHIZMAR: What did you think was wrong with you?

GALLAGHER: I didn't know. I just knew there was . . . *something* inside of me, this *bad* thing, and it just *needed*, and I couldn't tell anyone about it. I'd try to keep it locked up, behind a door, but sometimes I wasn't strong enough.

CHIZMAR: Did you enjoy hurting animals?

GALLAGHER: Not in the beginning . . . but that changed over time. It got easier. And I got better at it.

CHIZMAR: Was there anything in your childhood that might've ignited these types of thoughts? A starting point or catalyst of any kind?

GALLAGHER: You mean was I sexually or physically abused? Did my parents beat me or lock me in a closet all day? Did I fall down and suffer a head injury that rewired my brain? [shakes head] No. There was nothing like that.

CHIZMAR: What is your first memory of this "bad thing" inside you?

GALLAGHER: [long pause] I was seven, and I was at a friend's birthday party. His older sister was on the swing set in the backyard. She looked over at me and smiled, and I remember just standing there with my paper plate and cake, thinking: *I'm going to come back tonight and sneak into the house and crush* *your skull with a brick*. It just came to me, fast, like that. Why did I want to hurt her? I don't know. Why a brick? I—I don't know.

CHIZMAR: You were popular in high school. I remember seeing you at parties. Hanging out with both guys and girls.

GALLAGHER: [shakes head] That's because I was good at wrestling. Those people never really knew me, or even wanted to.

CHIZMAR: And all throughout those years—the wrestling matches, the homecomings and proms and graduation—you were fighting back those bad feelings?

GALLAGHER: [nods] Sometimes it went away for a week or two, but it always came back. Always.

CHIZMAR: I want to go back to college and Anna Garfield. Can you tell me what happened?

GALLAGHER: We were in love. We'd made plans to be together in the future. And, just like that, she wanted someone else.

CHIZMAR: And you wanted to hurt her?

GALLAGHER: Not then. I was too depressed. The ground had been stolen out from under me. I just wanted to somehow change her mind. But later . . . yes. I wanted to hurt her. I hated her for what she did to me, how she made me feel. And I hated myself, too, as a result.

CHIZMAR: You followed her around campus, broke into her car and dorm room, but you never tried to harm her physically?

GALLAGHER: Oh, I did, actually. Two times, that next summer, I drove up to where she lived with her parents, but I chickened out at the last second. Which made me hate myself even more.

CHIZMAR: Anna Garfield recently told a reporter that you had gotten rough with her sexually.

GALLAGHER: Yeah? Well, that's how she liked it. *She's* the one who asked me to tie her up. *She's* the one who asked me to choke her. I'd never done any of those things before her. Ask any of my old girlfriends.

CHIZMAR: The attraction to long hair . . . it was because of Anna?

GALLAGHER: You know, it's funny—I didn't even realize I was doing that until after I read about it later on.

CHIZMAR: [long pause] You know I have to ask you this: Why did you kill Natasha?

GALLAGHER: It was always going to happen at some point. I'd thought about it a lot when we were younger. I almost went through with it once about a year earlier. We were hiking at Loch Raven and I picked up a rock about the size of my fist. I came up behind her and was about this close [he holds his fingers a few inches apart] from doing it.

CHIZMAR: Why did you stop that day?

GALLAGHER: I got scared.

CHIZMAR: So what happened on the night of June 2, 1988? Why then?

GALLAGHER: [sighs] Look, I know you want me to say that something *dramatic* happened . . . like I felt some kind of other-worldly power surge go through my body, or I had a dream or heard voices. [Josh's eyes widen.] Or maybe the devil made me do it. But . . . no. That's not how it was. Earlier that day, I was working out at the gym, and afterwards, while I was in the shower, I saw everything so clear in my head—how I'd get her out to the woods, how I'd kill her, how I'd make it look like someone else did it, everything. It was all right there in a flash. I had plans to meet [Frank] Hapney after the gym, so I hung out with him for a few hours, and then instead of going home, I went to my parents' house in Edgewood.

CHIZMAR: And knocked on her window?

GALLAGHER: [shakes head] No. I was never outside her window. It was after midnight when I got there. I used my key and tiptoed in the front door and down the hall. We snuck out the same way.

CHIZMAR: The screen? The blood on her windowsill?

GALLAGHER: She cut her finger looking for a pair of boots in her closet. It was dark and she couldn't see what she was doing. I used my shirt to stop the bleeding and purposely left a little smear on the windowsill. Same time I opened up the window all the way and knocked out the screen.

CHIZMAR: Just like you'd pictured earlier in the shower?

GALLAGHER: Yes.

CHIZMAR: What did you tell her that night? How did you get her to go along with you?

GALLAGHER: She was fifteen years old. It didn't take much. I told her me and Hapney had been drinking at our old spot in the woods and he'd passed out. I needed her help getting him back to the car.

CHIZMAR: And then you led your sister into the woods and killed her?

GALLAGHER: Yes.

CHIZMAR: But not without a struggle. She fought you.

GALLAGHER: Yes.

CHIZMAR: [pause] And the other three girls from Edgewood . . . why did you choose them?

GALLAGHER: Pretty much the same reason. I saw them, and I *knew*. Right away. I knew I'd eventually kill them. And exactly how I would do it.

CHIZMAR: The police were unable to make any direct connections between your victims. You didn't know any of the other girls?

GALLAGHER: [shakes head] No. I saw Kacey Robinson walk out of the library one afternoon. She was by herself, and I was pulling out of Santoni's parking lot. I followed her home that day and watched her for the next week. The others were the same. I spotted Madeline Wilcox at a traffic light. The Riggs girl was playing hockey in front of the high school. Cassidy Burch was at the Stop and Shop buying a Diet Coke and a bag of potato chips. I was right behind her in line paying for gas.

CHIZMAR: And, besides the long hair, no single physical or personality trait tied any of them together?

GALLAGHER: [pause] The way they looked at me. The way they smiled . . . like they were making fun of me.

CHIZMAR: Annie Riggs identified the man who attacked her as someone much larger than you.

GALLAGHER: [shrugs] I was never big, but I was always strong and fast. The rest was all in her head. Just like the police sketch—it looked nothing like me.

CHIZMAR: Why did you cut off their ears?

GALLAGHER: Punishment.

CHIZMAR: Punishment for what?

GALLAGHER: For thinking they were better than me.

CHIZMAR: The police were never able to locate the severed ears. There are rumors that you . . . you ate them.

GALLAGHER: [shakes head] Never happened. I kept them in an old coffee can for a while, but they started to smell, so I dumped them in the Gunpowder. Catfish probably ate them eventually.

CHIZMAR: Posing the bodies became part of your signature. Why did you do that?

GALLAGHER: I wanted to leave them at peace for whoever found them. For the families.

CHIZMAR: The hopscotch grid, missing dog sign, pennies, and pumpkins . . . what was the significance? And the numerology?

GALLAGHER: [pause] I'm not ready to talk about that yet.

CHIZMAR: Why not?

GALLAGHER: Because it opens the door to something I'm not ready to talk about.

CHIZMAR: When do you think you'll be ready to talk about it?

GALLAGHER: I don't know.

CHIZMAR: Why did you bite your victims?

GALLAGHER: I don't remember biting any of them. I told the police that, but I don't think they believed me.

CHIZMAR: No recollection at all?

GALLAGHER: [shakes head] None.

CHIZMAR: So, at some point, did evading capture become a game to you? Taunting the police; leaving your mark on the memorials; calling my house and hanging up; creeping around Carly Albright's home.

GALLAGHER: I never went anywhere near Carly Albright's house. I never liked her very much. I'm not exactly sure why I did those other things. Maybe to distract myself from what I was really doing.

CHIZMAR: Which was what?

GALLAGHER: Killing those girls.

CHIZMAR: The media came up with a number of nicknames for you. "The Boogeyman" was the one that stuck. Were you pleased with that name or indifferent?

GALLAGHER: I was pleased. [pause] It seemed to fit, and that was the first time I was able to put a name to the bad thing living inside me.

CHIZMAR: You actually began to think of that part of yourself as "The Boogeyman"?

GALLAGHER: I did, yes.

CHIZMAR: What do you mean when you say that name seems to fit?

GALLAGHER: On the nights I hunted, I felt . . . different. I felt powerful. Bold. Invincible. At one with the night around me.

As if I could fly and pass through walls and make myself invisible.

CHIZMAR: You really believed you could do those things?

GALLAGHER: I could. I did. That's why they never caught me.

CHIZMAR: Do you think you're clinically insane, like some people have suggested?

GALLAGHER: [pause] You know, sometimes, I wish I were. But no. Something's wrong with me, but I'm not crazy.

CHIZMAR: How did you manage to remain so careful and not leave behind any evidence?

GALLAGHER: Common sense, mostly. I didn't want to get caught, so I tried to think everything through first. I wore surgical gloves, two on each hand, that I paid for with cash in Pennsylvania. I wore condoms. And I always bought a new change of clothes to wear on the nights I hunted. Paid for in cash at thrift shops. All basic stuff. Up until that point, the police were always a few steps behind. Honestly, my luck ran out that night at the cemetery. I knew I'd nicked my wrist on the fence, but it wasn't much more than a scratch. My shirtsleeve wasn't even torn. Later, when I checked at home, there wasn't any blood, so I'd figured I was good to go.

CHIZMAR: And the mask?

GALLAGHER: What about it?

CHIZMAR: You could've worn a ski mask or any number of other things to hide your face. Why make your own mask? Were you imitating a horror movie, as some people claim?

GALLAGHER: It was the Boogeyman's mask. It's what *he* wanted.

CHIZMAR: [pause] Going back to the night at the cemetery, if you weren't aware that the police had a sample of your blood in their possession, why did you stop after Cassidy Burch?

GALLAGHER: The same reason I hadn't killed anyone before all this started. I was able to keep the Boogeyman locked up behind that door. I was tempted after the Burch girl, many times, but I was able to fight it off. I even thought about killing myself a couple of times, but I didn't have the balls to do it. So I just kept holding that door closed.

CHIZMAR: Until Louise Rutherford in 2001, Colette Bowden in 2006, and Erin Brown in 2018.

GALLAGHER: [nods] Yes.

CHIZMAR: What changed? What was different about those women?

GALLAGHER: It was the same as before. I saw them all and I just *knew*—and I couldn't stop it from happening. I wasn't strong enough anymore. Nothing deeper or more mystical than that.

CHIZMAR: Was there a reason you didn't cut off their ears this time? Or leave anything behind for the police?

GALLAGHER: I didn't feel it was necessary.

CHIZMAR: Are there more women, Josh?

GALLAGHER: [long pause]

CHIZMAR: There are, aren't there?

GALLAGHER: Yes.

CHIZMAR: Will you tell Detective McClernan who they are? Where they are?

GALLAGHER: [long pause]

CHIZMAR: Will you tell me?

GALLAGHER: Not today.

CHIZMAR: Then when?

GALLAGHER: Soon. [pause] Maybe.

CHIZMAR: The families deserve closure. They deserve to know.

GALLAGHER: I said maybe.

CHIZMAR: Have you spoken to your mother since your arrest?

GALLAGHER: No.

CHIZMAR: Why not?

GALLAGHER: I haven't tried.

CHIZMAR: Do you miss her? Your wife and kids?

GALLAGHER: Yes. Every day.

CHIZMAR: How about Natasha?

GALLAGHER: Yes. I loved her very much.

CHIZMAR: Do you miss your father?

GALLAGHER: [long pause]

CHIZMAR: No?

GALLAGHER: I didn't say that. Of course I miss him.

CHIZMAR: According to your mother, you and your father spent an evening together a couple days prior to his death. What did the two of you talk about?

GALLAGHER: My mother asked me to try to find out what was bothering him. He wouldn't talk to her.

CHIZMAR: Besides the fact that his daughter had been murdered.

GALLAGHER: Besides that.

CHIZMAR: And what did you find out?

GALLAGHER: [pause, smiling] You know, don't you?

CHIZMAR: Know what?

GALLAGHER: You know what we talked about that night.

CHIZMAR: I'm not sure. I might.

GALLAGHER: Yes. Yes, you do. [pause, smile fading] That's why I asked to speak with you, Rich. You're clever. That's why people like to read your stories.

CHIZMAR: Trust me, I'm not that clever. You can ask anyone.

GALLAGHER: You are, though. And you know exactly what my father and I talked about. You know he saw something or remembered something and was getting suspicious. You know he was thinking about telling the police.

CHIZMAR: So what did your father see, Josh?

GALLAGHER: [long pause] He saw his ten-year-old son playing in the woods behind the house one day. He was so quiet, I never even heard him until he was standing right behind me. He cried out when he saw what I was doing to the dog. It was just a stray mutt I'd found down by the railroad tracks, skinny and full of fleas. I had it pinned to the ground with my knee and was choking it with both hands. I tried to explain, to tell him it was hurt, and I was just trying to put it out of its misery. At first, he seemed to believe me, or at least like he *wanted* to believe me. But then he saw the blood on my hands and what I'd done to the dog's ear with my pocketknife—and he *knew*. I'd never seen him so angry. He dragged me home by my shirt collar and we never spoke of it again.

CHIZMAR: Your father didn't commit suicide that night, did he?

GALLAGHER: [staring down at table] No, he didn't.

CHIZMAR: [long pause] Did you ever think about hurting me?

GALLAGHER: [looking up] Do you remember the day you were shooting baskets behind the high school and I drove up and joined you?

CHIZMAR: [nods] Yes.

GALLAGHER: Do you know that was one of the happiest days of my life?

CHIZMAR: How so?

GALLAGHER: [shrugs] It just was. Before that, I was driving around down by the water at Flying Point. Had my windows down and my stereo cranked up, and I felt good. No bad thoughts. No worries. No Boogeyman. I felt almost . . . normal. And then on my way back, I saw you shooting hoops and decided to stop. You were cool to me. Didn't say much, but you were nice. We played H-O-R-S-E and I beat you two out of three games.

CHIZMAR: [nods]

GALLAGHER: And when you had to leave, you told me to hang on to the ball and keep playing. You said you had three or four more at home.

CHIZMAR: I remember that.

GALLAGHER: A little later, on my way home, I remember thinking maybe I could stop. Maybe I could go somewhere to get help and when I got back, I could be like everyone else. Like *you.* [pause] But that never happened and—

GUARD: Excuse me. Time's up, Mr. Chizmar.

10

Lieutenant McClernan is waiting for me in the lobby after the interview. She hands me my cell phone, wallet, and car keys, and together we walk outside. The afternoon sun is high in the sky, but the temperature has dropped and there are fresh puddles in the parking lot. It rained while we were inside.

"You okay?" she asks.

"I think so."

"You did good. You got him started. Once that happens, they usually keep talking."

"He didn't answer a lot of the questions you gave me."

"He answered enough," she says. "And that business about his father . . . that's the first time he's admitted to his murder. How did you know to ask him that? It wasn't on the list."

Before I can answer, I stumble over my own feet and drop the car keys into a pothole filled with dirty water. Grimacing, I bend down and carefully fish them out, wiping my wet hand on my pants leg.

"You going to be okay to drive?"

"I'll be fine." I turn and look at the lieutenant. "He wasn't what I expected."

"They rarely are."

"I was sure he was going to say that his father told him he was adopted. The night Josh killed him." I shook my head. "But I don't think he has any idea."

"And we want to keep it that way for as long as we can."

I didn't say anything then. I just got in my car and drove away.

11

According to a 2009 study conducted by the Federal Bureau of Investigation, nearly 16 percent of American serial killers were adopted as children, while adoptees represent only 2 percent of the general population.

There's even a condition known as Adopted Child Syndrome that has been used as a successful legal defense in a number of death penalty cases where the accused has been adopted.

12

The main entrance to Green Mount Cemetery in downtown Baltimore resembles the outer gate of a medieval castle. The only thing missing is a drawbridge. As I sit in my truck in the parking lot, I keep expecting to look up at the twin stone towers and see armor-clad archers flexing their bows.

Finally, a few minutes past 5:00 p.m., a bright red Audi trailing a plume of dust speeds into the lot and pulls up alongside me. Carly Albright, dressed in an oversized winter jacket, baggy black snow pants, and pink rubber boots steps out of the car. She looks like a pregnant Eskimo.

I get out of my truck and make a show of looking at my watch. "You're late."

"Bite me," she says, pulling a faux-fur-lined hood over her two-hundred-and-fifty-dollar hairdo. "Some of us have jobs, you know."

"I have a job."

"Some of us have *real* jobs." She leans into the front seat of her car and comes back out holding a bouquet of fresh-cut flowers. "I should've bought fake ones. These'll be dead by tomorrow."

"Pretty sure they're already dead." I walk to the bed of my truck and pull out the miniature Christmas wreath I'd picked up at the florist on my way here.

"Nice," she says, and you can tell she means it. She takes my arm and we start walking.

"You expecting a blizzard?" I ask, trying not to smile.

"Oh, shut it," she says, nudging me with her elbow. "You know I hate the cold." She looks at what I'm wearing, which isn't much. "Don't blame me when you freeze to death."

Right on cue, the temperature drops a full ten degrees as soon as we enter the dark stone tunnel that marks the cemetery's main entrance. When we emerge on the other side, we're standing on a cobblestone walkway surrounded by almost seventy acres of ornate monuments and tombstones. What's left of last week's snowstorm blankets the rolling hills. If not for the Baltimore City skyline visible in the distance, we could be standing on a frozen hillside in scenic New England.

"I always forget how beautiful this place is," Carly says.

"Me too."

"When's the last time you were here?"

"Kara and I stopped by at the end of summer." I look at her. "You?" She shakes her head. "Not since the funeral."

"Come on," I say, starting to walk again. "It'll be dark soon."

"Any word from Lieutenant McClernan or Gallagher's lawyer?"

"Nothing yet."

Joshua Gallagher recently requested a continuation of our conversation from earlier this month. Despite my expressed lack of enthusiasm, Lieutenant McClernan and my literary agent are anxious to make it happen. Now it's just a matter of cutting through the usual spool of red tape.

"I wish he was here to see all this," she says.

"Not me."

"Why not?" she asks, surprised.

"I know he'd be thrilled to close the case, to get a killer off the street, especially this one, there's no question about that." I give her a shrug. "But I think he'd be disappointed it was Josh Gallagher. All this time, we were looking for a monster . . . but it feels like we found something else instead."

"He killed eight people, Rich. At least eight. I'd say that makes him a monster."

I nod my head. "You're right."

"You almost sound like you feel sorry for him."

"It's not that. I just don't . . . understand."

"Well, that makes two of us."

We walk in silence after that, eventually abandoning the walkway and cutting across open ground. As we punch our way through ankle-deep snow, I feel my socks soaking through, but I don't say a word about it. I'll never hear the end of it if I do.

"You know who's buried here?" Carly asks, finally breaking the quiet.

"John Wilkes Booth."

She stops and looks at me. "How the hell did you know that?"

"You told me at the funeral."

"Oh." She takes my arm and starts walking again.

At the top of a slight rise ringed by a grove of scattered pine trees, we come to a stop. "This is such a peaceful resting place," Carly says, looking around.

I immediately drop to a knee and use my hands to wipe away snow and ice and twigs from a modest granite headstone. When I'm finished, I place the wreath next to the marker and get back to my feet.

LYLE ALVIN HARPER
1938–2019
Loving Father

"Interesting," Carly says, leaning down and leaving the bouquet of flowers at the base of the marker. "No mention of his police career."

"I noticed that, too."

"Why do you think?"

"I think, at the end, he was a lot prouder of being a good father than he was a good cop."

She looks at me. "You miss him, don't you?"

"I do."

"When was the last time you saw him?"

"That's the thing," I say, wiping my eyes. "It's been thirteen fucking years. We went fishing the week after my father's funeral. It doesn't make sense that I feel this way."

"It makes sense to me."

We stand there in silence, staring down at the grave marker, lost in our private thoughts. Finally, I clear my throat. "You want to do the honors or me?"

She gives me a look, confused.

"Who's going to tell him we finally caught the son of a bitch?"

"Ohhh," she says, smiling. "And let you get all the credit? No thanks. I'll tell him."

She takes my arm again, gives it a squeeze, and rests her head on my shoulder. Our laughter echoes across the rolling, snow-covered hills. It's a good sound.

ABOVE: The Joppatowne town house where twenty-two-year-old Joshua Gallagher lived at the time of the murders *(Photo courtesy of the author)*

LEFT: Nineteen-year-old Joshua Gallagher at Penn State University *(Photo courtesy of Shane Leonard)*

ABOVE: Joshua Gallagher's Hanover, Pennsylvania, home
where he lived with his wife and two sons
(Photo courtesy of the author)

ABOVE: Joshua Gallagher on a job site
(Photo courtesy of Shane Leonard)

ABOVE: Fifty-four-year-old Joshua Gallagher's mug shot
(Photo courtesy of The Baltimore Sun*)*

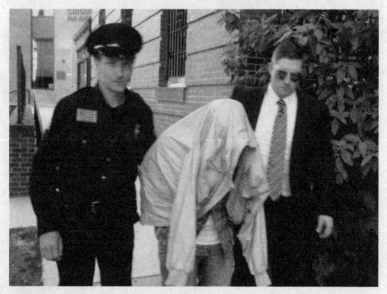

ABOVE: Joshua Gallagher being escorted out of the Harford County Courthouse
(Photo courtesy of Logan Reynolds)

Richard Chizmar

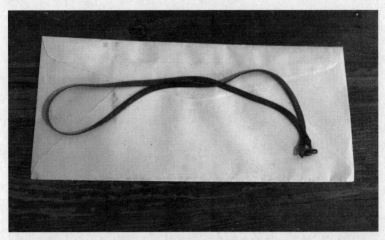

ABOVE: A gold necklace belonging to Madeline Wilcox found by police
in Joshua Gallagher's basement workshop
(Photo courtesy of The Baltimore Sun*)*

LEFT: Natasha and Joshua Gallagher
during a visit to the Penn State campus
(Photo courtesy of Shane Leonard)

RIGHT: Russell Gallagher holding a
young Joshua Gallagher
(Photo courtesy of Shane Leonard)

author's note

Beginning in August 1986 and continuing until the early months of 1990, someone entered the homes of at least twenty-five Edgewood, Maryland, women and touched their feet, legs, stomach, and hair while they were sleeping. When the women awakened, they found the man standing by the bed staring at them or lying nearby on the floor. In each instance, the man fled and disappeared into the night. Local police were unable to capture or identify the assailant until October 1993, when a former Edgewood resident jailed in Baltimore City on breaking-and-entering charges confessed that he was the so-called "Phantom Fondler," as many newspapers had taken to calling him. The man's fingerprints matched evidence found at numerous Edgewood crime scenes, and the case was finally closed.

That much of *Chasing the Boogeyman* is based on hard facts.

As are the myriad colorful stories of my childhood adventures and the loving observations of my mother and father and so many other cherished memories from the time I spent living on Hanson Road before walking down the aisle and marrying my high school sweetheart. The town of Edgewood itself, the stores and gas stations, the schools and parks, the neighborhoods and roadways, they're all real. They all exist. At least, they did back in 1988, when the bulk of this story takes place.

The rest of *Chasing the Boogeyman*—including, for example, the four murdered girls, the police investigation, the small town under siege, and characters such as Carly Albright, Detective Lyle Harper, and Joshua Gallagher—is nothing more than fiction. The result of an over-active imagination, a lifelong attraction to exploring the shadows, and a nostalgic streak a mile wide.

I've always wanted to write a novel set in my hometown. If you've read much of my short fiction, you already know that Edgewood plays a significant role in my storytelling catalog. As does Hanson Road, Winter's Run Creek, weeping willow trees, and countless other memories from my youth.

A couple of years ago, not long after moving into a new house, my wife, Kara, and I were looking at photos in our wedding album, when I made an offhanded comment about how strange it'd felt all those years ago to move back home after graduating from college. I remembered those months leading up to our wedding in vivid and affectionate detail. Of course, all Kara recalled is that I didn't help enough with the wedding invitations or any of the other preparations. "Except the food," she told me. "You were very involved in choosing the menu."

Shortly after closing the photo album and returning it to the cardboard box from which I'd discovered it, I felt another blast from the past worm its way into my head—the Phantom Fondler.

It was the first time I'd thought of him in years and it hit me like a bolt of lightning from a cloudless summer sky. Instantly, I flashed back to the series of cautionary headlines that dominated our small weekly newspaper and remembered how on edge the residents of Edgewood had become; how people started locking their windows at night and installing alarm systems; how worried and scared they grew that the mysterious intruder would one day soon escalate to doing more than touching his slumbering victims.

And that's where the idea for *Chasing the Boogeyman* was born.

Now, as many writers will tell you, some stories are born premature; you might have the skeleton of a decent idea and perhaps even a main character in mind, but all the rest—supporting characters, plot points, a beginning, middle, and end—is missing. Of course, many other stories are birthed plump and healthy; in these cases, all of the major plot points are in place, the complete roster of characters are present and ring true in your heart, and all that's left to do is to connect the dots and create a seamless and entertaining narrative. Still other tales, as rare as precious jewels, are born fully formed, as if merely buried in a mound of sand that needs only to be brushed away in order to discover the entirety of the story—crackling with life and energy and wonder—underneath.

Chasing the Boogeyman was like that for me—just waiting there beneath the surface.

Fully formed, brimming with mystery, and chock-full of surprises.

Surprise number one: for some unknown reason I immediately envisioned *Chasing the Boogeyman* as being told in the structured format of a true-crime book; in fact, presented as a "true story of small town evil" (which incidentally was the novel's original subtitle). Surprise number two: despite a well-earned reputation for being somewhat of a recluse and someone not very fond of the spotlight, I also *saw* with complete certainty that the story needed to be told from my own personal viewpoint. Twenty-two-year-old Rich Chizmar would not only serve as the narrator of the Boogeyman's dark story, he would also act as its conscience. Surprise number three: as a lifelong fan of true-crime books, one of the first things I usually do is flip ahead to the photo section— more often than not, positioned near the center of the book and presented in unsparing black-and-white imagery—to see what the real-life people and places involved in the crime look like. Studying those faces and crime scenes—the houses and alleyways and wooded areas—often serve to add another layer of reality and poignancy to the words I'm reading. I recognized from the very beginning that *Chasing the Boogeyman* would feature dozens of such photographs—and they needed to appear unquestionably authentic. The first thing I did to make this happen was to bring in the talented folks from Sympatico Media (a local production company I've been fortunate enough to work with on several movies). I furnished them with a lengthy, detailed shot-list, and they hired actors to play the roles of policemen, detectives, news personalities, and local residents. Then they spent two long days and nights capturing the majority of the images for this book. Several other good friends stepped up and volunteered to pose as the Boogeyman's victims. A young neighbor assumed the role of Annie Riggs, the Boogeyman's sole survivor. Because I run into my neighbor on a regular basis, I didn't have the heart to kill Annie Riggs. My son Billy and I managed to arrange and take the remainder of the photographs. Surprisingly, with all the various roles and moving pieces involved, we only made a single embarrassing mistake: one of the detectives from 1988 also makes an appearance in a photograph from 2020—and what do you know, he hasn't aged a single day.

So there you have it: the nuts and bolts and *how* and *why* of *Chasing the Boogeyman*. A hopefully unique and satisfying fictional melding of "this actually happened" and "this could have happened"—and a personal snapshot of a very special time in my life that took place in a very special small town. I hope you've enjoyed the journey as much as I have.

acknowledgments

As is always the case, I had a lot of help writing this book. I would like to offer my heartfelt thanks to:

Kara and Billy and Noah, for pretty much everything; my mother and father, whom I think of and miss every day; John, Rita, Mary, and Nancy, siblings and guardian angels; and my old friends from the Wood, blood brothers all, especially The Hanson Road Boys.

The Tiptons, for too many kindnesses to list on this page.

Annie Keele, Natasha Slutzky, Kacey Newman, Madeline Anderson, and Cassidy Ward, for lending their talent and trust.

Brian Anderson, Steve Sines, Doug Sharretts, and Melvin Futrell, for taking time out of their busy days to play make-believe.

Bev Vincent, Billy Chizmar (again), Robert Mingee, and Jeff Martin, for early reads and generous advice.

Brandon Lescure and Everett Glovier of Sympatico Media, for photographic excellence and acting mediocrity.

Gail Cross of Desert Isle Design for technical and design assistance.

Several unnamed members of the Federal Bureau of Investigation,

Acknowledgments

Maryland State Police, and the Harford County Sheriff's Department, for invaluable technical advice. You know who you are.

Dave Wehage, Deborah Lynn, Alex Baliko, and Matt and Nate Slutzky, for letting me pillage their personal photo albums.

Alex McVey, for the excellent police sketch.

The Keele family, for helping out with my crazy idea and putting up with their strange—yet charming—next-door neighbor.

Jimmy Cavanaugh, for being there from the very beginning.

James Renner, for fighting the good fight and the wonderful Foreword.

Stephen King, for friendship and advice.

Danielle Marie and Jason Myers, for friendship, tireless support, and encouragement.

The *Chasing the Boogeyman* "Street Team" for believing in this author and this project, and all their hard work.

Brian Freeman, Mindy Jarusek, and Dan Hocker, for watching over the store and keeping me in line. Not an easy gig.

Ryan Lewis, for being one of the good guys and navigating the never-ending maze that is La-La Land (as my father always called it).

Kristin Nelson, for working so hard on my behalf and always doing it with a smile in her voice. I'm not sure how she does it, but I'm immensely grateful.

Ed Schlesinger, for helping to shape *Chasing the Boogeyman* into a book I'm very proud of, and for doing it with such kindness and generosity.

And last but certainly not least, all the fine people of Edgewood, then and now, for giving me a place I can always call "home."